STRANGE COSMOLOGY

Small Worlds Book 2

By Alex Raizman

For my sister, Abbie, who always believed in me.

Table of Contents

Some say the world will end in fire,
Some say in ice.
From what I've tasted of desire
I hold with those who favor fire.
But if it had to perish twice,
I think I know enough of hate
To say that for destruction ice
Is also great
And would suffice.
-*Fire and Ice,* by Robert Frost

Prologue

A Debt Repaid

Ryan Smith thought that, as afterlives went, he had seen worse than Nav. The Slavic realm of the dead was not as oppressively dark as the endless war of Helheim, nor was it as imposing as the vast caverns of Hades. Mostly, it was barren, the kind of empty, frozen expanse that could only have been imagined by people that had lived in Siberia and wanted to come up with something *worse.*

Having visited seven other afterlives today, Ryan was developing some definite opinions. He preferred cold and ice to fire and brimstone. Quiet was better than howls and groans from the various inhabitants. And being able to enter without being attacked by an undead army was the biggest selling point of all. So far, he was ok with Nav.

My life is so weird, he thought. *Now, if I were a death goddess, where would I be?*

The only break in the seemingly endless landscape was a bridge in the far distance, and Ryan supposed that would be the best place to start looking for the lady of this realm. Ryan reluctantly began walking away from the doorway to his nanoverse, leaving his exit point further behind with each step and resigning himself to what might be a long search. He'd fulfill his bargain with the King of Hell when he delivered eight death gods and goddesses to the battlefield, and he had hoped that this last one would be relatively easy but had known better than to expect it.

After a half hour's walk, Ryan finally drew close enough to see that the bridge didn't seem to offer much of a clue. On the other side of the frozen river, everything looked exactly the same.

Maybe it's some kind of mystical thing, he thought. *I cross the bridge, and suddenly I'm in Morana's palace, where she'll give me three wishes and a cup of hot chocolate.*

He turned back toward his doorway, just to reassure himself that it was still there, and nearly jumped out of his skin when he heard a voice behind him.

"So...you're the delivery boy?"

Ryan yelped and whirled around, his heart pounding. A woman had appeared on the bridge, looking over the river. She turned to face him as he took a deep breath and tried to get control of himself.

At first glance, Ryan actually felt comforted. The woman had a matronly look, her soft features suggesting that she actually *might* be the type to offer warm shelter and a cup of hot chocolate. Then he saw the hard, black pits of her eyes, and wondered if she'd be more inclined to warm someone by tossing them into a fire.

"Morana?" Ryan asked hopefully.

"Yes. And you are?" Her expression dripped contempt, and Ryan swallowed hard.

"Ryan. Ryan Smith."

"Ryan...Smith," Morana said, tasting the name. She made a face, as if it was a particularly bitter flavor. "My. They're letting anyone have a nanoverse these days, aren't they?"

Ryan reflexively reached into his pocket, closing his fingers around his nanoverse. *You're a god, too,* he reminded himself. Sure, he'd only been one for a few weeks, but he still was a god. He'd battled a hundred handed giant, survived Enki's various traps and tricks, and nuked a small island in Canada. Was he going to let himself be intimidated by this random death goddess?

Her gaze narrowed, and Ryan realized the answer was absolutely yes. When her eyes flicked down towards his pocket, he felt a flicker of shame on top of the fear, realizing that grabbing for his nanoverse probably seemed weak and childish to her. Sometimes, being a new god felt a lot like being an uncool kid in high school.

"We should get going," Ryan said gruffly, ignoring his pounding heart and reddening face as he pulled his hand back out of his pocket. "You're the last one on my list."

As soon as the words were out of his mouth, Ryan realized they were a mistake, and Morana's eyes flashed in fury. An icy wind rose around her, turning her raven hair into a storm around her face.

"If I didn't need you to be free from this hell, I'd gut you for that insult," she snarled. "You dare suggest that I am lesser? I, the bringer of winter, the killer of Yarilo, the mistress of death?"

Ryan swallowed again. He scrabbled for his nanoverse again, needing the reassurance. *To hell with looking cool. If you have to fight her...crap.* Death gods followed different rules from other gods. They weren't reliant on their nanoverses, instead drawing power from the souls of the realm they claimed. Within that realm, they were not omnipotent, but they were far more potent than anything Ryan had ever tried to face before. If Morana decided his insult was worth losing her chance at freedom, he'd have to...

...have to figure out why she was laughing. It took Ryan a second to fully process that Morana's "angry goddess" pose had utterly collapsed, and that she was nearly doubled over with amusement. Again, Ryan felt heat rising in his cheeks.

"I'm so sorry," she gasped, wiping away tears. "It has been so very, very long since someone new visited my realm. Let alone someone I could mess with. Do you have any idea how boring it can get in here?"

Ryan let loose a deep sigh. "You really...you really had me going there for a bit. I thought you were going to kill me."

"Oh, oh no. My first chance to walk among the mortal world again? To gain worshippers? Freedom? You're absolutely safe." Morana chortled again.

Ryan shook his head. "Well, I know that Arthur has a pretty tight schedule for all this. Mind if we move along?"

Morana nodded and stepped off the bridge, joining Ryan on the frozen plain.

"How is the war in Heaven progressing?" she asked.

"Messy," Ryan said grimly. "Very, very messy."

As they trudged across the ice, he thought back to his last visit to the battle.

***

Ryan had completed his first six pickups as quickly as possible, barely glancing at the battlefield before darting back into his nanoverse. He had promised to free the captive death deities and bring them to join Hell's army but watching demons and angels do their best to destroy each other was definitely *not* part of the arrangement.

However, when he stepped out to deliver Hela, ruler of the Norse afterlife for the dishonorable dead, the demon Ashtaroth had caught his eye and beckoned him over, and it just wasn't politic to ignore Hell's general. Especially when they were, at least for the moment, allies.

Ashtaroth raised his sword in salute, and Ryan couldn't help staring as blood dripped from the sword onto the once pristine fields.

"You've barely stopped for an instant," the demon rumbled. "We appreciate your diligence, but you can spare a few moments to rest, and to appreciate the battle. After all," Ashtaroth's eyes gleamed, "this has been millennia in the making."

"I know, I'm just..." Ryan shook his head. The truth was that he didn't *want* to see the battle, but saying so would probably be insulting.

"I thought Graham Island got you used to war," Ashtaroth said, clearly intuiting the unspoken words.

"Can you ever truly get used to this?"

Ryan glanced at the battlefield, focusing on a tower still holding out against the horde of demons, its defenders in gleaming plate and fighting with spears of light. They looked so proud, so noble, so *glorious.* Ryan's allies, by comparison, were a mass of unholy flesh wreathed with hellfire. If this was a scene from a movie, it could not possibly be clearer which side was good and which was evil, not unless the director edited in labels over each faction.

When Ryan had promised to aid Hell in its war with Heaven, he'd been too focused on his own enemies, and his desperate need for allies, to think too hard about his end of the bargain. Now, he couldn't help questioning his "the enemy of my friend is my enemy" situation.

"Get used to this?" Ashtaroth gave him a wide grin, revealing rows of teeth that gleamed in contrast to his crimson skin. "I was born for this. It's like asking a wolf if they ever truly get used to the hunt. But I know how it affects you humans. What's that your people are fond of saying? 'War is hell'."

"Puns. We're standing in the middle of a battlefield, and you're making puns. You really are a monster," Ryan said, forcing a smile.

"You certainly didn't complain when we were fighting for you."

You were fighting other monsters then, Ryan thought. "I guess it felt different because it was my fight," he said.

Ashtaroth's expression turned serious. "And you knew the hows and whys of that fight and believed it to be of great importance. In this fight, however, it is you who are simply offering support without knowing all the roots of the conflict."

Ryan paused, considering. Arthur, the current King of Hell, wanted to turn it from a pit of evil and torment into a semi-respectable afterlife. Was this war about that, rather than a simple power grab? Was Heaven trying to force Arthur to take on the role of eternal torturer, maybe? One thing Ryan had learned since becoming a god was that all myths and religions were different - and more complicated - than he had believed.

"I should think you would be less quick to judge without full information. After all, Eschaton, I'm sure you are far from finished confronting those who misunderstand your desire to end the world."

"It isn't my *desire*," Ryan protested, "It's my *job*. And if I don't do it, something much worse will happen."

"Still, it will be hard to sit on that high horse, passing judgment, when you're laying waste to Earth."

Ryan winced. "It's different. It will be different."

"Oh? And please, pray tell, how is that any better than what we're doing here?"

As Ryan watched, Hela gestured towards the bastion. Swarms of half-rotted corpses, the undead monstrosities known as dragur, followed the gesture to descend upon the tower. "It won't be this horrible," Ryan whispered.

He spoke so quietly, he wasn't sure Ashtaroth heard him until the demon began to laugh. "It's the end of the world, Eschaton. It can't be anything *but* horrible."

"Right, but I'm... I'm going to do it in a good way," Ryan protested, keenly aware of how weak the objection was.

"And how does one end the world in a good way?" Ashtaroth asked.

Ryan turned away, back to the battle. The dragur were forming a ramp of their bodies, allowing the demons to clamber up the tower. He didn't want to watch but couldn't look away. *You played a part in this,* Ryan reminded himself.

Ashtaroth was still waiting for an answer, but Ryan didn't have it. He had to end the world, or the sun was going to explode, not only ending all life on Earth but making all future life impossible. Ryan intended to find a way to end the world while somehow saving as much of humanity as possible, but so far, he had no idea how to do that. "I'll figure it out," he said, as much to himself as to Ashtaroth.

The demon rolled his eyes. "As you will." For a moment, Ryan saw something almost like sympathy cross Ashtaroth's face.

"I suppose you should be going," Ashtaroth said after it became clear that Ryan had nothing more to contribute to the conversation. "We wouldn't want anyone getting the impression this is your war. You have enough complications, and Morana was never known for patience."

"I can't argue with that," Ryan said, turning his eyes away from the carnage. There were already two gods, Moloch and Bast, still at large and opposed to Ryan and his allies. Ryan was confident there would be others. The last thing he wanted was to add Hell's adversaries to his problems. With a nod to Ashtaroth, Ryan headed back to his nanoverse.

Soon, he would be done with this whole nasty business and able to get back to ending the world.

For some reason, that didn't exactly put a spring into Ryan's step.

***

Ryan had only given Morana the barest sketch of the fighting, but it was enough to fill the walk back to his door. The stars spun around them as they entered his staging area, the landing platform from which Ryan could oversee his pocket universe, where he truly was omnipotent. The staging area was also where Ryan was able to move his nanoverse through space and between realms, in a way he couldn't begin to understand, any more than he could wrap his head around the fact that he was inside his nanoverse, but his nanoverse was also in his pocket. His friend Crystal constantly told him to stop worrying about understanding everything and "roll with it", but sometimes it still gave him a headache.

Fortunately, Morana was happy to provide a distraction in the form of a question. "So, Uriel wasn't blowing smoke? There really is a new King on Hell's throne?"

Ryan nodded as he walked over to the console that controlled his nanoverse's movements. "Yeah, apparently. I've only met his representatives but given that Hell's armies are dancing to his tune, it seems pretty legit."

"Fascinating. Do you think he'll uphold his bargain with us?"

"Why would my opinion matter?" Ryan asked. "So far all you know about me is that I'm doing his bidding and that I'm apparently really, really easy to scare." He took a second to rearrange the staging area, summoning comfortable furniture, and even a few decorative elements.

Morana chuckled and took one of the seats. "Truth. However, you're also a god, and you've been free to roam about while I have been trapped in my realm. That gives you some credibility."

"Fair enough," Ryan said, setting the coordinates for the trip back to the battlefield. "I don't actually know the terms of your deal. All I know is that my friends and I have to pick you up and drop you off, because that was *our* deal."

"Our agreement was quite simple, really," Morana said. "You see, most of the death gods have been imprisoned for some time, as the result of some nastiness that I'd prefer not to discuss. Any of your sort of god could have used their nanoverses to free us, but few were inclined to do so, and our freedom was always of limited duration. If Arthur breaches the gates of Heaven, he'll have the power to free us permanently. In exchange for our help in the fight, he'll free us to gain new souls and walk the world once more. The second, to be honest, was more appealing to me. Nav has become a lonely place."

Ryan nodded thoughtfully. "That's a pretty good deal on both sides. I think he'll come through. He upheld his end of our bargain."

"Oh?" she asked. "And what was that?"

Finished at the control panel, Ryan took a chair across from her. "I needed an army. I had to deal with a bunch of...are you familiar with Varcolaci?"

Morana nodded. The Varcolaci were creatures out of Romanian mythology, a sort of middle point between werewolf, vampire, and goblin. They could tear a man apart like he was made from tissue and found death as inconvenient as an ill-timed nap.

"Arthur gave me a legion to fight the Varcolaci in exchange for transportation services."

"I see." Morana tapped her chin. "So, in your agreement, Arthur paid before you did?"

"Yeah," Ryan said, then frowned at the implication. "You're worried he'll back out on you because it happened in the other order?"

"Wouldn't you be?" Morana asked.

"Well, I'm fairly new to...all of this, really. I don't know how infernal deals work and what he can and can't back out of."

"But surely...oh my. You're still *Nascent,* aren't you?"

Ryan grimaced at the reminder. It was true, he was Nascent, a god that uncovered a nanoverse and was still undergoing the transformation into full godhood. It sometimes felt like it meant he was a child - which, essentially, he was. He didn't know half of what so many gods seemed to pick up on instinct, his divine senses were not as attuned as those of full gods...oh, and he could die without his nanoverse being destroyed. There was that little detail.

Morana gave him a sympathetic smile. "Apologies. It's been so long since I've met a Nascent, I've forgotten..."

"It's fine. I'm getting used to it."

"I should try to make it up to you, though," Morana said. "So, here's a bit of advice. You might meet someone named Ishtar. She's likely to try and convince you that you must end the world. It's absolute-"

"It's true," Ryan said firmly.

"Oh dear, you've already been taken in."

Ryan sighed. "I've had this conversation four times today. Sorry if I'm a bit short."

Everyone in the know agreed that Ryan was the Eschaton, the last god of an era. Unfortunately, opinions differed on what that meant. Some believed that meant there would be new gods, with different powers and roles. Others believed that no new gods would emerge. Ryan's friend Crystal, formerly Ishtar, believed that this meant it was time to end the world. Ashtaroth believed the same, and Ryan was pretty sure that meant that Arthur was on board but didn't know for sure.

For his part, Ryan agreed with her. Mostly. Her explanation made sense, and several people had tried very hard to kill Ryan based on the belief that it was true, so Ryan took that as a bit of confirmation. Granted, it wasn't much to go on, but...

Morana was giving him a wary look, and Ryan sighed. "Look, I'm not going to go crazy and start killing people. I promise. Right now, we're trying to figure out a way to save people, and we won't be doing anything rash when it comes to the apocalypse. Can we skip that part of the lecture, please?"

Morana sniffed. "I remember being Nascent. So sure I had all the answers, too."

Ryan rolled his eyes at the condescending tone. *Yes, Ryan, that will convince everyone you're not a child. Roll your eyes. You should throw a tantrum if you really want to sell it.* "So, once you're free, what are you up to next?" Ryan asked, hoping to change the subject.

Morana sniffed. "Something other than ending the world, I'm sure."

You walked right into that one, Ryan chided himself. "Oh, thank God, we're here," he said as the console started to flash.

"Odd choice of words," Morana said with a rueful grin, and Ryan couldn't help but agree with her. He opened the door for Morana, and they stepped out on the edge of the battlefield.

"Well," Morana said briskly, "looks like there's still plenty for me to do. Thanks for the ride." A chilling wind gathered around her as she strode into the fray.

Ryan deliberately turned his back on the fighting and came face to face with Athena. The Greek sculptors of ages past had done well mimicking her appearance, but no sculpture could have captured her energy and vitality, or her inherent grace. All the goddesses Ryan had met were beautiful, but Athena drew his eyes more than any other.

"Is that the last of them?" she asked, her voice tight. Athena had agreed on the necessity of working with Arthur, but Ryan knew that she was just as conflicted as he was, if not more so. He felt an urge to reach out to her and offer some sort of comfort, but held back, unsure if she would welcome the gesture.

He was glad he could at least give her good news. "Yup, as long as you and Crystal are done. Where is she?"

Athena jerked her thumb over her shoulder, and Ryan looked over to see Crystal perched on a rock and watching the battle. It was unusual to see her so still. A million years of life apparently left one with little patience for wasting time.

When he and Athena reached Crystal, Ryan saw that despite her relaxed posture, her expression was stormy. "I'm bloody glad that's over," she said. "Please tell me you lot are through so we can get out of here."

Ryan just nodded, and they turned to exit the field. It was time to seek different allies.

Chapter 1

Myrmidon Rising

The cold, antiseptic room shouldn't have made Bast think of the desert, but her dry, itchy eyes, swollen tongue, and parched throat caused her moments of half-sleep to be filled with images of sun and sand. When she drifted back to wakefulness, her stomach ached with Hunger so great, she almost wished for the desert of her dreams. At least then she could swallow sand to fill the emptiness in her stomach.

The sleep was never deep enough for her to actually pass into anything close to unconsciousness. She only got little tastes of sleep, just enough to leave her even more disoriented, trying to make sense of the fragments of conversation around her.

"...still alive, lending credence to the theory that..."

"...responsiveness to stimuli is..."

"...attempt again? The last time..."

It had been like that since she resurrected, and like the occasional smell of food inflamed her Hunger, the half-heard conversations drove home how painfully alone she was. They were talking to each other, and she wanted to cry out for them to acknowledge her. Talk to her. A hand on her shoulder, a whispered message; it didn't matter. She yearned for some interaction with these people, as badly as she wanted to tear their heads from their shoulders for subjecting her to this torment.

She didn't know where this place was. The last thing she remembered clearly was the battle on Graham Island. Being overpowered by Athena and her allies. Surrendering - actually surrendering - to *Athena.* That had been galling enough, but the fact that Athena had still driven her sword through Bast's stomach had been worse. When Bast had first awoken, she'd thought Athena was the one who had shackled and bound her and had put the mask on her face that prevented her from even speaking.

It's what Bast would have done if she'd been the victor. Better to restrain a foe than to destroy a nanoverse.

But then she'd started to have visitors. Individuals that walked around her, talking *about* her, never to her. She'd been denied any succor for her Hungers. No sleep, no food, no water, no interaction. She'd only been allowed air. For a mortal, this captivity would be fatal. For a goddess...she wouldn't be granted that relief. She could feel cool air brushing against her skin. At first, it had given her some hope she was outside, where rain would fall on her lips and quench her thirst, but she could also see a ceiling above her, oppressively close.

The owners of the voices drifted in and out like her consciousness. Sometimes she caught a glimpse of a white lab coat, or the edge of navy blue uniform. Nothing in those half-heard snippets of conversation gave her anything concrete to latch onto. They spoke almost constantly, it seemed to Bast. Or maybe she just couldn't remember the times when there was silence. *Say something to me. Talk to me. Just ask me a question, just say my name! Anything!*

She faded back into half-sleep, back to the desert that awaited her. Here she lay among sun-bleached bones that had been worn by the constant winds. Here she was half-buried in sand that should have seared her flesh but felt cool and distant. A scorpion scuttled across the sand near her, and with human lips, it said, "...extraction must be done carefully, we do not know how much more..."

The scorpion dissolved into the edge of a lab coat and a woman's voice. So close, the woman was *so close.* In desperation, Bast jerked her hands. To caress or throttle, even Bast couldn't say. It didn't matter. The chains they'd shackled her with clanked as soon as she'd reached the half-inch of movement they allowed her. She hissed as the edge of the shackles cut into her skin. The lab coat took a half step back and began to speak. Bast couldn't focus enough to make out the words. *Help me,* Bast tried to say. She'd beg, she'd plead if she could, but the skintight steel mask around her face arrested the motion. She made a noise, in the back of her throat, and it sent a ripple of agony along her ruined tongue and mouth.

She blacked out from the pain and found herself in the desert again. The scorpion was regarding her with curiosity, then skittered down to her arm. Bast watched, unable to move, as it stung. She wanted to scream at the sudden pain, but even here in this desert, her mouth would not move.

When she faded back into the antiseptic room, her head was slightly clearer. *I must have actually slept for a bit there.* Perhaps they had sedated her. Or perhaps she had gone mad. Was this place real? Or was the desert and its scorpions reality?

In this place, at least, she saw that she had been stuck with something: an intravenous drip providing nutrients she didn't need. She wanted to laugh, to scream, to curse whoever had thought that was required to keep her alive. It wasn't about the liquid or chemicals. It was about eating. Drinking. Feeling the gnawing in her belly fade away and feeling the dry sand on her tongue melt into soothing coolness.

No such relief was offered to her. Nothing. Bast felt herself drifting again, but not to the desert, and not to the lab. This was a memory.

"You're late," Thoth said, arms crossed, his fingers tapping with impatience. He'd abandoned the ibis head back in the third century, over twelve thousand years ago. Bast still found it odd to see him with a human face. It was even stranger to see him wrapped in the gleaming steel plate they favored in this land.

Bast shook her head to clear the rain from her hair. "You didn't want us relying on doorways," she countered. "I've been riding this damn horse for the last day, and you demand punctuality?"

The figure next to Thoth rolled his eyes. "This isn't important," he said. "She is here now. That is what matters."

Bast fixed the figure with a curious gaze. He was taller than either herself or Thoth, and broad of shoulders, with a thick golden beard that obscured most of his face. "Baldur, I presume? Or Thor?"

"Do I look like a blithering idiot, waving my hammer around and drooling?" Baldur rolled his eyes.

"There's enough rain in that bush on your face that I can't be certain about the drooling," Bast countered.

Baldur's retort was cut short by the approach of a final figure, wearing a thick green cloak. "We can cut the prattle," the woman said. "I found the trail."

Bast considered how unlikely that was in the rain, but held her tongue. If Artemis said she'd found a trail, then a trail had been found.

"I'm still not sure what we're dealing with," Bast said as she wheeled her mount around to follow the archer goddess. "All Thoth would tell me is that a monster had arisen." She didn't add the other part, the reason Thoth had asked her to join in this hunt.

He'd wanted a monster to catch a monster.

"Have you ever met a god," Baldur asked, "that could not slake their Hungers after reviving?"

Bast shook her head. "I'd never even considered the possibility."

"It happened here. Someone newfound their nanoverse. Survived long enough to undergo Apotheosis. Then the war with the Ottomans started."

"That was a year ago," Bast said with a frown. "How long is this story?"

"Short version," Artemis said, her voice sharp. "He was dismembered and entombed before he could revive. When he was finally released..."

"What?" Bast asked, her frown deepening. "So far, you've explained only how *he was denied feeding his Hungers. You haven't explained what that means!"*

"Look and see." Baldur gestured, creating a globe of light in the night gloom. In the center of the road was one of the spears favored by the local soldiers.

A man's decapitated head was impaled on the point of the weapon. His tongue hung from his lips, purple and swollen, and his eyes were wide with the terror he'd felt as he died. Bast shuddered as the skin squirmed from maggots writhing beneath the surface.

"Other Hungers develop in their absence," Thoth said quietly as they guided their horses past the macabre trophy.

Before she could ask for clarification, Bast saw a slumped figure ahead. The body of a young woman lay broken against an abandoned building, her skin desiccated and the color of parchment. Afraid to see more but unable to turn away, Bast leaned in, trying to find a cause of death. With growing horror, she realized with Thoth meant - there were two holes in her carotid artery.

"Damnit," Baldur whispered. "We're too late. He's become a full anthropophage."

"What was his name?" Bast asked, studying the woman's body with intense curiosity.

Artemis brushed the hair back from her face. "Vlad Dracul. These bodies are three weeks dead...the trail is colder than I feared."

A scorpion crawled out of the woman's wounds. Bast blinked. This wasn't had happened. This wasn't real. There hadn't been a scorpion, and it had been raining. There wasn't a dust storm. She hadn't been thirsty. It...

It was the desert again. And it was the sterile room that was her prison. The past and present ran together, and for a moment, Bast wasn't sure where any of the three began or ended.

Bast realized that, if this went on too long, she'd end up as mad as Dracul had been. She tried to find some comfort in the certainty that she wasn't mad yet. *Not yet.*

The door opened. Footsteps approached, and she tried in vain to turn her head towards the sound. For one wild moment, she was terrified, that it was the scorpion, grown so large it had to wear boots. *No. No, cling to this. The desert is a lie. This is real.*

"Is she ready to be drained again?" The authoritative male voice was familiar, and Bast knew instinctively that this was likely her chief tormentor. It was the voice of a man who gave orders and expected them to be carried out, a man who expects others to follow him straight to the gates of hell. *We'll see if they follow when I send you there.* Bast resolved to take no relief from *this* man, even if it was offered. This man had to die.

"Yes, sir. We should be able to get another two liters of ichor." It was a woman's voice. Bast had heard it before, multiple times. It was a gentle, almost motherly voice, but the speaker was a woman who always spoke of Bast as if she was a point of data, a statistical anomaly that needed to be forced into an equation. The disconnect between the tone and the words bothered Bast more than it should. It showed that this woman, whoever she was, was capable of compassion, of kindness.

She just had none to spare for Bast.

Why won't you even give me your names? It was another point of frustration that they never seemed to use names around her, always referring to each other by titles, or simply "sir." It couldn't be for fear of filling her Social Hunger - if they knew she had it, they would know enough to be sure that just knowing their names wouldn't fill it. *Some old superstition about names, maybe?* There had been times where men had believed true names had power. They were wrong, but...

"It seems to me that we should be able to fully drain each time. She's died once before, after all. She was dead when we pulled her out of the damn ocean. Why not just drain her and bring her back." The man's words should have formed a question, but his tone made it an imperative. Flat. He always spoke like that. He did not expect enlightenment, was not requesting it. He would understand what was happening.

You bastard, Bast though. *Look at me. Acknowledge me. I'm not your lab rat.*

The woman cleared her throat before saying, "We can't be certain she'll come back, Admiral. There are plenty of stories of gods truly dying. It seems safer to drain her as much as we can without killing her instead of..."

Bast felt her attention waver as another pang of Hunger overtook her. The desert began to return. Before it did, in a moment when she was between this place and the sands, she could hear their hearts beating in their chests. A steady pair of rhythms - wub-thub-wub-thub. *I'll rip them out when I get free. I'll rip them out still beating and then I'll be full.* She shivered at the thought, not from fear or disgust, but a wave of delight, and she reminded herself that she wasn't mad yet.

The desert returned. The scorpion was waiting, its tail poised over her arm, only this time the tail was a long, empty syringe. It was going to drain her ichor. It was going to drain her near death, but not all the way. She'd be weak for days afterward. Well, weaker.

It didn't matter. All that mattered was the Hunger, the need to get satisfaction.

She ignored the scorpion this time. There was a new element to the desert. High in the sky were a pair of suns, and they pulsed in time with that delicious sound. *Wub-thub. Wub-thub.* It sang to her, and Bast again reminded herself that she hadn't gone mad.

Yet.

***

The door to conference room 4B was adorned with a hand-lettered sign that gleefully proclaimed it the "Nerd Lair". Rear Admiral Dale Bridges paused to roll his eyes before reaching for the handle. He had allowed this breach in protocol so far because these consultants were not military, and the discipline Dale preferred would have made them miserable.

Long ago, Dale had learned that the happier civilians were, the better their results would be. Still, he had to take a deep breath and adopt a neutral expression before braving the "lair" that currently housed the United States military's most unusual think tank.

The rest of the base was a bastion of order, discipline, and efficiency, and the contrast made this room seem even more...weird. Dale still hadn't gotten used to the ever-expanding collection of posters; superheroes, supervillains, elves, dwarves, space marines, and all manner of nerd ephemera were rapidly covering every inch of available wall space. The conference table was littered with scientific reports and laptops mixed with stacks of comic books, graph paper, spiral notebooks, random post-it notes, and strangely shaped dice. Dale was pretty sure that some of these items were used to play some kind of game (and he certainly hoped that was the case with the dice), but he had absolutely no desire to learn the details. He had a feeling he was happier not knowing.

The tableau would have given a heart attack to most men of Dale's rank. However, the people in this room were useful, and skilled, and had unique perspectives Dale valued. He just wished they had some modicum of discipline.

To be fair, the professors and scientists were much more orderly than the comic book writers and genre fiction experts, although Dale had seen evidence that some of the academics were starting to slide towards the chaotic nature of their colleagues.

Doctor Shivani Pivarti, however, was not one of them. The Director of the recently formed Project Myrmidon was a no-nonsense woman who kept her person and personal space organized to a level that would have impressed the surliest of drill instructors. That attitude, combined with the fact that she'd been researching these entities for years before they'd become public figures - and managed to do so without letting the academic studies people took seriously suffer - had earned her the title of Director. Of everyone in the room, Dale preferred dealing with her. She could make sense of the chaos, and never let it impact how she comported herself.

Her opposite was Lazzario Littleton, who had become the unofficial leader of the comic book and speculative fiction authors. He was, according to the research Dale had conducted before bringing him in, "author of some of the most iconic storylines in modern comics", and that - combined with a strange sort of niche charisma - made the others of his ilk sit up and take notice. Dale has learned that while Lazzario was...different from the experts he was used to, the man had a keen intellect and surprising insights. Doctor Pivarti was currently giving him her full attention, even though his seemed to be equally divided between their conversation and a box of jelly donuts.

Lazzario's shadow and personal yes-man, Jake, stood nearby. Jake was a thin reed of a man with a prominent Adam's apple. Even in the cool air of the base, his forehead was beaded with sweat. It always was. Dale had wondered if it was due to a medical condition, but the more he observed the man, the more he put it down to Jake's perpetual nervous state.

Those nerves were not enough to prevent him from trying to flirt with one of Pivarti's researchers, a red-headed woman named Cassandra. At least, Dale thought he was trying to flirt. Jake was standing close to Cassandra and gesturing as he spoke, his hands shaking slightly. Cassandra, a pale young woman with thick glasses, seemed to be handling Jake deftly, politely smiling and laughing along with whatever story he was sharing. She was developing the glassy-eyed expression that seemed to go hand in hand with prolonged conversation with Jake, but Dale didn't think anyone was able to prevent that from happening. He'd even seen Lazzario's eyes glaze over when Jake got going. A fragment of their conversation cut through the din to reach Dale's ears.

"I understand that," Jake said, "but I really think an explanation isn't needed. The 'how' might be academically interesting, but from a practical effect-"

"From a practical effect," Cassandra said firmly, "it establishes limitations. In issue 186, you made it clear that Captain Blaster's powers could only..."

Dale tuned them back out. He understood that these digressions into comic book ephemera were part of the process this group used to understand the very real threats that they were up against, but for the life of him, he couldn't understand *how* they helped. *The how is only academically interesting,* Dale thought, then let the momentary amusement fade before cutting through the idle chatter.

"We need to be ready to move to live testing," Dale announced. Immediately, conversations stopped, and all eyes turned towards him. The team's expressions ranged from surprise to apprehension, and several glanced sideways at Pivarti and Lazzario, expecting one of them to respond.

They were not disappointed. "Why on Earth would we do that?" Pivarti asked, her eyes narrowing with frustration. "We're not ready yet."

Dale let out a long and ragged breath. "Doctor, you didn't watch the news today, did you?"

"I did not."

Dale punched a button on his tablet and took control of the flat screen monitor on the wall. A few more taps, and a video started to play.

The camerawork was amateur and shaky, done by some random person with a camera phone and a stronger desire for views than for self-preservation. A police officer was crouched behind his car door, using it as a shield as he fired down the street. The camera panned to follow the path of the bullets.

Everyone gasped, and even the ordinarily unflappable Pivarti had to adjust her glasses in a vain attempt to hide her shock. Coming up the street were a dozen human skeletons armed with spears and giant circular shields. "What the hell?" Lazzario whispered.

Dale didn't answer. More gunshots erupted in the street, and one of the skulls snapped back. Jake let out an excited whoop.

Then the stricken skeleton leaned forward, a bullet hole in the center of its forehead. It kept moving.

Dale waited just long enough for everyone to properly absorb the video. "The skeletons you're seeing have taken over Wilberforce, Ohio. The army is coordinating with a winged man claiming to be the Archangel Raphael, and he is telling them this is because Hell won a war against Heaven."

A few team members expressed surprise, and Doctor Pivarti opened her mouth again, but the Admiral cut them all off with a raised finger and a stern expression. He punched a few buttons on his tablet again, and a still image appeared. He gave everyone several seconds to take in the majesty of the winged man holding a golden sword raised high above his head, a beam of light shooting down from the heavens to meet the tip of his blade. Before him were a dozen human skeletons, holding their hands up as if to cover the eyes they didn't have. Bits of bone were being blown away from the skeletons from the sheer force of the light as if it were a wind scouring them clean.

"Holy shit!" one of the researchers gasped.

Dale nodded grimly. "And there's more." He worked his tablet again, and the image changed to a video clip. This one had also been taken from a camera phone, and while efforts had been made to stabilize the video, it still shook wildly. It showed a creature emerging from a second-story window. It had the arms and legs of a human, but mandibles jutted from its mouth, and from the base of the figure's spine was a thorax nearly as large as the being's torso. A pair of spinnerets at the base of the thorax affixed a thick strand of silk to the building.

Someone on the street screamed, and gunfire erupted. The arachnid humanoid propelled itself off the wall in a single leap and landed on a car. More gunfire punched through the roof of the vehicle, with flashes of light showing from the driver's seat. The arachnid tore through the thin metal on top of the car, and then the video cut out. "That isn't CGI, ladies and gentlemen. A group of these...things...have started an all-out civil war in Ghana. Their leader claims to be the Ashanti god Anansi."

Another image appeared, this one a still shot of Moloch, taken during the incident on Graham Island. "Remember him?"

"Yes," said Cassandra, who clearly didn't understand the concept of a rhetorical question, "that's Moloch. He was on Enki's team when-"

"That's correct," Dale interrupted. "He's in Venezuela building a temple to himself and gathering followers, probably to start *another* conflict, and the Antichrist and his cohorts were spotted in Greece doing God knows what. And that's all in the last twenty-four hours. Project Myrmidon needs to be on the fast track, starting yesterday."

Doctor Pivarti shook her head. "Sir, I understand that the increasing sightings of verified cryptids makes finding a more effective response seem more urgent-"

"It doesn't just *seem* more urgent," Dale snapped. "It *is* more urgent. Absolutely critical."

"-but Project Myrmidon simply isn't ready yet. Conventional means will have to last a bit longer."

Dale shook his head. "Every second that we wait just puts us further behind. The world's going to hell in a damn handbasket, Doctor. I want Project Myrmidon up and running *now*."

Pivarti's spine stiffened. "Sir, we have not finished testing for possible side effects. It is both dangerous and unethical to proceed without more data. We could inadvertently unleash monsters on the world, and perhaps find ourselves in an even worse position."

"And believe me, that's a major risk to take," Lazzario said, having finally swallowed his latest doughnut. "Like, ninety percent of the time you try something like this, you end up with horrible monsters."

"The monsters are already here," Dale replied. "Now we need some on our side. And this discussion is irrelevant because we have orders from the President. Human trials begin today."

For a few seconds, silence hung in the room as everyone digested the news of a directive from the Commander in Chief.

"Hey, I totally get that. Can't disobey the big guy." Lazzario shrugged. "But one of the things you want me to do is to let you know what could go wrong. I'm telling you that this pretty much screams 'horribly wrong'. Like, everyone's shouting at the movie screen wrong."

"Terribly wrong," Jake piped in. "Rushed super-soldier experiments are like, number five on the supervillain backstory checklist."

Pivarti pressed her lips into a thin line. "I agree with my...colleague, Admiral. The risks are-"

"Irrelevant," Dale said, already tired of this conversation. "Risks have to be taken right now. We're losing ground too rapidly. Don't tell me what we *can't* do because of risks, tell me how to minimize those risks."

Lazzario spoke up. "Okay, so a few things to consider when you're making super-soldiers then." He held up four fingers and began to tick them down with each point. "First, don't use an unwilling subject, use a volunteer. You don't want to end up with a lunatic running around with a hate-on for you. I know you probably won't do that anyway, but if I don't say it, I know I'm going to regret it."

"Absolutely," Jake added, nodding for emphasis. "Conspiracy theories will abound about any vanished person, which pretty much guarantees we'll be found out."

"Second," Lazzario continued after he was sure Jake had finished, "We're going to need intensive psych evaluations. I mean the works. Whatever kind of evaluation you use for astronauts? Take that, and then add whatever kind of evaluation you use for the Secret Service members that do POTUS protection. Then add whatever you'd want for someone who was watching your own child, Admiral. And then take it to the next level."

Jake nodded firmly again. "At least twenty. The best psychologists you can hush up. I cannot tell you how many times I've written stories where the super-soldier turns into a psychopath. It's pretty much guaranteed whoever you put though this is going to end up crazy. You need to make sure they're as sane as possible to start with. Whatever you think is enough? Add more."

"Third, make sure you've got someone in peak physical condition. The crème-de-la-crème, the best of the best. Doctor Pivarti has made it clear she doesn't know exactly what this is going to do to a person."

Dale idly wondered if Jake was going to nod so hard he snapped his pencil-thin neck. "There's a good chance that if we kill our test subject, we'll end up with some kind of horrible, undead monster that's going to eat our hearts or something."

"Fourth..." Lazzario trailed off, frowning. "I was sure I had a fourth point."

"Well," Dale said, "none of that should be-"

"Oh yeah, fourth!" Lazzario interrupted shamelessly, drawing a glare from Dale, who was used to being the one to interrupt, not being interrupted. "Pick people no one's going to miss. No friends outside of here, no family, no nothing. If this goes horribly wrong and they die, there's at least a three out of four chance that someone they care about ends up getting powers and becoming a foe for us later on down the line."

This time, Jake's head didn't so much nod as vibrate. "This is the most, the absolute most critical point. Dead family members are the unbreakable heroic motivation. Survivors never hang up the cape."

Doctor Pivarti frowned. "That hardly seems scientific."

"Doctor, we're dealing with gods and monsters. We saw demons fighting on an island in Canada. There are angels in Ohio, of all damn places." Lazzario shrugged. "We passed science about eighteen exits back, and are heading full speed towards Nuttyville, Earth, population 7.8 billion."

"You brought us here for a reason," Jake added, for once not nodding. Dale wondered if he was getting dizzy. "You brought us here because nothing like this has been tried in real life. In fiction, it's old hat. Trust us on these."

Dale nodded. "Consider your advice well heard and listened to. Doctor Pivarti, any other requirements on your end?"

She frowned. "My only concerns are focused on the subject's physical and mental well-being, Admiral. Which those two so...thoroughly covered."

"Excellent. Then you'll have your volunteers by the end of the day. Make sure you're ready for them, Doctor." Almost everyone in the room began to protest, but the Admiral just waited for it to calm down. "We will be taking all precautions," he assured them, "but we have our orders. Do the best you can with them."

"I'm ready, at least," Kathleen said, speaking for the first time. She slid a folder across the table to Dale. "You wanted uniforms that caught the right look. How's that do?"

Dale looked at the drawings inside and smiled. "Excellent work. Now it's time for the rest of you to step up."

Chapter 2

The Slopes of Olympus

Olympus was not an easy place to reach. To even gain entry, you had to go to the Core world - better known as Earth - location of Mount Olympus in Greece. From there, you had to find the cave that would let you transition over to the mythical realm of Olympus.

Ryan had nearly fallen over with shock when he saw what was on the other side of that cave. It opened on the base of a mountain that stretched up into the vacuum of space. Just looking up at it was enough to give Ryan a sense of vertigo. It was gray and barren of all signs of life, and too narrow for its height, at least compared to Earth's mountains. Almost closer to an obelisk than a mountain, although still a bit too wide for that description. The surface was spotted with cliffs and chasms that blocked any easy passage.

It was clear that the Greek gods weren't even remotely interested in company.

Seeing it had been bad enough. Athena's insistence that they actually *climb* it was something else entirely.

Ryan hauled himself over the lip of a sheer cliff, panting for breath. It was a reflexive action, not his Hungers settling in, which was for the best. If he or Crystal or Athena had needed to breathe, they would have suffocated miles ago. He wanted nothing more than to flop onto the flat ground in front of him and lay there until his arms and legs stopped screaming at him. *A few weeks ago you got winded climbing up the stairs,* Ryan reminded himself. His eyes went down the mountain. At this height, it was possible to see the curvature of the Earth, as well as the gentle blue glow of the atmosphere. *You just climbed to space. Are you really going to bitch about sore arms and legs?*

Apparently, the answer was yes. Ryan flopped onto the snow, panting for breath. He didn't *need* air anymore, but that didn't mean his body didn't want it. The snow was calming. Divine resilience meant the cold didn't bother him, so the snow was just something soft and cool to lay on. Soft, cold, and damp. And full of little rocks. Jagged ones. Groaning, Ryan decided the flop was going to be more uncomfortable than standing and stood up. *There shouldn't be snow this high anyway. We're out of the atmosphere.*

Ryan managed to get the panting under control, but he realized that he could feel the air rushing in and out of his lungs as he breathed. In space. Where there shouldn't be any air. *Well, it's not like Olympus obeys standard geography anyway,* Ryan reminded himself, trying - and failing - to dismiss a growing unease. It was easier when another world had a broken and cracked sky or was literally built on top of solid clouds. Ryan realized that the closer something was to normal, the more unsettling the abnormal was.

Crystal crested the cliff face, looking as sore as Ryan, and he had to catch her arm to keep her from stumbling. "You okay?" he asked, frowning.

"Right as rain, love." Crystal righted herself, giving him a smile, but he couldn't help but notice her eyes had a sunken look to them, one she'd worn increasingly often in the last few weeks.

Ahead of them, Athena turned to look over her shoulder. She caught the worried look Ryan gave her as Crystal dusted the snow off her hands. "Not too much further," Athena said.

"Good," Ryan responded. "I still wish we could have just opened doorways straight there."

Athena shrugged off the complaint without a trace of annoyance - if anything; she gave him a fond look. "If there are any of my kin still up here, they would have been mortally offended. If we want to earn their trust, we cannot start off by breaking ancient customs.

"After all this walking, Athena, some of them better be at the sodding top." Crystal's grumbling had a bit more of an edge to it than Ryan's did. *Lots of things Crystal's been doing have more of an edge to them.* Ryan felt a shiver that had nothing to do with the impossible space snow.

He and Athena had spoken privately and agreed that Crystal had been a bit off since Graham Island. Asking her about it got them nothing but jokes or sarcasm. Her last response had been, "When one million years old you reach, look as good you will not." Ryan had laughed and decided against pushing her further. *She'll talk about it when she's ready,* Ryan thought, then quickly amended that line of reasoning, *or at least, when she thinks it's worth sharing.* At least she wasn't trying to tell them to roll with it, although Athena was confident that was coming if they pushed her again.

To no one's surprise, the climb up Mount Olympus had done little to improve anyone's mood. Even Athena, who had made the trip before, was becoming short of patience. "I hope there is someone up there, Crystal, but as I have said - seventy-three times now, to be precise - I cannot be certain. I was cast out long ago and have not been back."

"Well, let's keep moving then. At least if it's empty, we can just use Ryan's bloody door to get out." Crystal muttered that last bit, and if Athena heard it, she paid it no mind.

The last bit of their journey involved scaling a wall of sheer ice. Ryan groaned at the idea of another cliff. *At least the last one was rock.* He was tempted to call for a pause to their trek but bit his tongue. As much as the idea of resting appealed to him, Ryan didn't like the idea of taking a break this high up. Some small part of him was convinced he'd fall asleep and roll right off the mountain. *Oh, hello, anxiety,* Ryan thought at the illogical fear, *didn't know you were still hanging around.*

"Maybe it'd be worth using a bit of power to cross this last bit?" Ryan asked.

Athena shook her head. "We're not coming up here as heroes or equals, Ryan. We're coming as supplicants who need a favor. If we charge up there in our divine glory, it will set the entire tone for the conversation. A tone we don't want. Have you heard of Bellerophon?"

"Can't say that I have," Ryan said after a moment of thought. The name sounded vaguely familiar, but he couldn't quite place it.

"He was a hero who tamed a pegasus. He was beloved by the gods...until he tried to ride that pegasus up this very slope. For his hubris, Zeus waited for him to get close, then struck him with lightning and let him fall to the Earth as a warning. If the mountain isn't enough of a clue, let me speak plainly: Zeus is not fond of uninvited guests."

"Okay, fine." Ryan sighed. "So we have to climb the whole way to show we're being properly respectful?"

"Yes," Athena said.

"Fine." Ryan fought back the urge to sigh again. *We need their help,* Ryan reminded himself.

"Glad you agree. Especially because you need to take point," Athena said, handing Ryan a pair of icepicks.

"Uh...what?" This entire time, Ryan had been relying on Athena to show him where it was safe to step. "Don't you think it'd be best if you want first? Or Crystal?"

"No," Athena said flatly. "I'm exiled from Olympus. I shouldn't even be here. And Crystal..." Athena trailed off and looked at Crystal, who shook her head. "Back when she was Ishtar, she did not exactly endear herself to Olympus. I think Hera might throw her off the mountain on principle."

"Ares always liked me," Crystal interjected with a sour note.

"Right up until the end. Believe me, he dislikes you as much as the rest now." Athena turned back to Ryan and shoved the icepicks towards him.

With a deep breath, Ryan took them and turned to start climbing. When they reached the base of the ice wall, Ryan looked over his shoulder. "Hey, Athena, how'd you get exiled?"

"Stop stalling," Athena responded.

"So what do I do with these?" Ryan asked, holding up the ice picks.

"Don't fall?" Crystal suggested with a smug grin.

"Very funny. Seriously, though. This is the first straight-up ice cliff we've had to face." Ryan looked up at it again and swallowed hard. The sheer ice was a new obstacle, and although he'd gained practice climbing over the last few days, this seemed orders of magnitude harder. *Ice is slippery.*

He tried very hard not to think about what falling down the mountain could do to him. Would he have time to twist reality? Or would he smash into rocks before he could, and find himself knocked senseless and tumbling miles down to the ground below?

"Relax," Athena said, giving Crystal a pointed look before turning back to Ryan. "You slam the pick in with each step. Drive it deep enough into the ice to support yourself, then climb up to the next. The claws in your boots will keep your feet from swinging too freely. Then repeat until you're at the top."

"That seems...easy enough." Ryan took a deep breath to try and calm himself. *Okay, Ryan. You've got this,* he thought with a confidence he didn't feel. Still, with Athena and Crystal looking on, he began to climb.

This was definitely harder than climbing actual rocks. That, at least, involved handholds he could trust, giant boulders that had stood for millennia. This was ice. Ice was treacherous, ice could crack. *Don't think about that,* Ryan thought. Every time he swung himself up to the next place to insert the pick, his heart skipped a beat. He was acutely aware that he was resting his entire weight on a thin piece of metal that was stuck into ice.

Don't look down, don't look down, Ryan chanted to himself and no sooner had he started the reminder than the urge to look down became overwhelming. He couldn't stop his eyes. Athena and Crystal were tiny specs beneath him. Even with superhuman stamina, his legs were singing with aches from the climb, and already his arms had added their voices to the chorus.

Wind whirled around him, tugging on his clothes. He was starting to sweat in spite of the cold, and the wind drove a bead of sweat into his eye. Ryan blinked, trying to clear the distraction. *You can do this.* He swallowed hard and swung the next pick.

It slipped.

Time seemed to slow as the ice pick broke free of the handhold he'd been about to create. Jagged shards of ice rained down from the impact site. He'd put his whole body into the swing, but the angle had been off, and all he'd managed to do was uselessly gouge a thin line in the ice. Ryan's stomach lurched as his feet swung wildly with the motion, and his heart dropped.

The remaining pick, the one supporting his weight, began to groan in protest. It wasn't supposed to support his entire mass, not when he was flailing like this. He could hear the ice beginning to shatter under the force. It was a high pitched sound, almost melodic.

If he couldn't regain his footing, it would be the last sound he ever heard.

Ryan's feet started to scour the ice below him, trying to get purchase, but in his panic, all he could manage to do was dig furrows. The single pick embedded in the ice was beginning to slant downwards, breaking free of its moorings, and Ryan was gripped by a horrible vision of falling - not just to the bottom of the ice wall, but down the mountain. He could see the pick breaking free at the exact moment his feet hit the wall, sending himself careening away from the wall to crash into the cliff behind Athena and Crystal. They'd turn, trying to catch him, but they wouldn't be able to grab him in time.

Ryan brought the free pick back up, hitting the ice with all of his might, fueled by divine strength and adrenaline enhanced fear. It was too much force. The ice shattered under the impact, slivers flying free and raining down on him. A couple landed on his eyes, and he was blind, and in that blindness, he lost track of logic or reason. He was sure he was already falling, just unaware of it. Any moment he expected to hit the edge of that cliff and then keep falling, impacting another ledge, then another, and yet another, until his broken corpse was finally free of the mountain and could fall all the way until it hit the atmosphere. If he was traveling fast enough, his body would ignite from the pressure at that point, leaving a blackened skeleton and a nanoverse that had once been humanity's last hope.

Ryan forced his eyes open and saw that he was still secured to the ice. The pick was at a terrible angle and starting to slide.

If Ryan had been able to concentrate, he would have twisted, Olympian pride be damned, but his panic was nearly full-blown mania at this point, and his divine powers required a moment of clarity to function. There was no time for clarity, there was no time for cleverness.

He swung the pick and heard it sink firmly into the ice. For several seconds, all he could do was stare at both picks, his arms trembling, his stomach rolling. Relief brought tears to his eyes. In spite of the cold, he felt hot, and he pressed his forehead against the cool ice. *I can't do this,* he thought. *I can't start climbing again.*

He'd faced hundred-handed giants on worlds of blasted iridescent sand. He'd grappled a mad god with more power than Ryan had ever imagined. He'd stared down a horde of vampire-goblins armed with weapons straight out of fantasy. None of those, nothing in those, terrified him more than the idea of trying to move his ice picks again.

Distantly, he heard someone calling his name. Athena or Crystal, he couldn't tell which. He didn't dare look down to check. Breathing as deeply as he dared, Ryan focused his ears on the sound. After a couple moments, he identified it. Athena's voice.

"Keep going!" Athena shouted. "I can see a ledge just a bit above!"

At least, that's what he thought she was shouting. She must have been doing some minor twist herself, making sure her voice could cut through the distance and roaring wind. It's what he wanted her to be saying, at least. Looking up seemed safe. Ryan forced his head away from the wall, his eyes watering at the effort of not going to either side and looked upwards.

It was there. Athena was right. Just a couple more handholds and there was the top of his climb. He just had to make his arm move. He just had to...

"I can't!" Ryan shouted, his voice coming out hoarse and cracked. He could barely hear it after it left his own lips. There was no way Athena and Crystal could hear it on the ground. If he could focus, he could twist...and if he could focus, he'd have nothing to fear.

His old anxiety spoke up then, an old friend whispering in his ear. At the worst points in Ryan's life, it had always been there like a good friend, happy to remind him that no matter how bad things seemed, it could still get worse. *If you don't move, you'll be hanging until you fall.*

That terror was enough to overwhelm every other fear. The last two handholds were taken with careful, trembling deliberation, a task that should have taken twenty seconds stretched over five minutes of real time and hours in Ryan's perception, and then he was hauling himself over the edge.

When he got to the top, he scrambled away from the edge and pulled himself into a trembling ball. *No more,* he thought. Any more passage up or down the mountain would be done with twisting and damn the Olympians if it offended them. He'd fight them all if it meant he didn't have to climb another step on Olympus, and he'd do it with a damn *smile* on his face.

Athena reached the top of the ice wall some time later. Ryan hadn't moved in the interim, and she knelt beside him. "Are you all right?" There was genuine warmth and concern in her voice.

The tears had turned to frost on his lashes, and Ryan hoped it just looked like he was brushing ordinary ice away when he wiped his eyes. "Just slam the pick in with each step, eh?" he asked. He'd meant for it to come across lighthearted and playful, but it just sounded bitter.

Athena's hand was on his cheek, and he leaned into the contact. It was soft and warm and human and everything Ryan needed in that instant. "I would have caught you. You know that, right?"

"It was kind of hard to think in the moment. I was sure I'd fall too fast." His voice was still high and hoarse, his heart was still pounding in his chest.

Athena smiled and laughed. She was doing that more often these days, Ryan realized. It was a nice change. She had a laugh that wrapped around you like an embrace. "Ryan. I've caught arrows with my bare hands. You think you could fall that distance too quickly?"

"I'm still mortal," Ryan said quietly. "I could still die."

"Yes," Athena said. She met his gaze and, in a tone that would brook no argument, added, "If I allow it to happen. Which I assure you, I will not."

Ryan took a final deep breath and nodded. "Thank you." She moved her hand away, and he felt its absence as strongly as he had the touch. "No more climbing."

"No more climbing," Athena agreed, looking over his shoulder. "We're here."

Ryan had been so paralyzed he hadn't even looked to see what was around him. He turned his head and found that the stone beside him wasn't a random boulder, but the step of some grand staircase, leading up to an immense facade. The doorway was flanked by columns, and Ryan's mouth fell open as he took in the enormity of them. He'd seen photos of the Parthenon and the Coliseum, and this facade seemed to be the primordial ancestor to them, related in the same way birds were technically dinosaurs. *I bet they were cheap knock-offs even back in the day, before they were ruins.* Through that empty door, he could see a city full of buildings on an enormous scale: columns that dwarfed the ones in front of him, stone buildings the size of skyscrapers, and statues that would overshadow Lady Liberty.

Athena spoke, and at first, he could hear the pride in her voice. "Ryan Smith, welcome to the Theopolis." On the last word, Athena's tone shifted, the pride turning to confusion and an undercurrent of fear. "What...no, that's not right," she finished.

Crystal approached as Ryan's eyes began to adapt to the splendor, letting him notice details he'd missed at first. One of the immense towers was leaning drunkenly, looking like it might collapse at any moment. Another had huge chunks torn from the sides as if some giant hand had punched holes in it. One of the statues had an arm proudly upraised, but it ended at the elbow. Amid all the ruins, this city of the gods was silent, save a wind moaning its way between the cracked and crumbling stones.

"What...what happened?" As soon as the question came out, Ryan realized it was stupid, as neither of his companions had been here in hundreds of years.

"I don't know," Athena hissed through clenched teeth, her fingers curling into fists. "I can't imagine what could have done...this" There was an undertone to her rage, a hint of deep pain. It gave Ryan a chill that had nothing to do with the cold air.

Crystal sighed, sounding more irritated than anything else. "How about we hold off mourning until we find out if there's anything to mourn, yeah? Maybe they just stopped the cleaning service. C' mon, we didn't climb all this way to bloody mope once we got to the top."

Without waiting for an answer, she stalked towards the ruins, leaving Athena and Ryan no choice but to follow.

***

Ryan's first experience with another world had been Cypher Nullity, the abandoned afterlife of Crystal's ancient people. There, he'd felt an overwhelming sensation that he was walking among the ruins of something that had once been great and grand. In some ways, the same feeling of kenopsia was worse here in Olympus. In Cypher Nullity the architecture had been alien and the ruins so unimaginably ancient that they were clearly something from another world, something scraped out of fiction and dropped in front of his eyes.

It wasn't the same with Olympus. Time had not worn away all the colors from the walls, and the banners that hung from windows were still brilliant shades of red and blue and green - although their edges had frayed into tatters, and insects had begun to eat holes in the cloth. One such banner broke loose of its moorings and drifted on the wind. Ryan reached out and twisted reality just enough to redirect it towards his hand. As soon as it met his fingers it began to dissolve, so worn that it couldn't stand even the gentle touch.

Athena stumbled beside him, and Ryan felt a tug on his arm. She'd latched onto his shoulder so hard her knuckles were starting to turn white. He'd never seen her like this before, and he began to ask what was wrong, but he saw that her eyes were glistening with withheld tears, and the words died on his lips. She wasn't looking at him but staring at the tattered fabric that had come to rest on the street in front of them.

Again Ryan started to speak, and again he stopped. He tried to imagine what it was like for her. What if he had left Saint Louis for hundreds of years, then come back to find the Arch shattered and laying in the Mississippi, and the homes empty and abandoned? What words of comfort could someone possibly offer him then?

He glanced at Crystal, whose mouth was pressed in a thin line. She just gave Ryan a barely perceptible shake of her head. If she had any words, it seemed, she was keeping them to herself. Ryan didn't think she did. Still, he felt an urge to do something, to do *anything.* Athena - brave, unflappable Athena, who had kept her calm after watching a friend fall to Bast's gunfire - could barely stand.

Ryan just reached up with his free hand and rested it on her fingers. It wasn't much of a comfort, but it was the only one he felt he could possibly offer.

After a few seconds, Athena gave a faint sniff and let go of Ryan's arm. "Come on," she said in a hoarse whisper. With that signal given, the three of them wove between columns. In some places, they had to pass under ceilings that were still held in place. In others, they had to walk carefully over the ruins beneath an open sky. A few of those colossal statues were visible as well, standing silent vigil over the crumbling ruins.

A fallen column of marble, covered with a spider web of cracks, barred their path. Athena stepped to the right of the column, and Ryan moved to follow her. Her back tensed slightly, and he altered his path to go around the left. *Don't intrude,* he thought to himself. Athena had let her barriers down more than Ryan had ever imagined she could. It would be best for her pride to let her have the momentary privacy.

Instead, he let his eyes drift upwards, trying to figure out what it had fallen from. This building only had four other columns and a ceiling. The columns were oddly curved, and some of the cracks in the ceiling looked deliberate, almost like it was...*A hand,* Ryan realized with a sudden shock. The columns weren't columns at all, but the immense digits of a hand from some statue.

Walking under the massive hand provided a new perspective of the statues' scale. Without a twist, even his newfound strength would not give him the ability to leap up and touch the palm he'd mistaken for a ceiling. He felt like an ant weaving its way between the fingers of a human. Down past the hand, where the wrist should have been, he could see the sandaled feet of the rest of the statue.

He had to pause to process the sudden perspective. He'd compared these statues to the Statue of Liberty, but now that he was among them, he realized that had been giving them too little credit. That statue would be a toddler compared to these, barely coming up to their kneecaps. It was dizzying in a way Cipher Nullity hadn't been, grand in a way that Officium Mundi couldn't hope to match.

This, without question, felt like a place that had housed *gods.*

He turned to find the path out from under the hand and came face to face with a stone bust of similarly immense proportions. It lay on its side, half-buried in the pavement. Ryan gaped. This was, without a doubt, the severed stone head of Athena.

No wonder she wanted to be alone, Ryan thought as he started moving again. Walking among the ruins of her former home would be hard enough. Coming face to face with her decapitated statue must have added a whole new level of surreality to the experience.

Sure enough, when he saw Athena again, her face was fixed into a scowl. She avoided Ryan's gaze, and when Crystal emerged from the other side, Athena stared straight ahead as she walked.

He chose to respect her privacy and looked away, his eyes falling instead upon an empty cart under a sign painted with faded Greek letters. Whoever had abandoned the cart had taken the contents. *Maybe it was an orderly evacuation,* Ryan thought. *Although if it was...why leave the cart at all?*

More questions with no answers.

Ryan was just getting ready to break the silence when someone else did. "Depressing, isn't it?"

Ryan spun towards the voice, to see a tall, bearded man emerging from a darkened doorway. The tall, two-pronged weapon he carried stirred something in Ryan's memory, but he couldn't quite place it. Ryan's heart started to pound, and he began to reach for the threads of reality to prepare an attack, but the newcomer simply looked them over and then swept into a mocking bow.

"Athena," he said, "it has been far too long, and...Crystal, it has not been long enough. And this must be Ryan the Eschaton. I must admit that I had expected someone grander."

"Hades," Crystal said flatly. "Since you're here, I assume the war in Heaven is concluded?"

"It is," Hades said smugly. "Arthur stands victorious, and the gods of death are free again."

"You have never cared about freedom, and never liked leaving your domain," Athena said. "Why are you here, instead of back in your kingdom?"

Hades gave her a thin smile. "It has been ages since I have had word from Olympus. Although I dislike this place and its politics, I do have some care for my brothers and sisters. As I had no need to come as a supplicant, it was no trouble to come and investigate."

"Any idea what happened here?" Athena demanded.

"Come." Hades motioned for them to follow him into one of the nearby buildings, a long, flat structure with massive pillars. The building was mostly intact, and the walls inside bore murals that reminded Ryan of the art he'd seen on Greek pottery: black and white, with a highly stylized appearance. They covered the walls from end to end, a dizzying array of stories depicted entirely in the artwork. Hades stopped in the center of the main room, next to a basin holding water gone green with stagnation. "I've found no trace of the others. I plan to ask the sisters if they know what has happened to our kin."

Athena's eyes moved away from the wall to meet Hades' gaze. "You know where to find the Fates? I couldn't find them after I was cast out."

"They reside in my realm. All the deities with the gift for prophecy got locked away with us. I guess Yahweh did not want the competition." He smiled without humor and reached into the pool of stagnant water. The algae covering it began to turn black, rotting away as he put a small amount of power into it. "I don't suppose you have any insight into what happened here, stern Athena?" It was an odd phrase but seemed to mean something to Athena, who blushed slightly.

"I wish I did. Have you maybe found a clue - anything - that tells what happened?" Ryan noted the touch of desperation in her voice.

Hades nodded. The black rot covering the pool was starting to melt away, slowly being replaced by bright blue. "Yes. Well, in a sense. I've found a complete lack of clues, which is a clue in and of itself."

"Oh, spare us the riddles, love," Crystal snapped, and Ryan wondered again about her irritation. *I'm being irrational,* Ryan thought to himself. Hades was getting on his nerves too, and the way Athena's face fell further with every word did nothing to alleviate that. Crystal just had less patience for it, clearly.

Hades stiffened as he looked at Crystal. "Fine. I've found no evidence of battle. I've found no destruction that couldn't be attributed to neglect. Whatever happened here, I believe our fellow Olympians left under their own power. I believe they could still be alive." He pulled his hand out of the water, which was now crystal clear.

Athena sagged slightly, her relief plain on her face. Crystal ground her teeth but kept her tone level. "Well, that's good news at least. Thank you for that."

Hades studied her a moment. "Yet you dislike it?"

"Too bloody right." Ryan motioned for her to stop, but Crystal plowed ahead. "Hades, we've got a situation here, yeah? I know you underworld gods are a bit tied up with your new freedom and all that, but if we fail the sun will literally explode."

Hades's eyebrows rose half an inch. "That's quite the claim. I suppose you have some proof to back it up?"

"I lived the last time it almost happened," Crystal said, her voice cracking like a whip. "I bloody damn well prevented it. You're a god of an underworld, Hades. Surely you know that humanity was not the first sentient race to walk this world."

"I do," Hades conceded. "Yet I hardly find that compelling proof we are in imminent danger of losing the sun."

Crystal looked ready to pull her hair out, and Ryan stepped in before she slapped the smug off Hades's face. "Hades, please, listen. Even if you don't believe us, we were desperate enough to go to Arthur for allies. We need help. Bast and Moloch are still out there, doing God knows what, and Earth's slipping into chaos. Help us find them."

Ryan had to admit to himself that it was nice to see Hades look thoughtful, nice to see *anything* from him besides smug dismissal. "Explode," Hades mused. "The sun is going to explode. Well, if you truly believe that, it certainly explains why you all are so driven."

Crystal nodded, her hands balling into fists at her side, "So if you have any insight as to where we might find the Olympians, or any other god, now would be a bloody good time to share it."

Hades thought for a long moment, and then looked at Athena. "Tartarus."

That one word made Athena gasp. "You think?"

As Hades made a gesture of affirmation, Ryan interrupted. "Care to explain to the Nascent guy?"

Athena and Hades both turned towards him. "Tartarus is a different underworld realm," Hades explained patiently. He walked over to one of the murals on the wall, depicting a vast pit with grasping tentacles and immense hands reaching out of it. Around the pit, divine figures, men and women alike, towered over smaller figures that Ryan took for ordinary mortals. "It never had a god. It was where we imprisoned the Titans eons ago, in the most secure prison we could devise." Hades's arm moved, drawing Ryan's gaze away from the pit to what was painted around it.

It was a maze, one so vast it dominated the entire wall. Ryan noticed one particular figure - a massive man with a bull's head instead of a human one - before turning back to Hades. "And you think the Olympians are locked up there? But if there was no fight, how were they trapped?"

"No, Ryan." Athena took over for Hades, and now her eyes were blazing with desperate hope. "In times of crisis, it's easy to convert a prison into a fortress. They must have gone there to defend themselves!"

"From what?" Ryan asked.

Hades and Athena shared a look, and Hades shrugged. "I'm not certain. Although..."

"Another pantheon," Athena said. "It's the only thing that makes sense. The Aesir or the Deva, most likely - I don't know any others that would have the numbers to drive our kin from this mountain."

"Perhaps," Hades conceded. "Although they might have gone because of something from within. If the locks on the Titan's prison had started to come loose, Zeus would take everyone there to try and reinforce the barrier."

"I'm sorry," Crystal interjected. "Are you saying it's possible the bloody titans are loose?"

"No," Athena said, and Hades nodded in agreement. "If they were free, they would be back on Earth by now. If Hades is right, then the Olympians are staying to make sure the barrier stays shut. If I'm right, it's because they still fear the threat that drove them to Tartarus in the first place."

It made sense to Ryan, although he didn't want to be the one to point out to Athena that neither scenario meant the Olympians were still safe. "Okay, we'll go there next."

Crystal grumbled. "Please tell me we can just take a bloody staging area directly there?"

"It wouldn't be much of a prison if you could, now would it?" Hades asked. Since the question was clearly rhetorical, he barely paused before continuing, "You have a bit of a trip ahead of you, I'm afraid."

"I know the way," Athena's voice was calm and full of purpose.

"Wonderful," Hades responded. "In that case, I take my leave. Best of luck." He turned, waving his hand. A hole opened in front of him - not a doorway, but a proper portal. Before stepping through it, he looked over his shoulder, "I would consider that perhaps not all of you are needed to investigate Tartarus. Given how pressing you believe other concerns to be, perhaps it would be best if some of you sought allies elsewhere."

"Wait!" Ryan said, drawing startled looks from the others. "We still need help. If you're not busy…"

Hades shook his head. "I have my own concerns, and I'm not going to throw them aside for some mad quest."

"It's not mad," Athena said, her eyes narrowing. "The entire world is at stake."

"Athena," Hades said with a sigh. "I thought you, of all people, would know better than to fall for Ishtar's nonsense. The world isn't going to end. You two," he indicated Ryan with a nod of his head, "are going to run around, following this madwoman, until you figure this out. Or are killed, permanently. I'm not interested in that."

Crystal snarled, "You just bloody said we should seek allies elsewhere because things are pressing. What'd you mean by that, if not the end of the world?"

Hades's eyes widened. "Ishtar. You and Enki broke the veil of secrecy surrounding divinity on national television. Arthur just secured victory for Hell and is going to be making mortals more aware of the reality of beings like us. As Ryan so keenly pointed out, Moloch is running free, and that monster needs to be put down. I have no quarrel with Bast, but she is your adversary, and the battle will likely be destructive. Others are moving openly. The world is changing, and for all your madness, I do like you. Your hearts are in the right place, although you are painfully misguided. I think the sooner you prove to yourselves that the world isn't going to end, the sooner you can start cleaning up your own mess - and then turn your talents to actually doing some *good* for the world."

None of them had an answer to that. Hades gave them a tight smile. "When you do realize that you're chasing shadows, come see me, and we can talk about the future. Or, I suppose, come to me if you get some actual proof this isn't madness."

Without waiting for a response, Hades stepped through the portal and into his realm.

Crystal broke the silence. "Much as I bloody hate to say it, he had one good point. We're lacking in allies, and we can't be sure we'll find the Olympian in Tartarus. Athena, love, how long is this trip?"

Athena bit her lip. "A week. Maybe more, depending on the obstacles we face. But if one of us attempts to go alone, it will prove much more dangerous."

"We're strapped for time," Crystal said, "If all three of us go off on a quest to Tartarus, and it turns out the Olympians aren't there, then we just wasted a sodding week we don't have."

"It's also the only lead we *do* have!" Athena retorted, her tone sharpening to match Crystal's. "The Curators will not give locations, and my kin remain our best hope."

"No, they aren't! We wasted an entire climb up the mountain, and now you want to go on another quest with no guarantee we'll find them." Crystal was squaring up now, her jaw set in frustration. "You just want to make sure they're okay and don't seem to understand that if we waste too much time, they'll die with everyone else!"

"Uh," Ryan said, knowing he had to speak before things got uglier, but having nothing more to add beyond that single syllable.

Fortunately, Athena hadn't earned the title "goddess of wisdom" for getting sucked into arguments, and Ryan's sound managed to stop Crystal from saying anything worse. Athena held up a placating hand. "Two days. We take two days to try to find other allies. After that, if we haven't found any, we try Tartarus. And if we have found help, then we can split up since it won't just be the three of us."

Crystal closed her eyes for a moment, and Ryan could have sworn she was counting backward. "Agreed. And that last comment was out of line, love. Sorry."

"Apology accepted, Crystal, but you were not entirely incorrect. I do want to make sure they are well, but I have not forgotten the importance of what we do." She offered Crystal a hand, and Crystal took it, relaxing slightly.

"Great," Ryan said. "So...where do we look for those two days?"

They both turned to him, and Crystal smiled. "I actually think I have a pretty good idea there. Tell you on the way, yeah?"

As soon as they agreed, she took out her nanoverse and opened a door, smiling as she held it open for them. Ryan caught a glimpse of Crystal's nanoverse, resting between her fingers and looking like just a typical black marble. When he did, for an instant, he felt the same revulsion he had for the cancerous mass that Enki's nanoverse had become. It was gone just as quickly, so he put it down to the stress of the looming end of the world and worrying about his friend's increasingly erratic behavior. Later, he would wish he'd paid more attention.

Chapter 3

Tangled Webs

Project Myrmidon's command center was buzzing with activity when Admiral Dale Bridges strode in. Computers hummed quietly and fingers tapped on keyboards, a constant undercurrent to the endless streams of conversation. Most of the attention was focused on the map spread across the back wall, covered with red, yellow, and blue dots.

"Can you confirm that?" someone was saying into a microphone. "Video, photograph...Yes? Excellent. And you think it's a chupacabra because...no, I understand. The video shows it actively sucking the goat's blood? Okay, I'll add it. Let us know if you see anything." The speaker typed for a moment, and a new yellow dot appeared in Phoenix.

Yellow, meaning there was a confirmed incident that did not require immediate attention. Something to watch.

The blue dots seemed to appear almost randomly, but there was a purpose to their madness. They were handled by a computer algorithm, scanning traditional and social media. Hashtags, photos, posts, and news reports that suggested relevant incidents were all on display. Dale tried to ignore the blue dots. Someone far below his pay grade would follow up and determine if they should be dismissed, or upgraded to yellow...or red, which signified confirmed incidents of note.

Despite his best efforts, Dale's eyes were drawn to the blue unknowns. *Too many...far too many.* If half those blue dots turned red, they would be overrun. With a determined effort, he turned his attention to the red dots: Ohio, Ghana, Sydney, Venezuela, and South Korea.

Ghana and Venezuela were of particular interest because those were the two spots where beings claiming to be gods were active. One was of a known entity; there had been confirmed sightings of Moloch in Venezuela. *At least one of these beings doesn't pretend to be anything other than a demon,* Dale thought grimly. He knew that, according to his mythology experts, Moloch was a member of the Canaanite pantheon who had been "turned into" a demon by later Christian writers. As far as Dale was concerned, he had always been a demon, just like all these other blasphemous entities. The one in Ghana was claiming to be Anansi, a fairly significant figure in the local mythology. He was regarded as a trickster, which to Dale sounded much like a deceiver.

Dale popped his knuckles in frustration, a habit he'd picked up during the first Gulf War and had never shaken. These beings were showing their true colors. Enki had claimed, when he first appeared on camera, that these "gods" had no desire to be worshipped. Ryan and Crystal had claimed the same thing. Yet here were two confirmed sightings, and what were they doing? Gathering followers. Sure, they might not be calling them worshippers, but at the end of the day, was there any difference between following a false god and worshipping it? You might not be actually saying prayers, but if you were taking advice from one, you might as well be praying to it.

It galled Dale that so many people were falling for the bullshit. Galled, but didn't surprise them. Humans, as individuals, were capable of great things. Humans in groups were only as great as those that led them, and they gravitated to whoever held the most authority. If someone claimed to be a god and could be convincing to the ignorant, people would follow, and people would draw lines and pick sides.

From where Dale was sitting, Moloch and Anansi were cut from the same cloth as Enki and Ryan. Both were building a religion, although Anansi was being smarter about it, more *subtle,* by not advertising his intentions. However, he'd plunged Ghana, one of the most stable nations in that part of Africa, into a civil war, and he'd done so with an army of spider monsters. Moloch, meanwhile, was openly seeking followers, and the monsters that he commanded were far more varied. They boiled down to the exact same thing: problems that Dale had to put down.

The blue dots were multiplying again, and Dale popped his knuckles harder. If he had access to the entire United States military apparatus, every satellite in orbit, and every single intelligence agent employed in the Western hemisphere, he'd still need a full year to confirm or eliminate just a single day's worth of reports. Those numbers weren't hyperbole; an analyst had told him exactly that. It was an impossibly large task, and there was no doctrine, no rules of engagement, for these kinds of threats. They were writing new rules as situations developed, protocols that had no precedent. Half of them had to be rewritten after they were tested and proved to be insufficient or outright failures. It was an organizational disaster.

In that, more than anything else, the nerds were earning their keep. They'd spent their entire lives thinking about how to fight threats that the military hadn't wasted time considering. Lazzario and Jake had worked with military analysts to create standard rules of engagement for unknown threats, and when they weren't working on project Myrmidon, they were going through a list of mythological creatures and their attributes, trying to come up with tentative plans to handle them. It was all based on speculation and best guesses, but it was a damn sight better than going in blind.

What they couldn't give Dale was the resources needed to handle so *many* threats. *We need better intelligence, so we can start triage,* he groused to himself. *Is a chimera worth engaging if it's staying away from civilization? Do we need to send subs to open fire on the akkorokamui before it moves into shipping lanes, or can we wait?* On those, the nerds could only speculate, and Dale did not trust speculation far enough to gamble the lives of his soldiers on it.

He was so distracted by the enormity of the task in front of him, it took him a moment to key into the actual feeling of the room. It wasn't desperate or frantic like he had expected. People were talking excitedly, and there were smiles and thumbs up. There was a palpable feeling of excitement in the air, almost electric in its nature. *What's changed?* He wondered as he waited patiently for security to finish confirming he was who he appeared to be - a precaution Lazzario had insisted on. "We don't know if there are shapeshifters, but myths are full of shapeshifters, and let me tell you, a single shapeshifter is all that we need to wreck our entire operation." Insights like that were why Dale considered the comic book expert to be a worthwhile investment.

Doctor Pivarti approached once he had cleared security. The younger woman - a term Admiral Bridges was finding increasingly useless with every passing year, since the doctor was in her forties and still young enough for him to mentally assign the moniker - had a tablet in one hand. Usually, the doctor was an exceedingly restrained woman, but today her eyes were practically gleaming. "Admiral. I finally have some good news for you."

Dale finally relaxed his death-grip on his fingers. "I've been waiting to hear that for some time, doctor."

"And I've been waiting to say it for even longer," she said, handing him the tablet. It showed the designs for a mechanical device that looked like a flattened backpack with straps across the chest. Dale studied it for a moment, not wanting to admit he couldn't make heads or tails of the thing. Fortunately, the doctor knew his limitations and started speaking after allowing him a good look. "We finished fabrication this morning. We finally figured out why our initial injections were unsuccessful."

The Admiral raised an eyebrow. "Oh?" He handed back the tablet.

"The ichor did take. It did change the genetic structure. We've actually seen some of those subjects display some low-grade abilities - the ability to run in excess of seventy kilometers per hour or lift up to five-hundred kilograms. Impressive results, but nowhere near the range we need."

Dale stared at her for a moment. "You just said you'd created literal super-soldiers. With a force of those, I could win almost any conflict on the globe. And I'm just now hearing about this?"

"Super-soldiers?" Doctor Pivarti cocked an eyebrow. "You've been spending too much time around Lazzario. I didn't say anything because you specifically told me you did not want your time wasted, Admiral. As impressive as these soldiers are, they aren't what you wanted. We're dealing with gods, or at least beings with the power to claim that title. They would tear these soldiers apart. You wanted me to reach out when I had real results. And now we do."

The Admiral debated if he should let the oversight slide. The doctor could be so literal sometimes that he worried about giving her instructions he hadn't parsed carefully. She should have notified him the instant she knew there was a way to create super-soldiers. Instead, she'd waited until now to tell him because they weren't precisely what he wanted?

Before he could open his mouth to object, the doctor was already moving on. "You see, the key was the Black Stone you brought in with the subject. It's been growing steadily, and we finally identified the radiation it's giving off." She paused for effect, showing a dramatic flair that Dale would have expected from Lazzario, not her. "It has the same signature as cosmic background radiation, but at a much greater intensity."

If she had hoped that would impress the Admiral, she was doomed to disappointment. "And that means?" he asked.

Doctor Pivarti's exuberance was unabated. "It means that this stone is somehow emitting the same energy as the rest of the universe, but in greater quantities. From a physics standpoint, it's..." She looked at his face, and the Admiral could see her resist the urge to roll her eyes. "The important part, Admiral, is that this harness draws that energy off the Black Stone and imparts it to our soldier. We're calling it a Prometheus Pack, after-"

"-after the man who stole fire from the gods. I do know my mythology, doctor. What effect will that have on our soldiers?"

"We've already exposed one of them to it in controlled doses. They get powers, Admiral. The way one subject described it, he could see the fundamental mathematics that governs reality, and manipulate them."

"Get me the nerds," Dale barked at a nearby sergeant. The man snapped to attention and scurried off. "Is the change permanent?" he asked Pivarti.

"No. It only lasts a short period of time from the initial exposure. That's what the Prometheus Pack does, Admiral. It drip feeds them a steady dose of this radiation. There are some side effects, but they seem to be minor."

"Go on."

"After draining the radiation, the soldier reports extreme thirst, hunger, drowsiness. All of those we expected. What we didn't expect was that the soldier would experience a high level of loneliness, bordering on a compulsive need for human companionship. We spent some time comforting him, talking to him, and by the end of it he was functional, but it was alarming. He also, ah..." The doctor trailed off.

"Spit it out, doctor. I need to know what we're dealing with."

"He propositioned one of the aides, sir. In rather crude terms. She's talking to HR now. We're reassigning her but keeping her within the project to avoid any allegations of discrimination. It seems to be a side effect of the loneliness, and the soldier was highly apologetic once he calmed down."

Dale pursed his lips. "Doctor, did he express *any* concern about his ability to...control himself?"

To his relief, Doctor Pivarti shook her head. "He was horrified at the suggestion. I think that with time for them to adapt, they'll be able to handle these side effects well. However, I do think Lazzario's point about mental stability was well made."

"Agreed." Dale moved on, relieved that they weren't accidentally creating a whole new breed of monsters. "So we can have bursts of them being...what did Lazzario call it? A 'reality warper.' And after that, they're merely stronger and faster than any human alive."

Doctor Pivarti shook her head. "Once he'd burned through his available store of the radiation, sir, he was no stronger than he had been before the ichor treatment. That came back once he'd eaten, drank, and slept, but it is a vulnerability to keep in mind. I'd strongly suggest we avoid deploying these soldiers as individuals, to compensate for that weakness. Otherwise, we run the risk of a lone soldier ending up as weak as a normal human in the middle of a battle."

Dale nodded in firm agreement, then paused in thought. "Doctor...do you think it's possible these other beings have the same limitations?"

Doctor Pivarti nodded. "I think it's a certainty. Perhaps they can be similarly drained of their powers."

"Excellent," Dale said, with as much emphasis as he could put into that single word. The idea of finally finding a weakness in these beings... *it's taken far too long, but we have something else we can use.*

Lazzario entered the room at a rapid clip, puffing as he headed straight for Dale. "Everyone else is on the way, sir. I just ran."

"I can tell," Dale said, regarding the man's red-faced and sweaty countenance. "We would have waited for you."

"Yes," Lazzario said, "which is why I ran."

Dale smiled in approval. "You can fill the others in. Doctor Pivarti, is our soldier ready for a demonstration of what he can do?"

Doctor Pivarti nodded firmly. "Follow me, gentlemen," she said, leading them out of the room.

***

Dale was pleased that Roger Evans had volunteered for the Myrmidon project. The man had shown a good deal of common sense in the retrieval of Bast's body, knowing it would be valuable even though they hadn't anticipated that she would revive. Dale had reviewed his service record after that, and everything in there made him a perfect candidate: he had done two tours in active combat zones and serviced with distinction, earning a Bronze Star, had no living family, had scored the highest marks on their psychological evaluation, and, in Kathleen's words, "will look damn good in one of our uniforms." As far as Dale was concerned, they couldn't have chosen better.

Which is why it was so annoying that Lazzario hated the choice. "He's too perfect, Admiral," he protested.

"I'm sorry, I don't follow," the Admiral said, as technicians helped Roger into the harness. "He meets all of the criteria you set."

"Yes, exactly." Next to Lazzario, Jake was nodding his head firmly.

"Care to elaborate on that?" Dale asked.

"It's rule one of this kind of thing. When someone is a perfect fit, there's something wrong. I mean, for god's sake, the man rescued a cat from a building in Kabul. He saved a damn cat, Admiral."

"It's too perfect. It's too arranged," Jake added. "It's almost certain that this is going to go terribly."

Dale could feel a headache coming on and fought back the urge to reach for the Advil in his pocket. "What was the point of the criteria, then, if you *don't* want someone to actually meet them?"

"Oh, we want someone who meets them," Lazzario said.

"No point to having criteria if we didn't," Jake added.

"Just not too well, if you know what I mean," Lazzario finished.

"I really don't," Dale said. "What do you think is going to go wrong?"

The two glanced at each other. "The thing is, Admiral, why does Captain Evans here *need* to be a super-soldier? He's already basically Mr. All American."

"Because he can't fight these beings yet, Lazzario."

"Oh, no, of course he can't. It's just..." Jake groped for the answer, looking at Lazzario for help.

"...we don't know how much stories influence these things," Lazzario said. "I mean, we're operating from the assumptions there's a degree of influence. Cycles of myth that turned into the basis for our modern tropes. The thing is, in all the stories, if someone is the perfect candidate to be a super-soldier, they usually make an *imperfect* super-soldier."

"So what, then, should we be doing?" Dale asked, unable to keep the frustration from his voice.

"Watching him closely," Lazzario said after a long pause. "I suppose it's a bit too much to really worry that narrative causality is actually that firm a rule. If it is, then we're pretty much screwed anyway, now that I think about it."

Dale frowned. "Why would you say that?"

Lazzario grinned. "Admiral, we're a super-soldier program in the desert trying to reverse engineer divine power and stuff it into a human frame. If tropes are laws, it's pretty much guaranteed that Captain Evans over there is about to turn into a terrible monster and kill us all. If the real world is operating under narrative law, we'll end up with a psycho killer no matter who we strap into that device."

Meanwhile, Doctor Pivarti stepped away from Evans and gave the Admiral a thumbs up.

"So objection withdrawn?" Dale said.

Lazzario and Jake shared another glance, then nodded reluctantly. "Objection withdrawn."

***

Inside a windowless concrete pillbox, Dale kept his eyes on the monitors showing Evans striding into the desert towards the designated testing area. Peripherally, Dale saw the two comic book specialists move to the back of the room like that would somehow protect them if something went wrong. It was almost amusing.

By contrast, Doctor Pivarti was perfectly calm. "Everyone ready?"

"Ready and eager, Doctor."

The doctor leaned forward and pushed a button to speak to Evans. "Captain. There's a rock to the southwest of you. I'd like you to make that rock go away."

On the screen, Evans nodded and turned to face the offending stone. It was about four feet across, a huge boulder that must have been rolled into the testing area for this purpose. He stretched out a hand, and Dale leaned forward, watching in fascination as Evans wiggled his fingers for a moment. The harness strapped to his body began to glow.

Then the boulder exploded with a deafening peal of thunder. Dale reflexively jumped backward, then mentally chided himself for reacting just like the civilian consultants.

Roger stood there, hand still outstretched. Dale stared, his mouth hanging halfway open in shock as the debris from the boulder settled onto the ground. The display had been impressive, and he needed to process what he had seen, which was not an easy thing to do. A man - not a demon, not a god, but a man that Dale *knew* - had stretched out his hand and a bolder had detonated like a claymore.

That last word helped his rational brain kick into gear. It really had been like a claymore: a shaped charge. The rubble wasn't spread around wildly; instead, formed a narrow cone. *He turned it into a shotgun blast of rock,* Dale thought, marveling at the realization. *If anyone had been standing on the other side...*

Doctor Pivarti leaned forward and spoke into the microphone. "Well done, Captain. Now, there are hostiles to the east. Deal with them."

As soon as she mentioned hostiles, cardboard cutouts of men popped out of the desert. Before she finished the word "east", Evans leapt to the side and extended his hand again. Some force Dale couldn't see cut one of the cardboard men in half before she could finish the word "them". Evans gestured again, and the other two were struck by balls of flame that flew not from Evans's fingers, but instead materialized behind them and streaked into their heads. Everyone in the pillbox stared at the flaming remains of the "hostiles".

"Thank you, Captain." Doctor Pivarti said smoothly. "Now, tell me, what exactly did you do there?"

The Captain's voice came clearly through the speakers. "For the boulder, I applied a kinetic force, but at irregular pacing. I...well, I selectively told chunks of it they wanted to move away from me but applied slightly different forces to each one so it would tear the boulder apart. For the first of the hostiles, I pressurized the air and sent a stream at the target at about 15,000 psi. For the other two, I pulled all the oxygen in the air into a single point and increased its temperature, then sent it in their direction."

Dale leaned toward his own microphone. "Why did you start the fireball from behind them? Why not just form it directly around their heads, or just hurl it at them?"

Given how quickly the answer came, it seemed Evans had anticipated the question. "We're dealing with beings that have been doing this for thousands of years, sir. I have to assume they've seen most of the tricks. I went with an assault from behind so they won't see it until, ideally, it's too late. It's the same reason that, even though it's frowned upon, it's a sound tactic to shoot from behind."

Lazzario, who had finally moved up with the others, nodded and chimed in, "The logic is sound. I mean, even with these powers, he's got a hell of a learning curve. Anything he can think of, the enemy has probably already seen and dealt with. The trickier he is, the better his chance of succeeding."

"Excellent," Dale said. "And how do you *feel,* Captain?"

"Hungry, sir." There was a pause. "No, it's more than that. I feel...great, but also like I haven't eaten all day. I'm thirsty, to the point where it's distracting. And...I feel isolated. That's fading while we're talking, but it definitely was strong immediately after doing three different alterations to reality in such quick succession."

Dale glanced at Pivarti, who was nodding. "This is in line with previous experiences," she said. "I think we're very likely going to want to make absolutely sure we equip them to deal with these needs. Backpacks with straws for easy hydration. Food beyond normal rations to satiate this strange hunger. And always, always working in groups to deal with the loneliness."

"I wouldn't send someone against one of these things alone unless I had no other choice," Dale said, drumming his fingers on his knees in excitement. "How soon can we have more ready?"

"We have three additional harnesses prepared, awaiting your orders."

Dale nodded. "Get them equipped and start their training. I want all four ready to deploy tomorrow." He stood up and glanced at Pivarti and Lazzario. "It's time to start pushing back. Any objections?"

If they had them, they knew better than to voice them.

***

New York had seemed like the best city to visit, since virtually no one stood out here, even if their faces had been plastered on the news. *At least, that's the theory,* Ryan thought to himself, scanning the street. His phone began to beep with dozens of notifications.

He'd been cut off from the core world for so long, they were all coming in at once now. "Sorry," Ryan muttered, remembering how much the phone had annoyed Athena back when they'd gone to meet the heresiarch, "but I have to check this."

Crystal shrugged. "I don't know about you two, loves, but I burned enough power climbing up and down a bloody mountain to be a bit peckish. Can we find somewhere to eat?"

Ryan nodded absently as he unlocked his phone. They started walking down the street as Ryan scrolled through the notifications. Most of them were-

"Street," Athena muttered, bringing Ryan up short.

"Right, thanks."

Most of the notifications were from friends tagging him in various videos of himself, demanding to know what was going on. Using "friends" in the loosest possible terms - college classmates, former coworkers, his sister, who was beyond furious at him at this point, and...Jacqueline. He just stared at the notification in mute surprise for a few seconds, unable to process it. Jacqueline hadn't spoken to him much since the breakup, not that he'd exactly tried to reach out. A six-year relationship falling apart didn't lend itself to an easy friendship afterward. But here she was tagging him in some ANN article? *She has to know I'm not the damn antichrist,* he thought, pulling up the notification to see what-

"Light changed," Athena said. Ryan took a step further, and Athena's hand snapped out to catch him on the chest before he could actually enter the street. Surprised, he looked up. Traffic continued to zip by.

"Why'd you tell me the light changed?" Ryan demanded.

"Wanted to see how aware you were of the world around you," Athena said with a smirk.

Before he could retort, the light actually did change, and they began to cross the street. Annoyed, Ryan looked back to the notification. Jacqueline's message was simple. "You know this guy?"

Ryan couldn't fathom why she had done that. It wasn't like they were friends. *Probably just curious.* That didn't sit right with Ryan, but there were more important things to worry about. Like the headline of the article: "Man claiming to be Anansi starts Civil War in Ghana."

Eyes widening, Ryan opened the article. The picture directly under the headline showed soldiers opening fire on an indistinct shape. Ryan couldn't make out the creature's form, but whatever it was, it clearly wasn't human. Humans only had two arms. He skimmed down to the article.

Accra, Ghana - For the third day, government soldiers clashed with arachnid humanoids in the service of a man claiming to be Anansi, the ancient Ghanan trickster god.

"Lamppost," Athena interjected, breaking Ryan's concentration. Frustrated with himself, he stepped to the side to dodge the obstacle as he kept skimming the article.

He responded to Jacqueline's tag with a simple, "Nope, but I have some friends who might. TY for the heads up." Then he looked at his companions. "Either of you know Anansi?" he asked.

Athena curled her lips in apparent distaste. "I can't say I do, but I know his type."

Ryan blinked. "His type?"

Athena nodded. "Trickster gods. They're devious, underhanded, and like getting the last laugh whenever they can. Loki, Anansi, Hermes, Puck, Morgan Le Fay... they're all like that."

"Anansi's one of the nice ones, though," Crystal interjected. "Like Prometheus, Coyote, Hare...they like getting their laughs in, but they're good people."

Athena sniffed.

"He's also the first god we've heard break cover since Enki died," Crystal remarked. "That makes him a potential recruit we actually know how to find."

As they stepped into a restaurant, the smell of freshly baked bread, sizzling steak, and barbeque sauce reminded Ryan that a mountain as high as Olympus was a pretty steep climb, even for a god.

The conversation lagged as they tended to the business of settling in and ordering food. The break gave Ryan a chance to consider Crystal's point. Taking the help of the first person to come along was how they'd gotten saddled with Moloch last time and look how that had gone.

After the waiter left, Crystal resumed the discussion as if there had been no interruption. "And I always liked Anansi. I mean, we haven't spoken in a few hundred years, but he was always a fun bugger to have around."

"He's a Trickster," Athena repeated. She managed to lace that last word with enough scorn that Ryan wondered if Anansi's ears were burning even across the Atlantic. Both Crystal and Ryan waited a moment, but Athena seemed to think those three words should settle the argument.

Ryan couldn't help asking, "But since you've never met him, and Crystal knows him...?"

"I know his ilk. Tricksters, as their name implies, should not be trusted."

Ryan met Crystal's gaze, and she only shrugged and rolled her eyes. "I'm not a big fan of discounting someone because they belong to a group," Ryan said carefully.

"Please," Athena said. "Tricksters are something you *chose* to become. It's not something you're born into. It's not like being the Eschaton. If someone was a god of murder, would you think it fair to judge them based on that?"

Ryan grimaced and looked at Crystal. "What are your thoughts?"

"We kind of have a dearth of options, love," she said.

"Last time you thought that way, didn't you end up allying with Moloch?" Athena asked, echoing Ryan's earlier thoughts.

"Okay, low blow. You're not wrong, love, but it's still a low blow."

Athena gave her a cold smile. "It still proves my point. Tricksters are treacherous. It's in their nature."

Ryan swallowed and looked at her. "Wait, if it's a choice, how can it be in their nature?"

"Well..." Athena stopped and frowned. "We just don't know if we can trust him." From the look on her face, she knew how weak her argument was starting to sound.

"I'm not saying we should repeat the Moloch mistake, love," Crystal jumped in. "Bloody hell, I learned my lesson there. But we should at least give it a chance. Just...make sure we spend a bit more time talking to him before we dash off into a life or death fight, yeah?" Athena opened her mouth to object, but Crystal wasn't done. "Besides, you're not exactly a paragon of good decision making. If you want to bring up Moloch as bad judgment, don't forget you teamed up with Enki, and he's leagues worse."

Athena stiffened at the reminder. "I certainly haven't forgotten that, Crystal," she said through clenched teeth.

"Okay," Ryan said, drawing out the word before things could get heated. Athena and Crystal were staring daggers at each other, and it felt like the tension was going to erupt at any moment. "Why don't we all dial it back down to eleven, okay?"

For a second, Ryan didn't think he'd gotten through to them, as their gazes were still locked in mutual fury. Then Athena took a deep breath and glanced at Ryan, then back at Crystal. Athena sighed. "What does that article say he's doing?" It wasn't an apology, but it seemed enough to mollify Crystal for the moment.

"Uh..." Ryan shrugged. "The headline says he started a civil war, but that doesn't seem as clear from the article."

"The things Tricksters do are rarely clear," Athena said sourly.

Ryan raised an eyebrow. "You really have a problem with Tricksters, huh?"

"You say it like it's a bad thing," Athena countered, her voice harsh. "Having a problem with Tricksters is just being smart."

"I dunno about that, love. It seems to be a bit past the point of rational," Crystal chimed in.

Athena ground her teeth. "I expected you to understand, Crystal," she said. "Everything is a game to them. You really want to hinge anything important on the word of a Trickster?"

"We don't have many other options," Ryan said, not pointing out that so far, Athena hadn't done much to convince them that Tricksters were anywhere near as bad as she claimed. "And I'm not saying we go up to him and say 'you seem trustworthy. Come, let us tell you all of our secrets'. I'm just saying we should talk to him, find out what's going on, and go from there."

Athena scowled but conceded the point. "Fine. Anything else on the phone?"

Ryan returned to checking his notifications, eating mechanically once the food arrived. It wasn't long before he came across a tag that made his blood run cold.

"Moloch Establishes Venezuelan Cult," he read aloud.

Both Athena and Crystal gave him sharp looks. "Any more details?" Athena asked through gritted teeth.

Ryan skimmed the article. "There's something about a national park: 'El Ávila National Park has been cordoned off by the Venezuelan military'. Um...Authorities think Moloch has holed up in there, but it's a pretty big area to search."

Athena nodded. "We can't let that go unattended. We at least need to know if he's in there, and what he's doing."

"Too bloody right there," Crystal said, leaning her elbows on the table. "Ryan, I think you should go talk to Anansi. He'll like you. Athena, you can go be sneaky in Venezuela and check on Moloch."

"And what about you?" Ryan asked with a frown.

"I've got a third lead to pursue. Someone I expected to help us out back during that mess with Enki. I want to make sure she's okay, and if she is, I want to know why the *hell* she didn't answer when we called for help."

"Who?"

Crystal shook her head. "Not important, love."

"It sounds pretty important to me," Athena objected. Then she cocked her head. "Oh. Of course. Dianmu."

Crystal nodded firmly.

"Dianmu?" Ryan asked.

"One of the few people who have remained friends with Crystal throughout the millennia," Athena said. "I honestly was surprised when you showed up without her. I'd warned Enki to plan for her."

Crystal's eyes flashed. "If she got hurt because -"

Athena held up a placating hand. "He said he didn't want to pick a fight we didn't need, so we could deal with Dianmu if she showed up."

"And you trusted him?" Crystal spat.

"Woah," Ryan jumped in, "Crystal, I thought we were past all that."

Crystal's glare softened, but only slightly. "I'm just saying that if my oldest friend is dead or worse because of you, we're going to have a sodding tough conversation."

"If Enki had gotten to her," Athena said, choosing her words with evident care, "he would have had a third nanoverse to add to that abomination he made. I'm sure she's fine."

Crystal took a deep breath. "You're right." Athena gave Crystal an expectant look, but if she was waiting for an apology, it didn't seem to be forthcoming. "Anyway. Ryan to Anansi. Athena to do some recon on Moloch. And I'll go check on Dianmu and find out what the hell happened there. After we have dessert."

Chapter 4

Blight

As soon as Crystal was alone in her staging area, she let out a long breath.

"Switch to real display."

She knew what to expect, but still watched closely, hoping that this time would be different. *C' mon, love, you're too old for that level of self-delusion.* The display shimmered, and the colors began to run like rain. The image of her nanoverse went from being a young and healthy universe, full of bright stars that were alive and brimming with energy and potential, to something Crystal had never imagined possible.

The stars should have been brilliant white and yellow and red, just like in the core universe, and as her nanoverse had always looked before. Now, though...the first star she saw as the real view asserted itself was the pale purple of a bruise. Other stars were an unnatural green, looking like pools of algae floating in the void. There were red stars, but instead of flame-red of red dwarves, they were a deep crimson that made them look like spots of blood. A scattering of yellowish stars reminded her of pallid, sick skin.

Stellar matter stretched between the stars in immense gas clouds, making the entire galaxy look like a great mass of unhealthy flesh, a tumor that stretched across the sky. Crystal shuddered. After the battle with Enki, she had needed to do a Crunch and restart the nanoverse, but it should never have reformed looking like this. At first, she had thought could be a passing change, a strange new stage of early universe development, but as the nanoverse progressed and grew, that hope had faded rapidly.

So your nanoverse looks like a bunch of infected open wounds, love. This can't possibly be a problem, yeah? She bit her lip. *None of this should be possible. Yet here it is. How?*

That question was the one that was eating at her the most. There had to be a cause for this, something behind it. Was it just that she was getting old? No god had ever endured for as long as she had, at least not to her knowledge. Maybe this was a natural part of a nanoverse's life cycle if it stuck around as long as hers. Just as flesh and bone broke down after years of use, no matter how healthy the mortal was, maybe entire universes succumbed to natural decay. Crystal frowned as she considered it.

"It's possible," she said aloud. As soon as the words were out of her mouth, however, she decided they were wrong. Yes, it was possible that mere age had finally taken its toll, but that rang false to her. If it was age and wear and tear, it should have happened gradually over time, each iteration showing more and more signs of this unhealthy universe. This abrupt change, on the other hand, couldn't be attributed to pure entropy. *Especially not when a better answer exists.*

Enki's dual nanoverse. The unnatural abomination he'd formed by taking over Tyr's nanoverse and merging them together, making him so powerful they'd needed a nuke to defeat him. Crystal remembered destroying it, how *wrong* it had felt. How she'd gagged to touch it, how it had taken so much effort to destroy the damn thing when it should have just been an act of will. She'd thought it was done after that, but now...*It was a contagion,* she thought, *like popping a pox pustule on a plane. I let all of it out in my nanoverse, then collapsed damn thing around it, bringing all the foulness into one place, and let it infect everything right from the bloody big bang.*

That answer, as much as it disgusted her, at least made sense. Well, at least it made sense in a "none of this should be happening, so normal logic doesn't really apply here" kind of way. Nothing else had changed, at least not that Crystal knew about.

She'd considered telling Ryan and Athena. She really had.

And how exactly does that conversation go? "Hey, loves, my sodding nanoverse is going to hell. No, you can't do anything about it. Yeah, I think this is probably my last bloody go around. Go ahead and worry about it. It's not like we have anything better to do." Crystal kicked one of the chairs of her staging area, needing to lash out at *something*.

It didn't help.

The truth, Crystal had to admit, was that she'd gotten used to being the expert. Whenever someone needed to know something about godhood, they'd been able to turn to her. Oh, sure, they often *hadn't,* and it usually ended up being a giant bloody mistake for them, but there wasn't any element of the divine experience she wasn't intimately familiar with, either from going through herself or watching some god or another endure it. Nascency. Apotheosis. Hungers. Pantheons. Different categories of gods. Even the longing for the release of mortality that came in a god's twilight years. She understood it all.

Unfortunately, nothing in her experience had prepared her for this. Nanoverses followed a very predictable pattern from birth to death. There were exceptions, of course. Enki's merger of two nanoverses had proved that beyond a shadow of a doubt. He'd done something she'd believed, she'd thought she had *known*, to be impossible. But at least that had just been a difference of degrees. Enki had become stronger than any other god had ever been, but in the end, it had only been a matter of fighting him, overcoming him, and destroying his nanoverse. None of that fell outside the range of what Crystal knew.

This? The stars in her nanoverse turning the colors of diseases, the stellar matter spreading like an infection? It was so far outside her knowledge it might as well be written in gibberish. It was like she'd woken up one morning to find gravity pushed instead of pulled. *No, not that.* She'd still have context for that. It was like she'd found gravity suddenly caused people to burst into flame. There was no frame of logic for it.

Why now? Of all the bloody times, why now? If it had been a different time, she might have gone to Athena to brainstorm. Or to Dianmu. Or, long ago, even Enki. *That's a sick joke now,* Crystal thought with a grimace. He was the cause of this, even if he hadn't meant to be. Now Crystal had to clean up his mess, and it had become *her* mess. But who could she go to now? Now, when the others needed her to have all the answers?

"I didn't ask for any of this," Crystal said to the empty staging area. She was surprised at how bitter she sounded. It had been millennia since she'd resented being the last Eschaton. Those scars had healed with the passing of countless eons. Or at least, she'd thought they had. It seemed they were still rawer than she had imagined. *I didn't have anyone to guide me through this. Just...*

No. Crystal wouldn't think about him now, not after so long. There was no point to dredging up ghosts from before the dawn of man.

"You need to quit bloody whining," Crystal said, her voice the sharp reprimand she'd use on a small child. She tried not to think about how often she was talking to herself. "They need you to hold it together."

That was the rub, she realized, the real heart of the issue. Ryan and Athena, and anyone else they could convince to join up with their side, needed her to be the knowledgeable one. They were trusting her about the end of the bloody world, and that was quite a bit to ask people to take on faith. The last thing their group could stand right now would be doubts about her ability to manage her own nanoverse. *So you'll just have to bloody deal with it. You're omnipotent, aren't you? Get out there and sodding fix it.*

"Drop into real space," Crystal said, watching as those cancerous stars stalled in their orbits. She took a deep breath and teleported herself to the nearest one.

This star should have been a red dwarf, with a temperature of a few thousand kelvins. Up close like this, it should have been blindingly bright. Instead, it shone with a sullen, purple luminescence that bathed the orbiting planets in an unnatural ultraviolet glow. Crystal held out her hand. *Best to start small. Let's get this star right.*

She focused her will.

The moment she did, a sickeningly strong wave of nausea hit her. She doubled over in empty space, heaving into the void. If she'd had anything in her stomach, she was certain she would have lost it. Instead, she had to fight down a burning sensation and the taste of bile in the back of her throat. *No...* she thought, shaking from more than just illness. She was supposed to be omnipotent here, she was the Goddess of this universe. Nothing was beyond her!

Crystal straightened and braced herself. She extended her hand again, ignoring the way the tips of her fingers trembled.

Change, she thought, giving words to her will.

The nausea hit her again, but she was ready for it this time. It still caused her stomach to churn, and she could still feel stomach acid burning in her throat. *No. No, no, no. You are stronger than this. You are the bloody master of this universe.* The star still shone with that disgusting purple light. Her outstretched hand was shaking so violently, she could feel it in her back. *You are not going to resist me,* Crystal thought. Another retch tried to escape her throat, and she fought it down, clenching her jaw so hard she could hear her teeth strain under the pressure. *You. Will. Change!*

The star shimmered and, with reluctant slowness, began to change. Crystal felt a surge of triumph and pushed even harder. It might take her thousands of years local time to fix every star, but that would be only days in the real world. Whatever was wrong with her nanoverse was correctible! It would just be a minor inconvenience.

The last bit of purple faded from the star, and Crystal let go of her will with a fierce smile.

Before her eyes, the star popped back to the purple color. "No!" Crystal screamed in the vacuum. It shouldn't be possible.

But it was. It had happened. Somehow, her nanoverse was resisting her will.

Crystal teleported back to her staging area and lost the battle against her stomach. Unable to stop herself anymore, she threw up.

It took her a few minutes to finish shaking. What had just happened was beyond impossible. *There's that damn word again.* She took refuge in the only thing she could find. Something within her power, something that didn't have anything to do with the corruption eating at her nanoverse - something that she was confident she could accomplish.

"Set course for China." Crystal felt some relief saying that, as part of her wanted to get out of her staging area, a feeling she didn't think she'd had since becoming a goddess. She glanced up at the diseased colors of her universe. Frowning, she muttered, "Put the color filters back in place."

The stars and galaxies above her shifted again and looked once more like a normal nanoverse.

You can't avoid it forever, you know. Crystal shook her head to dispel the nagging voice. Whatever was going on with her nanoverse had to be dealt with eventually, if that was even possible. And if it wasn't...then she'd just have to hold on until it was time to end the world. *I can do that, at least,* Crystal told herself. *I've waited too long for a second chance, and nothing is going to get in my way.*

Chapter 5: How to Make Friends and Influence Gods

The sunlight momentarily blinded Ryan as he stepped out onto the streets of Accra, a wave of dry heat washing over him as he blinked to let his eyes adjust. The light and heat were just short of oppressive, and he needed a little bit to get used to the change. *Well, it's not the worst thing sunlight's ever tried to do to me,* he thought as his vision cleared.

His nanoverse's doorway connected to the bathroom door of an out of business gas station. A bright yellow "Coming Soon" sign was displayed over the entrance, and he caught a few curious looks from pedestrians as he stepped out of what was supposed to be an out of commission building. He raised his hand in a quick, friendly wave, and got a few nods in return. The universal maxim of "act like you belong, and people will assume you do" was in effect. It helped Ryan mask his surprise and a little bit of shame. Before this, his entire view of Africa had come from movies and TV shows. He'd been expecting to see some level of abject poverty around him.

Instead, what he found was, well, a city, much like the ones he had known his entire life. There were only a few details that jumped out at him as being foreign. The gas station prices popped out right away: the sign proclaimed that gas was ₵4.19 per liter, as opposed to the dollars and gallons Ryan was used to. Aside from that, the trees weren't the ones he knew; they were lower to the ground and their leaves were different shapes. Beyond those details, the most surprising thing was how normal it all looked. While Ghana hadn't quite reached full developed nation status yet, it was well on the way, and it showed.

Ryan pursed his lips as he realized that, with the end of the world approaching, this country probably wouldn't get a chance to be classified as a developed nation. Decades of work and planning brushed aside because he'd become the Eschaton.

You're not here for the sights, he reminded himself. He started walking, weaving among the pedestrians crowding the streets of Accra. He put on his best "I'm a clueless tourist" face, gawking at everything like he'd never seen it before. In truth, he was still struck by how ordinary it all seemed. To his left was a brown apartment building, laced with balconies. They were mostly empty, and Ryan couldn't blame anyone for wanting to stay indoors in this heat. There were still people on the streets, walking and talking, although they were doing so with the general lethargy that comes from heat. The accents were different, and Ryan found them warm and melodious, something he could listen to for days on end.

Unfortunately, he didn't have days to listen. *I have to come back here someday,* Ryan thought, then scowled as it occurred to him again that there was an excellent chance there wouldn't be an Accra to go back to when this was all done. Depending on how the world ended, this city might not even exist anymore. *But the people will,* Ryan thought with a surge of determination. *Damnit, these people will. I might not ever be able to save Accra, but wherever we take its people, they'll be alive.*

He did his best to push off his anxiety about how difficult that would be. Fortunately, a distraction presented itself as he saw his destination was on the left. The building was an unassuming structure with a stylized spider painted in the window.

Before barging in unannounced, Ryan took a moment to survey his surroundings. No one seemed to be paying him much attention, but something was raising his hackles.

There. Two men, sitting in a nondescript car. They looked like they were both reading on their phones, and if it weren't for his divine sight, he would have believed it. However, the car was sending out radio signals, not just getting them, which screamed "undercover cops" to Ryan.

Of course cops are watching who goes in and out of here. Their best-case scenario involves an actual cult of literal spider people. Their worst-case scenario is an attempted coup by a hostile god, and the whole world knows what we can do now. He hoped they hadn't recognized him - half the world still thought he was the actual Antichrist - but it was too late to do anything about it.

Instead, he headed inside.

He entered a clean and well-kept waiting room. A pair of fans sat on the floor, keeping air circulating. The radio was on, and Ryan could hear a newscaster discussing the current weather. There was a TV connected to the wall as well, showing some game show Ryan didn't recognize. Ryan headed for a man sitting behind a desk at the far side of the room. A small brass nameplate on the desk proclaimed him to be Kwadwo Commodore.

Ryan hadn't mastered the ability to decode and speak languages yet. Athena and Crystal had tried to teach him, but there hadn't been enough time between all the chaos. Thankfully, English was the official language of Ghana. "Hello," he said, smiling.

Kwadwo gave Ryan a puzzled look. "Can I help you, sir?" His voice carried the same accent Ryan had heard from most of the people on the street.

"Yes. I'd like to speak to Anansi."

Kwadwo tensed slightly, and his hand reached for his phone. Ryan couldn't read minds, but this guy's thoughts were written all over his face. *Get rid of this jerk as quickly and politely as possible*. "Of course, sir. And who may I say wishes to speak with him?"

"Ryan Smith. A fellow god."

Kwadwo paused, and for a moment Ryan thought the man recognized him and was either frightened or impressed...then realized that he wasn't so lucky. He just thought Ryan was a lunatic, one of probably a dozen he'd dealt with today alone.

"Of course, sir. I'm sure we can make an appoint-"

Ryan didn't twist too hard. Just enough to change the direction of every photon in the room so they converged in a sphere above his outstretched palm. The man's smile vanished, and his eyes widened into a bulge. "Sorry for the theatrics," Ryan said, "but I'm kind of in a rush. Maybe he could squeeze me in?"

The ball of light vanished, and the man inclined his head towards Ryan. "I'm very sorry for my doubt."

"No need to apologize, Kwadwo. You could not have known he was what he claimed to be." The voice came from the door at the back of the room and out stepped a new man. He was African, about Ryan's height, and his build was leaner than most gods Ryan had met so far. His hair and beard were both cut short and streaked with white. He wore a gray suit, the top two buttons of the shirt undone, and regarded Ryan with an amused glint in his eyes. There was something in his bearing that made Ryan feel like he was intruding, a proud, regal posture that got Ryan to feel like he was underdressed for the occasion.

"Anansi, I assume?" Ryan made himself smile, although he wondered how many times he'd have to deal with someone stepping out of a hidden alcove.

Anansi inclined his head in agreement. "Ryan Smith. Kwadwo, clear my appointments for today. I have a feeling I am going to find myself quite occupied." Anansi stepped back through the doorway without waiting for a response, and Ryan followed.

Inside was a sitting room with a low table and cushions on the floor. Another door sat at the back end, and Ryan suspected that it would lead to Anansi's staging area. The other god motioned for him to take a cushion. "I'll ask that you forgive me for not revealing myself sooner. I wanted to take your measure."

Ryan took a seat, and Anansi did the same. "Really? That was a test?"

The grin Anansi gave him wasn't cruel, but Ryan got the impression he was being laughed out. "Life is a test, Nascent. Sometimes, it is just more direct than others. I find it is very educational to see how a man treats those that could be seen as beneath him."

Ryan nodded slowly at that. "So how'd I do?"

"Polite, but overbearing. Very American. Could have been much worse." Anansi's eyes sparkled with amusement.

"Well, I've only been a god for a few weeks. Haven't gotten a chance to get more arrogant. Give me a couple decades, I'm sure I'll be lurking in doorways and testing random strangers."

Anansi roared with laughter and reached over to clap Ryan on the back. "A sense of humor! I think I'm going to like you, Ryan Smith."

Ryan couldn't help but give a genuine chuckle of his own in return. The man's laughter was infectious. "I hope you do, Anansi. Because I need your help."

Anansi's eyes narrowed, although his smile didn't waver. "Straight to business? Also very American. I just came out of seclusion to re-enter the world, and you wish to drag me into your battle with Enki?"

"No." Ryan shook his head. "Enki is dead. But the world is going to end, and most of the gods are sitting on the sidelines. We need your help."

Anansi's smile faded, and he leaned forward to fix Ryan with a laser-focused gaze. "Yes. I received missives from both Enki and you. Both told vastly different stories, Eschaton. I had hoped to hear both sides before making my decision, but you have slain the opposition, so now I may only hear from you." Anansi's gaze did not break as he reached under the table and pulled out a pair of beers. He slid one to Ryan. "Drink with me and tell me your tale. Start at the beginning, Ryan Smith. At the end, I believe I will know if you can be trusted or not."

Ryan cracked open the beer. "And if I can't be trusted?"

"Then, I will take no pleasure in ending your life." Anansi opened his own drink.

After some thought, Ryan took a drink. *Well, best be honest. He said to start at the beginning...* "So, as long as I could remember, I was being followed by a guy in a suit, right?"

It turned out to be a wonderful thing Anansi had cleared his day, as the story carried them long into the night.

***

Crystal stepped out of her nanoverse, trying to remember the last time she had been in China. It had been...*No, I'm sure I've been here since the awful business with the bloody opium. Wasn't I?* It bothered Crystal that she couldn't remember. She was dimly aware of a child scrambling away from her arrival and a woman scowling at her from a doorway. That seemed less important than her uncertain memory. *Didn't I come here during the first World War? Or was I somewhere else then?*

Crystal shook her head, trying to clear it. *I was here back in 1978!* She thought triumphantly. *It was 1978, because they unbanned Shakespeare, and I wanted to see Othello in Mandarin. I bloody knew I'd been here since the Opium Wars.*

Satisfied to have answered her question, she finally began to take in her surroundings. China had made some astonishing progress in regard to poverty reduction in the last thirty years, but in Crystal's one million years of life, she had not encountered a city without a slum. Guangzhou was no exception. She had noticed over the years that the experience of the urban poor was fairly universal; the only thing that marked the area as being uniquely Chinese were the characters written on the signs.

She'd find who she was looking for here. Crystal frowned, remembering what Candia had told her, back before this had all started. "A goddess must guard against callousness." Guangzhou's "urban villages," the euphemistic names for the slums, were the kind of place where a degree of callousness was needed to protect yourself to the human suffering that surrounded you.

"There she is! The ghost woman!" a young voice said from the alley.

Crystal turned to face the speaker. The child she'd barely noticed earlier had come back with a woman in tow, and when Crystal turned towards them, the child scampered behind the woman's leg. The woman was about Crystal's height and possessed the sort of effortless poise that was usually associated with dancers or gymnasts, moving smoothly to protect the child from this intruder.

She looked like she was in her late twenties until you looked at her eyes. Those eyes belonged to someone far older than her apparent age. It was the best way Crystal had learned to spot gods. No matter what they did, their eyes always looked old.

Everything about her was clean and neat. She was wearing jeans, sneakers, and a white t-shirt that seemed too spotless for this alley, and her hair was short, coming just down to her chin, serving as a perfect frame for her face.

"That's no ghost," the woman said kindly. "That's a very old friend of mine."

"Very old?" Crystal snorted. "I'll try not to be insulted, Dianmu."

"As if you were ever that easy to insult, Crystal." The woman – Dianmu, goddess of lightning - smiled. "You're scaring my people."

"Sorry about that, love. It's been a rough few weeks."

Dianmu nodded. "Why don't you go to the other children, Hui? Let them know I have a guest, but we're still eating at noon sharp."

The boy nodded vigorously and glanced over at Crystal. "Sorry I thought you were a ghost," he muttered before dashing away.

Dianmu smiled after him. "I suggest we wait for privacy to speak," she said to Crystal.

"I think that's for the best, love." Crystal followed her down the alley.

***

Nothing about Dianmu's apartment indicated that it belonged to a goddess. Crystal supposed you could call it a penthouse suite since it was on the top floor, but that term typically conjured images of rooftop pools and glass panel windows overlooking a beautiful view. You expected to see some tosser in a suit swirling brandy in a penthouse.

You could never imagine anyone doing that here. For starters, it was nowhere near that large. It didn't take up the whole floor; several other apartments shared this floor with Dianmu, although it was larger by several degrees than the apartments below it. It was clean and well maintained, but it had a lived-in feeling that you'd never get in a penthouse. There were tiny, almost imperceptible scuff marks on the tile floor, and minuscule grooves worn into the wall where someone had repeatedly traced their fingers along the drywall day after day.

The living room had a single futon in it, comfortable-looking but with faded stains from years of use and exposure to the sun. The only thing that made the apartment unusual was the lack of electronics. No television, not even an old and bulky model. No computer fan whirring from an unseen office. Only the lights, a clean but ancient window AC unit, and a small refrigerator made any use of electricity.

The room was laid out with this in mind, Crystal realized as she took a moment to take off her shoes. The futon was placed to get the maximum amount of sunlight during the day, and from the indents worn into the cushions, whoever sat in it preferred to read by daylight. No end tables were placed near the unused outlets, instead sitting in easy reach of the futon.

Most gods and goddesses preferred, if they dwelled among mortals, to decorate their homes with art and antiques, pottery and paintings - the trappings of luxury from bygone eras. Dianmu had forgone that. Instead, she outfitted her apartment with the trinkets that one accumulates over the course of...living. There on the end table was a photo of Dianmu with two smiling, gap-toothed boys. Next to it was a framed newspaper article about a new police captain in the Guangwei Subdistrict of Guangzhou, the man in the photo bearing a striking resemblance to one of the children. *Father? Brother? Or just that little boy all grown up?*

Crystal noticed that the theme was repeated throughout the room: framed photos of Dianmu and a child, each sitting next to a connected item. A college admission letter here. A second photo of a smiling adult in a lab coat, and so on. Children, and then success as adults.

"Who are they?" Crystal asked.

Dianmu smiled. "Children of the district. Ones I was able to help."

"That's... that's great, love," Crystal said with genuine warmth, although she couldn't keep a tinge of jealousy from creeping into her voice.

Dianmu evidently heard it. "You helped people too, Crystal."

"I did, yes, but never..." Crystal gestured towards the photos. "I help people. You change lives."

"We all do what we can," Dianmu said. "Are you Hungry?"

Crystal shook her head. "Thank you, though. Just got back from Olympus."

Dianmu raised an eyebrow. "One would think that a journey like that would inspire Hungers, not be a reason to not have them. Then again, it has been some time since I've heard word from there. How are the Olympians?"

"Missing. Looks like for some time, actually." Crystal didn't bother to hide her grimace. It was one more mystery she didn't have an answer to, one more problem that was weighing her down. *So many stupid, trivial things. The world is going to end. I don't have time to chase after missing gods.*

Dianmu studied Crystal's face, "You're serious?" she asked. "I'd heard rumors, but I assumed they would have turned back up by now."

Crystal nodded. "Only ones I've seen lately are Athena and Hades, and they haven't been near Olympus in quite some time. Looks like the Olympians left centuries ago, and never came back."

"So it doesn't relate to your current...problems?" Dianmu asked delicately.

"No." Crystal flopped onto the futon. "I almost wish it did. There's no time for another mystery right now, love."

"How bad is it?" Dianmu asked, sitting next to Crystal. She sat with the same natural poise Crystal had always associated with the storm goddess, who always seemed to be hyper aware of where her body was and what it was doing. Usually, Crystal found it charming. Right now, she felt an overwhelming temptation to kick her. She tried to shake off her edginess and focus on the conversation.

"Very bad." In spite of her best efforts, Crystal felt anger bubbling up. "Enki almost killed me twice. Damn near killed the bloody Eschaton. Hell, if he hadn't gone for a sodding double-cross, he might have had us. Twice. We had to drop a nuke on him."

"Crystal..." Dianmu said, reaching out.

"Where were you, Dianmu?" Crystal snapped, the anger boiling over. She was nearly shouting and couldn't find it in herself to care. There had been too much going on to dwell on Dianmu's absence back then, but it had cut more deeply than she'd realized. "I had to ally with *Moloch.* Which turned out to be as bad as it sounded. I didn't expect many people to show up. But you – I was counting on you."

Dianmu withdrew her hand. "It was that bad?"

Crystal gave her a curt nod. Suddenly, she wondered what she was doing here. What explanation could possibly make her trust Dianmu again, after she'd left Crystal behind on the most important days of the last million years?

"Then I am truly sorry I couldn't be there. By the time I got your message, the battle on Graham Island was over. I assumed that meant it was the end of it." Dianmu's voice was sincere, her eyes full of sorrow.

"Where were you that a curator couldn't get to?" Crystal spat. She'd expected a lot of excuses from Dianmu, but not such an obvious line of bullshit. "Because they're even better than us at getting to wherever they bloody want. I've had one of the wankers show up when I was in my nanoverse before, so please, tell me where you were that you couldn't get a sodding message!"

"Dead," Dianmu said simply.

Dianmu couldn't have cooled Crystal's rage better if she'd thrown her into a glacier. "Oh." Crystal coughed and felt herself flush. "I'm sorry for-"

"Jumping to conclusions?" Dianmu asked with a sparkle in her eyes. "Don't be. If you didn't, you'd hardly be you."

Crystal found she couldn't meet her friend's eyes at the moment. She instead let her gaze wander back to the photos that adorned the walls, young adults that Dianmu had helped get out of the slums and into new lives. *Yes, that's an excellent way to feel less guilty for being judgmental,* Crystal thought. *Remind yourself of all the reasons you were just a massive git.* "Still, I am sorry. I should have known...I shouldn't have assumed. What happened?"

Dianmu settled back, and Crystal felt a smile tug at her lips. Dianmu did love a chance to tell a story.

"People were going missing," Dianmu began, "In too great a number to be accounted for by normal means. It disturbed me, and then became extremely concerned when I realized they were all people either living on the highest or lowest floors of their buildings."

Crystal frowned and nodded in understanding. "A predator," she said. Monsters that prey upon humans tend to avoid exposure. They knew that if humanity banded together, enough of them would be able to kill any threat - especially now, in the modern day, when humans had so many weapons. To prevent detection, they tended to attack from below the ground or from the air.

Dianmu's poise cracked as she clenched her hands with hard, cold anger. "Not many things can come from both above and below. Even fewer that would risk hunting in a city.

"Except for anthropophages," Crystal said, her voice mirroring Dianmu's fury. The thought of them disgusted Crystal to her core. They were vile creatures. The best-known examples of anthropophages were vampires, although there were others. Aswang, werewolves, wendigo, just off the top of her head. Unsurprising, since anthropophage literally translated to "eater of men".

Dianmu nodded in agreement. "However, the pattern didn't fit one of their ilk. You know the old tale that vampires need to be invited in to enter someone's home?"

Crystal nodded. It was a myth she was familiar with, but she'd never learned any factual basis for it. Then again, she hadn't exactly ever made a study of vampires. She'd just killed them.

"In my dealings with anthropophages, I've learned it has some vestige of truth in it. Of course, they do not require an invitation to enter your home, but they do prefer it. It means they have your trust, that your guard is down." She shook her head. "They would never need to focus on the ground floors, and would never, ever risk having to fight their way through a horde of panicked humans from roof to floor. I honestly was at a loss of what could be causing it. Anything more monstrous, and the risk of being caught is much greater. Even if mortals don't target you, you risk drawing the attention of a god or goddess. Which, of course, this one had, but at first it managed to utterly confound me."

Dianmu sighed and looked out the window, where a bird had landed and begun preening. Crystal didn't recognize the species but was still surprised to see it. Birds were rare in the dense parts of the city, preferring instead to inhabit the less settled portions outside the town. "Then, the first body was found. It was labeled as a ritualistic gang killing, which is what municipal police across the world use most often to describe monster killings."

Crystal frowned. "I've seen what monsters can do. You're telling me the cops write that off as being bloody gangsters?"

"What else are they supposed to do?" Dianmu asked. "If they say it's a cult, they'll have a panic on their hands. If they say it was a wild animal, in a city as densely populated as this, people will call them incompetent or liars - and they'll still have a panic on their hands. If they blame it on gang activity, however, people can sleep safely. They can tell themselves, 'I never angered any gangs, nor do I know anyone in a gang. There is no risk to me.' They might become frightened, they might cry out about the crime, but ultimately, it's criminals killing other criminals. It's a safe lie to cover the real horror."

Crystal's frown deepened, and she rubbed her temple. "Bloody hell, that sounds far too plausible."

"You've never paid much attention to the aftermath. You show up, fight the monster, and leave the humans to fend for themselves," Dianmu said.

Crystal thought she heard an accusatory note in that, but decided she was just paranoid. If Dianmu was angry with her, it wouldn't be like the lightning goddess to be subtle about it. *Although she's not in her role as a lightning goddess right now, is she?* Crystal reminded herself. It was easy to forget that, for all the flash and pomp of the storm, Dianmu had another association - that of hidden crimes.

"One thing I've learned over thousands of years," Dianmu continued, "is that human nature never changes. We like our nice, comfortable lies more than the hard, brutal truth that we are as vulnerable as anyone else. When a civilization is exposed to that truth, panic always follows."

Crystal pursed her lips. "I didn't even sodding think about that."

"What's wrong?" Dianmu asked.

"You're right, love. You absolutely bloody are. And during the whole mess with Enki, we all appeared on bloody national television."

Dianmu nodded. "I do feel the fallout from that is still floating in the air, waiting to fall to Earth."

Crystal scowled and shook her head. That was a problem for the future. "So...a body was found?"

"Yes," Dianmu said, quickly picking up the thread of her story. "I was able to get my hands on the police report. The victim's brain and liver had been removed. That told me everything I needed to know." She gave Crystal an expectant look.

Crystal cursed. "Fangliang," she whispered. They were a rather unique creature, demons that savaged corpses to feed on those two organs. And when they couldn't find bodies...well, they were not above making their own.

Dianmu nodded. "Fangliang. Have you ever dealt with them?"

Crystal shook her head. "Believe me, love, I would have told you if I had. Hell, for that matter, I would have been asking you to come along when I did.'

"True. Well, they favor being below ground, but they can fly through the air on transparent wings. It was the only thing that fit, although I was surprised they were operating in a city. The only way to kill them permanently is to bury them alive. Otherwise, they keep reforming and coming back at every full moon."

"So you had to take it alive and bury it?"

"Yes. And that was my plan, when I delved into the burrows it had dug in the foundation of a condemned building. Find it, capture it, and bury it." Dianmu's eyes flashed at the memory. "I wasn't expecting an entire nest of the creatures. Over three hundred of them."

Crystal let out a low whistle. "How did that go undetected?"

"They were spreading out their hunting and focusing on poorer areas. They were organized, and they were *smart."*

"So that's how you died?" Crystal asked, "Sheer numbers?"

"Oh, no." Dianmu's smile took on a fierce edge. "I don't know if I could have defeated three hundred of the creatures in combat. But I didn't need to. I had come to bury them alive, after all, and the building above us was condemned."

Crystal stared, her mouth hanging open. "You collapsed a building on yourself to take them out?"

"Yes. One of the beams impaled me, and I had to immolate myself so I could resurrect back in my nanoverse."

"Bloody hell," Crystal whispered. After a few seconds process how casually Dianmu was talking about being buried, impaled, and immolated, she let out a soft breath. "Dianmu? I think you spent too much time around me."

Dianmu laughed softly. "Hardly, Crystal. I'm reasonably certain I was perfectly capable of stupid plans long before I met you."

Crystal nodded, then paused to think. Something in Dianmu's story seemed off to her. "Pretty big coincidence, happening right around the time I needed your help."

"Oh, not in the slightest. I went back after I resurrected. Human sacrifices were used to summon and focus the creatures."

"Moloch," Crystal spat.

"I'm almost certain of it. Other gods who resort to such abominations at least have the shame to hide it."

"I'm sorry for assuming."

Dianmu waved the apology away. "Think nothing of it. You had no way of knowing, and...well, you know what I thought about your belief in the end of the world. I could see where the assumption comes from."

"So you still don't believe it?"

Dianmu shook her head. "I trust you, Crystal. You're a friend. But the idea that any one of us could have the power to end the world... it's hard to swallow."

"I suppose it was too much to hope for." Crystal sighed.

"Cheer up," Dianmu said with a twinkle in her eye. "I never said I wouldn't help you."

Crystal's forehead furrowed. "Why-"

"If you're right, and the world can be ended, then your reasons must be right as well, and it must be protected. If you're wrong...then the only real threat here is gods like Enki who believe you and try to stop you. In short, the only real threat is to *you.* Either way, you're in danger."

"That's not the entire reason, though, is it?" Crystal asked. "You're holding back something."

"You won't like the other reason," Dianmu said, her smile vanishing. "It's a bit offensive."

"I spent the last few weeks dealing with Enki, love. I doubt you'll be able to offend me too much."

"Fair," Dianmu said. "And you won't let this go if I refuse to tell you. I know you, Crystal."

"So save us both time and tell me."

"As long as I've known you, you've believed the world was in danger. That an Eschaton would arise, and that you'd be responsible. It kept you going where other gods have given up and sought oblivion. I'm worried what it'll do to you if it turns out you're wrong."

"Worried I'll snap?" Crystal said, trying her best not to let her hurt show. She looked out the window again. The bird was gone now, having flitted away to wherever it made its nest, or wherever it found food. Crystal, at that moment, envied it more than she could say. The bird lived a simple life, with simple concerns. *Wouldn't that be nice for a change?*

"Yes," Dianmu said simply. "And, as your friend, I want to be there if that happens."

Crystal sighed. "I should have left that one alone."

"I warned you."

"Yeah, you did." Crystal shook her head, not in denial, but to clear it. "Well, love, as much as I don't like that answer...I'll take it. I need your help, and even though you think I'm crazy...I could use another friend in all this."

"And if nothing else, I can give you that."

The smile that spread across Crystal's face was far from forced. "Well, then. Shall we be going?"

Dianmu answered by rising. "I'll need to leave some instructions behind before I go. To make sure these people are cared for. And I promised the children a noon meal. Then...yes. I promise I will be beside you in your next fight."

***

Under ordinary circumstances, entering El Ávila would be easy, but these were not ordinary times. Athena crouched in an alley just across from the park, watching the soldiers. These were not bored men trying to do the minimum amount of work. They were sharp and alert, their eyes scanning for possible intruders. *If they were not actively impeding me, I'd approve,* she thought. The military had cut off public traffic entirely, and there were armed blockades at every point of entrance.

Usually, Athena wouldn't worry about the soldiers. It would be simple to turn herself invisible and phase right past them. Doing so, however, would burn her divine power. The mission was only supposed to be reconnaissance, but there was a risk of being seen by Moloch, his cultists, or his monsters. If she found herself in a fight, she'd need every scrap of power she could hold on to. If she could find a mundane way into the park, she would take it. If she couldn't, she would have to burn power rather than be stuck outside or forced into a fight with the soldiers who were just doing their jobs.

Movement drew her attention to a pair of teenagers creeping towards the perimeter, scampering behind cars to avoid detection. She caught a glimpse of their faces: the boy frightened but determined not to show it, the girl full of excitement. Athena tensed, surveying the soldiers.

One soldier in a portable watchtower had spotted the couple and was already raising his assault rifle. Athena reached out, ready to forget her need to conserve power and intervene, but it was too late. A short burst of automatic weapons fire cut through the air.

The bullets sparked off the ground a few feet to the left of the teens, who froze with fear. Athena let out a sigh of relief as soldiers swarmed over the pair. The troops weren't shooting to kill.

"On the ground!" a soldier screamed in Spanish. "On the ground and your hands over your heads!"

Crying, the teenagers complied. The soldiers reached for their backpacks, tearing them open with the gentle care of a wolf with a rabbit's carcass. Athena watched as the usual harmless goods fell out of the packs - pens, notebooks, cell phones, and black hooded robes inscribed with red thread. *Oh,* Athena thought grimly as the soldiers began to cuff the two. *That's what they're looking for.*

"You are under arrest for association with the cult of Moloch," one of the soldiers intoned.

As soon as the words were out of his mouth, the pair's crocodile tears dried up. "We have rights!" the boy shouted.

One of the soldiers brought a rifle butt down across the boy's face. "You're trying to sneak into a national park and join a terrorist group. Shut the hell up about your 'rights', son."

"You'll regret that," the girl hissed through gritted teeth. "Moloch will-"

She stopped abruptly when the soldier raised a rifle butt. Another soldier reached in and grabbed his arm before he could strike her, too. "C' mon. They're kids. Let's just take them in."

Satisfied the soldiers weren't going to execute the two teens in the street, Athena began to creep down the alleyways near the perimeter. *No point trying to get through here. They're on alert.*

The next group of soldiers had the same rigid professionalism. *I think I'll end up waiting too long if I keep trying to find a slacker*, Athena thought.

Before she could begin to formulate a new plan, something rustled in the bushes within the park. The soldiers' reaction was immediate. They whirled to face the sound as spotlights lit up, illuminating the area. The soldiers opened fire, repeated staccato bursts of five rounds each until the magazines were empty.

Then they waited, watching the patch of shredded bush. Athena waited with them, turning on her divine sight. There was definitely something in the bushes-

They rustled again. The moment they did, the soldiers launched an RPG directly at the source. Dirt, plants, and bits of flesh were thrown away in an explosion that set people in the surrounding buildings screaming.

Then there was no movement.

Stars of Olympus, Athena thought. *They plan to keep out anyone and everyone, and then assume all motion inside is hostile and respond with extreme prejudice.* It made a cold sort of sense. There were many creatures that could kill on sight or give minimal time to react if they became aggressive. It would mean the death of countless innocent animals, however, and if anyone was still in the park...

This is taking too long, Athena decided. *I need to get inside.*

She gave her nanoverse a squeeze, more for luck than the little power it had accumulated since she last drew from it and rendered herself intangible and invisible so she could ghost her way into the park, past the watchful eyes of the soldiers.

***

Athena had read up on El Ávila National Park as she left the city before she completely lost cell phone service. As much as she disliked the portable phones, she had to admit that they occasionally had their uses. She just wouldn't admit it to Ryan. One thing she had found interesting was the park's biodiversity: Wikipedia had informed her that it had over five hundred bird species, a hundred and twenty mammal species, twenty amphibians, and thirty reptiles, on top of eighteen hundred different plants.

As impressive as Athena found that factoid, she was reasonably certain that cockatrices were not a normal part of the local ecosystem. This beast was clearly a new addition.

Athena pressed herself against a tree, her heart pounding. She winced at the sound of the beast's feeding, a sound like gravel being put through a woodchipper.

If I'd rounded the corner when it was looking up, that would have been me. A goddess was not immune to the cockatrice's petrifying gaze. Being caught would be a disaster; since she wouldn't technically be dead, she wouldn't reform. Instead, she would stand frozen until someone found her or the world ended.

The shroud wouldn't protect her, so she'd dropped it. The creature would easily see her even with the protection, and the fact that it was alive and hunting meant she was safely out of the military's range. *I'd trade a thousand armies to be rid of this thing, though.*

The cockatrice raised its head to swallow some of its prey. That gave Athena a chance to look; so long as she avoided the creature's gaze, she was safe. It was still an effort to make herself take the risk, but she needed to know more about what she was up against. Cockatrices came in a wide variety, some more dangerous than others.

This one was easily as tall at the shoulders as Athena herself, with thick, long legs that ended in wicked talons. Its wings looked too small to let the creature fly but would spread out for balance as it chased down its prey. Its feathers were the bright red and yellow of a creature that held no fear of any predator. It was as she'd feared: a Spartan Cockatrice. Stronger, faster, and with a particular taste for human flesh.

Athena whipped her head back behind the tree as the cockatrice finished its meal and glanced around. *Stupid risk, looking for that long.*

Sweat began to bead on her forehead. There were few monsters that could terrify Athena, but this was one of them.

Okay, she assured herself. *You don't need to fight this monster. You just need to move around it.* She took a moment to roll her shoulders and steady her nerves. *On the count of three. One. Two* - just as she started to move, the cockatrice raised its head and angrily asked the forest "Booooraaaaaaaak?" Athena slammed herself back against the tree, stifling a gasp.

When the trees did not respond to its inquiry, the monster turned back to feeding. Now that it seemed again intent on its food, Athena started to move again. She was still terrified, but she hadn't come here to cower behind trees all day.

"Kaaaawooook?" the cockatrice asked, popping its head up.

Athena threw herself to the ground behind a low shrub and bit back a curse. *Really?* She asked herself, fear turning to fury as she made sure no part of her body was exposed to the creature. *What is it sensing?* Cockatrices were not known for being easily distracted from their meals. In fact, Athena could only think of two things that would distract them more than once: a mate in heat, or a predator it actually feared.

She shrunk back further into the trees as the bushes began to rustle in front of the creature. *Looks like I'll be getting an answer soon.* She took a deep breath, readying herself for whatever might be emerging.

A staff burst out of the brush and slammed into the soil. Grey tendrils began to creep from the point of impact, withering nearby plants. A gnarled hand, wrinkled and covered in warts and liver spots, clutched the stick in a violent grip. It shook slightly as it supported its owner, who began to follow the staff out of the dense underbrush.

Athena's entire body tensed. She pressed her body further against her cover and deliberately suppressed her reflexive breathing. *Moloch,* she thought with a mixture of anger and dread. She was perfectly motionless, rooted to the spot, her eyes glued to the monstrous god.

If anything, Moloch looked even more hideous than when Athena had last seen him. His sunken eyes were deeper, blacker pits. His skin seemed leatherier and more worn. His lips cracked into a horrific smile, and Athena was sure his teeth were even more yellow, rotten and twisted to the point of being sickening. His smile sent a chill down her spine. Had he seen her?

Her mind raced, forming plans in case Moloch had spotted her. In a straight fight, she could trounce him. Most gods could, as Moloch rarely practiced direct combat. However, this wouldn't be a straight fight. They were deep in a natural habitat that Moloch had controlled for weeks. There was no telling what variety of monsters he'd summoned or created to aid him.

The forest covered Moloch's back with shadows, and in those shadows, Athena saw a thousand imagined horrors. Gorgons coiled around trees, fangs glistening with petrifying toxins. Minotaurs hunching behind brushes, their breath steaming even in the tropical air. Namean lions crouching in the deepest recesses of shadow, ready to pounce. Moloch was a threat because of everything that could be behind him, and in terrain he had taken as his own, *anything* could be behind him.

If he had seen her, he didn't give any immediate sign. Instead, he studied the cockatrice. Athena felt an irrational surge of anger. The creature had popped its head up every time she'd tried to move, and here it was calmly eating with *Moloch* behind it.

Moloch licked his blistered lips with his pale white tongue. "Well...what do we have here?"

For a moment, Athena was convinced that Moloch was speaking to her. She prepared to do one solid twist of reality and engulf herself in enough flame to burn her body to ash in an instant. If she got lucky, the fire would spill over into immolating Moloch as well. If she didn't, she would at least avoid being taken-

"Kaaaaaaaaarrrrrkkk!" the cockatrice screamed. After a second, rational thought overrode blind panic: Moloch was talking to the monster, not to her. She hadn't been spotted.

Yet.

She relaxed slightly as Moloch began to circle the cockatrice. It kept its head and eyes focused on the malformed god, but he kept his head moderately bowed, watching the cockatrice out of the top of his vision without making actual eye contact.

Athena wondered if this is what other gods felt watching her wield a sword, seeing someone move with the absolute competence of a seasoned master. Athena had no idea how he was managing to keep the cockatrice in his peripheral vision without triggering its petrifying gaze, but the motion seemed as natural to him as drawing a blade was to her. There was a reason that Moloch was the god of monsters. At that moment, she could almost have respected him if he hadn't been so loathsome.

"You're a beautiful creature. Such a pity." Moloch rasped.

The noise the cockatrice made in response was unlike anything Athena had ever heard: a sort of defiant whistling, mixed with overtones of gravel being run through a blender. The cockatrice began to turn slowly, keeping its eyes fixed on Moloch. When its target stubbornly remained flesh and blood, the cockatrice cocked its head like a confused dog. Athena could almost hear its thoughts. *This has always worked for me before, but you're not turning into bone, which is damned rude of you. Can you please freeze in place so I can eat you?*

Moloch did not oblige the cockatrice's request, much as Athena wished he would. Instead, now that the cockatrice had turned a full one hundred and eighty degrees, Moloch's form began to run like hot wax. He straightened, and his emaciated form filled out and expanded to become taller, with broad shoulders and solid muscles. His dirty grey hair brightened to gleaming silver. In less than a minute, he had changed from a withered, disgusting creature to the ideal image of a god.

Transformation complete, Moloch held his hand out towards the brush. "Send the Aspirants forth." His voice had changed to a resonant baritone full of power and authority.

He's disguising himself in front of his cultists, Athena realized. *He knows that people are more likely to follow someone attractive. Clever.*

Two men and one woman emerged, carrying primitive weapons. Moloch's symbols covered their naked bodies, tattooed on their faces and drawn in blood on their limbs and torsos. Athena's mouth went dry, and she wondered how many new horrors would await her. Moloch's cults had taken many forms over the millennia, but they'd always included warriors like these. Stripped of all vestiges of society, monsters in their own right. Athena had never faced them herself, but she's seen the aftermath of their raids: blood so thick on the ground it turned the soil to mud and viscera arranged into mockeries of divine sigils. She'd heard of them breaking phalanxes and making berserkers turn and flee.

He called them Godslayers.

While Athena couldn't take her eyes off the new arrivals, the cockatrice didn't notice them. It was transfixed on Moloch's outstretched hand, waiting for him to make a move.

Moving his hand slowly back and forth to keep the cockatrice's attention, Moloch began to speak to his followers, using the gift of the Primordial Speech, the language all of mankind once spoke. Although no mortal mouth could form the words anymore, gods could make use of it, and be understood by all mortals. "You stand here, willingly outcast from the society that rejected you. You stand here, clothed as newborns, wearing naught but viscera. You stand here, with weapons you have made with your own hands, so they are extensions of your body. Are you prepared to forsake all you had been, and be fully reborn as my children?"

All three gave a slow, deliberate nod.

"Good. Then prove your worth." He snapped his fingers and twisted, vanishing from the cockatrice's vision.

It gave a confused coo as it turned back towards its meal, only to find three more humans there. Either because it knew they were only human or because it was frustrated by Moloch's disappearance, it didn't display the cautious curiosity it gave Moloch. Instead, it immediately lunged forward.

The woman had a pair of stone hatchets, one gripped in each hand and held low to her side. The man on her left had an enormously thick stick slung over his shoulder with a rock so large it could almost be called a boulder, and the man on her right held a spear wrapped in thorny vines.

Athena watched the fight with disgusted curiosity. The cockatrice lunged towards a man wielding an enormous club, but it was cut short when the other man slashed at its neck with a spear wrapped in thorny vines. It spun to face the new threat, giving the woman an opening to cut at its eyes with one of a pair of stone hatchets. The three worked together so well it looked almost choreographed.

The cockatrice reeled back, one eye ruined and leaking blood. It took a couple of steps back, but the humans pressed the attack. The spear-holder waved his weapon in its face, drawing its attention, as the club-bearer swung at the monster's feet. There was a sickening crunch as one the hammer blows landed, crushing delicate bones. The cockatrice gave a sound of agonized fury and turned to run. But the woman had been circled the monster while her companions attacked and struck its face with full force.

Athena didn't want to watch the remainder of the fight but found herself unable to look away. The Aspirants took turns, pummeling the beast. At least twice, Athena saw them deliberately avoid killing blows. They wanted it to *suffer*. The cockatrice's motions became increasingly panicked and erratic. It gave a few more screams and clawed and bit with every ounce of energy it could muster, but with each attempt, those attacks became weaker. Fainter. Its strength was failing, and it knew it.

Finally, it became too much. The cockatrice collapsed, and with a triumphant scream, the woman buried both her stone hatchets in its head.

"Well done, my Children," Moloch said. More people, dressed in black robes and bearing the same facial tattoos, stepped out of the bushes. Athena realized that if she had taken refuge on the other side of the clearing, she would have been trying to hide among Moloch's followers.

The newcomers presented the victorious Aspirants black robes, and Athena took a moment to study them. It was a diverse group. Twenty people, counting the three Aspirants, thirteen men and seven women. She saw a variety of nationalities, and other than the tattoos and robes they had little in common.

The entire group moved in a practiced silence as they began attaching ropes to the cockatrice's corpse. Once it was secured, they turned as one and dragged the body along the forest floor. Moloch strode after them with the bearing of a king being preceded by his retinue.

Athena waited a good while before daring to move. If nothing else, she now knew better what Moloch was doing down here. Once Moloch's followers had taken the cockatrice back to where they were holed up, they would feast upon it.

It explained so much about his feared Godslayers: their inhuman strength and durability, the way their weapons could penetrate divine resistances, and their own unnatural defenses. If fighting a human or mundane animal, Athena could snap her fingers and stop their heart with a simple twist. Gods and monsters couldn't be impacted that way, and neither could mortals who had consumed enough monstrous flesh.

Moloch was building an army.

Athena decided that was enough reconnaissance. There might be more she could discover, but further solo investigation would be too risky, and Ryan and Crystal needed to know that Moloch was preparing for war.

Behind her, someone cleared their throat.

She whirled around, feeling hopelessly exposed and unprepared. A handsome man in camouflage tactical gear, including a Kevlar vest, was aiming a gun directly at her chest.

"Pallas Athena," he said, "It has been some time."

Then she noticed the stylized falcon symbol over his chest and took a closer look at his features.

"Horus," she said, keeping her tone carefully neutral, despite her racing heart. She was almost positive that Horus would never work with Moloch, but these were strange times, and his appearance here was odd. "It definitely has been a long time. I'm surprised to see you here. Would you mind pointing that gun somewhere else?"

His gun did not waver. "I suppose you may be surprised. I cannot say the same, Pallas Athena. I have been looking for you. How our reunion goes will depend on your answer to one simple question."

"And what might that be?" Athena was already shifting to a defensive stance. She'd been ready to immolate herself, but that had been against Moloch and unknown monsters, and before she had vital information. If she had to fight Horus, the odds were much better.

"Simple. Where. Is. Bast?" Horus snarled, and Athena realized he was half-crazed with...hope? Fear? Some strong emotion, but she wasn't sure which. This meant she couldn't know what answer he wanted, leaving her only the option of telling the truth.

"I haven't seen her since I killed her."

Horus took a long time studying her face, looking for evidence of a lie. When he saw none, he lowered the gun.

"Tell me everything."

Chapter 6

Drip

Bast hadn't seen the desert in hours. Or was it days? Time still lacked meaning. *I slept.* Bast focused on that fact, held it in her mind, a tiny sliver of hope. The exhaustion had finally won out against the discomfort. She'd fallen asleep, she thought, although it might have been an accumulation of small naps, drifting in and out of the desert. She didn't remember sleeping, but so much of her time was static...*It doesn't matter,* Bast told herself firmly. What mattered was that she had slept. Now there was no more sleep. No more dreams.

No more distraction from the raw scraping of her tongue in her mouth.

Her thirst was omnipresent, overwhelming hunger and loneliness. Overwhelming most rational thought. She imagined she could hear water everywhere. The gentle rush of fabric as the last of the researchers left reminded her of rainfall. The rush of air from the air conditioner sounded like a distant waterfall. The greatest torment was the pipes above her. Sometimes they rushed with water, right over her head. Every time they did Bast stared at them, transfixed, trying to will them into disgorging their contents. Everything made her think of how badly she wanted something to quench that thirst, how much she needed some relief.

Even the blood she heard in the researcher's veins.

The door closed, and even that temptation was gone. Nothing. There was nothing. No relief coming. Not now, not ever. Sleep was the final Hunger she could have filled on her own. Thirst, food, and socialization were all denied to her. Bast blinked as tears started to form, tears that were too dry to help. They were just a salty sludge that burned her eyes.

In frustration, Bast began to struggle against her chains again. The cold steel was unyielding. If she had her full power, she could have snapped them like paper, torn them like flesh. Knowing the difference between what could be and what was drove her to further frustration, and she started to slam her head back against the table. Each impact let loose a ringing clang. She didn't know what she was trying to do. Breaking the steel around her skull would be as impossible as snapping these chains, and the helmet was cushioned so she couldn't even hurt herself.

She fell back, no longer moving, exhausted. Fear began to well up in her, fear that she had pushed herself too hard, that she would need to sleep again, that she would have to go back to the desert. *No. Please, no.* There was at least some relief in not needing to sleep. It was *something.*

After a few minutes, Bast relaxed. Her body was tired, but her mind was alert. She wouldn't need to sleep.

She was just helpless.

Bast started to occupy her mind with fantasies of escape. She skipped the escape itself, as she had no idea how to accomplish it. Once she figured that out, fantasy would become reality. In the meantime, she focused on what would happen immediately after she broke free. She would *show* these people what it meant to anger a goddess. Legends would be told for *millennia* of the hell she unleashed upon these buildings. *No, there will be no legends. No one will be left alive to tell them.*

Unfortunately, the fantasies could only sustain her for so long. Just as they began to fade into despair, she felt something on the edge of her sensation. It was like drumbeats over the horizon, throbbing in the distance, although it wasn't quite a sound. It was something familiar.

The distraction was enough to fight away the depression for a moment longer. Bast reached out towards the sensation, straining to try and place it. Without her power, it was maddeningly out of reach. Bast growled in frustration, and then it suddenly fell into place. It was familiar because it was hers - her nanoverse! Somehow, wherever it was hidden, someone had activated it. She braced herself for the rush of energy, but instead, she felt the power race away from her, going elsewhere. It was like watching distant lines of lightning streak away. Bast tried to scream in frustration, but all she could do was whimper. *What are they doing? That shouldn't even be possible! Who dares? I'll kill them, I'll tear out their hearts, I'll feast on their...*

A small trickle power broke away from the flood, as if it sensed her desperation. It streaked through walls and floors and jumped to where it belonged. Bast clutched that tiny fragment of power as tightly as she dared. It was a droplet in the vast ocean that she used to have, and the moment she used it, she'd be tired again. It would mean going back to the desert.

Unless...

Bast stared at the pipe above her, her heart pounding. If this worked, she'd still need to sleep, but maybe it wouldn't be a desert she visited.

Bast took the deepest breath she could manage in the damned restraints and sent that little droplet of power away. A tiny needle of force, a minuscule fraction of her will made reality, streaked along the path of her gaze and hit the pipe with a metallic ping.

Her eyelids started to droop. Reality began to run like water as her exhaustion returned. She forced it away, forced herself to fight the sudden resurgence of sleep. There was time for that later. Right now she needed to watch, hoping she hadn't wasted the only bit of power she might ever get. If she had, she thought she might go mad. If it didn't-

Drip

A lonely drop of water detached itself from the pipe and let gravity do its work, bringing it to its final resting place: Bast's dry, chapped lips.

She forced her mouth open just enough to let that drop run between her teeth. It dissolved on her tongue, barely even registering, and certainly not taking the edge off the thirst.

Five agonizing minutes passed before...

Drip

Another drop fell straight into her mouth, and Bast felt a surge of joy.

One Hunger was being met. One weakness was being removed. *It might take days, but I'll get there. I'll finally have one of my Hungers addressed...and when my mouth is less parched, maybe I can truly sleep. And once I've slept...*

Drip

This time her tongue darted out to meet the drop, and she let herself smile while waiting for the next one.

Once I've slept, I'll find out who dared to treat me like a lab rat.

Chapter 7

The Spider and the Fly

"That's why I'm here; we figured I was the best choice to head to Ghana and make contact with you." Ryan took a deep breath. Until he'd started telling the story, he hadn't realized how much he'd been through since finding his nanoverse. He'd left out their concerns about Crystal's health and Athena's mistrust of tricksters, and a few other details that didn't seem important, but otherwise, he'd told the other god everything.

Anansi stroked his chin, "I see." Anansi drew the two words out as if he was contemplating every letter. Ryan waited for him to continue, but Anansi seemed to believe that settled the matter.

"Uh..." Ryan began, and Anansi smiled and raised a finger to stop him.

"I assumed you had questions for me as well. Was that incorrect?" The words could have been judgmental, but Anansi's tone was honestly curious.

Ryan paused to think of what he was missing, then felt stupid as he realized what Anansi was getting at.

"Right." He took a deep breath, deciding to go with the most uncomfortable topic first. "The news is claiming you're trying to start a civil war here. What's really happening?"

Anansi cocked his head slightly, a small grin spreading across his face. "You seem to be implying that I am not starting a civil war here. Why is that?"

"Because it wouldn't make sense for you," Ryan answered without a trace of hesitation. "I mean, I could be wrong, but you don't strike me as power-hungry. You might start a war if there was a just reason, but Ghana is one of the most stable countries on the continent. I don't see a motive for conflict."

Anansi's head remained tilted, but the edges of his eyes crinkled. "You think you know me so well when you were the one that did most of the talking?"

Ryan nodded. "I did most of the talking, but you said a lot too." Ryan held up three fingers and began ticking off points. "You frowned hard when I mentioned Enki was working with Moloch. You clenched your fists when I talked about the mummies in Grant. You relaxed when I said we drew Enki out to a deserted island." He lowered his hand. "All of that could be faked, sure, but we spent hours talking, and it'd be exhausting to fake your reactions the entire time. So I think that adds up to a man who doesn't like chaos or needless violence."

Anansi's laugh was deep and rich. "You see much, Ryan Smith, and you pay attention. You are correct: I do abhor needless violence, although do not think that means I fear to 'get my hands dirty', as it were." He met Ryan's eyes, his mirth vanishing. "I did not mean to start a conflict here. But when I announced who I was, the worshippers of Jehovah and his Son thought I was spouting blasphemy. When they saw my children, they thought them to be demons. And when they opened fire, I acted to defend what is mine."

Ryan nodded slowly. "The spider-people the news was talking about, they're your children?"

Anansi shrugged. "After a fashion." He reached into the pocket of his coat and pulled out a well-worn photograph, handing it over to Ryan.

At first glance, it looked like a human. An unusually tall one - he towered over the individual next to him, and his limbs were long and lanky - but just a human. Then the details began to pop out at Ryan. What he'd first mistaken for shadows were actually two large fangs jutting out from his lips and down his chin. The figure's eyes weren't just hooded, they were black as pitch and almost lifeless, ringed by tiny dots that gleamed like secondary eyes. To top it all off, what Ryan had first taken as armor was a dark gray carapace that had replaced most of the man's skin. It was a seamless blend of spider and human, and Ryan found it both fascinating and slightly nauseating.

"They're my worshippers," Anansi said.

***

Hector Ross settled back into his seat. The cushion was soft leather, molding to his body perfectly as he got comfortable. In his time with the United States Marine Corps, he'd ridden in all manner of military vehicles. He could have described them in a variety of ways, but before today, comfortable had never been one of them.

It appeared being part of project Myrmidon had perks beyond becoming the deadliest weapon in his country's arsenal.

"Everyone, attention," Roger Evans said from the front of the plane, motioning them to gather around. "Just got word that we have authorization from the Republic of Ghana for this little operation."

"So?" Diane said, lounging in her chair. She'd gotten increasingly insubordinate since becoming a Myrmidon. They all had. The shrinks were wondering if it was some kind of feedback from having divine blood in their veins, a personality shift coming from Bast. Hector didn't worry about that. As far as he was concerned, having the power to make reality his bitch was enough reason to let discipline slack some.

"I'm with Diane, sir," Hector said, leaning forward to rest his elbows on the armrest and prop up his head. "We were going in either way. Sure, it's nice that we won't be violating sovereign airspace, but...why should we care?"

Andrew Palmer answered before Roger could, giving them all an incredulous look. "Don't you see? That means this isn't a stealth mission anymore."

Diane and Hector shared a wicked grin as Roger nodded in confirmation. "As far as the government of Ghana is concerned," Roger said, "we'll do less damage than a prolonged civil war. We're to try and contain the fight where we can, but..."

"But we showed them the footage of Graham Island, and they don't want things going nuclear," Diane interjected, glancing over at Roger. "That sound right?"

"Pretty much," Roger replied with a small grin. "And that's one thing that needs to be crystal clear. Under no circumstances are we to replicate a WMD, unless the hostiles do it first. Everyone got that?"

Nods all around, Andrew's a bit more sullen than the others.

"We wouldn't survive ground zero anyway," Hector said. "The eggheads still have no idea how Smith and the others pulled that off."

Roger nodded gravely. "And that's the other thing I want to stress. Smith has a few weeks' experience on us, at a minimum, and possibly months. However, before that, he was a civilian. Shouldn't be too tough to deal with."

"I wouldn't underestimate him," Hector interjected. "He's fought against other gods before and survived."

"True, but I think we can handle him. Anansi, on the other hand...according to our mythologist, no one knows when Anansi first emerged. Legends of him go back thousands of years. He's got millennia of experience."

"Yeah, most of them when the height of military technology was spears and swords," Diane said, rolling her eyes and sitting up straighter. "And even when guns were around, they were mostly muskets and shit. I think we have a few tricks he won't see coming." She mimed firing an assault rifle.

Hector nodded in agreement.

***

"You...turned people into this," Ryan asked, staring at the picture in shock. "That's...why? This is some straight-up Kafka body horror."

Anansi's smile had a brittle edge. "Because people were on the news shouting about how the world would end. Gods were coming out of the shadows. Monsters were returning. I had to keep my people safe. I am but one being. For all my power, I cannot be everywhere. This," and he gestured to the picture, "protects them. They're able to survive so much more than normal humans. Seeing as the gods who are actually going to end the world are at a loss for how to keep people safe, I stand by my choice."

"You... I'm sorry, I'm having trouble understanding. They're monsters!" Ryan exclaimed, then quickly backtracked as Anansi's eyes hardened. "I mean, that's how people see them. They look monstrous. I'm sure they're perfectly fine. Or, at least, as good as they were before?"

"I knew I would be exposing them to such... judgments," Anansi said, his voice flat and unyielding, "and they knew that when they accepted my gift. But I did not deceive them. They chose this for themselves as a way to survive the apocalypse. And if you cannot save the world, I will rest easy knowing that I did what I could to at least save this small sliver for as long as they can endure."

Ryan winced. "I'm sorry, I didn't mean to offend."

"I've found throughout my life that very often, men say offensive things and then try to hide behind their ignorance. They act like it excuses them from having said something offensive." Anansi reached over and pulled the photograph out of Ryan's hands, putting it back in his jacket pocket. "It does not. Do not say you did not mean to offend."

"Well. Okay." Ryan shook his head. "I've never seen a person partially transformed into a spider before. It's...unsettling."

"I think, Eschaton, that you should become accustomed to being unsettled."

***

"Maybe you're right, and Anansi's out of touch with modern tech," Roger allowed, "or maybe he's already seen it all. There's plenty of brushfire conflicts across the globe that a literal shapeshifter could have slipped into and out of without anyone noticing. Do we really want to go in assuming he doesn't know what we can do?"

Diane scowled again but shook her head. "So the plan is the same, but less subtle?"

"Damn right. We hit the ground, we move fast, we hit hard. Full auto - let our new strength compensate for recoil. Get in closer than we're used to, because the further away from our target, the more power we drain with every attack Double check before we drop, make sure you have ichor rounds loaded."

"Already done," Hector said with a yawn.

"Then triple check," Roger said firmly. "I don't want things going to shit because we run out of power and end up standing there with our dicks in our hands."

"I'd like to see Diane manage that," Andrew said with a chuckle.

That broke the tension a bit with a round of laughter. Diane made a rude gesture and gave Andrew an anatomically improbable suggestion, which caused the soldiers to laugh again.

As the mirth died down, Roger walked over to the window and looked out at the African coast. "One more thing," he said, his voice low, forcing everyone to lean in. "We've been instructed by command to recover more of those Black Spheres. They want them to power more Myrmidons." He gave them a look of wide-eyed innocence. "I don't know about you, but if I was one of those freaks, I'd put that thing where no one could find it. Don't you think?"

Hector opened his mouth to speak, then saw the considering frown on Andrew's face, and the way Diane's forehead was furrowed. Hector paused to let his own gears turn, considering a little more carefully.

Right now, the four of them were the best weapons anyone had against these gods. They were unique; as a group, they were one of a kind. If Project Myrmidon had more of those spheres, there would be more Myrmidons. They'd lose that unique quality. They'd, in essence, just be grunts again.

"You know what, sir?" Hector said into the silence. "I think you're absolutely right."

"Good," Roger said as the others nodded agreement. "Thought you might. We'll check for them, of course, but if we can't find them, we'll at least have two new bodies for the eggheads to play with. Drop's in five."

"Yeah," Andrew said, "about that. I noticed a bit ago that this damn plane doesn't have any parachutes."

"Parachutes?" Diane said with a grin. "What kind of punk-ass god needs a damn parachute?"

"Drop's in five," Roger repeated. "Final gear check, and then we hit the ground hard. Let's see how 'gods' die."

***

Ryan took a deep breath. "Can I get a hand with pulling my foot from my mouth? It tastes like a shoe, and that's not the best flavor."

Anansi erupted in warm laughter, so infectious that Ryan found he couldn't help but join him. "Okay," Ryan said, "so you're turning your worshippers into spider people to help them avoid the apocalypse. I'll be honest, I didn't even know that was possible."

"I am over five thousand years old," Anansi said with a twinkle in his eyes. "And just recently, I encountered something I believed impossible."

"What was it?"

Anansi reached into his pocket and pulled out a cellphone. "I can push this piece of glass a few times and have almost any food I want brought directly to me. Impossible is a word that I would hesitate to ever use, Ryan Smith. I think you'll often find that the difference between the possible and the impossible is just a matter of time and determination."

"Makes sense. Well, given your motivation for turning people into those...hybrids? Is that the right term?" Anansi nodded, and Ryan continued, "How would you like to help make sure I don't screw up the end of the world too badly?"

Anansi thought, and Ryan leaned back and didn't interrupt. He didn't want to rush things, although he was keenly aware that he had spent most of his twenty-four hours already.

"I think that I will," Anansi said finally, "if you promise me a couple things."

"If I can, I will."

"A careful answer. You're taking to being a god quite naturally." Anansi continued, "Two things, then. First, I will make sure that my people are cared for. If the world is ending, and your mission cannot save them, I will take time to ensure their safety. If possible, I'd like your promise of aid for that."

"If at all possible," Ryan agreed. "I don't know how crazy things will get, but I will do everything I can to give you that time."

"That is all I can ask. And that you don't interfere if I must break away to ensure their safety."

"I wouldn't dream of it," Ryan said without hesitation. "Hell, if it comes down to that, I'll be glad to know at least some people are going to make it out."

"Good. As for the other...I'd like to ask a question. You had a life before all this, yes?"

"I mean, yeah, but it wasn't much of one." Ryan said, frowning as he tried to follow Anansi's logic.

"Oh, but it was yours. Yet in your tale, you did not mention it once. No family, no friends. As far as your story was concerned, your life only involved Nabu, and then you were a god." Anansi's gaze was intense, and Ryan couldn't maintain eye contact. He found himself looking at the floor as Anansi continued, "You want to save the world, but you have removed yourself from it. Letting yourself get completely engrossed in being a god, so much so you are losing what it means to be human. Talk to the people you are trying to save so that you do not lose sight of that which matters."

"You want me to...what? Go to a bar, spend some time making friends in a park? Because I'm a bit busy-"

Anansi cut Ryan off with a firm shake of his head. "Even now, you misunderstand. Deliberately, I think. You will go talk to your family, your friends. Reconnect with the people you care about."

Ryan let out a long sigh. It was what he was afraid Anansi had been getting at, and he tried to deflect as best he could. "It's been crazy. I can't be sure there will be time to go talk to them."

Anansi shrugged. "Maybe it will be hard. But in the long run, you will save more time if you have me as your ally, I can assure you of that. If you do not...well, then you will at least not have to make time to see them."

"You'd really refuse to help us if I don't make time to see my friends and family? Seriously? With the entire world at stake?" Ryan felt the heat rising in his voice and tried to clamp it down.

"Yes, Ryan Smith, I would. Because if you do not, I believe you will become as dangerous as Enki. You are not grounded. You do not have anything in the world to make you want to save it, other than the abstract notion of good and evil. But war, it has a way of eroding the abstracts. Anchor yourself, so you do not lose your way."

Ryan found the strength to meet Anansi's eyes again, but they were unyielding. Ryan let out another sigh, though this one was less frustration and more resignation. "Fine. I agree to your terms."

Anansi smiled. "Then, I will work with you. I do have some questions, though. For example-"

Before Anansi could finish, he was cut off by the sound of shattering glass from the front room.

***

Wind whipped Diane's hair back as she flew towards the target, streaking through the air like a superhero. Well, almost. They weren't really flying. It was a controlled fall, using tiny amounts of divine power to alter their vectors towards the target. She grinned fiercely. It was still closer than she'd imagined possible, at least since she'd been a kid.

The city of Accra stretched beneath them, everything looking small and toy-like from this height. Part of her brain insisted she should be able to reach out and pluck the cars below like they were hot wheels. *I wonder if I could,* she thought, imagining using her divine powers to create a hand made of energy.

The ground was getting closer with every second, and the cars were starting to look too big for that to work. Plus, it would be a pointless waste of power. *Unless I threw a car into the building. I bet that even with everything Anansi's seen, he never imagined a car flying through his window.*

It was a fun thought, but it wouldn't work, even if she was strong enough to toss cars like that. Police had cleared the road leading into Anansi's office, giving them a clear field of operation. Diane twisted reality one last time, to make sure she was on target, and then began to prepare for impact.

Each of her companions did the same, and their fall jerked to a halt a few feet above the ground as they zeroed out their acceleration an instant before impact. Diane absorbed the rest of the fall by letting one hand drop to the ground to stabilize herself.

There weren't any more signals needed. Each of them hurled tear gas grenades into the store's front window.

***

Ryan whipped his head towards the door. There was a gentle hiss in the air, and they could hear Kwadwo let out a surprised shout that quickly turned into coughing.

Ryan was on his feet, reaching into his nanoverse and pulling out a sword, while Anansi summoned a pair of daggers. "Do you feel that, Ryan?" the other god whispered.

Ryan did. It was a strange feeling, like the sensation from fingernails on a chalkboard without the sound. Whatever was out there was weird and unnatural and *dangerous.*

"I think we should-" Ryan began.

He was cut off by a staccato burst of gunfire, muffled by the walls. Ryan slammed himself to the ground as bullets zipped through the air over their heads, filling the space they had just vacated. He could hear shattering glass from the front room, and white gas began to pour through the holes in the wall.

Ryan felt his heart pounding. Kwadwo was still coughing, and Ryan heard glass being crushed under boots.

"Ryan Smith and Anansi!" A voice shouted. "Surrender peacefully or die, by order of the United States of America."

By order of the what? Ryan thought, glancing at Anansi. When he first heard the gunfire, he'd expected terrorists or some kind of fanatics. Soldiers, however, were a different matter. Anansi gave Ryan a questioning look, clearly unphased. Ryan told himself he wasn't scared of the men outside, a lie he was sure he'd eventually believe. He had never imagined going to battle with United States soldiers. *They opened fire on a building in a crowded city. That back wall didn't magically stop bullets. They could have killed someone. Screw that noise.*

Ryan gave Anansi a nod and scrambled over to the wall to peer through the holes. In the other room, Kwadwo was on his hands and knees, still coughing. A soldier walked over and grabbed his hair, forcing his face up. "It's not one of them, sir," the soldier said.

Good, Ryan thought with relief. *Now they'll let Kwadwo go and-*

The soldier's rifle swung up in a lazy arc until it was pointed directly at Kwadwo's face. Before Ryan could even think to act, the gun erupted. Kwadwo's head jerked back, a red mist spraying out of the back of the skull, and he collapsed in a lifeless pile.

Anansi's face turned to stone, and his eyes flared with sudden rage. He rose to his feet in a smooth motion and reached out to begin a twist.

"Come out now, or you will be destroyed!" the authoritative voice demanded once again.

Ryan answered the demand with a twist of his own. He began to manipulate the equations governing the wall's momentum. Right now it was unmoving, but if he changed the velocity from zero meters per second to one hundred...

His twist fell into place, and the wall exploded outwards, sending wooden shrapnel flying towards the attackers. Anansi's twist followed, and the splinters curved in the air, random debris becoming guided missiles. "Here we are, you son of a bitch," Ryan said, stepping out to see what they were facing.

The shrapnel had never reached their destinations. They were embedded in the floor around the feet of the intruders, and Ryan couldn't even begin to fathom how that had happened. The soldier in front was a young man, probably in his early twenties, with sandy blond hair and a hard glare. His hand was outstretched, although Ryan could see nothing in it.

There were three others with him: an extremely tall dark-haired man, a woman with a malicious grin, and a squat man with deep-set eyes and a bored expression.

Each of them wore a harness over their fatigues, some strange device that glowed with a faint light. With his divine sight, Ryan saw that the equations around those things were monstrously complicated, far beyond anything Ryan had seen before. Whatever they were, they were clearly unnatural.

What sent a chill down Ryan's spine was the soldiers' complete lack of shock at the display of power. He and Anansi had just turned a wall into homing missiles, but these people seemed...unimpressed. No matter how disciplined a soldier you were, that couldn't be something you were *used* to. *What the hell are you and why aren't you shitting your pants in fear?* Ryan thought.

It didn't matter. He would *show* them why they should be afraid. He began to twist again. Beside him, Anansi was doing the same. The stony expression on his face had broken, and every line of his body radiated fury. Ryan began to relax. Whatever they were, they'd managed to piss off Anansi and - The soldiers had also grabbed equations, each making a different manipulation. Ryan lost control of his own twist in shock, and the pillar of fire he'd been preparing fizzled out into a heatwave that rolled over his opponents. *They're... they're gods?*

Ryan's hand shook as the god-soldier's equations began to fall into place. Bolts of lightning burst through the ceiling, and Ryan threw himself to the side, the twin bolts electricity arcing to scorch the floor he'd just vacated. The bolts targeting Anansi were intercepted as the Trickster redirected his twist upwards, creating a barrier. The impact drove Anansi to one knee, as Ryan hit the floor and rolled.

Four of them. He and Anansi were outnumbered two to one, and that first attack had nearly fried him. He could only imagine how close Anansi had come to being hit, but from the way his eyes widened, it had been closer than Ryan would have liked.

"Shouldn't talk about my mother that way." This was the authoritative voice, but it wasn't demanding now - it was harsh and menacing. "Dead or alive. Go!"

Ryan started to get to his feet, but the government-sponsored gods were already manipulating equations again, and he threw himself back to the floor as four fireballs appeared on each side of him, racing inwards to explode where his head had just been.

They weren't just outnumbered. They were also outgunned. These gods were throwing power around like they didn't care about their Hungers, and as long as they kept that up, he couldn't see how he and Anansi could survive this.

The harness on one of the gods serving the United States government glowed brighter as she began to twist equations. *Some kind of monitoring tool, or enhancing her power?* Ryan wondered. He couldn't make heads or tails of it, especially when he had more pressing concerns.

The woman hurled a sphere of solid air at Ryan, and he rolled to the side. It missed him by mere inches. Driven by reflex, Ryan kept rolling. Bullets slammed into the ground beside him, and he barely stayed ahead of the fire.

The assault was relentless. Ryan finally managed to scramble into a crouch, just as the woman thrust out her hands and sent another arc of lightning towards him. He dove again, wishing that he could at least *get off the damn floor*, and threw out his hand in a desperate twist of equations.

A burst of air, followed by a quick transformation of the air to a mixture of sodium and water, created a rolling fireball. Windows exploded across the street, and the two soldiers Ryan was dealing with were thrown out the windows.

Oh, holy crap, that worked, Ryan thought. This twist was one he'd wanted to try, although he'd hoped to test it in less desperate circumstances.

As a bonus, he had cleared out the tear gas and smoke in the room. Ryan could see better now, and finally had a chance to stand up, so he took a moment to take stock.

It occurred to him that the soldiers were attacking too *fast.* They were making mistakes with their twists and burning power like it didn't matter when they ran out. *These guys are rookies,* Ryan realized with a start. It was comforting at the moment, but it should be impossible - Ryan was supposed to be the newest of the new guys.

A problem for later. Ryan turned, intending to help Anansi, but then he saw the two soldiers charging back into the room, looking more annoyed than injured. *Divide and conquer. I can't worry about Anansi – I have to assume he can handle it. I have my own problems.*

His opponents switched roles, the man letting his gun dangle as he began twisting equations while the woman unslung hers to take aim. Ryan tried to dodge, but suddenly his movements felt sluggish and heavy. Bullets slammed into his chest, and pain radiated from the impact. He knew this was it, that his brief tenure of godhood had ended, and he'd lost his chance to save humanity.

Then he looked down and saw three bullets hovering over his heart, but no actual wounds and no blood. He blinked, focused, and saw the equations delineating an air pressure bubble protecting him. *Anansi.*

Acting to save Ryan had put Anansi in a vulnerable position, with the other two soldiers about to fire on him. Adrenaline kicked in, giving Ryan the ability to move. He reached out and heavily ramped up the magnetic attraction between the two guns aimed at Anansi. When the soldiers opened fire, the guns were pulled to point towards each other, spoiling their aim.

Unfortunately, the two men stopped firing before they could mow each other down. Instead, they let go of their guns, which slammed together before clattering to the floor. Anansi was moving, and Ryan returned his attention to his own opponents.

The woman was readying another twist, but Ryan didn't have time to follow it, because, at that moment, the man threw a bolt of lightning. *Shit!* Ryan threw out his hands and amped up the positive charge beneath the woman's feet. The lightning arced away from Ryan, negative being called to positive. She clenched her teeth in pain as the bolt struck her, and the harness around her chest sputtered before the light went out.

Ha! I'm better at math than you, Ryan thought with a surge of exaltation. The woman snarled and held up her hand again, ready to try another attack...but nothing happened. Her eyes widened in shock.

Realization struck Ryan, and he shouted, "Anansi! Their harnesses give them powers!" The woman hoisted her assault rifle, opening fire, but Ryan was already rolling and twisting, gathering a lightning bolt of his own.

HIs remaining empowered opponent had vanished, so Ryan tossed the lightning at Anansi's attackers. It split in two, targeting both of them. The tall man held out his hands and grounded the bolt with a positive charge on the floor - *Shit, they learn quick* - and the squat man simply tossed his rifle at the attack, letting it intercept the bolt.

Anansi saw the opening. The spider-god leapt the distance between himself and the tall soldier, landing with his feet on the man's shoulders. The soldier brought up his hands to try and ward off Anansi's attack, but he was too slow - twin daggers lanced down and plunged into the harness. Anansi kicked off the soldier, sending him to the floor while Anansi flipped away. The harness went dead, and Ryan let out an excited whoop. The odds had just changed completely. One on one, and he and Anansi knew their opponents' weaknesses.

"Fall back!" The man who had been attacking Ryan shouted. "Fall back now!" He hurled another canister of tear gas towards Ryan and Anansi.

Ryan rolled his eyes and stepped into the spreading cloud. *Tear gas didn't work, you haven't realized that yet?* He could see the commander was twisting equations and prepared to counteract whatever attack the man threw. Right now the soldier was altering molecular formulas. *What are you hoping to accomplish?* Ryan wondered. The commander was turning the main component of the tear gas, 2-chlorobenzalmalononitrile, into a much simpler formula. CH4.

I know that compound. CH4. It's...Methane! Ryan snapped his fingers in excitement at placing it.

Then his face fell as it hit him. Methane.

Shit.

Ryan and Anansi both saw the woman open fire into the cloud and desperately grasped onto threads of reality. The first few rounds did nothing, but the fifth or sixth round struck something metal, which produced a spark. That spark found the methane and did what heat and methane were known to do best, which was exploding with enough force to demolish the building they were in, sending the roof briefly upwards before it collapsed down on the two gods.

Ryan's last-second barrier was enough to keep him safe, but it was a near thing. "Anansi?" Ryan gasped, straining against the weight of the rubble.

He heard a reply, though he couldn't make out what Anansi said. Ryan dropped his barrier and zeroed out gravity for everything except himself, making the rubble weightless. It was still a complicated process to push his way through, as chunks of the building kept bouncing around and barring his path.

By the time he was free, their adversaries were gone. At least Anansi had freed himself too and was brushing plaster dust out of his eyes. Ryan rubbed his cheek, and his hand came away with a thin smear of blood. He could also see a few scrapes and cuts on his companion.

He replaced the gravity around the debris slowly, letting it settle gently back to Earth. After all, somewhere, under the rubble, was Kwadwo's body. "This is monstrous," Ryan whispered hoarsely. He looked around with his divine sight. "There aren't any people around. The local government must have cooperated, evacuated the area while we were talking. How did we miss that?"

Anansi, staring at what remained at the building, and the surrounding area, didn't bother responding. Ryan couldn't blame him. It looked like a warzone. Nearby structures had bullet holes and shattered glass, and a pipe had burst in the street, spraying water into the air. A few pieces of paper were still fluttering in the breeze, blackened and charred by the explosion.

Anansi's face was a mask of sorrow when he finally broke the silence. "You see now part of the reason we have hidden for so long. When gods clash..." Anansi didn't finish the sentence, instead moving his hand in a sweeping gesture that encompassed the wreckage around him. "The only one to die here was a mortal man. A good man."

Ryan walked over to Anansi. "I'm so sorry I brought this to you. I'm sorry about-"

Anansi shook his head to cut Ryan off. "Did you know they were following you? Did you know they existed?"

Ryan shook his head.

"Then do not apologize for the evil other men do, Ryan Smith. Do not apologize for not knowing the future. They are the ones who will have to answer for Kwadwo's death."

Ryan stepped up behind Anansi and put a hand on his shoulder. "And I promise you, Anansi. They will pay for that."

Chapter 8

Divine Council

Ryan stepped out of his nanoverse, the obsidian sand of Cypher Nullity crunching under his feet. He craned his head back to enjoy the sight of the alien worlds drifting through the broken sky above, crossing impossibly fast across the black lines of lightning that permanently scarred the air.

Unlike the last time he was here, there wasn't that forlorn, empty feeling of kenopsia. This place was still a dead, desolate world, but it no longer felt abandoned. *Perhaps because it has a purpose again,* Ryan mused. Anansi stepped out while Ryan was still taking in the sights.

"Over six thousand years old," Anansi murmured, "and I still find new marvels in hidden corners of the cosmos."

Ryan chewed his cheek before responding. "Does it ever get old?" he asked, his voice quiet. "After millennium upon millennium, do you ever look at things like this and think 'oh, bah, another marvelous alien world?'"

Anansi chuckled and shook his head. "Never. At least, not for me. I feel immensely sad for those gods that do lose that wonder."

Ryan nodded in agreement. In the distance, he could hear the others in conversation. "Guess we're the last ones to arrive."

"One thing I don't understand," Anansi asked as they walked. "Why this place? Among all the cosmos, why here?"

"Well, for starters, it's free real estate," Ryan said, looking over at Anansi and waiting for a laugh. When Anansi met his amusement with blank patience, Ryan winced. *Right. Pop culture references aren't great for immortals.* "I mean that literally in this case. This used to be the Lemurian afterlife. Since there's no more Lemurians, and there hasn't been in ages, it's empty. There was a hecatoncheires here, but Crystal and I took care of it."

Anansi gave Ryan a curious look, and Ryan corrected himself. "It was mostly Crystal, but I helped."

Anansi raised an eyebrow.

Ryan sighed and explained, "I'm sure my screams were very distracting."

"I saw you fight a hecatoncheires on the news," Anansi said. "I didn't doubt that you had helped. I appreciate the honesty, though." He flashed Ryan an impish grin.

"Anyway," Ryan said, forcibly changing the topic before he embarrassed himself into oblivion. "We wanted somewhere that wasn't being used by anyone, and no one besides the people here knows it exists. Others can't find us if they don't know where to look. It was Athena's idea to use meet here."

The gods were gathered in a building near the Reliquary of Squandered Dreams. Ryan skirted around the Reliquary, giving it a wide berth. He'd stepped in there the last time he was on Cypher Nullity, and for his troubles had been rewarded with a sight of what his life would have been like if he'd lived without regret. He would have married Jacqueline after confessing that he saw a suited man following him at all times, would have had children with her...and then the world would have been swallowed by the Sun going supernova.

He had no interest in reliving that experience.

Instead, he headed into the place Crystal called Hall of Forlorn Contemplation. To Ryan's eyes, it looked like a cathedral designed by a madman - a massive structure that looked almost organic, with spine-like supports placed at regular intervals and the worn stone of the walls giving the appearance of flesh stretched between them. The walls were spotted with stained glass windows that allowed light to filter into the room.

The building's interior was less menacing than its exterior had suggested. The fleshy theme did carry over, with the columns looking like stacked femurs and the ceiling covered in a webbed pattern that reminded Ryan in of veins and arteries. But millions of years of dust covered the whole thing, creating a softening effect that made it more sad than creepy, a haunted house that had fallen into depression with no one to torment, desolate for so long it couldn't bother to try to frighten those who were now inside.

Inside he found Athena and Crystal had been joined by not one, as expected, but *two* new gods. Ryan assumed that the woman standing slightly apart from the others was Dianmu, but the man sitting near Athena was a mystery. Ryan started slightly as he noticed the man's military gear, and only relaxed when he saw the lack of a harness. He glanced over to Anansi. "I don't know that guy," he whispered.

"Horus," Anansi replied, also keeping his voice low. "I'm a little surprised to see him here. He and Bast have a...complicated history."

Ryan wanted to ask more questions, but Athena had spotted them and motioned for Ryan and Anansi to join the group. Horus's attention was on Crystal, and he gestured firmly as he spoke. "I know Moloch is a threat, but we need to find Bast. If she is working with him, there must be a good reason. She may very well be in danger."

Before Crystal could respond, Athena turned to him, her eyes narrow and harsh. "Bast *murdered* Tyr right in front of us, knowing Enki was going to destroy his nanoverse, Horus. You're in denial."

"You can't know that for certain!" Horus said, his voice matching the anger in Athena's eyes. He had turned to face the Greek goddess, but it was Crystal who responded.

"Sure, we can't read her mind," she said, "but she buggered us. Hard, and not in the fun way. Which means Enki had her trust, so we have to assume she was complicit in the whole thing, yeah?"

Horus scowled. "I know her. She wouldn't-"

"Incorrect." Athena interrupted, "You *knew* her, but by your own admission you haven't seen her in three hundred years. People *change*, Horus. Surely you aren't the same man you were in the 1700's?"

Ryan shared a look with Anansi, and they altered their course. Since Dianmu was off to the side, away from the group, and not embroiled in a heated argument, talking to her seemed infinitely more appealing than joining the others at the table.

He offered Dianmu a hand. "Ryan Smith. I'm the Eschaton, apparently," he said in a low voice as Horus began to rebut Athena.

Dianmu's handshake was firm but friendly. She moved with an easy calmness that contrasted with Athena's steady deliberation and Crystal's energy. "Dianmu," she said.

"Good to meet you. How long have they been at it?" Ryan asked, looking over at the table. Crystal had picked up the thread of the argument again, once again pointing out it was safer to assume Bast had gone evil.

"Only about fifteen minutes," Dianmu responded, glancing over at Athena, "although I get the feeling that it was a longer discussion before Crystal and I joined in."

"Gotcha." Ryan wasn't sure what to say next, so he was glad when Anansi decided to jump in.

"Anansi. I don't think I've had the pleasure." He offered Dianmu a hand, and she shook it with a bit more caution than she'd used with Ryan.

"No, we have not. But I still know you by reputation, Trickster." Her tone was still friendly, almost teasing. "My husband and I were still married when he had his run-in with you."

Anansi considered for a moment. "Leigong? You were married to him?" Dianmu nodded, and Anansi chuckled. "Back then, I was more prankster than Trickster, I'll admit. How long did it take him to find all the feathers?"

"Five decades." She shook her head, her face a combination of bemusement and frustration. "And another two to be certain he really had found them all. He wasn't amused."

"And that's why I avoided China for the next three thousand years," Anansi said.

"A wise choice. I don't think he had forgiven you, even by then." Dianmu turned towards the table and frowned. "As nice as it is to meet the two of you, I think we had best step in before this argument repeats itself for the fourth time." Although her tone was still polite, it now carried a tiny hint of irritation. She grabbed her glass of water, moving towards the table without waiting for a response.

"Perhaps we can set this argument aside?" Dianmu said when they reached the others. Her voice was level, but firm enough to cut through the argument. They all looked at her. "It's becoming obvious that neither side will convince the other, so allow me to ask a question that I think everyone has overlooked: do any of you actually know where to find Bast?"

Reluctantly, both Athena and Horus shook their heads.

"Then perhaps we can wait until we have some idea of where she is to argue about what should be done with her?"

"Especially since we have bigger problems," Ryan chimed in. All eyes moved from Dianmu to him, and he shifted uncomfortably under the attention. "Hi," he said, turning to Horus. "We haven't met. I'm Ryan Smith."

"Do you always introduce yourself with your full name?" Horus asked. "It makes you sound like a simpleton."

Ryan pursed his lips. "Oh, I'm so glad you decided to join us. Between Crystal, Athena, and I, we have plenty of snark, but we were lacking in any outright assholes. Good to know that role is being filled."

Horus's eyes narrowed. "Little-"

"Athena!" Anansi said brightly, stepping between Horus and Ryan to offer Athena his hand. "It's wonderful to meet you finally. It's been on my to-do list for at least seven hundred years."

Athena took and shook his hand like he'd offered her a live snake, and she was trying to crush its skull. "Anansi," she said in a cool voice, her smile tight and strained. "I'm a bit shocked to hear you wanted to meet so badly."

"Well, you were the mastermind behind the Trojan horse. When Hermes told me about that, I laughed for days. A war goddess employing Trickster tactics? I had to meet you."

If Athena's smile got any tighter, it would snap. "Cleverness is not the sole domain of Tricksters," she said. Crystal discreetly nudged Athena's calf under the table, and Athena made herself relax with a visible effort. "Still, I appreciate the compliment. Apologies if I seem rude. There are three stories about me that are repeated the most often, that being one of them, and sometimes I wish I was known for anything else."

Behind Anansi, Horus had calmed down. He gave the Trickster a gruff nod. "Haven't seen you seen the Punic Wars, Anansi."

"Same," Crystal piped in. "You kind of dropped off the grid, love."

"Hardly," Anansi said, shaking both their hands in turn. "I just realized warfare was never going to be something that appealed to me. I prefer the version we have in stories - much less death, much less chaos, and much more heroism."

"Better to leave the warfare to those of us that are good at it," Horus said with a laugh. He clapped Anansi on the back and then shot Ryan a resigned glance. "Eschaton. You mention a greater threat. Explain."

Do you even know how to ask questions, or do you just demand things? Ryan wondered. Aloud, he said, "There's an army being made that poses a serious threat to us."

Crystal and Dianmu only looked worried, but Athena's mouth dropped open in shock. "You encountered them too?"

The question made Ryan sag. "I was really hoping they only had the few Anansi and I fought. If they were in South America, then we've got a bigger problem than we realized." Anansi nodded in agreement.

"Well, it's hardly surprising they were in South America," Horus said, seemingly willing to put aside his argument with Athena for the moment. "Moloch is behind them."

"Oh c' mon!" Ryan nearly shouted - not at Horus, but at the universe. "Moloch is working with the United States military?"

That took Athena and Horus aback, and they glanced at Anansi as if seeking confirmation. "The United States military is involved?" Athena asked.

"Well, yeah," Ryan said, tilting his head. "I mean, they had US flags on their uniforms."

"Uniforms?" Athena's forehead wrinkled. "When I saw them, they were naked or just wearing plain robes."

"Except for the harness, I assume?" Anansi asked.

"Harness? No, just the tattoos."

"What tattoos?" It was Ryan's turn to furrow his brow. "None of the ones we fought had tattoos, at least not that we could see."

"Oh bloody hell in a handbasket!" Crystal snapped, getting everyone's attention. "Athena, tell us what you saw. Then, Ryan, *you* tell us what you saw. Because I'm pretty sure you're talking about two different sodding things!"

Dianmu reached out and put a gentle hand on Crystal's arm. Crystal pursed her lips as she took a deep breath. "Please," she added, and Dianmu smiled.

"Very well." Athena began. She told them about arriving in Venezuela and sneaking past the soldiers waiting to ambush anyone going in and out of the park. Crystal cursed when Athena mentioned the cockatrice.

"Wait," Ryan interjected. "It can turn us to stone?"

Athena nodded. "Even the gods aren't immune to the powers of beings like that. It's why we sent Perseus to dispatch the original Medusa."

"It gets worse," Horus added with a grim face. "If you fall to one of those things, you are not truly alive or dead. You do not resurrect because you don't die. Mortals will die - they'll suffocate because their lungs don't work - but gods? We remain trapped until someone destroys the statue."

Ryan shuddered at the thought.

"Oh, and just to add to that, love," Crystal said with false cheer, "you're aware the entire time. Unable to move, unable to breathe, unable to do anything but stare ahead until your statue is destroyed by the elements or your nanoverse undergoes heat death unless someone comes along and breaks you so you can resurrect." Crystal shivered. "That was not a fun decade."

"I'm just glad I found you," Dianmu added before turning to Ryan. "If you were to get caught by one of these things...I suppose we'd have to leave you trapped for a few years to ensure you had undergone Apotheosis before we destroyed the statue, to ensure you did resurrect."

"And by that point, the world probably would have ended anyway," Anansi said with a shrug. "So...stay away from cockatrices."

"Yeah...I think I got that, thanks."

Athena nodded and picked up the story with Moloch's transformation and his followers killing the cockatrice and ended with Horus's arrival.

Ryan glanced around. "Mind telling me why that's bad so I can join you all in grim silence?"

Apparently, humor wasn't the right idea here. Athena just sighed before explaining. "By letting his followers feast on such beasts, Moloch's giving them resistance to divine powers. We won't be able to directly alter their biology, and their weapons will be harder to defend against. They may even gain some powers from the creatures."

"In time, they'll become monsters themselves, and only divine flesh will satisfy their hunger," Horus added. "I've dealt with their like before."

"I'd like to hear about it," Ryan said, by way of a peace offering.

"Yes. That is why I mentioned it. Because I intended to tell you." Horus gave Ryan a level stare.

Ryan just rolled his eyes and withdrew the olive branch now that Horus had broken it over his knee.

"It was back during the period your historians call the Bronze Age collapse," Horus began, leaning forward on the table. "After the Olympians and their Titanomachy destroyed civilization as we knew it."

Athena clenched her fist but didn't interject. Ryan looked at her askance, and Athena only gave him a curt shake of her head.

"A few of the survivors of Ugarit fled across the Nile, to settle south of our dominion," Horus continued. "After what had happened to their city, we were inclined to allow them to stay there. Ba'al was nowhere to be found, and we hoped to incorporate them into our faith and kingdom. We didn't know they already had a god they worshipped. Mot. Their death god. Mot saw an opportunity for conquest since he was now without a Pantheon. He started to feed his followers on the flesh of monsters in secret, hunting them down for his people.

"I don't know if Mot knew what he was doing to his followers at first. I'd certainly never heard of such a thing before, and it surprised even Ra. They came storming up along the Nile. It wasn't a large army, no more than a thousand, but…" Horus took a deep breath, his eyes getting a distant look. Ryan got the impression he was peering back through time to the war that had raged. "But they were able to resist our manipulations of the elements. Many of us weren't able to even harm them. Our soldiers had other problems. The followers of Mot could leap over walls, break bronze in their hands, and snap a man's neck with a blow.

"That was the end of the empire of Egypt. We had survived the aftermath of the Titanomachy, we had survived the predation of the Sea Peoples, and we had survived while our allies and enemies fell around us, but this was the final straw. We were able to kill them all, down to the last man, but our empire didn't recover for centuries from the ravages that war left on our country." Horus shook his head, dispelling whatever memory had held his attention. "That's the power of these *things* Moloch has created. They can break empires and cut down gods. They're superhuman."

"Damn," Ryan said, slumping his chair. "Anything else we need to know to fight them?"

"You?" Horus said, scoffing. "Your best action would be to stay behind your betters, Nascent. You have much to learn before you fight these things."

"Actually," Ryan said, stiffening in his chair, "we already did. Right Anansi?"

Anansi sighed deeply, looking at Ryan. "Unfortunately, what we fought was something new. What the followers of Moloch do, it's an old practice, one most gods banned long ago - and why we allowed the creatures of legend to be locked away."

"Until Arthur set them free," Ryan muttered, making a note to have words with the King of Hell if he ever got the chance. He addressed the larger group. "Anansi and I didn't face that - we were up against something different, something new. The United States government has found a way to make gods out of technology and sent a squad of them against us."

Athena put a hand to her mouth, and Dianmu leaned forward. "Elaborate, if you will?"

So Ryan told his story, with Anansi adding details Ryan had overlooked. He started with the tear-gas grenade going through the window and ended with the explosion. "The good news is," he added, "if you can get the harness off them, it's pretty much instant power down. Also, they have to have a power source, which means it's finite. If you know what you're dealing with, you can probably outlast them."

"I'm not certain about it being finite," Anansi said. "We didn't see any evidence of that."

Ryan thought for a moment. "You're right. I'd love to get a better look at one of those harnesses."

The other four goods looked confused, and Ryan stood up, pulling a wooden rod out of his nanoverse. "Here, I'll show you." He began to sketch a crude stick figure in the dust on the floor of the Hall. "They have guns, some kind of assault rifle," Ryan said, adding a line coming out of the stick figure's hands, "and they carry smoke grenades. Probably other weapons as well, although they seem to prefer to keep one hand free to twist reality." Ryan drew a question mark over the other hand. "The harness goes across the chest like this," Ryan continued, drawing an X over the figure's chest and adding a few more lines. It was rapidly turning into a scribbled mess.

Anansi glanced at the drawing. "There's a strap across the back," he added.

"That's right here," Ryan said, pointing to one of the lines.

Anansi regarded him flatly. "That's a strap across the back?"

Ryan nodded.

Anansi looked at him for another long moment, then started to laugh. "As much as I'm enjoying watching your artistry, perhaps I could try?"

"Fine," Ryan said, dropping the stick. Anansi reached out and began to twist. A perfect image of the leader of the soldiers appeared floating over the table. "You can do *holograms,"* Ryan sputtered, "and you let me scribble with the stick?"

"You were having so much fun," Anansi said kindly. "I didn't want to disturb you."

Ryan flushed as even Horus grinned.

Crystal snorted. "Well, that's brilliant. So we've got theovores and super-soldiers. Sounds like a lovely time."

"And there's still the end of the world, let us not forget," Dianmu said mildly. "Although if push comes to shove, that problem could solve the other two." They all looked at her, and she shrugged. "I'm not advocating it, but it sounds like the world *must* end. If these factions cannot be faced, then perhaps they can be erased during the End Times."

"I don't think so," Ryan said, surprising even himself. He took a moment to catch up to his own subconscious. "If we're going to end the world peacefully, which is still the plan, it's going to be delicate work. I'm sure of that. We can't risk doing it while either of those groups could beat down the door and interrupt us."

The other gods looked doubtful until Crystal spoke up. "If he's saying that, then he's right. I didn't have anyone to explain the eschaton stuff to me when it was my go-around, loves. But I do remember some things just making sense like that, yeah?"

"Also," Dianmu mused, "there is the problem of Ryan's Nascency, which is evident to any god who faces him.

"It is?" Ryan asked.

Dianmu's eyes widened. "You were not aware?"

"No," he admitted, and Dianmu wrinkled her nose as she looked at both Crystal and Athena.

"There's been a lot to cover," Athena broke in, "and not a lot of time."

"I see," Dianmu replied. "Well, having *successfully* mentored more than a few Nascents over the years, I've become something of an expert in the process."

Ryan noticed Athena's eyes narrow as she watched Dianmu. *What's that all about?* he wondered.

"When you have completed Apotheosis," Dianmu said to Ryan, "your blood will turn to divine ichor, which any god will recognize at a glance. For now, it is quite clear that any one of us could permanently destroy you."

"And if these soldiers are using our powers somehow," Horus put in, "they might be able to figure it out, too."

"Meaning," Ryan said gloomily, "that I could be right in the middle of executing the perfect plan to end the world..."

"And have your head blown clean off," Crystal finished. "So we can't just go around ignoring nasty people who want to kill you."

Athena nodded in agreement. "Then it seems obvious Moloch should be our first focus. The entire United States is a large area to search, and I at least have some idea where Moloch's base may be."

"What about Tartarus?" Ryan asked. He hated bringing that up, but if Athena felt she couldn't talk about it...*someone needs to remind her we do care about that.*

"My kin will have to wait. Moloch is a greater threat." Her voice was neutral, but Ryan knew it was tearing her apart, not knowing what happened to the Olympians.

"All right!" Crystal said, clapping her hands. "So we have a plan? Well, not a plan, but at least a vague idea what we're doing next?" Everyone nodded. "Great. Let's try to make that into an actual plan then, loves. We've got two main problems: Moloch and the super-soldiers in America. Is there anything else we need to take care of?"

Anansi gave Ryan a pointed look, and Ryan grimaced. "There is one other thing. I made a promise I need to fulfill."

Athena looked at Anansi, then back at Ryan. "And what oath did you make, Ryan?" she said, her every word slow and chosen with the utmost care.

"Nothing bad, I swear," Ryan said before Athena could draw some terrible conclusion. "Anansi merely brought an excellent point to my attention...namely, that I still have family out there I've been ignoring. Throughout all of this. And, well, since the world could end...I should probably reconnect with them, to make sure I don't lose focus on why I should care about saving the world."

"Oh." Athena thought for a moment and nodded. "I think he may have the right of that."

"Too bloody right," Crystal said, her voice a bit harsher. "Ryan, I kind of assumed you didn't have a life."

"Thanks," he muttered.

She continued as if he hadn't spoken. "You're immortal, you nob. Or you will be. You'll live for thousands and thousands of years, but your friends and family *will* die, and that'll be the last you see of them. If you have them, you should be spending time with them." Ryan was taken aback by the heat in her voice, and by her face, Athena was as well.

"I will," Ryan said, holding up his hands in a placating gesture. "Promise."

"Oh, yes, you will. I'm going to make sure you do. This is *important*, Ryan." There was a fire in Crystal's eyes, one Ryan hadn't seen in a while. He could only nod in agreement.

"She's right," Dianmu said. Her voice wasn't as heated as Crystal's, but it was every bit as firm. "The transition to Apotheosis can be alienating. Maintaining a connection to your mortal life is vital, in my experience."

Horus snorted, pulled out a knife, and began trimming his nails. "What a load of sentimental crap. We forge connections as gods. Better to rip off the Band-Aid when it comes to your mortal life. They'll die before you know it, anyway."

"Yes," Dianmu said, her voice icy, "because the god who has spent the last two thousand years throwing himself into every war that happens anywhere is a paragon of well-adjusted divinity."

"Spare me that, Dianmu," Horus shot back. "This idiot is who you all believe we have to depend on to save the world, and you want him to go hug his family? We don't need that. We need *action.* There's no time to sit around singing campfire songs. We need to deal with Moloch, we need to deal with these toy soldiers, and then we need to find Bast."

"Okay, you know what?" Ryan snapped. "I've just met you, and I'm already getting sick of your shit, Horus. You don't know anything about me."

"I know everything I need," Horus said. "You're Nascent. You're weak. And you're not all that bright."

"Horus," Athena said. She sounded calm, but it was the dangerous calm before a storm. "In all the millennia I've known you, you've been wrong about many things. So have I. However, that might be the most incorrect thing I've heard you say since you propped up the Ptolemaic dynasty."

From the looks around the table, Ryan realized that must be a reasonably biting insult. "Who-" he started to ask.

"A long story full of decadence, incest, and interfamilial murder," Anansi said quickly. "Like that show with all the naked women and dragons, only with fewer dragons and more murder."

Horus growled, "An insult the idiot needed explained to him."

"An idiot who was instrumental in outsmarting Enki," Athena said firmly. "A coward who had only a pointed stick and harsh language when he faced down a god who had merged two nanoverses. A Nascent who faces death with less fear than some full immortals I know. I know your feelings on Nascents, Horus - you believe they should be locked up in a pyramid until they undergo Apotheosis, so they cannot be harmed. I know you spent your own Nascency in the exact same way." She stood up and leaned forward, her face inches from Horus. "Call Ryan a coward again. I dare you."

Horus met her gaze. For a long instant, Ryan thought they would start fighting. Then Horus looked away. "Not worth my time," he muttered.

Athena sat back down, content with letting Horus save face.

"Now, then," Crystal said, clapping her hands for attention. "Here's the best plan, I think. I'll see Ryan safely to his sister. I don't like the idea of him traveling alone with those government goons running around. While I do that, the rest of you lot head to Venezuela and see if you can track down Moloch. Sound good?"

No one argued. As they were getting ready to go, Ryan turned towards Athena and gave her a shaky grin. "I'll be honest, I kind of wish I was going with you."

"Even though you'd have to face Moloch, who could kill you?"

"See, that's the thing," Ryan sighed. "Moloch *might* kill me. But after everything that's happened so far? My sister *definitely* will."

Chapter 9

Wheels Within Wheels

Drip

Bast licked her lips again, as she had every few seconds for the last several...she didn't know. Hours? Days? Weeks? No, it couldn't be that long. Days seemed most likely. With the way her captors turned the lights on and off at irregular intervals, it was impossible to be sure, but she had overheard that some team - Project Myrmidon - had been dispatched again, which meant enough time had passed for them to have a mission, come back to the base, and head back out again.

The important thing was that it had been long enough that she was no longer thirsty.

Having one of her Hungers finally met nearly brought her to tears. She'd held on to that feeling, crystalized it, and smuggled it in the back of her mind. She might need it later.

Drip

Her tongue lanced out reflexively, and while it was still good to have liquid, she realized that it was not sustainable. Eventually, it would become a form of torture, the slow and intermittent dripping driving her slowly madder. *Mad. I'm not crazy yet.*

With her vigor somewhat renewed, she'd taken note of the lab technicians that scurried about her cell and drew her ichor. She'd been able to pick up their names, and even hints of their personalities. All four had a tendency to forget she was in the room as they experimented on her. They clearly didn't realize that she was alert. Aware.

Waiting.

Eugene always had something to complain about, no matter what happened or what breakthrough they'd made, and moved with a slow and cumbersome gait that was punctuated by sighs. Cassandra was his opposite, an excitable woman who would always counter his claims with a burst of obnoxious optimism that made Bast want to rip her heart out and shove the organ, still beating, into her mouth and chew and chew and...

Drip

The water droplet brought Bast's mind out of its obsessive spiral. She licked her lips and continued her list of techs. Grace had a high and light voice that made it sound like she was constantly daydreaming if daydreams involved theories and formulas instead of empty-headed thoughts. Liam was a nervous man with a slight stutter. When he held drinking glasses, they clattered together, and he often asked one of the others to do something delicate, which suggested to Bast that he had some kind of muscular difficulty.

Liam and Grace had some sort of romantic interest, and they'd whisper to each other when the others weren't around, sharing private thoughts and sweet nothings. When they did, their hearts would pound, twin drums of young love...or at least young lust. Bast could swear she could see the two hearts, even though they were behind and above her, miniature suns that promised an end to all want.

Knowing who they were was important. She needed that for the next phase of her plan.

Drip

Again, her tongue took in the minuscule amount of moisture. It hadn't become irritating yet - the memory of that thirst was still fresh. However, she no longer *needed* it. That Hunger had been satiated. But those drips of water would serve one more purpose, so Bast could endure as long as necessary.

Eugene and Cassandra were in the room now. They'd been quiet for the last few minutes, the only sounds the gentle pecks of fingers on keyboards and the constant song of their beating hearts. Eugene finally broke the silence.

"I'm going to take this batch of ichor to the centrifuge, not that it'll really get us any new data. Going to, though, just so I can log it. Shouldn't be more than twenty, tops."

"Okay!" Cassandra chirped. "I hope the experiment goes well! You never know, today may be the day we have a breakthrough."

Bast's mind raced. Twenty minutes. She had decided that Cassandra was the easiest mark, so this was the opportunity she'd been waiting for.

Drip

She licked her lips once more. Now it was time to act.

Bast subsumed her pride and called upon that crystalized feeling from earlier, the stored joy at having her thirst quenched that nearly made her cry. She let herself fully feel the memory now, that joy causing her eyes to fill. Once the tears were running, she let out a noise. It was high pitched and muffled, a pained sound more suitable to a wounded animal than a goddess - or even a human.

Cassandra shrieked and glass shattered. Bast wanted to curse, desperately hoping no security would come bursting in. But the only sound was Cassandra's pounding heart. *Lub-dub-lub-dub-lub*

Drip

Lub-dub. Lub-dub. As Bast cleaned away this latest drop, Cassandra came closer. "Did...did you say something?"

Twit, Bast thought, and let out the noise again. Cassandra leaned over her. Better than Bast had expected. It had felt like an eternity since Bast had last seen anyone's face.

The woman wasn't precisely what Bast had pictured. She was bespectacled, which fit Bast's mental image. However, Bast had imagined her being blond and sunny. While her face wasn't unfriendly, Cassandra had jet black hair and heavy eyeliner that darkened her eyes.

That didn't matter. What was important was the way Cassandra's face contorted with a mixture of concern and surprise. "Oh my God, you're crying!" the woman exclaimed.

Bast moved her head as much as the restraints allowed. It was barely anything, but enough to get a message across. Cassandra looked torn, and Bast could imagine why. If these four hadn't been able to divorce themselves of their humanity, they wouldn't have been chosen for this task. But there was a difference between ignoring the corpse-still body of a monster and ignoring a moving, weeping figure who had been strapped to a table for who-knew-how-long.

Cassandra bit her lip, and her brows pulled down. "I can't... what's wrong?"

She recoiled slightly from the anger in Bast's eyes, pulling herself out of Bast's line of sight in the process. "Of course. You can't speak. I don't-"

Drip

Cassandra's face reappeared, her jaw set. Whatever she had decided, she'd decided it *firmly.* It was almost adorable, like a puppy certain it was going to catch its tail this time. "Know what...wait, did water just fall on you? Blink once for yes, twice for no."

Bast gave a single blink.

"Is that the problem? Is the water bothering you?"

Blink-blink.

"I'll let maintenance know. How long has that been going on? Oh, duh, you can't tell me. Sorry, I...sorry. I'll go tell maintenance." She stood up, and Bast felt a surge of panic that lent real fear to this sound, more of a plaintive one than before. Cassandra froze.

"You... don't want me to go?"

Blink.

"You're lonely, aren't you? No one to talk to?"

Bast blinked again, and Cassandra shook her head. "Of course you are. We've had you strapped down here for *ages* now, and we were told not to talk to you no matter what." Cassandra hesitated. For a moment, Bast feared she'd stop there, but Cassandra plunged ahead. "I suppose this doesn't count as talking to you. More...talking at you. Anywhere, there hasn't been any evidence that your powers are conversation dependent."

Drip

Bast licked the water away as Cassandra continued to chatter. "It's not that we don't want to talk to you - I mean, if you're really Bast, you must be over three-thousand years old, I can't imagine what you've seen, what you could tell us! But they're worried about what you could use against us. We still don't completely understand how your power works." She let out a nervous laugh, and a few seconds of silence followed.

Drip

That seemed to spur Cassandra to action. "Why don't I just email maintenance, but I'll stay here? I can talk to you while I work - we're trying to identify the chemical composition of your blood. Er. Well, it's not blood. It's ichor. It's fascinating - have you ever analyzed your own blood?"

Blink-blink.

"Oh, my, well..." She started talking about amino acids and exotic chemicals. Bast clung to every word with the same desperation she had felt licking those drops of water as they fell.

And slowly, as slowly as those pathetic drips had taken care of her thirst, this near-incomprehensible technobabble began to help Bast to feel less alone.

Two Hungers down.

Drip

***

Dale stood at the head of the room, watching a video feed, his hands clasped behind his back. He watched his soldiers engaged with Anansi and Ryan until the room exploded into a ball of fire and the image froze. "Your camera was damaged after this, correct?" he asked, his eyes still on the screen.

Roger Evans cleared his throat before speaking. "Yes, sir. The damage from shrapnel was extensive."

"Then please," Dale said, turning around to face the room, "explain to me what happened next. Most importantly, explain to me why we do not have a confirmed kill on either of these entities."

Dale looked around the room at the moment of silence that followed. It was the first full meeting of the Myrmidon Team since the operation in Ghana. Dr. Pivarti was sitting at the other end of the table, her fingers steepled in front of her face. Lazzario and Jake were side by side, of course, looking at some notes on a tablet instead of directly at the Rear Admiral. Kathleen had one of the Myrmidon's uniforms spread across her lap, her curled hair hanging around her face as she studied the fabric. Dale could barely see her lips moved as she put a finger through one of the holes. Carmen, at least, knew how to behave at a meeting, and was sitting with her attention fixed on the four Myrmidons.

For their part, all four stood at attention.

"The building collapsed, sir," Roger said, picking his words with the unique care only used by men delivering bad news to their superior officers. "We hoped that would prove sufficiently fatal. And, more importantly, Hector was caught by some debris. Had a piece of rebar driven through his gut. It was *my* assessment that we should preserve the life of one of our own, even at risk of failing the mission."

Bridges noted the subtle emphasis on the possessive pronoun there and gave Roger a slight nod of approval. "I appreciate it when a man can own their fuckups, Evans."

Roger's face hardened. "Sir?" he asked, that perfectly innocent question that always means "I don't want to get in trouble for saying 'have you lost your damn mind, sir?'"

"Your concern from your men is a credit, soldier. I'll grant that. However, and correct me if I'm wrong, your concern was for Hector Ross, yes? The same Hector Ross who, not eight hours after what you describe as an impalement, is standing right there to your left, correct?"

"Yes, sir," Roger said, and Dale once again found himself approving of the man he was dressing down. *You made a bad call, Roger, and I can't let that slide. But I can't fault the logic behind that call.*

"Tell me, Captain. Do you now believe Hector Ross was in any immediate danger?"

"Not knowing what I know now."

Dale pursed his lips. "And did the explosion also damage your radio equipment, Captain?"

"No, sir."

"I see." Dale paced the room, then turned to put his attention fully on Dr. Pivarti. "Doctor, let me ask you. *If* Roger had radioed back for assistance, what would you have told him?"

"That the injury was nowhere near as severe as it appeared. There was plenty of time for termination of the two hostiles." If Dale looked annoyed, Dr. Pivarti's face was a thundercloud. "There was no reason to abandon the mission."

"If I'd been briefed on how quickly we heal, I would have radioed," Roger snapped, temper finally flaring. "I was only told we were tougher than before. That did not indicate to me any kind of improved healing ability."

"If you had read the full report-" Dr. Pivarti began.

Roger wasn't interested in letting her finish. "Begging your pardon, ma'am," he said in a tone that meant he couldn't care less if he had her pardon, "but we were given seven hundred pages of briefing material. All known myths on Anansi. All known information on Ryan Smith. Everything we knew they had been up to since emerging. Everything you knew about our abilities. Everything we could knew or suspected about other known hostiles, including Athena, Ishtar, Moloch, and several deities we haven't even seen yet. I had to prioritize the reading material and delegate. I gave Hector the folder on our abilities."

"So you're blaming him for your decision being misinformed?" Dale demanded.

"No sir," Roger said, his tone icy. "He had a foot long piece of steel shoved through his gut. I'm shocked he remembered his own name."

Dale took a deep breath. "Have a seat, all of you. I understand, Roger, I do. And Hector, I'm glad you've made a full recovery. But you need to understand that injuries that would normally cause a withdrawal no longer apply."

"At what point, then, do we pull out?" Roger asked, his voice a shade warmer. "Doctor, do you know what we can and can't recover from?"

Dr. Pivarti shook her head. "The only way to know for certain would be to subject you to various injuries and watch you recover. I imagine everyone here agrees that would be a bad idea." She didn't wait for the nods before forging ahead. "However, I think there's a good standard to apply. As long as you still have power in your harness, anything short of an injury to the brain or heart should allow you to heal."

"And what if power is running low on the harness? Will we heal without it?"

Dr. Pivarti sighed. "I'm not certain, to be honest. We'd need more testing to be sure."

"Do the tests you can without risking anyone's life," Dale said briskly. He motioned back to the screen, where the video switched to an aerial view of the ruined building using thermal imaging. "As you can see here, two heat signatures crawled out of the wreckage. Before a response could be launched, they entered a door and vanished. Can someone explain that?"

No one spoke up immediately, and Dale crossed his arms and waited.

"Oh...wait." Lazzario's voice broke the silence, and he leaned forward, drumming his fingers on his desk. "Is it really that simple?"

"Is what simple?" Dale asked.

"They have portals," Lazzario said, snapping his fingers, alive with excitement. "That's how they get around so quickly, and why they're so hard to pin down! They can open portals. One...hang on. Admiral, zoom in on the doorway they went through, at the moment they did."

Dale did. Lazzario studied it, his smile spreading. "See right here," he said, pointing to one side of the door. "The temperature changes right as they step through, like they'd opened the door to somewhere cooler."

Jake nodded. "It fits the available data. It explains those structures they built on Graham Island, too; they must have needed them for rapid transportation."

Dale frowned. "Explain."

Jake looked at Lazzario before speaking. "Well...they stepped into a doorway, yes? Maybe they need a real doorway to vanish. So they built those big fortresses so they would have doorways if they needed to make a hasty retreat."

"It's possible," Dr. Pivarti added. "Although we don't have enough data to support the idea that doorways are needed. I do think we can agree they have some sort of ability to create portals."

Carmen frowned. "There's...enough lore to support it, I suppose. Most of the myths weren't concerned with how gods got places, except for chariots and boats for various sky deities."

"Which means," Dale said, picking up the conversation and wrestling it back onto the most important topic, "that once we engage, we cannot guarantee they'll return to a given location. We have to assume that once they escape, they could be anywhere."

"Not anywhere," Lazzario said. "We'll need to pinpoint where they go. They could have a limited range, and we might be able to exploit-"

"It rained on Mars," Kathleen said, almost too softly to be heard.

Everyone turned to look at her. She didn't look up from her sketchbook, despite suddenly being the center of attention.

"I read about it. It rained on Mars. Had scientists all over the place wigging out." She shrugged. "Gods going to Mars and making it rain could explain it."

Lazzario frowned and glanced at Jake, who was nodding furiously. "They could be *anywhere,*" Jake said mournfully, "and that shoots my doorway theory to hell. Unless...there are structures on Mars?"

"Sir, if I may?" Roger Evans asked, interrupting before Jake started spinning conspiracy theories. He was holding up a folder labeled "Ryan Smith".

Dale nodded for him to go ahead.

"Trying to chase beings that can teleport between cities - all the way to Mars, potentially - is going to be the next best thing to impossible. We need to get them to come to us." He pulled a photo from the folder and tossed it onto the table. "Or we just wait somewhere they're bound to go. It won't work with most of them, but we have data on Smith's previous life."

Dale picked up the photo. It showed a short-haired woman in her twenties who he recognized immediately. Agents had been dispatched to interview her, but she'd been useless. "You want to bring her in?" Dale asked.

Roger shook his head. "We do that, Smith comes at us with every single being he's buddy-buddy with and raises eleven different kinds of hell, sir." Lazzario and Jake both nodded in agreement. "So we put a small team on watching her. We wait for him to show up. Then..." Roger held up a hand and curled it into a fist. "One less 'god'."

Chapter 10

Brotherly Love

"Kind of like old times, isn't it?" Ryan asked with a smile. They were back in Crystal's nanoverse, the stars dancing around them. It looked different from the first time he'd seen it. Younger, full of bright stars and spiral galaxies that danced and spun in intricate patterns. He remembered that she had restarted her nanoverse after Graham Island and reflected that there was something extraordinary about an early universe.

"How do you figure?" she asked, following his gaze to the galaxies above them. For a second, he thought he saw anxiety flit across her face, but it was gone so quickly Ryan assumed he had imagined it.

"Just riding in your nanoverse," he said, "with no immediate tension looming over our heads. No reason to worry that when we step out, someone is going to ambush us...Is it weird to be nostalgic about a few weeks ago?"

Crystal put her tablet aside and smiled at him. "No, love, it isn't. Nostalgia's a funny thing for us - when the years start losing meaning, you can get nostalgic about five minutes ago and not have any of us laugh at you."

"Yeah, but I haven't lost meaning to the years yet," Ryan said. "Yet here I am, thinking about last month as 'man, those were the days'."

Crystal chuckled. "Well, what did you expect? Your entire bloody life was boring as sin, from what you've said. Then you were constantly in danger. So, of course, you romanticize the one time in between those two points when things were interesting but not terrifying."

Ryan considered for a moment and nodded. "I guess that makes sense. And hey, even better, it's a time before my sister has ripped my face off."

Crystal rolled her eyes. "Ryan, love, I completely understand your desire to avoid facing the music there. I also don't care." She went back to working on her tablet.

"Uh..."

"I had a family once." Crystal's voice was harsh, and she stabbed at the touchscreen like she was going to put her finger through the device. "Back in Lemuria."

Ryan grimaced. This entire time, he'd been complaining about *having* to go see his sister, stressing about how angry she would be, and Crystal was...well, he wasn't sure what she was feeling, but it didn't take a genius to put together that it wasn't anything even on the same planet as good. "What happened?"

Crystal didn't look up. "That's the thing, Ryan. It's been a million years. I don't know anymore. I don't remember my brother's name, my parent's faces, my sister's laugh...I don't even remember if I had more than one of each." She shook her head. "Actually, I'm pretty sure I had to have multiple brothers and sisters. We laid eggs, so it's pretty obvious we had clutches. I probably had more than one of each. Probably. But I don't have any idea." Crystal stabbed her tablet a few more times, and Ryan was left to wonder if she was actually doing anything with it, or just using it as a prop to hide her anger. Poorly.

"I'm sorry," he said after a moment.

Crystal sighed. "I realized I couldn't remember them around seven hundred BC. I tried for a while to recall anything, any detail...but after a while, it hit me. I was mourning the *idea* of them. I'd actually mourned *the people* hundreds of thousands of years before. But if I had a chance to go back and see them again, to remember them? I'd do anything for that." She looked up, and Ryan could see what she had been trying to hide. Her eyes were glistening with repressed tears.

He didn't know what to say, but Crystal didn't seem interested in his opinions. She kept talking. "So go see your sister, Ryan. Hold on to the memories, as long as they last. Because they don't last forever, and neither will she."

They sat in silence for a couple minutes, Ryan desperately trying to come up with something to say. Before he could figure it out, Crystal said, "We're here."

Ryan stood up, but Crystal wasn't moving. "If we're here, let's get this over with?" he asked.

"You go ahead, love. It occurs to me that I might not be the best person to bring to a family reunion, yeah?"

Ryan frowned. Something about her tone was off. "You sure about this?"

"Absolutely," Crystal said in that same odd tone. "Just go on ahead. I'll be along in a bit, once introductions are made. Figure this is a good chance to check on my nanoverse."

It finally clicked for Ryan what was off in her voice. It was too cheerful, too polite...too strongly faux British. "I could use some moral support in there," he said, "In case my sister-"

Crystal's eyes hardened. "Ryan, love, she's your bloody sister. You're being a total wanker about this. Just go. It'll be brilliant. Family matters, yeah?"

"I'm just-" Ryan started to say, but she cut him off with a sad smile and a wave towards the door.

"Go, Ryan. I'll come back after I'm done."

"Okay." Ryan took a deep breath. "Take care, Crystal. And thanks."

"You too," Her smile widened. "Now go! I'll see you afterward. Hug your sister for me."

***

Laying on her cheap, overstuffed couch, Isabel Smith realized she'd come to loathe social media. It used to be her morning routine to spend her first half-hour of consciousness lying in bed, scrolling through Facebook and Instagram, her phone held over her head until she was fully awake. The omnipresent threat of dropping her phone on her face helped her avoid falling back to sleep, and she'd usually find a few funny pictures or interesting animal facts to share with her friends.

These days, every message, tag, share, or comment she received was about Ryan. Someone - and if Isabel ever found out who she was going to throw them off her eleventh story balcony - had told the press that she was Ryan Smith's sister. *The* Ryan Smith that had been all over the news. Then that dipshit at the local paper had run an article with her photo in it, ending with "at time of press, Isabel Smith had declined to comment."

"You should either turn over you're brother or chug bleach, bitch. Your a monster," she read aloud from a comment on one of her posts.

Her fingers flew to the touch keyboard. "Amazing. You managed to use *both* versions of 'your' incorrectly. I'd applaud the stupidity, but I imagine loud noises startle you easily."

She sighed as her thumb hovered over the post button. It would feel so good to hit it, but after thirty seconds, the good feeling would fade, and she'd just have to deal with trolls all day. Instead, she set the post to "only friends" and deleted the jerkoff's comment.

"Declined to comment" was such a nasty little phrase. Isabel had thought that was the best thing to do. Max, her lawyer friend, had *told* her it was the best thing to do. But with the rest of the article painting her as a vapid millennial that didn't care about what was happening with her brother, "declined to comment" looked a *lot* like "didn't care."

The media had moved on quickly. There were angels in Ohio, spider people in Ghana, photos of the Kraken eating a boat in the Pacific, and gods. So many gods. She might be related to one of the more interesting ones, but with so much else going on, human interest pieces like "family members" didn't get the clicks "Three harpies carry off cow in Montana" did.

She'd hoped that would be the end of it, but the internet and the government had not forgotten, and she wasn't sure which was worse.

Her phone beeped with a text from Claire. "Asshats trolling you again, hon?"

Isabel bit her cheek and considered the words carefully, finally settling on "Yup." It was a curt response, one that brooked no room for discussion.

"I'm sorry," was the response, followed by a frowny face emoji to show *how* sorry Claire was. "Have you heard from him yet?"

"No, I haven't, because my brother is a jackass," Isabel growled at the phone. What she typed was "nope," then sat back and stared at the three dots letting her know Claire was responding.

That was the thing. The trolls, the conversations with government agents, getting fired from her job, she could *handle* all that if she'd known Ryan was okay. Instead, it felt like he was the only person on the planet who *didn't* want to talk to her.

The three dots resolved into a message. "Well, if you need company, I've got a bottle of Moscato with your name on it."

Isabel put the phone down without responding. She wasn't in the right headspace to deal with that right now. She was afraid she would end up taking her anger at Ryan out on Claire, who didn't deserve it.

Older brothers were supposed to be jerks. That was the way of the world. They gave you noogies and wrestled with you and made fun of you for watching *Clarissa Explains it All,* yelled at you for bothering them when their friends were over, and destroyed your Animal Facts binder.

But Ryan *hadn't* been that brother. He'd sat down and listened to her explain the intricate social structure of her dolls and had cared enough to ask two days later how Ms. Buttercup's Revolution against the Pixie Queen was going, and if Ms. Buttercup wanted some back-up from the Power-Rangers. He'd watched *Clarissa* with her. Well, he'd actually played his Gameboy while she watched it, but he'd never made fun of her for it.

Even after the whole...thing with his imaginary friend had gone too far, he'd still taken her to dinner after he got out of high school every Wednesday when their parents worked late.

And now he's completely ignoring me. Isabel felt tears well up and furiously blinked them back.

Her phone beeped again. Claire. "I just hate the thought of you being alone during all this," followed by a heart.

Isabel typed: "Thanks, Claire. But...I don't think it would be good to be around you right now." She considered it, then backspaced. "Thanks, Claire. But I'm fine." Again, she hesitated and then deleted the message.

She knew that Claire was sincere and honestly cared about how Isabel was coping. However, the last thing Isabel wanted to do was see her ex, precisely *because* she wanted to see her ex. They'd ended things for the right reason and broken up was broken up. Isabel was not going to fall back into a relationship that didn't work. If it had been years...then maybe. Things can change in years. But no one changes that much in a couple months. She tried again: "Thank you, Claire. Really. But right now would be a terrible time. I'm not in a great place and might do something that would hurt us both in the long term."

This time, she hit send.

Anyway, Claire was still going to Korea to teach English in the spring. When Isabel realized she didn't want to go with her, that had brought everything that wasn't working in their relationship to the forefront.

One more reason to be mad at Ryan. His dumb ass had been part of the reason she hadn't wanted to go. *Granted,* a part of her that insisted on being fair chimed in, *the vast majority of the reasons were having no job prospects and not knowing the language and not wanting to move halfway across the world with someone you weren't sure was right for you.*

Isabel hushed that particular inner voice. Being mad at her brother was more comfortable than being scared for her brother, so he was getting the blame for everything right now.

"I understand," Claire sent, "and I'm sorry. If you do need company though, let me know - I promise I won't let things get weird."

Lots of people were saying that these days. "I'm sorry." At least Isabel knew that Claire actually meant it.

Isabel typed her reply. "You're always weird. It's part of your charm." Before she could hit send, there was a knock at her door.

Isabel sighed and stood up, glancing in a mirror to make sure her hair wasn't a complete disaster. It was probably Agent Francis or Agent Brown or someone from the alphabet soup out there, and she didn't want to look like a couch goblin in front of them. They didn't seem to be taking her seriously as it was.

The knock came again. "I'm coming," Isabel shouted. "I swear to God, if it's you government assholes again, I still don't know where the hell my good for nothing brother-" She threw the door open, ready and willing to unleash her anger on whoever was out there.

Her mouth fell open. He had shorter hair than she remembered and was holding himself differently. His eyes weren't darting around nervously, his shoulders were back, and he'd lost about thirty pounds. But there was no mistaking her brother.

"Ryan?" she asked softly. A flood of emotions swept over her, weeks of fear and anger and frustration in a tidal wave that threatened to drown her.

Ryan's face lit up. "Heya Izzy."

"Is it really you?" she asked. She reached out, her hand trembling. *I've snapped. I've gone insane. There's no one outside my door, and people are going to see me waving my hand at empty air.*

"Yeah, it's me," Ryan said. "You cut your hair."

Isabel ignored that last bit, although she did note it was the kind of inane observation her brother would make right now. She touched his shoulder, making sure that he was solid and real.

"Yeah, it's me," he said again.

Isabel nodded once, then curled her fingers into a fist and punched him in the chest.

Ryan rocked back on his heels. Back in the day, Isabel had been able to throw punches that could knock him on his ass. These days, after gaining godhood and getting his ass beat by Enki, they didn't hurt as much as they once had.

The fury in her eyes did plenty of that. "You asshole!" She hit him again. "No call, no text, nothing!" Tears welled in her eyes as she pulled back to hit him one more time. "The news is calling you the Antichrist! I have reporters and government goon breathing down my neck twenty-four-seven! I missed so much work I got fired! And the whole time the only reason I know you're alive is because I keep seeing you on the news! You. Prick!"

The punches were actually hurting now, but she was winding down. Ryan took a deep breath. "You're right, there's no excuse. Best I can say is I'm sorry, and I'm here to make up for it."

She regarded him for a moment, then gave him a fierce hug. "Don't think this means we're okay, jerkwad. But I'm so glad you're all right."

He hugged her back, thinking that if anyone had been observing from the outside, they would have one of two reactions. If they'd been an only child, they never would have believed two people could go from screaming and punching to hugging this quickly. If they'd had a sibling, they would have nodded in complete understanding.

Mentally, Ryan thanked Anansi and made a note to do that in person. He felt his own eyes begin to sting, and he hugged his sister tighter. "I know. I'm going to tell you everything. Can I come in?"

They broke the hug and wiped their faces. "Yeah, yeah. Come in," she said.

He did, and she gave him another light punch. "Still?" he asked.

"I think I have the right to hit you whenever I want for the rest of our lives." Isabel looked like she might be joking. Might. "So what the hell happened to you?"

"I became a god. With, like, actual powers and stuff," he said, shrugging in embarrassment at how pretentious it sounded. It hadn't before, but saying "I'm a god" to his sister felt...wrong.

She stared at him, her mouth hanging open. "You know, if it weren't for what I saw on the news, I'd think you'd finally lost your mind. I'm going to need a drink for this, aren't I?"

Ryan nodded. "I'll take one too."

He surveyed her apartment, decorated with black curtains and neon paintings of abstract shapes flowing into each other. She motioned him into the kitchen, the only part of the apartment Ryan could see that lacked anything bright neon unless you counted the pink bowls sitting in the sink.

"You get water, jerkwad," she said. "I'm not sure if I'm going to share my booze with you. So. What the hell happened?"

He thought for a moment, and reminded himself that this was his sister, he could skip some steps. "So, remember that imaginary friend I had that never went away? Well, it turned out he was something called a Curator and was named Nabu..."

***

Isabel was resting her chin on her hands as Ryan finished the story. She was also chewing her lip, a habit she'd had since childhood, and Ryan had long ago learned to let her finish her train of thought if she was doing that. She hadn't hit him since he'd gotten into the apartment, and he didn't want to give her reason to start up again. *You make it sound like she's some kind of violent psycho,* he thought, suppressing a grin.

After several minutes, Isabel spoke. "So. I need to make sure I understand this."

Ryan nodded for her to go ahead.

"Your imaginary friend from childhood was real. You found a marble that is actually a universe and got pulled into a fight with actual gods, and you're armed mostly with the power of math. Now you beat the main god you were fighting, but his BFF who eats children is still out there, so you have to fight him. All of this is because the freaking world is going to end, and you want to not kill everyone in the process. That about sum it up?"

Ryan shrugged sheepishly. "Pretty much. Although it seems kind of silly when you put it that way."

Isabel rolled her eyes. "You think? Ryan, are you sure you haven't gone nuts and joined a cult?"

"I am. I can prove it if you want."

His sister's eyes narrowed. "How?"

"I can zero out your personal gravity. You'll float like you were in space."

Her eyes lit up. When she was ten, Isabel had decided she would be an astronaut. This was at least more realistic than her previous life goal of being a unicorn, which had been an improvement over her last ambition to own "a million billion dogs". While she'd eventually decided on a different career path, she'd never gotten over her fascination with space. Offering her the chance to experience zero gravity was like offering her an early Christmas. "Okay, if you can do that, I'll believe the whole thing."

Ryan nodded and held out his hand, twisting. Manipulating gravity was the first trick he learned, and it remained one of his favorites. The effect was immediate: her clothes and hair started floating loosely about her, and her startled motion at the sensation sent her spinning into the air.

For a moment she just floated, stunned, and Ryan hoped she wasn't going to freak out or start throwing up. When her head bumped gently against her ceiling, Isabel began to giggle with childish glee.

"Ohmygod." She pushed off the ceiling, letting herself drift towards the floor. Spinning to bring her hands down, she let her fingers touch the carpet and pushed herself back upwards. She was barely able to speak, instead just letting out a delighted "Weeeee!"

Ryan smiled as his sister bounced around her apartment, alternating between delighted laughter and various "wee" s and "woo" s of excitement. It hadn't been long since he'd gotten his powers, but everything had been so crazy, so hectic, so...high stakes, that he'd never really thought about taking some time to just revel in the joy of what he could do.

Seeing his sister burst into another round of laughter as she overshot her living room and landed on her back on the hallway wall, he resolved to do so.

"So, believe me?" he finally asked, once she'd calmed down. He'd gone into the living room after she'd maneuvered in there, sitting on the couch while she floated a foot over the coffee table.

"Oh my God, yes. This is amazing! How long can you keep me up here?"

Ryan held out his hands. "Reality eventually pushes back against any change I make, but as long as I'm nearby, I can keep it up almost indefinitely. If it was a more complex equation, I'd start getting Hungry soon, but gravity is pretty simple."

"Hungry, not tired?" She turned herself slowly, so she was facing him but still floating.

"Yup. Although it's not just food hunger. Thirst, tiredness, the need for air, loneliness – those are all what Crystal called Hungers. I don't need to worry about any of them unless I push myself too hard."

Isabel bit her lip again. "Loneliness? You don't get lonely anymore?"

Ryan shook his head. "I think it's why gods don't go crazy after a century or two. Once you become a god, you don't need to socialize, unless you burn through enough divine power. You still can if it's something you enjoy doing – or at least, enjoy doing as much as you did before you got your nanoverse – but it's like..." He groped for an analogy. "It's like eating really good chocolate, not because you're hungry or even have a craving, but just because you like the taste. And reading a book or watching a movie or any kind of art falls under that too."

Isabel gently tapped the coffee table to set herself spinning while she thought, then stopped herself by catching her foot on the ceiling fan. She gave him a solemn expression that was somewhat spoiled by her being upside down. "Okay. Then I'm not mad at you anymore."

Ryan blinked. He'd hoped the zero-gravity ride around her apartment would get Isabel to consider letting go of the anger but hadn't expected anything so abrupt. "Why not? Not that I'm complaining," he added hastily, "but it seems sudden."

She nodded. "I know, but it makes sense that such a sudden, major change to your psychology would probably throw you for a loop, and you'd forget little details like letting your little sister know you were trying to stop the goddamn apocalypse. Ahem." She sighed, and then held her hand to her mouth as the force of the sigh sent her drifting back. "It's the only thing that explains you being such an inconsiderate jackhole, and it's something I can forgive you for. So like your new bestie likes to say, roll with it."

That got a laugh out of Ryan. He considered objecting but honestly couldn't figure out if she was right or not. Maybe that *was* part of the reason he hadn't reached out to her. "Thanks, Izzy. I appreciate it."

"No problem. Of course, this goes away if you don't take me with you."

Ryan sputtered. "I'm sorry, what?"

Her face hardened. It was hard to take the glower seriously as she was floating sedately across her apartment, but no one could glower quite like his sister. "I'm coming with you, Ryan. I won't get in the way, I'll stay safe in your pocket universe staging area thing, but I'm coming with you."

"No, absolutely not. If I die and you're in there, you'll be trapped forever, and if it gets destroyed, I don't even know what would happen to you."

Isabel shrugged. "And if you die and I'm not with you, I'll burn to death when the sun explodes. At least this way I'll know what's going on."

Ryan felt himself getting ready to argue but instead took a deep breath to really think about it. If Isabel was with him, he'd also know she was safe; after all, if the government could find her, so could Moloch or Bast or anyone else was after him. *And if she's in your nanoverse and you have to end the world violently, you can be sure she'll survive.*

Something of what he was thinking must have shown on his face, because Isabel tilted her head to the side and said, "Woah. You just went down a dark road in your head. Care to share?"

Ryan sighed. "Not really, just an ugly thought. But all right, you can come."

Isabel relaxed. "Good. Just don't forget I'm just a mere mortal and will need to be fed and watered and all that."

"You sound like a houseplant," Ryan said. Isabel glared while she tried not to laugh, and he raised his hands in a gesture of surrender. "Don't worry, I won't forget. We'll make sure you're covered. Think I can even make you your own room and stuff."

"Good. I shared a room with you that one summer when Mom and Dad remodeled. Not an experience I want to repeat." She stuck her tongue out at him, and Ryan returned the gesture.

"One thing to think about," he said. She leaned forward in the air. "I found the last nanoverse of the Old Age. Once we finish all this, it'll be the New Age, and new nanoverses might start appearing right away. If I find one, which isn't very likely, but possible, would you maybe..."

"You're asking if I want to be a goddess. You're actually asking like I might say no?" She gave him an incredulous look.

Ryan's face was severe. "Izzy, it's a one-way thing. You'll be immortal, which means everyone you know and love - aside from me - you'll see die. You'll see civilizations end, and you'll be there when whatever comes next rises. You'll be forgotten and-"

Isabel cut him off. "Wow. You really haven't had a chance to enjoy this at all, have you? Ryan, you're a freaking god. Who cares about all that? Sure, it'll be sad, but you get to make the world better - and have the power to make a difference. And get to be awesome while you do it."

For a few seconds, all Ryan could do was open and close his mouth, and then he chuckled. "I should have come here sooner. Thanks."

"No problem. Now let me get closer to the ground, turn on gravity, and then I'll start packing."

Ryan did, and once she was back on the floor, she headed to her room and began throwing things in a suitcase.

"Hey," he called. "You know I can just make new clothes for you out of the air when we're in my nanoverse, right?"

"Yup. And I've seen your fashion sense, and oh my God I do not want that. Plus, it's not just clothes."

Ryan did notice she was grabbing other things in her mad frenzy. "What else?"

"Sentimental crap. Like the stuffed bear Dad got me before the accident. And the photo albums I took from the house. Stuff that we can't replace in a brand new world."

Ryan was surprised by hard that hit him. It hadn't even occurred to him that he'd lose those things, but now that she'd brought it to his attention..." Thanks."

"No problem. I still have your stuffed T-Rex, want it?"

She wasn't looking at him, but he could only nod, unable to talk past the lump in his throat. She looked up at him and gave him a soft smile. "We'll get through this, Ry. The same way we did when Mom and Dad passed."

"Yeah, we will. Thanks, Izzy."

"No problem. Dork." She stuck out her tongue again before going back to packing, and he laughed.

As he did, he decided one thing. No matter what happened, he was going to find a way to give his sister immortality.

At that moment, there was a knock at the door. "That must be Crystal," he said and headed towards it.

"Okay. I'm almost finished in here; just give me another minute or two."

Ryan opened the. "Hey, Crys-"

One of the government-made gods was standing there, and Ryan couldn't see the harness he had worn before. What he could see was an assault rifle pushed directly into his face.

"Goodbye, Mr. Smith," the man said, and squeezed the trigger.

Hector admitted to himself that the "Goodbye, Mr. Smith" was a conceit that could have gotten him killed, an action-movie one-liner that should have been beneath him. It had felt so...right, though. *I need to tell the doctor about that.* She was very interested in any potential psychological bleed through.

That momentary lapse had made the kill less clean than Hector would have liked. Ryan's head had twisted up and to the side before Hector had finished pulling the trigger of his M-16, so his three-round burst hadn't hit straight on. The first bullet had torn a hole in the side of the target's face, and the second had removed the nose. He couldn't see the mess the third one had left, buried under the hair, but Hector was confident he must have put it into the temple.

I didn't think it would be that easy, he reflected, somewhat bemused, as the man who would have ended the world lay unbreathing on the floor. Hector reached over to his shoulder and hit a button. "Primary target down. I repeat, Primary target down. Civilian still presumed in domicile – requesting orders? Over."

"Proceed to eliminate all targets," the voice of Admiral Bridges replied after a moment. "Cannot risk the sister inheriting powers after the death of primary target." A pause followed by a simple message. "Well done. Over."

Although Hector Ross didn't like the idea of killing a woman whose only crime had been having the wrong brother, his chest swelled at the praise. "Roger, sir. And thank you. Proceeding to eliminate. Over." He stepped carefully over the unmoving corpse.

He'd heard a scream from the bedroom when he'd opened fire. This would be easy, and Hector promised himself he'd make it quick.

Then a hand grabbed his ankle, and Hector realized he had celebrated too soon.

Chapter 11

Darkness Falls

Crystal sighed as Ryan disappeared. If she was honest with herself, she had been hoping he'd balk a bit more and give her a reason to turn it into a serious row. One that might take a few hours to resolve.

Anything to delay having to go into her nanoverse. After her last unsuccessful attempt at cleaning up the corruption, the thought of facing it again made her feel physically ill.

You should have gone with him. There were plenty of reasons to do so. Ryan was alone and exposed, he could be in danger! *Yeah, right, Crystal. What are the odds someone attacks while he's visiting his sister? You're just trying to make excuses.*

If she didn't deal with this now, there was no telling when she'd next get the chance. Her resolve had strengthened when she saw Ryan staring at the fake projection of her nanoverse, and she'd felt a momentary terror that he had seen through the illusion. But now that he was gone, she was having trouble getting started.

Crystal took a deep breath, a habit that hadn't faded after a million years. Some things are too ingrained to ever really go away, and the slow inhalation was inherently calming. *There has to be a reason for its resistance. There has to be a cause behind it.* It was just a matter of finding the cause, then applying her will to fixing *that* problem. It would be so easy.

So why are you shaking?

Crystal pushed the thought aside, then set her staging area to drop into her nanoverse. "Initiate real display," she said firmly.

It was even worse once she was actually in the flow of her nanoverse. The stars, filtered through that grotesquely yellow interstellar gas, pulsed like horribly infected sores. It made her want to retch just looking at it.

Oddly, she also started to feel more relaxed. The sickly green and purple stars were disgusting, but they had a strange beauty. It was like admiring a painting by Bosch or Goya; the thing depicted in the art was horrible, but you could appreciate the subtle brush strokes, the interplay of light, the way tendrils of solar flame reached out like a grasping hand to eradicate an entire planet...

Should you really fix it? Crystal asked herself. *I mean...it's an utterly unique thing. It's beautiful. Would almost be a shame-*

Crystal raised a hand and struck herself in the face, hard enough to make her ears ring. The fog cleared, and she saw this monstrosity for the horror it was. Her hands shook.

What the hell was that? Deal with this, Crystal. You have to, before...

Before those strange thoughts came back. She needed an anchor, something to remind herself of what was at stake. Grasping at the first idea that came to mind, she did something she hadn't done in over three thousand years and allowed her body to melt back to its natural appearance.

After so long, it felt like going back to a childhood home that had been remodeled – familiar, but oddly different. She stretched, enjoying the comfort of her original form. She looked at her hands, covered in fine green scales and possessing three fingers and two thumbs. Gold and red feathers covered her head, and she inhaled deeply through the four vertical nostrils that sat between her golden, slitted eyes. Her tail feathers bristled in satisfaction at, well, existing again.

I wonder what Ryan and Athena would think of me like this? Hell, I wonder what I think of me like this? It was a silly, useless thought, as these days she felt more like a human than like the last of her old kind. *Bloody hell, I can't even remember what we called ourselves. I guess Lemurian would be the English term, but that's like calling Humans Earthlings.* Sometime in the last million years, she'd lost the word, just like she'd lost so many other memories.

So many things lost. An entire world. Because she hadn't been smart enough to figure things out in time.

Suddenly, it was uncomfortable to be in this body again. Part of Crystal wanted to return to the human form she'd come to think of as herself. Crystal decided the discomfort would help her stay focused on what mattered: cleaning up this mess. Resolved, she dropped into her nanoverse and stepped into the vacuum of space. Or at least, what was supposed to be the vacuum of space. But there was something she didn't normally associate with the empty void that quickly drew Crystal's attention.

There was a *wind blowing* through space and hitting her with icy gusts. She also sensed some kind of strange matter all around her, too small to be seen. It was everywhere but dispersed into individual microscopic particles, instead of conforming to the laws of physics and clumping together. In her nanoverse, only Crystal should have been able to subvert the natural order, but this, like so many other things, was not her doing.

Crystal held out her hand and asserted her will, ordering the strange matter to coalesce.

Nothing happened. She stared at her empty hand in mute confusion. After the incident with the star, she'd expected some resistance, but this...whatever was here had just ignored her will. It was like stamping on a cockroach and being thrown across the room.

A curious side effect of her sudden fear was the reminder that, in this body, she had two hearts. Both were pounding.

Okay, don't panic, Crystal thought, panicking. *Let's see what's going on here.*

She focused her vision, bending light to create magnification. It worked, which was a huge relief, and she studied one of the strange particles.

It was a cell. Or a bacterium. Some kind of living organism. It didn't look exactly like anything Crystal had seen before but was similar to a nerve cell but covered in cilia that allowed it to – somehow – traverse interstellar space. As she watched, it divided into two.

The sight made her shudder but wasn't enough to spur her into taking action. *You want to patiently observe and learn. You are not frozen with fear.* Crystal hoped if she repeated it enough, it would be true.

After a minute, the cells divided again. She broke into a cold sweat. *If they divide every minute like that...bloody hell, how much longer do I have before they literally fill my nanoverse?*

They must have been here before but hadn't been numerous enough for her to notice. She was convinced that these were the *root* of the problem. Somehow, these...what were they? She decided to call them "Phoberia" because they certainly scared her enough to deserve the name. Somehow, they were imbued with a spark of her divine will. Now that she was focused on one, she could sense it thrumming inside of it, a nucleus of her own power. She was dimly aware she'd detected it ever since stepping out of her staging area, but it was like hearing your own heartbeat. You turned it out because it was a part of you.

Experimentally, Crystal winked one out of existence. It vanished. Then she focused on a larger group, asserting her will to remove all of them. Nothing happened. So individually, they were virtually powerless, but as they multiplied, they had a collective force all of their own. They were doubling by the minute, so even if she spent the rest of eternity in here, she'd never be able to defeat them individually.

And you're just sitting here gawking at them, Crystal thought, pushing herself past her fear and into rational thought. She could trigger a cataclysm, engulf her entire Nanoverse in a black hole so it would be annihilated, and then trigger a crunch from the outside. However, two problems came to mind. First, she wasn't sure the Phoberia would allow it. More importantly, doing so would end trillions of lives. A crunch should only be done if it was absolutely necessary.

Experimentally, Crystal teleported herself into deep space, far away from any inhabited worlds, and tried to create a singularity.

It should have been simple. This time, though, she could feel the resistance, an immense wall of willpower, something hateful and malicious barring her from exerting her will. *No.* Crystal thought, her teeth clenching. *You will not fight me. This is* ***my*** *nanoverse. You will break!*

She screamed into the void as she pushed her all power against the resistance. It rebounded, and all of her force slammed into her. She shrieked in pure agony, and for a few minutes, everything went dark.

Eventually, Crystal opened her eyes and slowly gathered her wits.

That shouldn't have been possible, but it had happened. She was too late.

Despair welled up in her, threatening to drown her. The collective will of the Phoberia outmatched her own power. She *couldn't* beat them, not now. She had no good choices left. If she reset her nanoverse, maybe she could destroy them...along with every person living here.

If it comes to that, tell Athena and Ryan what's going on, and have them lock you up before the corruption spreads too far. Except...if she didn't wipe out the Phoberia, wouldn't they eventually kill everyone anyway? Without any predators, they would spread unchecked until-

Wait.

She had been pitting power against power and was overmatched. But there were other ways to remove an organism. The Phoberia were ready for a contest of wills, but were they prepared for something more mundane, like a more traditional predator?

It would have to out-evolve the Phoberia and be able to hunt them in large enough numbers...*No, not a predator. A pathogen. Specifically, a virus...a viral phobophage.*

She might not be able to hunt and destroy the individual cells, but a rapidly spreading virus...yes. She willed one into existence and magnified her vision again to watch. It latched onto the Phoberia...and the Phoberia exuded pseudopods to engulf the pathogen before it could attack. Crystal swore. *Okay, no, don't give up.* She created another version, giving it a more rapid attachment system. The Phoberia couldn't engulf it this time, but the phobophage was unsuccessful.

And so it went. Viruses were created, the Phoberia countered. She felt her panic grow with each failure. Finally, she had incorporated everything she could think of: a sliver of her divine will, the ability to produce thousands of copies of itself within a minute, and rapid movement to move between clusters of Phoberia.

If this doesn't work...I don't know what hope is left. Taking a moment to calm her nerves, she sent it at the Phoberia.

Her little virus dodged pseudopods and latched onto the cell's outer wall. The Phoberia deployed antibodies, but the virus adapted. It injected divine DNA into the Phoberia, and Crystal watched, holding her breath.

The Phoberia erupted, spilling the virus out into interstellar space.

If Crystal had been standing in a gravity well, she would have collapsed from relief. As it was, she just went kind of...limp. *I did it.* She waved her hand, a tiny bit of her will causing the virus to begin multiplying as it traveled.

"Take that, you wankers!" she shouted into the void. The virus would evolve more rapidly than the Phoberia, and it would clear out the infestation in a few centuries, which would pass in a mere few minutes back in the core world. Then she could come back and put things to right without their resistance.

There was a nagging doubt that this was too easy, but Crystal pushed it aside. She'd pulled it off. The hard part was over. She could fix it!

At the moment, there was nothing she could do. She needed to let the virus do its work, and she should catch up with Ryan.

He probably hadn't even noticed she'd been gone.

***

I'm dying. The thought felt like it was coming from somewhere far away. Ryan was dimly aware that dying would be a bad thing. There was something he was supposed to do.

Right now, though, the pain seemed far more critical.

I wonder if I'll see Arthur, that distant part of Ryan wondered. It was unlikely he'd wind up in Heaven, not after invading it. Or maybe that wasn't actually a sin. Ryan wasn't a biblical scholar, but he was pretty sure none of the commandments expressly forbid assisting the King of Hell in invading Heaven.

"Proceed to eliminate all targets. Cannot risk the sister inheriting powers after the death of primary target. Well done. Over."

That's not how nanoverses work, Ryan thought through the fog of pain. There was something else in that message, something that felt like it should be important, but-

"Roger, sir. And thank you. Proceeding to eliminate. Over."

Eliminate. That word cut through the agony encasing his brain, and it was replaced with realization that turned to white-hot rage and panic. This man, this monster, was about to go kill his sister. Before he even realized he was moving, Ryan grabbed the soldier's ankle.

"Not. My. Sister," he said. Or he tried to say. What came out was something along the lines of "Ooot Eye Isssstah." He couldn't seem to get his jaw to close all the way. He didn't think the soldier could understand him, but the emotion cut through the slurred words. Then the soldier went white and swung his gun towards Ryan's skull.

Maybe if he had just fired, instead of taking a second to aim carefully, he could have killed Ryan. But that extra moment gave Ryan time to twist.

First, he heated the gun to 2000 degrees Kelvin, more heat than Ryan had created in a single equation. The bullets detonated, spraying molten metal into Hector's face. The second twist, as Hector screamed and clawed at the burns, increased the strength of gravity on the soldier by a factor of ten. He fell to the ground next to Ryan, struggling to rise. Ryan saw Hector reach out, trying to twist to save himself.

He was going to kill your sister. Just for being your sister. No mercy. The rage Ryan felt was even more profound than when he had seen that decadent lump of an emperor sitting on the throne of the Empire, claiming to speak in Ryan's name.

Ryan grabbed Hector's hand. "This is mine now," Ryan hissed.

Hector Ross gave him a pleading look and Ryan jerked his arm. He was rewarded with a satisfying crack of bone and Hector's scream. He crawled on top of Hector and grabbed his head with both hands, then began to slam it into the floor. It cracked against the hardwood. Ryan slammed it again, rewarded with another thump. He kept going.

"Ryan!" Isabel screamed, grabbing his shoulder and trying to pull him back. He stared down at Hector. The man was a mess, his face red and bruised, his breathing shallow and hoarse.

The sight turned Ryan's stomach. Hector needed to die. But now that he was defeated...*Do I really have it in me to beat him to death?*

He realized he didn't.

Shock and adrenaline kept Ryan from passing out and allowed him to scramble to his feet.

"Oh. My. God." Ryan glanced over, his jaw still hanging open. Isabel had a gun, dangling at her side in a shaking hand. Her eyes glistened with tears. "Ryan?"

Ryan just nodded, the gesture sending lances of agony through his head. "There. May be. More. Get away from. Windows. Crystal. Hopefully here. Soon." Each word was a fresh hell and making them understandable was a new level of agony.

Isabel took a deep breath, nearly heaved, got herself under control, and nodded. She was sobbing now, barely able to form words between the tears. "Bathroom. Come on. I have...first aid. Jesus. Oh my God, Ryan. Come...oh my God."

***

The screen still showed the final image Hector's body camera had managed to catch before they lost the feed: the Antichrist looming over Hector, looking like something out of a horror movie. Blood ran from his shredded lips, his jaw hung askew, and his teeth showed through the hole in his cheek.

So close. They had been so close to defeating that monster, but there he was, this so-called god, showing his true colors in his mutilated appearance.

"Damnit!" Dale shouted, slamming his fist on the desk. Several aides jumped at the explosive sound, but Doctor Pivarti just raised an eyebrow.

"He is severely wounded," she said. "We may still have a chance to make this come out right."

"Come out *right*?" Dale snarled. "He's certainly killed Ross by now, and probably destroyed the harness. We are *well* past things coming out right."

He rewound the video to the last thing Ryan Smith had said.

"There. May be. More. Get away from. Windows. Crystal. Hopefully here. Soon."

"Can someone break that sentence down for me?" Dale asked, his voice now dangerously calm. "Did we at least learn anything from sending a man to his death?"

"W-well," Lazzario stammered. "We've got confirmation that Crystal is still working with Ryan. And she'll be arriving soon...or, at least, he believes that."

Dale pinched the bridge of his nose. "I was hoping for something not painfully obvious."

It had seemed perfect. The watchers they'd placed on Isabel Smith's apartment had reported the arrival of Ryan Smith, acting totally unconcerned about any possible threat. It was the perfect chance to engage the target without allies. It hadn't even seemed like a trap, just the bastard being overconfident.

"It's a shame," Pivarti said, studying the image on the camera. "Hector barely managed to utilize the energy in the harness."

Bridges whirled on her, pointing an accusatory finger in her direction. "A man is *dead,* Doctor Pivarti, and you're worried about the *harness*? It was your idea to send him in alone!"

The soldiers and support staff in the command center got very quiet and did their best to appear focused on something else. Fingers flew to keyboards, eyes turned to screens. None of them wanted to be ordered out, so they tried to look intensely busy. Dale wasn't surprised. Soldiers were worse than teenagers when gossip was involved, and the Admiral and the head researcher for Project Myrmidon having it out in the command center was as juicy as it got.

Right now, he couldn't care less. He was literally shaking with rage and wanted to hurl the doctor out of the building.

"A decision I stand by, Admiral," she said with her usual lack of deference. "We only had one of the upgraded harnesses ready for action. We also had a priority target, as you pointed out. If I recall correctly, you barely objected to sending Myrmidon B into the fray."

"It was a calculated risk," Dale spat. "But you told me he could survive. That the harness was ready for use."

"And I stand by that as well. Ryan was far faster than we anticipated. Before seeing this footage, could you imagine he'd be able to move like that?" The doctor pushed a button on a control, rewinding the footage to the moment Hector pulled the trigger, then began to run the feed in extreme slow motion.

"Why are we watching this again?" Dale asked.

"Watch," Doctor Pivarti said. "That weapon has a muzzle velocity of seven hundred and thirty meters per second. Given the short distance, the bullet would be traveling at about the same speed upon reaching the target."

Dale watched as the Antichrist's head began to move. Even slowed down to this degree, the motion was preternaturally fast.

Pivarti continued. "To get the bullet to hit somewhere non-vital, Ryan had to move his head about six inches. That placed his cheek in line with the bullet and allowed him to open his jaw." On the screen, Ryan's mouth widened in just as the bullet touched his cheek.

"What's your point, Doctor?" Dale asked through clenched teeth.

"Simply this," Pivarti said as the bullet tore into Ryan's face and explosively exited the other side. "Given the distance involved, Ryan moved his head at approximately seventy meters per second. No one could have predicted that speed, Admiral."

"It's your *job* to predict these things, Doctor," Dale growled.

"No," she corrected, "it is my job to predict what I can based on the data we have. We have new data. That will enable me to make more accurate predictions."

"Hector is dead, doctor! Don't you *care*?"

Doctor Pivarti froze. "Of course I care, Admiral," she said softly. "I just watched a man die in front of us. I've never imagined something so horrible, but we all react to grief differently. I choose to shield myself with facts. I choose to focus on what I can do to make sure this *doesn't happen again*."

"And what, have you learned? Anything even *remotely* useful?" Dale asked

"Actually, yes." Doctor Pivarti rewound the video again. "Ryan is attempting to evade the bullet here. He's trying to get clear of the path. Which means that seventy meters per second is the *maximum* speed he could make this motion; otherwise, he would have been able to completely evade it. We have a top speed for these things now, Admiral. That gives us something we can use."

That, at least, Dale could understand. It did little to alleviate his fury at the doctor, but it did allow him to at least reign it in. *You need to keep it under control,* he told himself. He pointed at one of the aides. "You. Michael, isn't it?"

The man nodded and licked his lips.

"We evacuated the upper floors of the building before moving in?" Dale asked.

Michael nodded.

"What about the lower floors?" Dale added.

"No one evacuated them, sir," Michael said, finally finding his voice. "We didn't see a need."

"Tell the ground team to begin the evacuation. I want someone in every elevator in that damn building, I want people on every stairwell, and I want the building empty in the next five minutes." Dale smacked his fist on the desk again.

"Sir! Yes, sir!" Michael practically jumped to grab his microphone and begin relaying Dale's orders.

"What are you doing?" Doctor Pivarti asked, her voice calm.

"We still need to take out the primary target. I want to minimize civilian casualties. Once we have the building empty, we can send in every ground troop we have in the area. Cut Ryan down. He's half dead."

Pivarti pursed her lips. "Might I suggest a different tactic, sir?"

The doctor never called him "sir". It put Dale on edge. "Given that your last suggestion got a man killed, Doctor, I'm not overly enthused at another one."

"I want to make sure no one else dies," Pivarti said firmly.

Dale bit back a sharp retort. If the doctor's suggestion was actually sound..." Go ahead," he said.

"You're evacuating the building anyway, so send in gunships. Your soldiers can go in later to confirm Ryan's death. But he's surprised us once already. I'd rather not put more men at needless risk."

Dale considered her for a long moment. Her suggestion made sense. The Antichrist had proven to be surprisingly resilient, and they didn't have any of the other Myrmidons on the ground. They hadn't wanted to risk them with inferior harnesses.

"Do it," Dale snapped to one of his aides, knowing the order would be relayed. "Get gunships into place, and the moment the building is clear, have them open fire. High explosives."

And pray to God they get the bastard this time, Dale thought, turning back to the screen. It had switched to an aerial view of the apartment building, and people were scurrying out like ants disgorged from their hill.

"Sir," said one of the aides. "You should see this." The man handed Dale a tablet.

It showed the current location of the Myrmidon B harness. "Get this to the deployment team," Dale said. "Now."

"What is it?" Pivarti asked.

"The harness is moving. That means Ross might have survived. If so, I want him out of that building as quickly as possible. Then we light the place up."

***

The cloying, damp heat of the tropics pressed in around Athena. This part of El Ávila National Park was densely forested, and the trees' proximity added to the oppressive feel of the place. Moreover, with the site becoming increasingly infested with formerly mythic beasts, she couldn't help regarding every tree and bush with a wary eye.

At least this time she was not alone. Anansi, Dianmu, and Horus changed the odds of any possible encounter considerably, and not in a monster's favor. Horus has also demonstrated a keen eye for detail, and he had been the one to spot Moloch's trail at the site of the cockatrice's death.

"Are we making *any* progress, or have we been walking in circles for the last hour?" Horus snapped, and Athena took a deep breath.

She was grateful for Horus's skill, but definitely *not* for his company.

Dianmu rolled her eyes, and Anansi chuckled under his breath. Athena forced her jaw to unclench. "Well, Horus, we have been traveling in a straight line. We are following the trail you discovered. These are both unchanged from your last inquiry."

Horus growled, "If you would let me have the lead, I would not need to ask, Athena." His tone dripped with condescending frustration, and for half a second, Athena wondered if she could blow his head open with a single bolt of lightning, or if it might require two or three.

"When she let you have the lead, my friend, you set a pace none of us could match," Anansi said, his tone patient. Athena appreciated the Trickster's ability to remain calm. Horus had turned into a falcon when he tried to lead, something Athena had deemed an unacceptable waste of energy. Since falling back in the line, he had continuously needled her about their path, even though she was confident he knew they were going in the right direction.

"You could have kept up if you'd exerted yourselves," Horus snapped, before sinking into sullen silence.

Athena took a deep breath. She reminded herself that Horus had other concerns. That he was worried about that murdering bitch Bast. That he was only here because he thought they would be the quickest way to get him to his goal. Unfortunately, reminding herself that Horus was feeling protective of Tyr's murder was doing nothing to improve her mood.

Some gods improved their temperament over the centuries. Horus has just grown more impatient and condescending.

"Might I suggest a compromise?" Dianmu asked. Athena and Horus both looked at her. "Horus, why not scout ahead to make sure we are on the right path, while Athena leads our group on the ground?"

"That's what I *wanted* to do," Horus said, although he had said nothing of the kind. Without waiting for Athena's response, he turned into a falcon and flew away.

Athena let out a sigh, releasing her irritation at Horus for taking Dianmu's suggestion - and at herself for not thinking of it sooner - without waiting for confirmation. "Thank you, Dianmu. I was...struggling to contain my frustration."

"I know, dear. It's why you both missed the obvious option. You two have history, I take it?"

Athena nodded. "When Alexander seized Egypt, the Olympians went to war against their deities to ensure he could control the region. I personally clashed with Horus multiple times and cut off his hands in one fight. He never quite forgave me for the injury."

"I can't imagine why," Anansi said to Dianmu in a stage whisper.

She felt her cheeks redden. "They grew back," she muttered defensively, "and it was millennia ago. I've gotten over him putting an arrow through my eye." Knowing how absurd she sounded, she stopped talking before she said anything worse.

"I wonder, Athena, have I done you some wrong?"

Athena hadn't heard Anansi's approach, and she started. She glanced sideways at the other god, who was giving her his usual friendly grin. Dianmu had fallen back, perhaps sensing Anansi's desire for a private conversation.

"Seeing as this is our first time meeting, I can't imagine how you could have," Athena said briskly.

He nodded. "Yet you seem to be uncomfortable around me. There must be something about me, either a past action or some inherent quality, that is the root of your dislike."

Athena huffed. "You're a Trickster and a Spider. Every dealing I've had with either has gone poorly for me."

"Ahhh," he said, smiling. "Did you not turn poor Arachne into-"

"It wasn't about the weaving thing." Athena snapped with more heat than she intended. *Careful, Athena,* she told herself. There was no need to start a fight, and Anansi hadn't done her any wrong. In fact, he'd been nothing but helpful so far. "I'm sorry, Anansi. It's not fair, I know, but..."

"...once bitten, twice shy. The euphemism typically implies dogs, but I think it may be even more relevant with spiders."

Athena chuckled and surprised herself when she realized it wasn't entirely forced. "The bite is often worse in that case, yes. But I'll try to be better about it."

"Do not worry. I am just glad to understand the concern. So if it wasn't the weaving, why did you turn Arachne into a spider?"

"You enjoy asking uncomfortable questions, don't you?" Athena said, although there was no heat to it.

"Of course. Trickster, as you pointed out."

Athena chuckled mirthlessly. She remembered that day all too well. The surge of power. Artemis' warning. The piles of the dead. A terrible punishment. "I'm afraid I'll have to decline to answer. There are some things I don't talk about."

If Athena's answer upset Anansi, he didn't show it, instead giving her a slight nod of understanding. "For the best, I think. Look," he pointed ahead. "It appears our feathered friend has found something."

Athena glanced ahead and saw Horus change to his human form long enough to urgently wave them forward. Then he returned to the air, and the others picked up the pace.

They covered the next kilometer in total silence. Athena's heart sped up, and her chest tightened as the pre-battle thrill began to build. She reached out into her nanoverse and plucked a simple straight sword, taking long, slow breaths to keep the anticipation under control.

Then they broke into a clearing and saw what Horus had found: a building towering so high into that Athena was amazed they hadn't seen it sooner. The tiered building resembled the ancient ziggurats of this region, but the stone was smooth and recently cut. Each layer was supported by immense pillars in the Canaanite style, long and ridged with deep grooves. The entrance was a simple archway with spikes inlaid into the stone, and each spike bore the skull of a different animal.

It was definitely a temple.

Horus landed and changed form again. "Do we wait for the others, or do we go ahead?" His voice was a low whisper, barely enough to be heard even though they huddled closely together.

"I would suggest caution," Dianmu said, her voice tinged with worry. "We do not know how many of these resistant cultists Moloch has created. Crystal and Ryan would greatly improve our chances."

"While you have a point," Horus countered, "we also don't know how many more he could create if we wait."

"I will defer to the war goddess in this," Anansi said, "but I would advise caution as well. We do not know what dangers we face."

Athena considered for a moment. "We get closer and attempt to look within. Caution is important, but if there are limited foes, striking before their reinforcements could arrive may be our best option."

For the first time since they arrived in Venezuela, the other three all agreed with her. Horus didn't even give her a dirty look, which was a blessed relief. They crept up to Moloch's temple and climbed the first tier until they reached an open window on the east side of the building.

It was empty within, at least from what they could see, but lit by a strange glow. Athena nodded towards Anansi, then pointed ahead. *Get a closer look* was the unspoken message.

The god nodded and turned into a spider. Although massive – nearly half a meter long – it would draw less notice than a man. She waited, her heart pounding until he skittered back into view and resumed his human form. "It has been emptied. You may want to see this for yourself, however," he whispered.

Athena went in, followed by Dianmu and Horus.

In the center of the temple was a vast pit, full of bones covered in soot and char. Athena didn't need to look closer to be sure that at least some were human. *Moloch does love sacrifice,* she thought, her stomach turning. It was possible to draw power from the ending of human lives. Possible, but horrific, as it consumed the soul in the process. Once, Athena had complete control over a practitioner of human sacrifice, and she had handed out the worst punishment she had imposed over the course of her long existence.

If given a chance, she would do far worse to Moloch.

She didn't need to wonder why Moloch had needed the extra power. Along the back wall of the temple was a portal, more than large enough to accommodate a man. Such things were used to enter places inaccessible by nanoverses, and the list of such places was short. Each one was a place of power that had been locked away so that gods could not easily access it, because of the high potential to do harm from such locations.

Wherever he had gone, Moloch would be far more dangerous when he returned.

Chapter 12

Hope Springs Eternal

Cassandra stepped into view, smiling at Bast. "Let me just finish setting things up. I'll get the mirror. Everyone else has gone home or to their rooms for the evening, so we shouldn't be interrupted." Cassandra's voice was more certain than it had been at first, although there was still a slight tremor in her tone.

Before this, had you ever broken a rule in your life, Cassandra? Bast wondered.

That kind of question was too complicated for their limited communication. Still, Bast let some of the tension drain from her back and arms. It was a relief to know that Cassandra was alone. When the other lab assistants were there, they still talked about Bast like she was a fascinating new slime mold.

It was appalling.

That thought was cut off by a sound growing closer. The creak of poorly oiled wheels and...

LubdubLubdubLubdubLubdub

Cassandra's heart always raced when she was this close to Bast. Even though Bast was beginning to gain her trust, it still made the young researcher nervous. *Or is it excitement? Does doing something so bold give you a thrill of the taboo?*

Bast suspected it was a little bit of both.

The mirror appeared in front of Bast's face, angled on the end of a multi-segmented metal arm. This was the primary way they could communicate. The mirror let Bast see Cassandra as she worked, and let Cassandra see Bast's eyes as she blinked her responses. One for yes, two for no, three for elaborate, and a rapid series of blinks to indicate Bast just needed to clear her eyes. It was simple, but it was effective.

It was also low risk. Even though the rest of the laboratory was empty, there was still the possibility of someone stopping by. The changed position of the mirror might arouse suspicion, but far less than Cassandra leaning over Bast to stare into her eyes.

"So I've got a few questions for you if you don't mind me starting there?" The last few words went up in a questioning tone that betrayed the young woman's uncertainty. Bast actually appreciated that. She *should* be uncertain around Bast, given that - for all she had done for Bast's comfort these past few days - she was still one of the goddess's captors.

And questions would be better than the alternative. As much as Bast appreciated having the woman there, it was hard to follow Cassandra when she started talking about biology. Cassandra was working long hours, often staying after her fellow researchers had left. From what she'd told Bast, she'd justified it to Doctor Pivarti, the head of research, by saying she thought she was close to a breakthrough when it came to...something involving a lot of biological terms. Something about changes to mitochondrial DNA in Ichor. When she started rambling about her theories to Bast, it helped fill the Social hunger, but it was painfully dull.

Bast blinked once in affirmation. Questions were fine.

"Thanks. So, I've meant to ask you...and I'm sorry if this is uncomfortable, but are we going to have any problems now that you've had some water?"

The question was so unexpected, Bast had to give Cassandra three blinks to get her to repeat the inquiry. *What on Earth are you talking about?* she thought. Bast hadn't even realized Cassandra had connected the drops of water to her drinking. Her eyes narrowed. *This one's more intelligent than I thought.*

"I mean..." Cassandra bit her lip, misinterpreting Bast's expression. "Sorry, this is really uncomfortable, and kind of gross."

Realization dawned on Bast, and she was glad Cassandra couldn't see her face. The sheer indignity of being *asked* if she needed something as base and mortal as a chance to use the restroom...if Bast had been free, she might have snapped Cassandra's neck for the simple insult of it all. The mental image of Cassandra laying on the ground, her head twisted at an unnatural angle...Bast felt her hands tightening into fists.

Where's ***that*** *coming from?* Bast asked herself.

Before Cassandra could elaborate on the question, Bast gave two deliberate blinks, then immediately regretted them. If she'd lied, Cassandra might have taken steps to allow Bast to relieve herself, which might have led to an opportunity to escape. Well, it was too late now. Besides, the actions Cassandra would have probably been willing to take would have been undignified and overly restrictive.

"Oh, thank God." Cassandra practically slumped in relief. "I mean...is that offensive? Mentioning the Abrahamic God?"

Bast blinked twice again. The truth was, she just didn't want to think about that whole mess, and everything that had come from the spreading of Christianity and later Islam, including forcing most of the Pantheons to go into hiding from a mass of humanity that no longer tolerated the belief in gods other than the "one true God", and she *definitely* didn't want to try and communicate the complexities of that through awkward blinks while strapped to a table.

"Okay, glad to hear it." Cassandra rolled out of Bast's vision for a moment, giving the goddess an unobstructed view of her workspace for the first time. The text on the computer screen was unreadable in the reflection, unfortunately. However, Cassandra did bring personal effects to work. There was a picture of the woman holding a black cat at an awkward angle, lifting it from beneath its forelegs like one would pick up a human baby. Unlike a child, however, the cat looking like it was trying to decide if it was enjoying the attention or getting ready to claw its mistress's arms until she put it down.

Knowing cats, Bast strongly suspected the latter happened mere seconds after the photo was taken.

Adjacent to that photo was one of Cassandra in a black dress, her hair in an impressively sophisticated style, with a man's arm over her shoulder. The man wore a tuxedo, and a frowny face sticker had been stuck over his face, which told Bast everything she needed to know. Next to that was an older photo of a much younger Cassandra, next to a smaller child with a mouth rimmed in frosting.

Cassandra rolled back into view and followed Bast's gaze. "Oh, the photos?"

Bast blinked once.

"That's my cat." Cassandra flushed. "Um. She's named after you. I didn't know goddesses were real back then, I just thought I was being clever naming a cat after a cat goddess. Is that a problem?"

Bast blinked twice. If someone was going to name an animal after her, she preferred they at least named the right animal. If it had been some mangy mutt, that would have been a different matter entirely.

"Oh, good." Cassandra's face relaxed some, although her cheeks remained a bit red. "She's a real treat. Hard to photograph - every time I try, she decides the camera is a toy, and I end up with a blurry mess. That's the best photograph I have of her. Remind me to show you the scars she gave me after that one - never tried picking her up like that again."

The amusement in Bast's eyes was real. *Knew it.*

"Do you have some kind of special affinity for cats? Or did you get associated with them for another reason?"

Bast waited patiently for Cassandra to realize the mistake. The woman was smart, there was no doubt about that. But her curiosity meant this wasn't the first time Cassandra asked a question to which there was no way to answer with simple blinks.

"Right, sorry." Cassandra tapped her chin. "Okay, do you have special control over cats?"

Bast blinked twice. As frustrating as communicating like this was, it was infinitely preferable to no interaction at all, and just like the slow drips of water had gradually quenched her thirst, this was slowly chipping away at her need to socialize.

"Were you associated with cats just because you liked them?" Cassandra asked.

Bast considered how to best answer, and finally blinked once. It had the virtue of being partially true, although it wasn't a complete answer. Bast had been associated with cats because she'd had a cat head, thanks to some low-grade transformation. That had been in vogue at the time. She'd chosen a cat, however, because she liked the creatures. They were tiny engines of destruction, the perfect murderers, and they also were utterly absurd.

Cassandra grinned. "A woman after my own heart."

Lub-dub, lub-dub, lub-dub

Don't say that word! Bast silently screamed. She did her best to convey amusement with her eyes, but the mention of the word and the sound of Cassandra's heart pumping in her chest set her stomach rumbling with hunger

Cassandra chattered away, and Bast pushed the thoughts aside.

Soon, Bast thought. *Soon, I will feed.*

She just wished she knew what she wanted to eat.

***

Crystal stepped onto the street outside of Isabel's apartment building, enjoying the feel of the sun on her skin. It was a crisp California day, warm but not overwhelmingly hot, with a gentle breeze coming in from the beach.

She took a deep breath. *Job well done. Now I just need to-*.

The thought was cut off as her shoulder blossomed with a flower of agony. Crystal screamed at the sudden pain and stumbled back, dropping to one knee. It was only then that the sound of the gunshot reached her ear, a deep, echoing report that bounced off buildings. *Oh, you sodding little bastard,* Crystal thought, hissing against the pain. A second bullet hummed through the air like an angry mosquito, inches from her ear.

Crystal phased out of reality.

A single bullet had nearly dropped her. *Think, think, oh damnit that hurts.* Crystal took a deep breath, and her ichor spewed from the wound.

Ichor. Of course. The gods had known for millennia that arrowheads forged with ichor were deadly, so any mortal who'd figured out the trick had met with a nasty end, as well as any he dared to tell. That didn't mean the secret couldn't have been rediscovered, though, and there was no reason it couldn't work with bullets, too.

Whoever had shot her was using ichor rounds. There wasn't any time to worry about how they had them or how they figured it out. Right now, she had to worry about her shoulder, which was bleeding ichor at an alarming rate, and the fact that ichor rounds could still hurt her while she was phased. That thought cut through the pain and gave her feet the energy they needed to move. A third bullet punched a hole in the concrete where she'd been standing.

Crystal stumbled behind a car, heart pounding. Her mind worked a mile a minute, with the kind of clarity that only came when you were at imminent risk of death. It was unlikely that some random person had ichor rounds. That meant those damn super-soldiers Ryan had talked about were here. Which meant Ryan was in danger, possibly even dead, from the precise threat Crystal had said wouldn't be a problem.

No, Crystal, don't focus on that. You have to save yourself, then you can save him.

The first thing she had to deal with was the wound in her shoulder. Gritting her teeth, she reached into the open wound and began to hunt for the bullet. It was an agonizing process, but after a few seconds, she felt it between her fingers. She inhaled deeply, exhaled, and *pulled*.

Okay, she told herself. *Okay. That was bad, but you're fine now, love. You're fine. You're good.*

The ichor erupting from the wound told a different story. Crystal was starting to feel lightheaded, and the last thing she needed was more pain, but the only way to stop the bleeding was going to involve a *lot* of pain.

Resolved, she put her hand over her bleeding shoulder and turned up the heat. Her already faint vision went dark for a moment from the sheer torment, but she didn't lose consciousness, and she kept the phasing effect up. By the time her shoulder was cauterized, she was weeping silently and breathing in hitching gasps.

C' mon, love, push through it.

Gunfire punched holes in the car, then traced its way down the street. The shooter clearly wasn't sure where she had gone, so they were firing in the blind hope of hitting her. If they kept it up long enough, they'd be able to pull it off.

Right now, all Crystal could do was hold her ground. She pressed her hand against the side of the car and twisted atomic numbers. Cheap aluminum turned into carbon, and she rearranged the molecules to form a solid barrier of graphene between herself and the shooter.

The effort made her drop the phase. She was fully vulnerable now, but her barrier should protect from the ichor rounds. She leaned against the car and took several deep breaths in rapid succession, then moved her injured shoulder. The agony was immense, but it moved. Small favors. She could still use the arm. Barely.

The gunfire stopped, and Crystal forced herself to wait. *They'll want to check the area. And when they do...I can get moving again.*

The waiting paid off. After a couple of minutes, a pair of soldiers walked to the place where she'd been shot. One of them crouched down to look at the splatters of ichor. Gritting her teeth, Crystal dropped a field of invisibility over herself and one of the soldiers and then bent light to plunge them both into darkness.

The man screamed and flailed about blindly, but Crystal could still navigate by the equations she saw. Even with only one good arm, it was easy to pull the rifle from his grip and smash the butt against his nose. She wielded the weapon like a baseball bat, hitting him in the face and arms until he collapsed.

Crystal kicked him out of the range of her invisibility and dropped the darkness so she could observe.

"Oh...shit." The remaining soldier whispered, moving to stand over his fallen friend. "I have hostile contact out here!" He shouted into the radio. "Repeat, I have hostile contact!"

From the radio, a voice responded, "Copy that. Where's the damn target?"

That must be the sniper that shot me in the first place, Crystal thought, waiting for the right moment. The soldier replied, "Target is invisible! Repeat, the target is-"

Crystal shifted the invisibility field over the remaining soldier and gave him the same treatment she'd just given his companion. A bullet buzzed through the field, but Crystal was already moving.

"Respond! Anyone there?" The radio squawked, and Crystal took a grim satisfaction at the panic in the speaker's voice. "I need support! Omega is on-site! Repeat, Omega is on-site!"

Crystal didn't wait to hear anything else. She ran towards Isabel's building, dropping her invisibility once she hit the lobby. The directory gave her Isabel's apartment number - eleven stories up.

She hit the stairs hard and began vaulting up them as fast as she could, taking them three or four at a time. Each step sent a fresh jolt of agony through her shoulder. She was seeing black spots by the fifth floor and was barely standing by the eleventh.

As she staggered out of the stairwell, she heard helicopters in the distance. She groaned and pushed herself down the hall. *Not yet...not yet. Need a bit more time. Just a few more seconds.*

There was a bloody path leading from an open door to the elevator. Crystal stared down at it, trying to make sense of what she was seeing. Who had been hurt? Ryan? His sister? Someone else? The blood trail looked like someone had been dragged.

A bullet tugged Crystal's hair as it missed her by inches. She jerked her head up to see a woman standing in the doorway with a revolver.

"Will everyone please stop shooting me?!" Crystal shouted.

The woman dropped the revolver in shock. "Oh my god, you're not military!" Isabel screamed. "Oh Jesus, oh God, please tell me I missed."

Crystal couldn't help it. She started laughing at the absurdity of almost being shot by the woman she was trying to rescue. "No, love, I'm not the sodding military," she choked out, "and you did miss. I'm Crystal."

"Right, Crystal. Sorry. Oh God. Please, save him!" Isabel's eyes were wide, and tears were streaming down her face. She looked like she was holding onto sanity by a fishing line that could snap at any moment.

Those three words slapped the laughter out of Crystal. "Save him? What happened?"

"He got...shot. In the...his face. His face got shot off. I got him in the bathtub but he's not breathing but you all don't need to breathe so I don't know what-"

Crystal brushed past Isabel and went through the apartment to the bathroom. Ryan's body lay there, and Isabel hadn't been exaggerating. With his cheeks blown out and his mouth hanging open, he looked like a corpse.

*Ryan, no no no...*Taking a deep breath to steady herself for the worst, Crystal reached down to his pocket and felt his nanoverse.

It was still solid, not the crumbling sand that would have indicated a dead Nascent.

"He's alive, but barely." She turned to Isabel, her face hard. "Isabel. I need you to do exactly what I say, follow my every cue. We can get out of this alive, and I can save him. Maybe. But only if you do everything I say, without hesitation. Can you do that?"

Isabel nodded rapidly, tears still pouring out of her eyes. "His face...oh God his face."

Crystal stepped forward and grabbed the other woman by the arm, forcing Isabel to look her directly in the eyes. "Isabel. Listen to me. I am a million years old. I've been waiting a million years for your brother. Do you believe, for a single goddamn second, that I'm going to let him die?"

Isabel shook her head.

"Good. Now. You still listening? Your brother is a god. He can heal from anything, so long as he doesn't actually die. His wounds are bad, but he won't bleed out. That means that if we get him out of here, he is going to live, and so you are. But the only way that happens is if you focus and follow directions, okay?"

This time, when Isabel nodded, Crystal could see a small thread of rationality behind her eyes. She'd hold up, long enough.

"Good. Get me a glass of water and something I can eat. Now."

True to her word, Isabel ran off without hesitation. Crystal took a few moments to tear down the shower curtain and begin fastening a sling to carry Ryan. *Can't just toss him over my shoulder, need my hands free.*

Isabel returned as Crystal was finishing. She didn't speak, just thrust a bottle of water and a protein bar in Crystal's face. Without a word, Crystal grabbed both and downed them as quickly as she could. The helicopter sound was getting louder.

"They'll do. That's two." Crystal furrowed her brow. "Still not enough. I need a bit more. Still Hungry. Don't have time for a nap."

Isabel stared at her with wild eyes. "Hunger? Right, what can I do?"

Crystal's mind raced. Once the helicopters opened fire, they were done for. She didn't think she could hold off a missile right now. Thinking frantically, she squeezed her nanoverse for a bit more strength.

"Remember, love," she told Isabel. "Everything I say. No hesitation."

The helicopter was almost there, and Crystal just wasn't strong enough to deal with it. Her Hungers were clamoring for attention. Even with the food and drink, she needed a nap, and she needed some human interaction. The first one was out of the question, and for the second...

Oh, duh, Crystal. She turned to Isabel. "I need you to kiss me."

Isabel gave her a confused look. Crystal believed Isabel had been sincere in her intent to follow everything Crystal had said without question but hadn't anticipated one of those requests being so incongruous. "I'm sorry, what?"

"I can explain later, love. But the helicopter will be able to start firing in under a minute, and I'm too weak to save us, but if-" Crystal's explanation was cut short as Isabel grabbed her and pulled Crystal's face to her own. They locked lips and embraced. For a handful of seconds, nothing else mattered but that kiss, drowning out the fear and pain and tiredness and sound of approaching aerial annihilation. Instead, there was an electrical surge flowing between them, one of the purest and most potent ways two people can connect.

Before they got too wrapped up in it and got blown to pieces, Crystal broke the kiss and smiled. "Okay, yeah. We're good."

Isabel blinked a few times. The human contact seemed to have helped her get a better grip on reality for the moment...or maybe everything was so crazy that Isabel was just kind of floating along with the madness. "The Hungers, right?"

"Doesn't matter." Crystal said. "That was wonderful, love, really. So now I need to grab your brother-" She bent down in a fluid motion and put the shower curtain sling over her good shoulder, leaving Ryan hanging across her back like a huge bloody purse. Literally bloody. Isabel turned to the sink and threw up.

"-and now I need to save us both. Take my hand." Crystal used her good arm for a quick twist to reinforce the curtain and stick it to her body. That should prevent Ryan from coming loose. Should.

After the kiss, it didn't seem anything Crystal suggested would seem odd. Isabel grabbed the hand on her bad arm, and Crystal fought to keep the pain off her face.

"What...what are we doing?" Isabel asked.

Crystal turned to face her, the smile growing even wider. "Something incredibly, insanely stupid."

"What-" Isabel began to ask, but Crystal was already running, pulling Isabel along into the living room. The helicopter was coming into view; they literally had waited until the last second.

As they ran, Crystal gestured. Isabel's sliding door exploded outwards, sending a hail of supersonic glass flying towards the helicopter. The helicopter launched a missile at that exact moment, and the force Crystal had used to break the door hit the rocket. It detonated halfway between the helicopter and the apartment.

To Isabel's credit, she didn't stop running when the helicopter exploded. She did start screaming, however, the kind of scream that didn't stop. Crystal gestured again, hitting the head of a second missile with a twisted equation.

She slapped a negative sign on its acceleration, thinking through the process. *Negative acceleration isn't a real thing. It's just the opposite direction from its current path. Which means the front of the missile is going to meet the back of the missile right about -*

The missile flattened into a pancake and violently exploded.

The helicopter pilot wasn't an idiot. He didn't waste another rocket on them. He instead switched over to the minigun slung under the helicopter's belly. Crystal's heart sunk as she heard the whirring sound of the gun warming up.

Crystal and Isabel were almost on the balcony, Isabel now screaming actual words. "Crystal we're on the eleventh floo-*ohmygod*!"

As a hail of bullets flew toward them, Crystal threw out her hand and sent the railing of Isabel's balcony ripping free of its moorings at Mach six. She and Isabel followed, although at a much slower speed.

The helicopter pilot was likely ready for most things. Crystal figured there's no way they'd let an amateur fly on this kind of mission. However, nothing in his training could have prepared him for a hypersonic balcony railing.

The two objects collided in midair, and the impact sent the helicopter spinning away. Two other helicopters were moving into position, but gravity had a firm grip on Crystal and Isabel at this point, carrying them towards the ground.

Isabel resumed her wordless screaming as Crystal whipped them around so she could face upwards. The effort of holding on to Isabel's hand was pure agony at this point, but if they were connected, that was one less twist Crystal needed. With a quick gesture, she sent shards from the balcony flying at the other two helicopters. Both of the vehicles were met with a hail of shrapnel that was alive and spiteful. One began to spin out of control. Crystal dealt with the remaining helicopter by twisting gravity. Suddenly, everything near the remaining helicopter regarded it as "down".

Loose objects from the building's roof, the shrapnel of the crashing vehicles, and the two remaining helicopters all slammed into the last adversary, turning the entire mass into a giant fireball as fuel tanks ignited.

Crystal twisted gravity around herself, Isabel, and Ryan. The new, weaker gravity carried them safely to the ground as Crystal reached up and did one final twist, encasing the three of them in a protective shield of air as debris rained around them.

Isabel looked up at Crystal, her eyes full with a mixture of shock, terror, exhilaration, and awe. "Oh my God," she said, her voice hoarse.

"Goddess," Crystal corrected. "Come on. We still have to finish saving your brother."

Chapter 13

Recoup and Regroup

Crystal slammed her doorway shut behind Isabel. She didn't waste any time calling up a bed for Ryan. The shower curtain she'd used for an impromptu sling was slick with blood, and Ryan's breathing was coming in short, shallow gasps.

"Oh my God," Isabel gasped, getting her first good look at her brother since the initial attack. Crystal didn't blame her. She'd seen some severe injuries in her day, but this was a fresh horror. Isabel started to gag, and Crystal summoned up a bucket.

"Whole thing finally hit your limit, love?" Crystal said absentmindedly, already forming a variety of tools to begin work on Ryan's face.

"Yes. How – I mean, is he..." Isabel didn't seem to be able to finish a sentence. Again, Crystal couldn't blame her.

"He's alive, and he'll be all right. I think." Crystal looked over her shoulder and gave Isabel her most reassuring smile.

It didn't seem to work particularly well. Isabel was pale and shaking slightly.

She wiped her mouth before asking, "You think? Sorry, I don't mean to sound...ungrateful, it's just ...shouldn't we get him to a doctor?"

"I just jumped off a building and took out three helicopters before I hit the ground, and you think I can't doctor?"

"What? How are those even *remotely* connected?" Isabel gave Crystal a wide-eyed stare.

"Damn, was hoping you wouldn't think of that," Crystal said lightly, turning back to Ryan. "Yes, they are different skills. But Ryan's past a doctor's ability to help at this point, mainly because a doctor will be working based on normal human biology, yeah?"

Isabel nodded in agreement, which was a relief because that was a complete fabrication. The truth was that if they took him to a hospital, those government super-soldiers will be all over them before they could sign the paperwork.

Crystal continued, "As long as I can get Ryan to stop bleeding, it'll be fine. He'll have some nasty scars that he'll probably want to shapeshift away, but that's it." Crystal began to thread a needle. "I've done post-battle surgery on gods before, so this is an old trick."

Isabel nodded slowly, then said, "Wait. If he can shapeshift the scars away, can't we just wake him up so he can shift himself healthy?"

Crystal shook her head. "Doesn't work that way. You can't shift away damage. He could turn into a dog right now if he was awake, and he had actually learned to shapeshift into an animal, but it would be a dog with a missing nose and holes in the cheeks."

As Crystal began to stitch. Isabel turned around and made another retching noise again, although it just sounded like a heave.

Isabel kept her back turned. "But...well, why? Why can't you just...fix it?"

Crystal chuckled but didn't pause in her stitching. "You and Ryan are definitely related. Love, you're standing in a pocket universe between my nanoverse and reality, your entire life just got turned upside down, your apartment is being raided by the government, and you're worried about the minutiae of divine shapeshifting." Although the words were mocking, her tone was kind, almost sympathetic. "Trust me, love. It's better if you just roll with it."

Isabel laughed, too, but it had a manic edge. "Ryan s-said you loved t-that phrase."

"He's not wrong." Crystal cut the string and prepared to move over to the other cheek. She didn't start yet. In her head, she began a countdown as took off her gloves. *Five, four, three, two-*

Isabel's laughter turned to sobs. "Oh God, this is so fucked up."

Crystal stepped over and put her hands on Isabel's shoulders. "I know, love, I know." She took Isabel in her arms. "You just about had the worst bloody introduction into our world that I've ever seen. Let it out."

"N-no," Isabel said, starting to push away. "You should be...Ryan-"

"Isn't bleeding any more. He's fine right now, he's stable." Crystal glanced over to Ryan to make sure that was true. Calming Isabel down was important, but Ryan's life had to come first. The whole world was depending on it. Seeing that he was in no immediate danger, she continued, "Love, he got an ugly injury, but there's no major blood loss anymore. He's not going to get an infection, he's not going to bleed out, and right now he's too unconscious to be in pain."

Crystal held Isabel until the tears were under control.

"Thanks," Isabel said.

"You're welcome. Are you okay now?" Crystal asked.

Isabel sniffed and wiped her eyes with the back of her hand. "God, no. I don't even know what that *means* right now. But I'm not falling apart. Take care of him."

Crystal patted her on the shoulder before getting back to work on Ryan's cheeks. She hoped Ryan would shapeshift instinctively once he had healed enough because otherwise, he was going to have some brutal scars. It was an ugly sight, the kind of chop-shop surgery that you got when your surgeon wasn't actually trained.

Crystal finished the last bit of stitching on Ryan's cheeks. "There we are. Now just to bandage up that nose and he should be good."

Isabel turned around and looked at her brother hesitantly. The end result wasn't pretty, but he at least looked alive, and the holes in his face were sewn shut. Still, she shuddered and looked away. "Thanks. I mean...for everything. You saved our lives."

Crystal shrugged. "You're very welcome, love. Ryan's a friend, and you're family of a friend. Oh, and if Ryan dies everything gets blown up and I've wasted the last million years, so I guess I can't claim it was entirely altruistic."

"Fair enough," Isabel said with a sound that was almost like a laugh. Almost. "Oh, God, my apartment..."

Yeah, they're definitely from the same family, Crystal thought as she unwound some gauze for Ryan's nose. "Well, don't beat yourself up over it," she said, "You kind of had some other things on your mind, yeah?"

"What?" Isabel forced herself to smile. "You think my brother b-bleeding from the face in the bathtub and helicopters shooting missiles at my living room somehow justifies me forgetting about my luggage?"

"You know what?" Crystal said, laughing, "I suppose when you put it that way, it does seem rather silly."

"Well, in my defense, a strange woman did throw me off a balcony."

"That absolute bitch!" Crystal exclaimed.

"So...what happens now?"

"We wait for Ryan to wake up. I'm not going to risk cauterizing the wounds. It would be excessive right now; that's really only a battlefield fix. Once he's up, we find out where he put his doorway so he can hop down into his nanoverse and use the time differential to heal up quickly, and then we rendezvous with some of our friends who are looking for Moloch. After that, love, if I'm honest, we'll be winging it."

"Okay. I appreciate the honesty at least."

Isabel still looked unsteady, and Crystal could hardly blame the poor woman. She'd probably been holding on by a thread ever since Ryan vanished and reappeared by the news. Then, when her brother finally returned, everything had gone to hell with alarming alacrity.

"Now," Crystal said, "do you think you could be okay for a couple hours?"

"Alone?" Isabel asked, her voice cracking.

Crystal winced. "Oh, no, that's not what I meant at all! I'll still be here with you. Just...I've gotten most of my Hungers taken care of, but if I'm going to fully recharge, I need to get some sleep in."

"Oh." Isabel's face fell, but then she forced a smile. "I don't like the idea of being even relatively alone right now. But... I'd feel infinitely better if you were at full strength." She sat on a chair and pulled her legs up, wrapping her arms around her shins. "So, please, do. It's safe here, right?"

Crystal nodded. "There isn't a force between Heaven and Hell that can break into a god's staging area. I could drop the doorway in the core of the sun, and it wouldn't even feel warm on this side."

"Please don't," Isabel said. "Get some sleep. Please."

"Wake me up if you need to. For any reason. Ryan would kill me you had some sort of meltdown and I slept through it."

Isabel gave her a thumbs up. "I'll be all right."

Crystal nodded and called up a bookshelf. "If you need to take your mind off things..."

Confident she'd done everything she could, Crystal formed a bed and climbed in. In seconds, she was sound asleep.

***

Ryan's first conscious thought was *Isabel.*

He started reached up, heart pounding. *They're going to kill Isabel, they're going to kill my sister, I have to get up.*

He could hear someone saying his name, grabbing at his outstretched hands, trying to hold him back...

His vision cleared. Crystal hovered over him, saying his name repeatedly. "Ryan! Ryan, it's okay love. I got there in time. She's fine."

That penetrated the fog of pain and fear, and he relaxed. He wanted to ask a question, but Crystal gently put her hand on his mouth. "No, Ryan, don't. I'll explain, just...give me a thumbs up to show you understand, yeah?"

He raised the requested digit, and she relaxed. "You got shot in the face. You'll be fine, but if you try to speak right now, you're going to tear open the stitches, okay?"

Ryan nodded. The motion sent a spiderweb of pain lancing through his head, and an involuntary groan escaped his lips. Crystal winced.

Isabel stepped into view. "What's wrong?" she asked, her forehead creased.

"I asked him a yes or no question, and of course he nodded. My mistake, love."

"Well, it's not your fault he's a dumbass." Isabel fixed Ryan with a firm glare that belied the moisture in her eyes. "Don't nod, dumbass. And don't glower at me for calling you a dumbass. On top of that, since I'm giving you orders, don't you dare get shot in front of me again, or I swear to God I'll put itching powder in your underwear again, okay?"

Ryan slowly raised his hand to give her a thumbs up, then with even more deliberate care rotated his hand to extend his middle finger. Isabel choked out a laugh, with the edge of a sob, then stuck her tongue out at him.

"He's going to be okay," Isabel said to Crystal. "Unfortunately, he didn't learn anything."

Crystal had watched the entire exchange, and her smile was about as wide as Ryan had ever seen. "Oh yeah," she said, "You two are definitely siblings. Okay, Ryan, do you feel up to standing up? I want to get you back to your staging area. Thumbs up for yes, down for no, sideways if you're not sure."

Ryan considered for a moment, then held his thumb up.

"Okay. So here's the plan. I get you back to your staging area. You'll heal faster there. Otherwise, you'll heal at human speed, and you do *not* want that delay, yeah? You'll know you're fully healed when you can reshape your nose. Isabel stays here with me, we go check on Athena and that lot, and you join us when you're ready. Same way to signal your answer."

Ryan held his thumb out to the side.

"Lemme guess, love. You want your sister to come with you, yeah?"

Ryan gave Crystal a thumbs up.

"Not a good idea. The fastest way to heal is to stay asleep. That means if Isabel needed anything, including to *leave* for any reason, she'd have to wake you up to close the door behind her. When you're healing like that, it's going to be damn hard to wake you. She could end up trapped without any way of escaping besides causing you further injury." Crystal bit her lip and looked at Isabel, whose face had gone pale.

"I think I'll stay with Crystal if you'll be okay on your own," Isabel said in a small voice.

His eyes wide, Ryan gave a thumbs up.

***

Crystal poked her head out of her doorway to check for any remaining military presence. Law enforcement, including several men in suits, were on location, but no military. Apparently, the army had cleared out and left things to the cops and feds.

No super-soldiers, she thought. *I wonder how they're going to spin opening fire on an apartment building.* She made a mental note to ask Isabel to keep an eye on social media for that. The poor woman clearly had a good head on her shoulders, but was massively out of her depth, just as any other mortal would be. Giving her something to do would help Isabel wrap her head around things.

And it would be good to know what Isabel could find, because Crystal had questions. Somehow these soldiers had been ready for fighting gods, better than any mortals Crystal had ever encountered. There were two possible answers, neither of which Crystal liked. One was that they had struck a deal with some power, a god or goddess who was working with to take them down. That would be bad, but manageable. It also seemed less likely. Try as she might, Crystal could not come up with a god or goddess who would be dumb enough to give mortals the secrets of ichor. The other, more likely explanation was that the military had captured a god or goddess somehow.

Later, Crystal. Worry about that later. Let's get Ryan to his nanoverse.

Reaching out, she did a modified version of her earlier bending light trick, this time creating a corridor between her doorway and Ryan's. She let enough light in so they wouldn't be moving in total darkness. Invisibility was useless against gods, as they'd see the twists that created it, but against mortals, it was damn useful. Since there were plenty of armed men around, discretion seemed prudent.

"Okay, we're clear," she said, poking her head back in.

Ryan was standing with his arm draped over Isabel's shoulder, so she could support his weight and make sure he didn't pass out during the walk. Crystal moved smoothly over and took the other side, and they gently led Ryan down the pathway towards his nanoverse. Crystal could see how hard he was fighting to keep his eyes open.

Once inside, the staging area created a bed out of the floor. Ryan's head drooped, and the weight on Crystal's shoulders increased. "C' mon, love, you're almost there."

"Mhrnhl," Ryan said, blinking at the bed. "Bed?"

"Bed," Crystal said. "We're going to help you in." It took both of them to make sure Ryan just didn't dive face-first into the pillows without thinking. Once he was actually in the bed, Crystal pulled off his shoes, and Isabel threw the sheet over him.

"You're sure he'll be okay in here?" Isabel asked.

Crystal squeezed Isabel's shoulder. "Positive. Now, Ryan, set your doorway to close itself in...sixty seconds."

A countdown appeared on one of the screens, and Crystal and Isabel hurried out.

Back in Crystal's staging area, Isabel let out a deep breath and then slumped. Crystal moved to support her, putting an arm around the other woman.

"It's okay," Crystal said. "He'll be fine. And he'll be back before you know it."

Isabel nodded, and Crystal led her over to a couch.

"I'm just..." Isabel said, groping for the right words, "It's... I've never seen him like that, y' know? He was in a car accident once and got banged up pretty bad, but that's it. He was always so nervous about one thing or another, and so he never really did the stupid things guys do, so he didn't get hurt, rarely got sick...is that because he was going to become a god?"

"Nope," Crystal said, settling onto the couch beside her. "He was one of thousands the Curators thought might find the last Nanoverse and kick off the end of the world, but it wasn't because of anything special about him. They just have gotten really, really good at predicting outcomes over the millennia. Hell, the Curators could have been wrong, it could have been some other random person."

"Oh," Isabel said. "I dunno, I guess with gods being real, I figured prophecy was involved or something."

Crystal laughed. "We don't have any special ability to tell the future. But after hundreds and thousands and thousands of years, you get really bloody good at spotting patterns, love. Some, like the Furies, are so good at it even we call them prophets, so it really seems prophetic to the average bloke who doesn't have the benefit of that much experience."

"Drat," Isabel ran her hands through her hair. "I normally hate spoilers, but I'd love to know how this whole thing ends. If I'm going to be okay and my brother is and the world is..."

Crystal patted her arm reassuringly. "Isabel, love. Most gods give up on immortality after ten or twenty thousand years. I don't know any who stuck around for more than a hundred thousand at most. But I have. You know why?" Isabel shook her head, and Crystal reached under the other woman's chin to make sure their eyes met. "Because I wanted to make damn sure that everyone would be okay this time around. So I can't see the future, and I can't tell you what's absolutely going to happen, but I can tell you that I didn't wait around a million years to cock it up now, yeah?"

Isabel laughed and held Crystal's gaze for a few moments longer before brushing a strand of hair behind her ear. "Thanks. So I guess we need to go to Venezuela now?"

"Oh, we already are. But I want you to stay here when we get there. For all I know, it's turned into an active war zone."

"No problem here." Isabel leaned back. "Is there anything I can do?"

"Not at the moment, but maybe after this. How good are you with a computer?"

"Pretty good. I'm no leet hacker girl or anything, but I know my way around a search engine and various websites and such."

Crystal smiled. "Good. I'm absolute rubbish, and Athena...honestly, I can't even talk about it. As soon as I can, I'll take you somewhere with internet access, and you can do some research for us."

"All right," Isabel said. "What do you want me to look for?"

"See what you can find out about Myrmidon, the government's spin on the attack on your apartment, any references to Bast after the Canada fight – anything. Right now we're completely in the dark in regard to those things, and we need to know what's going on."

"I can do that," Isabel said. "What about while you're gone?"

Crystal smiled and pointed to an enormous pile of newspapers in one corner. "I'm a bit behind on the old school research, too."

"Who would have thought," Isabel said, "that even gods needed support staff? I'm on it. Be careful out there."

Chapter 14

The Shadow of Shadu

"This is pointless," Horus growled. "We don't need all four of us to guard this damn portal."

Athena rubbed her temples. The worst part of listening to Horus gripe was that he had a point. "Horus, we've been over this. If the others return-"

"I know," he snapped, cutting her off.

Athena dug her fingers into her thighs to keep them from Horus's throat. While Dianmu and Anansi watched the portal, ready for something to come out and attack them, Athena and Horus stayed alert for any threats that might emerge from the jungle. Athena was really, *really* regretting her watch partner.

"Then you just said that to irritate me?" Athena asked, unable to keep the frustration down.

"Just wanted to make sure my objection was still being disregarded," Horus said, crossing his arms across his chest. "I'd hate to think you'd changed your mind and-"

This time it was Horus who was interrupted, by a shout from Dianmu. Within the temple, a doorway had appeared between two piles of skulls.

Athena scrambled to her feet. "Everyone get ready!" she shouted, preparing to incinerate any hostile.

Anansi held up his hands, and Athena saw an elemental swirl around him. Dianmu reached into her nanoverse, pulling out a wicked glaive longer than she was tall, and Horus unslung his rifle and took aim. Athena had to grant him one point: he could put aside his grudges when there was a threat.

The doorway opened, and Crystal peered out. "Oh, bloody hell," she said. "Should have given you a warning. It's me, loves, you all can calm down."

Athena breathed a sigh of relief as she let go of her prepared twist. "Glad you could make it," Athena said, then noticed that Crystal was alone. "Where's Ryan?"

"He's alive," Crystal said with a tight smile. "And he'll be fine, love. He sort of...got his face shot off."

"I'm sorry, could you repeat that?" Anansi's asked. "His face?"

Crystal nodded. "One of those military gods, the cheap knock offs of the real deal? Sort of shot him right in the face. It didn't kill him, but he's taking a little bit of a break in his nanoverse to heal up, yeah?"

"And the military gods? Do they die like mortals, or will he be back?" This was Dianmu, whose face mirrored Anansi's concern.

"I can't tell you," Crystal said. "He was gone by the time I got there, but I got to have some fun with attack helicopters and snipers. Armed with bullets that could hit me even when I was phasing. Ichor rounds."

The four exchanged glances. "Tell us everything," Athena said.

When she finished, there was a moment of stunned silence. "Never before," Horus said, his voice a harsh whisper, "have mortals been able to bypass our phasing. How is this even *possible?*"

Crystal chewed her lip. "Well...if you smelt metal with a bit of Ichor, you get weapons that can still injure us when we're phased. Same as how we can fight each other, and monsters can still hurt us, even if we're phasing."

"But that would require them to have a source of ichor," Horus scoffed, but at the same time, Anansi and Dianmu shared a worried look.

Oh no, Athena thought, *we might lose him.* She was surprised to be so worried about the possibility. She didn't like Horus, but he was a valuable ally.

Horus continued, "They can't just scoop it off the ground. Ichor dries and becomes useless too quickly. How would the..." He saw Crystal's face, and his eyes went wide. "No. You don't think...they have her?"

"They have someone. I'm sure of that," Crystal said. "Most of the Olympians are in Tartarus, and most of the Asgardians haven't left Asgard in nearly five-hundred years, but beyond that, there are plenty of other gods who've been quiet so far in all this. The presence of Ichor doesn't mean they have Bast."

"But you think they do!" he snapped.

Athena could see Dianmu's hand tighten on her glaive and couldn't blame the storm goddess. The veins on Horus's forehead and neck were bulging.

Crystal winced and held up a placating hand. "No, I don't. We detonated a nuke to stop Enki. They would have had to wait to go in for fear of radiation."

Horus pursed his lips and turned the thought over. "We have to find her," he said, his voice far more plaintive than it had been before. "Then we'll know."

The look of shock on Tyr's face as Bast had trained the gun on him flashed through Athena's mind, but she bit her tongue on her immediate sarcastic retort. "We do need to find her. But Moloch's portal is right here, and we do not know how long it will remain open, or where it leads." She nodded towards Horus. "Besides, as you pointed out earlier, if she was working with Moloch before, she must have had a reason. It's most likely she and him are together."

Hope ignited in Horus' eyes, but Crystal interjected before he could speak.

"Portal?" Crystal asked, tilting her head.

Anansi, who had been standing in the doorway to the interior room, stepped aside to give Crystal an unobstructed view of the pulsating ring of energy. She let out a low whistle.

"Oh. Yeah, we should probably deal with that first."

Horus clenched his fists so tightly, Athena wondered if he'd draw blood from his own palm.

"Have you gone mad?" he spat. "They're draining ichor from one of us to make weapons, and you want to focus on Moloch?"

Horus had gone from desperate to enraged in a fraction of a second, and his screaming was almost painful to hear. Athena took a step back. He sounded like a lunatic, raving at them. Not wanting to wait for him to act, Athena reached into her nanoverse and drew out a sword.

"Oh, so that's how it is?" Horus asked her, instantly switching from a scream to a dangerously low hiss.

"Horus," Crystal started to say, but he cut her off.

"No. I want to hear it from you, Athena. Do you intend to cut me down?"

"Only if you force me to," Athena responded, doing her best to keep her voice calm. "Horus, you're irrational."

"It's your fault she's even there," Horus said. He met Athena's gaze, and his hands clenched and opened at his sides.

"Yes."

Horus tensed his entire body, and Athena prepared herself for his attack. Crystal and Dianmu also seemed ready for an outright brawl.

Anansi, however, was not. "Horus," he said, his voice level, "there's much we still do not understand. The battle happened in Canada, but these soldiers are American. We do not know where Bast is, just that she is somewhere within the second and fourth-largest nations on Earth. Probably. It would be unwise to drop everything to find her when we are on Moloch's trail."

Horus's nostrils flared. "I don't care about Moloch! I am here to find Bast, and for no other reason."

"Then you are a fool," Dianmu snapped. Every head turned to look at her, but she did not take her eyes off Horus. "Moloch clearly wishes to establish dominance after the end of the world. Do you think you would fare well under that? Do you think *Bast* would want to live in Moloch's nightmare world? You saw what he has created here, the sacrifices he made for power."

"But-"

"No," Dianmu said, her voice still razor-sharp. "There is no room for 'but' here, Horus. Moloch must be stopped before the world can end, so he does not gain control. Anything else - you, any of us, and Bast - must be secondary. Ensuring the Eschaton's survival is the only thing that is more important than that."

Horus glared at her, and for a moment it seemed like he would leave in spite of the logic.

"Horus," Athena said, keeping her voice as gentle as she could. "You know Dianmu is correct. But I promise you, as soon as Moloch is dealt with, we *will* find Bast."

Horus spat on the floor. "You only want to find her so you can kill her."

Athena felt her fists clench, and slowly forced them to loosen. "I swear to you, Horus, that if you are with us when we find her, I'll stay my hand." The words left a sour taste in her mouth, but against Moloch's army, they needed whatever help they could get. *Even if it means allowing Bast to live.*

Horus relaxed. Slightly. "Very well," he said. "I will stay with this until Moloch is defeated. And will expect your aid in finding Bast afterward."

"Brilliant," Crystal said, smiling at everyone. "This is good, yeah? We're one step behind Moloch after all. How long could it take to catch him?"

Anansi's eyes sparkled. "I fear now that you have said that, we will find it even harder. Murphy's law, yes?"

"Oooh, good point, love. Knock on wood then." Crystal tapped the top of her own skull.

Even Horus smiled – slightly – at the joke. "So now we wait for the Eschaton and go in?" he asked.

Athena shook her head. "We've waited long enough. Ryan can catch up when he's healed."

"Agreed," Dianmu and Anansi said in unison, and even Crystal nodded.

"Then it's settled," Athena said. "Let us be done with this."

***

Athena led the way through the portal and hit the ground in an immediate roll, barely registering her surroundings as she dove for cover behind a wall. When there was no immediate sign of danger, she began to cautiously examine her surroundings, starting with the wall itself. It was made red stone streaked with orange marbling, unlike anything she had ever seen before. She looked up and saw a night sky was lit by a trio of small moons. The air reeked of ash and ozone like a forest fire sparked by a thunderstorm. Wherever they were, she was sure it wasn't in the Core anymore, or any realm she knew.

Athena risked peering over the top of the wall. This realm was as empty and silent as Olympus had been, but without the long-abandoned feeling. The walls were broken in places with scars that still burned hot, curling plumes of gray smoke rising from stone and soil. She took a deep breath and noticed the coppery scent of blood. In the distance, she heard the crackling of a fire.

The ground had great furrows carved by divine manipulation of reality, too straight and narrow to be by any natural tectonic movement. Athena could see more of the marbled blocks, shattered and cracked, and bodies littering the ground.

This was the silence of a battlefield after the fighting was done.

"We're too late," Anansi said quietly, and Athena nodded.

"Shadu," Crystal whispered. "It's Shadu, the otherworld of the Canaanites. Their version of Olympus."

Athena pointed to Crystal, Dianmu, and herself, then at a tower that still seemed intact. When the other women nodded, Athena pointed at Anansi and Horus, and then at her own eyes. At their nods, she slipped out from behind the wall and began to advance carefully, hugging the ground as much as she could. Crystal and Dianmu followed suit.

The first body they reached was once of Moloch's Aspirants. He was a young man, perhaps twenty. His eyes stared unblinking at those three dots in the sky, and his face was twisted into a rapturous smile that clashed with his spilled entrails. Flies were already landing on him. Athena shuddered at the sight. She'd been on battlefields since before recorded history and only left them after the collapse of the Byzantine Empire, yet the sight of anyone who had died this violently still filed her with a mixture of pity and revulsion. That smile didn't help matters. It was *wrong.* Dead men should either look at peace or horrified.

They shouldn't look so damn *happy* about things.

They came across more of Moloch's followers, their bodies battered and broken, eyes staring blankly at the sky. One was covered with burns along half his body, charred so profoundly that his hand was nothing more than a blackened skeleton. Another's long hair stood straight up, and her corpse still smoldered.

"Mortal weapons didn't kill these soldiers," Athena whispered to Crystal.

Crystal's expression was queasy, but she studied the corpses carefully. "No marks from monster claws or teeth, either. Only one thing causes injuries like this."

Athena had been hoping Crystal would disagree with her own conclusions, but no such luck. Divine power had killed these men.

Dianmu had moved slightly ahead, and now she waved them over. She stood over a broken body, and as Athena drew closer, she realized she knew this man - or had known him, more accurately.

"Who is he?" Dianmu asked, reading Athena's expression.

Before responding, Athena knelt beside the body. If not for the gaping wound on his throat, it would have been possible to believe he still lived. "Marquod," Athena whispered, her voice thick.

Crystal hadn't seen his face yet, and at his name, she came up short. "Who the bloody hell would kill Marquod?"

"Moloch." Athena spat out the name.

"But why?" Crystal's voice was on the edge of cracking, and Dianmu was giving them both a concerned look.

"Marquod was a god of dance and laughter," Athena said, gently closing his eyes. Marquod had been staring accusingly at the heavens as if he had died wondering why he deserved this. "He was always smiling, always had a joke on his lips, and he-" Athena struggled to finish the sentence.

"He was fond of the lost and broken," Crystal said, swallowing hard. There were tears in her eyes. "If you know someone who knows Marquod, you know a deity that's been exiled."

"I'm sorry," Dianmu said quietly.

Crystal nodded appreciation but turned back to Athena. "His nanoverse?"

Athena shook her head, trying to keep her tears in check. "Gone. I pray that it's just rolled under a rock somewhere." She smoothed his hair back. "I'd like to see him dance again."

It's always the gods like him, Athena thought. *We war gods and storm gods and death gods and thrice-damned tricksters, we get out of these things all right in the end. It's the dancers, the laughers, the dreamers - they're the ones that suffer.*

Athena clenched her hands until her nails bit into her palm. There would be time to mourn Marquod later. For now, she had to make sure the living gods remained that way. "Come on," she whispered.

At the base of the tower, Athena wrapped herself in a bubble of solid air and pulled herself to the top. Dianmu followed, and Crystal signaled for Anansi and Horus to leave cover and join them. The tower wasn't tall, only five stories, but it would offer an excellent view of the entire area.

When they reached the top and turned to survey the battlefield, Dianmu gasped, and Athena had to grab onto a parapet for stability. It was a slaughterhouse, the likes of which Athena hadn't seen since the fall of Constantinople. Dozens of dead. From up here, Athena couldn't tell the difference between Canaanite gods and Moloch's zealots. They were just broken bodies lying in the soil of this strange realm. Athena reached into her nanoverse to pull out a pair of binoculars. Instead, she retrieved a spyglass, but it served her purpose. She scanned the terrain, looking for signs of life.

She found none. As far as she could see, the five of them were the only things moving here, other than the flies that were preparing for a feast.

"Athena," Anansi said after a moment, leaning in. "What do your elf-eyes see?"

Athena continued her scanning without pause. "I am not an elf, and this is a spyglass. But so far, no sign of movement."

Behind her, Crystal let out a semi-hysterical giggle. Athena was familiar with gallows humor, although it had always struck her as disrespectful. Especially when she didn't get the joke.

"I think we're safe," she finally, collapsing the spyglass back into her nanoverse. "Moloch got what he came for. He's gone."

"How do you know?" Horus asked, tilting his head slightly.

"There's a portal at the other end of the field. He didn't leave that one open, but there's a pile of bodies near it."

Crystal looked thoughtful. "Why leave one portal open, but not the other?"

Dianmu answered the question before Athena could. "It seems he wanted us to see, and know what he did here, but did not wish us to follow him any further."

"Well," Horus said, sourly. "This has been a waste of time. We received his message, and now we've lost him. We need to go back and start looking elsewhere."

"For Moloch, or for Bast?" Athena asked, her voice harsher than she'd intended.

Horus shook his head and held up a hand, his mouth twisting sourly. "Stay your anger, Gray-Eyes. We seek whoever we can locate, so it will depend on what clues we find. You have my oath, Athena, is that not enough?"

I had Bast's oath too, Athena thought, but aloud she said, "Of course. My apologies – I just dislike our failure here."

Crystal took a step towards her, her mouth open. Whatever platitude she was about to utter was cut off by a sharp click.

Athena understood instantly and started to shout a warning as she grabbed threads of reality, twisting with desperate need.

She barely saw the shock cross Crystal's face before the world went white. The air bubble Athena had tried to throw around them was only half-formed, and the soupy air compressed and battered the gods. Athena's vision went black, and she lost track of what was happening.

She hit the ground moments later, the impact snapping her back to full awareness. The last of her improvised shield vanished, and her head rang from the explosion. She looked around wildly, trying to find any of her companions. Her hasty shield might have protected them too, or it might have come too late. She didn't know.

Debris from the tower rained down around her. Athena cursed when a stone struck her forehead and drew blood. She hissed in pain and twisted, searing the wound shut. She briefly lost her vision again as her eyes watered.

When they had cleared, she saw that the portal they had used to enter had gone dark. For a moment, Shadu seemed even quieter than before. Then more explosions rocked the remains of other towers and structures. Athena dove for shelter, and then twisted to form a full, solid shield.

Turning, she came face to face with the corpse of another of Moloch's zealots, a woman with silver blond hair and another of those damn smiles plastered across her lips. Athena's lips curled in disgust, and then her mouth dropped open as the corpse's neck began to writhe as if maggots were crawling under the skin. Athena scrambled away as the woman's head tore free from her shoulders and took flight, entrails trailing like tentacles grasping at empty air. Athena reached into her nanoverse to draw a sword as the head hissed raged at her, showing three-inch fangs.

Penanggalan. He made penanggalan. It's a trap. And I led us right into it.

***

When the tower exploded, Crystal was flung away from the others, hurling off the tower and through the air. *It was a bloody trap, and I triggered it,* she thought. *Stupid!*

The ground rushed up at her, and she quickly twisted to lower her gravity before she splattered against the hard stones. She touched down gently, scanning the horizon for any possible threats. *It can't just be that one explosion. Moloch wouldn't have left it to chance that we'd stumble across it.*

She'd landed close to Moloch's exit portal, an area that had been relatively untouched by the earlier battle. She didn't see the others, although a speck in the distance might be Horus in falcon form. Athena, Dianmu, Anansi...*you have to assume they're okay,* Crystal told herself. Until she knew otherwise. There wasn't anything she could-

A clap of thunder tore through the air. *No, not thunder. That's a sonic boom. Someone's fighting.* Of course. Moloch must have left monsters waiting somewhere. Crystal turned on her heel to rush in that direction and felt a hand grab her foot.

Reflex kicked in, and she leapt upwards as hard as she could. With her personal gravity still decreased, the motion carried her a good twenty feet into the air. She held out her hands, realizing how horribly exposed she was. If anything else was laying in wait, she'd just announced her presence as badly as if she'd screamed.

But there was the immediate threat to deal with. Crystal reached the apex of her leap and scanned the ground.

The "threat" was half-buried by rubble. It was a man. He could be one of Moloch's, or he might be a Canaanite survivor. Either way, he'd have information.

She landed and took a tentative step towards the man. "Hey. Hold on a second, let me get you out of there."

When she cleared the stones away from his head, she saw an older, bearded face. It was a face she knew: Resheph, the god of plague. "Ishtar?" he asked, his voice weak.

She quickly began clearing more of the rubble. "In the flesh, love. Don't try to move, you look like you're in a right state. I'll have you out in a jiff."

"No...time," he coughed, a phlegmatic sound that made Crystal shudder. Usually, the sick didn't particularly bother her, but hearing Resheph cough used to be a death sentence. He'd been able to concoct diseases that even gods couldn't resist. The black plague had been his idea, his plan to stop the advance of Genghis Khan.

The revulsion must have shown on her face, but he shook his head. "No...illness...I wouldn't..."

"I know," Crystal said, lifting a piece of debris and tossing it aside. The others would have to get along without her until she freed him. "Just an old reflex, yeah?"

He nodded slightly, a slow gesture that caused him to scrunch his face in pain. "Moloch. It was-"

"Yeah, he's been a right pain in my arse for a bit now," Crystal said as she lifted another stone. "No need to waste the energy – I'm here because I was following him. I don't suppose you managed to infect him with anything nasty?"

Resheph shook his head as Crystal heaved the last rock from his stomach. This revealed why Resheph was having so much trouble speaking, and Crystal did her best not to let her horror show. He'd been impaled, a spear driven straight through his spine and then broken off by the collapsing rubble.

"He took them," Resheph managed to spit out, ichor leaking from his mouth.

"Took what? We saw Marquod earlier..."

Resheph shook his head, and Crystal went silent to let him continue.

It took him a bit to manage to speak again, and in the silence, Crystal could hear the sounds of distant battle. *I shouldn't be wasting time. He's out of that mess, so he'll keep. I should be getting back to-*

"The...verses. He took them."

Crystal winced. "So he's going to destroy them," she said. This wasn't how things were supposed to be. Enki had escalated every fight to life or death, and now Moloch was continuing that tradition.

All these ages, Crystal thought, *we managed to war without final death. Now, all that has changed.*

"Monsters," Resheph said. "Heard him talking...to his followers. They were going to..."

"Oh no." Crystal wanted to be sick. Moloch was a master of crafting monsters out of dead gods. With all the nanoverses he'd have from his attack here... he'd have an army. Hecatoncheires. Dragons. Medusae. Probably things she couldn't dream of - and he'd have an entire *pantheon's* worth...He would be unstoppable. "Did he say where he was going?"

Again, with great effort, Resheph shook his head.

"Okay. Did he take yours?"

Resheph smiled slightly. "No. Managed to...bring building down...on myself." He tapped a pouch on his belt. "Got it right-" the last word was cut off by more of that disgusting coughing. A chunk of viscera flew from his mouth, and Crystal turned her eyes away.

"Okay," she said, her mind racing. "Resheph. Other gods, my allies, are fighting for their lives. I need to get back to them. Your spine is severed, love. How do you want me to deal with that?"

He didn't need to think about it. "Do it. Quick."

Without waiting, Crystal brought her sword down into Resheph's skull. The sound was sickening, as always, but she maintained eye contact until the light went out in Resheph's eyes. She reached down and scooped up his nanoverse before a quick twist set his corpse on fire.

It was a choice she'd made before when the injury was bad enough.

Without wasting any more time, she turned and headed towards the sound of battle, moving in giant leaps augmented by her decreased gravity. She just hoped she would be in time to help.

***

The penanggalan's entrail tentacles whipped at Athena. She surrounded herself with a bubble of air and pushed herself away, the tentacles slapping against the barrier. They didn't find purchase, and the penanggalan hissed in rage while surging to close the distance between them.

Athena rolled to get more distance, slashing her sword through the air. A few of the tendrils went flying away, and the penanggalan recoiled from the blow.

Around her, more torsos were detaching from bodies, their heads whipping around to focus on her with eyes full of malice. *Worry about them later.* The one in front of her was closing the gap, spittle dripping from its screaming mouth.

Athena hurled her sword directly at her attacker's skull. A quick twist as she let go of the sword and the weapon let out a sonic boom as it accelerated.

The sword didn't just punch through the penanggalan's skull. It *detonated* it, and a red mist erupted from around the penanggalan. The creature's entrails fell to the ground limply.

Useful knowledge, Athena thought, already moving again. She hadn't been sure the destruction of the head would be fatal. The immense sound, coupled with the rather gory display, gave the other penanggalan pause. Athena seized on their distraction to leap with all her might, propelling herself further out of the circle with a gust of air. Midair, she held out her hand and called her sword back to her. It flew into her grip, and she was barely able to bring it up to meet the bite of the next attacker. *They're fast,* she thought as the two halves of the skulls fell to the ground, revealing three more creatures closing the distance.

The penanggalan didn't appear to be stupid. They weren't rushing in as blindly now that Athena had felled two of their brethren. Instead, they attacked from different directions, keeping their grasping entrails extended so she couldn't just block them out. Athena felt their slimy lengths brush against her arms and fought desperately, finding herself losing ground with each strike.

And still more came. Like the hydra, for every one she cut down, two or more filled the gap. One of them got its tendrils around her arm, and before she could cut herself free, it yanked with a strength that caught her off guard. It didn't quite pull her off balance, but it did propel itself close.

Athena felt fangs sink into her arm. Another tentacle wrapped around her leg and yanked, and a penanggalan bit deeply into her calf. Athena let out a cry of pain, and a third wrapped its entrails around her waist and bit the back of her neck. Already they were drawing strength from her, feasting on divine Ichor. Too much longer, and she would be too weak to keep the fight up.

Fortunately, Athena fought well in close combat.

She grabbed elemental threads with her free hand. This wasn't an intricate weaving, pulling in threads to create a delicate construct. This was a direct, brute force transmutation of Air into Flame.

The world exploded around her. A thin layer of elemental Water protected her from incinerating herself, but the impact of the sudden flame drove her to her knees. The penanggalan that were attached to her screamed as they burned. The remaining swarm hesitated at the display, floating out of her reach to study her with beady eyes.

Athena took a slow breath, steadying herself and rising to her feet. She'd beaten back the first assault and had bought herself time to think.

The penanggalan weren't all waiting to see what she would do next. Several of them broke away and latched onto some of the bodies that still littered the battlefield, and when they finished feeding on a body, it became a new penanggalan and joined their ranks.

Athena swore. Some of the creatures were fully fed, hale and healthy and brimming with blood, and she could see the excess energy swirling around them as a sickly mass of crimson smoke. That was going to make them far more dangerous than the first group.

She reached up and twisted as several dozen penanggalan turned to face her. She sent shards of stone hurtling at them, a barrage of bullets flying from the ground. The penanggalans' writhing intestines lashed out, batting the projectiles away before they could reach their targets.

They're too fast, Athena thought as they snarled in excitement and began to rush in. She changed to direct twists of Air, blades of condensed wind cutting into the approaching monstrosities. They bled but endured the strikes and continued to advance. What would it take to kill them?

A tendril wrapped around her arm again. This time, when the penanggalan tugged at her, she went stumbling towards it. Her sword flashed, but another pair of tendrils whipped around her sword arm. The twin penanggalan began to tug her from both sides.

Then the pressure on the right vanished, and Athena swung her sword around and rammed it through the face of the penanggalan still attached to her.

Dianmu had arrived, her glaive flashing down on one of the monsters. It didn't cleave the penanggalan as neatly as Athena's sword had, but it did the job.

"I got your message," Dianmu said with a fierce grin.

"Nothing quite like a sonic boom to give away your location." Athena got back to her feet, breathing heavily. "The others?"

Another penanggalan moved in. Athena dropped to a crouch to ready herself for the charge, and Dianmu raised her glaive. Before either of them could reach it, a rolling buzzsaw of air caught it mid-flight. Anansi stepped into view, that implacable grin still on his face. "Hopefully, Horus and Crystal are on their way," he said. "Want to see how many we can take out before they get here?"

Athena threw her sword again, adding the supersonic twist to accelerate it towards a new target. Anansi's confidence was appreciated, although she suspected it was feigned. The penanggalan were brutally effective killers and outnumbered the gods significantly. Athena doubted it would be easy.

The one she'd targeted caught her sword, proving her point. It tossed the formerly supersonic projectile aside and snarled as it dove. Athena reached into her nanoverse to grab another blade, her teeth gritting in determination.

"Let's," Athena said to Anansi, raising her sword.

The three gods rushed to meet the penanggalan in a clash of steel on flesh. Athena hacked with her sword, only barely aware of Dianmu and Anansi in her peripheral vision. The penanggalan in front of her croaked as she shoved her blade down its throat. She had to duck as another one groped for her neck. She swung the sword upward and slammed the impaled penanggalan against her new adversary. They burst like ripe fruit.

Athena leapt up, tentacles passing through the space she had just vacated and tossed a blade of air down beneath her. It severed some of the appendages, but now the penanggalan were racing up to meet her. She flipped her feet up behind her and descended with her sword held out, slashing at the brutes as they drew closer. A tentacle wrapped around her ankle and she had to curl up to break it free, exposing her back to the mouths below. Two latched on to her, one biting into her side and the other her shoulder and Athena shouted in pain as they started to feed.

She kept her back downward as she hit the ground. It drove the wind from her but turned her attackers into paste. She rolled, but another creature managed to get its tendrils around her throat. Anansi's daggers sliced them away before they could constrict. Athena slashed out with her sword, freeing Dianmu from one that had latched onto her arm with tentacles and fangs. Dianmu's glaive flashed and completed the circle, cutting away a third that was veering towards Anansi.

The penanggalan were taking advantage of their numbers, wrapping around the trio, forcing them to fight back to back. Anansi threw daggers from his nanoverse, imbuing each one with an animating force that let them harry the penanggalan. Dianmu lanced out with her glaive, stabbing at any creature that dared get too close. Athena kept her slashes up, cutting the tentacles down.

And yet, their numbers barely dwindled. One of them began to snatch Anansi's flying daggers out of the air, hurling them back at the Trickster. Athena heard him grunt as one sunk into his shoulder. Another got its tendrils wrapped around Dianmu's glaive and with an immense surge, pulled the weapon free from her grasp. Dianmu sent out a stream of lightning to strike the creature, but they were closing in. Athena struck with her sword, only to find the mass of tentacles closing around her arm, immobilizing it, pulling her closer to a penanggalan's waiting maw.

Athena raised her free hand, pressing it against the penanggalan's forehead and keeping it at a safe distance. Her palm was slippery with blood and threatened to slide off at any moment. The penanggalan snarled and snapped at her. This one was the strongest yet, and she could feel her elbow start to bend under pressure. It was getting closer.

No, Athena thought, pushing down as hard as she could manage. She laced her fingers in the monster's hair, stopping her hand from sliding any further.

Her arm started to tremble, and she couldn't get her other hand free to twist. She gritted her teeth and planted her feet, pushing with all her might against the penanggalan's head. It was strong enough to contend with divine strength. *Something* had to give.

And then, one by one, she could feel the penanggalan's hairs tearing loose under her grip. Just as her handholds were about to break free, the penanggalan's head jerked back, and it slumped to the ground. The pressure on her arm relaxed, and the sharp report of gunfire reached her ears.

Horus had entered the fray, taking a position on one of the nearby towers. His assault rifle was swept across the battlefield, constantly finding new targets. Athena could see he was twisting reality around the barrel of his gun, doing something to the bullets. It didn't matter what. She had an opening now, and with her arms free, she slashed at another monster.

Horus had drawn attention with that attack. A dozen of the creatures were taking to the air and swarming towards him. Horus threw up a barrier between himself and the monsters, then emptied his magazine into a pair of them. Athena had to give him a nod of respect. He was opening holes in his barrier as fast as the weapon could fire and closing them behind the bullets. She'd never seen someone pull that off with anything faster than an arrow. His attackers slumped to the ground, and he tossed the gun aside to switch to a melee weapon.

Then a penanggalan grabbed Athena by the throat and began to pull her in. She stifled a new surge of panic and swung her sword, severing the grasping appendages. It let out a hiss of anger and pain, which she cut short by embedding the blade in its face.

For the first time in the fight, no new opponent rushed in to take the place of its fallen kin, giving Athena time to look around the battlefield. There were still a few penanggalan active, but most were lying on the ground in various states of destruction. As she watched, Anansi cleaved another in half from chin to skull, and Dianmu electrocuted three with a bolt of lightning thrown from her recovered glaive.

A new swarm started to rise from the corpses, the fully fed penanggalan from earlier. Athena didn't even have the energy to curse this time. Every last bit of strength she had would be needed if she'd have a chance to survive-

The thought was cut off by Crystal striding onto the battlefield, drawing a sword and shouting. "Oy! Looks like you couldn't take those three down; maybe give me a try, yeah?"

The Penanggalan hissed and surged towards her as one. As Athena watched, Crystal leapt among the penanggalan like a sylph, flitting and flowing between them. Her slender sword sliced the eye out of one of her attackers as she jumped over the encroaching entrails of another, letting her foot connected with that attacker's nose. As she landed, she flipped her blade out to intercept another in a single fluid motion, so quick that the second penanggalan was cut in half before Crystal's foot touched the ground.

A tentacle lanced out and wrapped around Crystal's ankle. That was when Athena moved, throwing a twist of air to sever the appendage before it could throw off Crystal's balance.

The swarm was converging on Crystal, freeing the weary gods to grab bows from their nanoverses and open fire.

The penanggalan fell like flies before the barrage.

Chapter 15

Consequences and Considerations

Athena wanted nothing more than to fall back into the soil and sleep for the next year. If it hadn't been so badly soaked with monstrous blood, she might have actually considered it. "Everyone accounted for?" she asked.

Crystal was breathing heavily and leaning on her sword for support. She wiped some sweat-soaked strands of hair back from her face and looked up at the other gods. "Sorry for the delay!" she said, her voice full of forced cheer. "Thanks for saving a few for me."

Anansi stood up, pulling a dagger out of a dead penanggalan with a sickening lurch. He had a dozen small injuries and one deep wound on his left bicep, where one of his attackers had gotten its teeth deep into the muscle. "I would have killed them all on my own, but I would have-" he grunted in pain and shook his head. "But I would have hated to deny you the fun."

Dianmu flicked her glaive, clearing it of blood. Deep bruises were starting to form on her arms and neck. She rubbed at her eyes. "I'm not in the mood for the japes," she said to Anansi, though her voice wasn't unkind. "Thank you. All of you. That swarm was...trying."

Athena could feel multiple injuries throbbing for attention. *If there had been a few more, or Crystal and Horus had been a bit later...we might have lost someone.*

Dianmu limped over to Crystal, using the butt of her glaive as a walking stick. "I trust you had something fairly important to keep your attention?" she asked Crystal.

Crystal gave her a good-natured grin. "Your trust is well placed, love, because I did." The smile faded quickly as Crystal focused on the news itself. "I ran into Resheph. Moloch came here to kill off his own pantheon and scoop up their nanoverses."

Athena swore. It was a slaughter on the scale of nothing she'd heard of before. Theomachies - wars between gods - were not unheard of. The Aesir had warred with the Deva in a conflict that had lasted a century and was remembered in both their respective faiths into modern times. The Olympians had fought with the Titans and caused the Bronze Age collapse. Sekhmet had nearly wiped out the Lower Kingdom in her personal war against the rest of the Egyptian pantheon. Yet even in those bloody battles, and the more genteel conflicts that had followed, Nanoverses were rarely taken. It was...monstrous.

"You think he means to create a newly merged nanoverse with all the ones he recovered?" Athena asked.

"Maybe," Crystal said, frowning. "He has at least a dozen now. If he does what Enki did, he'll be damn near unstoppable, but..."

"But?" Dianmu prompted after Crystal trailed off.

"Resheph was talking about monsters," Crystal said, pursing her lips. "If Moloch plans on taking them into his nanoverse and...well, popping them to create monsters, from an entire pantheon this old..."

"That is more his style," Athena said after some thought. "No risk to him, and at the same time, a massive increase to the power he commands." It made a disgusting amount of sense. He'd be unimaginably dangerous with that many newborn monsters at his disposal - although...

"It would still be better than if he merged them," Dianmu said, echoing Athena's thought. "Do you really think he won't?"

Crystal nodded. "I've been thinking about it. We assumed the fight with Enki was, well, winnable, because he was predictable. But what if that wasn't it? What if he was just overwhelmed by how much power he was holding, so had to stick to his classics, or copying someone else?"

"You think Moloch doesn't want that to happen to him," Anansi said, stroking his beard and frowning.

"It makes sense. Moloch's never been big on direct conflict." Crystal fiddled with her hands as she worked through the thought. "He's like Enki, in his own way. Rigid and stuck in his habits. Sure, if he merged that many nanoverses he'd be..." Crystal swallowed. "Well, I don't want to think about how strong he'd be. But what would he do with the power? He would benefit more from an army of monsters."

"So there's a chance," Anansi said. There was a note of hope in his voice, one he was trying, and failing, to suppress. Athena couldn't prevent herself from feeling the same surge of hope. It was a powerful drug, and one she tried to avoid imbibing too often, but in this case...

Athena looked at Crystal. "Do you really think Moloch might want to avoid that risk?" she asked, knowing the hope was showing and not caring. "With so much to gain, he'd let fear stop him from seizing that much power?"

Crystal considered for a long pause, then slowly nodded. "There's a lot of bad names you could call Moloch. Bastard. Prick. Asshole. Monster. Jackass."

"Would-be-tyrant," Dianmu added.

"Murdering coward," Anansi contributed.

They all looked at Athena, who frowned in thought, searching for the right phrase to sum up her feelings on Moloch, "Sociopathic traitor not fit to lick the paws of the lowliest, flea-bitten cur to have ever begged for scraps."

"Nice," Crystal said. "We could probably list them all day. But none of them are 'idiot' or any of its variants, yeah? If Enki succumbed to sensory overload from two, Moloch would be driven mad by thirteen."

Athena let out a long, steady breath. "I hope you are right," she said. "Because I don't know how we could possibly defeat someone with that much power. The three of us barely bested Enki, and only survived doing so by turning his power against him. Even with six of, I doubt we could defeat Moloch if he managed thirteen."

"If it took three people to beat someone with one extra," Anansi said, "then we'd need at least...what? Thirty-nine gods if Moloch went for broke?"

A falcon flew down from the sky, shifting into Horus as it landed.

Dianmu sighed. "Let's assume for now that the merger is not his goal. Then he would have another reason for taking these nanoverses, and creating monsters seems to be the most logical intent."

"Maybe," Horus said, "he's just eliminating our possible allies."

"Good of you to join us," Athena said. "Did you find any other survivors?"

Horus shook his head. "They're all dead, and their nanoverses are gone."

Silence reigned as the gods considered the implication. An entire pantheon, gone. Nothing like it had ever happened before.

"I saved Resheph," Crystal said in a small voice, tapping a pouch at her side. "I killed him and destroyed his body, but his nanoverse is safe. He'll resurrect there safely, so that's..." She trailed off.

Athena suddenly realized that something like this *had* happened before. Enki had done the same thing to his old pantheon. Crystal was the only survivor.

Was this what it was like for you, Crystal? Athena thought. If not for the others, she would have gone over to hug her friend. Instead, she said, "It is *something*. Maybe he can tell us more, once he resurrects."

"I don't think we can afford to wait," Dianmu countered. "Moloch will be moving onto the next stage of whatever he's planning."

Anansi nodded. "He only has a few days before he has to worry about these gods resurrecting and coming to reclaim their nanoverses, so he can't dawdle too much. And I think there's a flaw in your theory, Horus."

Horus bristled. "I'd love to hear a better explanation, old spider."

Anansi sighed. "I do not know. But if he was seeking to deny us allies, he chose a poor method for doing so."

"Anansi is right," Dianmu interjected before Horus could argue. "If we tell other gods what happened here, they'll begin to fear Moloch will come for them even if they mean to stay on the sidelines. It could be a rallying cry for our cause. He *must* have a plan for those nanoverses."

Horus looked like he'd just taken a swig of stale, sour beer. "Fine. Then we need to figure out for sure what he's doing with them. That will help us find him and deal with him permanently."

Again, no one was sure what to say. Horus was right about that...but it didn't get them any closer to an answer.

Crystal opened her mouth, but whatever thought she had was cut short. At that instant, breaking the silence that had fallen over the group, the darkened entry portal surged back into life.

Immediately the five gods scattered, surrounding the portal and assuming defensive positions. *This can't be happening,* Athena thought. *Another attack? Right now? We're too tired.*

Then, to her immense relief, Ryan dove through the portal, sword in hand. They watched as he rolled behind cover, unknowingly parroting Athena's earlier entry.

It wasn't a bad call; in fact, it was precisely the right call when going through an unknown portal. However, doing it when no adversaries were present struck Athena as so...so *Ryan* that she had to smile. "It's all right, Ryan. The fighting's already over."

"Oh," Ryan said, his cheeks flushing slightly from the theatrics. "Okay, good. Everyone okay?" Athena nodded with the others, and Ryan let out a sigh of relief. "Great, glad to hear it. So...what happened?"

Athena shook her head. "We'll fill you in. But right now...we have Hungers to attend to, and there's nothing left for us here. Let's head back to the core before this portal goes dark again."

***

Some of Dale's contemporaries had trouble with presidents who had never served in the military. Many even went so far as to talk about them, in private, with outright contempt, calling commanders-in-chief who had never been commanded "cowards" and "dilettantes". Dale thought those opinions were far too extreme. The President's job was so immensely complicated that anyone who held the office would lack knowledge and experience in some areas; if it weren't the military, it would be something else, and a different group of people would be privately rolling their eyes.

However, that didn't mean that Dale *enjoyed* dealing with a president who had never been on the front lines, or even the back lines, had mostly been leading the country during a time of peace and had no practical understanding of the need for, and the difficulties of, rapid military response.

Especially when that President was dressing him down.

"Let me recap in simple terms," President Thomas Mason snapped. "You identified Ryan Smith, Antichrist, god, superhero, or whatever the hell he is, entering his sister's apartment building."

The President paused, waiting for a response. Dale held out as long as politeness allowed, then kept it to just a simple, "Yessir," because that was what you said when the President asked you a question, even if it was a question you had already answered.

"And, upon getting this information, without consulting this office, you decided to engage the target?"

"Yessir."

At that, the President of the United States of America, the leader of the free world, slammed his hand on the desk like a teacher trying to get the attention of an unusually thick student. "You *unilaterally authorized a strike on U.S. civilians on U.S. soil?!"*

"Yessir." It was amazing how politely insolent two syllables could sound with enough practice.

President Mason growled. "Admiral. You...how do you think this is acceptable? For God's sake, man, you launched missiles on an apartment building. It's on the evening news! Have you seen it?"

Dale had seen it, but before he could say so, the President started a replay. Dale decided the best move was to shut up and watch, yet again, a news report on the destruction of the apartment building.

"This amateur footage clearly shows a United States Navy Helicopter, the X91 'Barn Owl' opening fire on this apartment complex. Witnesses claim that their cell phones were confiscated after the incident, but this live-streamed video was already available online. There are unconfirmed reports that three Barn Owls were destroyed by a counterattack. The Navy has refused to comment on the incident, but the President has scheduled a press conference at seven PM EST."

President Mason glared at Dale. "Seven PM EST, Admiral. Now, please, tell me what the *hell* I'm supposed to say to the press about what happened here?"

"The truth, sir?" Dale said, his tone slightly less stiff. If the President was asking for his advice, he wasn't going to terminate project Myrmidon, and he wasn't going to court-martial Dale. *Not yet, at least. He might still do it once this is all over. But until then...*

"The truth? That one of my Admirals launched a strike on United States soil, and I knew nothing about it?" A vein bulged in the President's forehead.

"No, sir. That Ryan Smith, the super-powered terrorist responsible for detonating a nuclear device in Canada, was in that apartment. That we cleared the apartment building of civilians before we attacked."

"And that after all that, Ryan Smith is still alive and out there?" Mason asked, clenching his hands into fists. "That we *failed*?"

"That we attempted," Dale replied. "That we only failed because those cowards in Congress won't allow the needed funding to truly deal with a threat of this magnitude. That the threat is still at large because we're operating on a shoestring budget, and we could have had him if the bleeding hearts had not drug their heels."

The truth was, Project Myrmidon was already funded for the next decade. It was a small operation and was able to rely on technology they were developing in house. However, the truth wasn't necessary at the moment. The President needed an answer that would mollify the public and appease his base, and Dale's suggestion would do that. Emphasize the size of the threat, the precautions taken to ensure public safety, and then blame Congress. Really, it would be a politician's dream soundbite.

"All right," President Mason said after a moment. "I can sell that. But no more of this, Admiral. No more attacks on American soil."

"I can't promise that, Mister President," Dale said carefully. "Right now, every piece of intelligence we have on Ryan Smith is based on his connections within the United States. We can't predict anywhere he might go outside of our borders, and that means we'll always be one step behind."

Dale tried to think of a way to argue that the failure in Ghana was worse than the defeat and California but couldn't figure out how to do it. He decided that it was best not to mention that incident at all.

The President sighed. "No more missiles, Admiral. No more explosives. You get your job done with the Myrmidons, and if that means you have to sit out a possible engagement, then that's what you do. No attacks on the target unless the Myrmidons are ready to handle the situation on their own. Am I clear on *that,* at least?"

"Yes, sir." This time, the two-word answer held no insolence. In truth, the attack on Ryan had driven home what both Lazzario and Pivarti had been telling Dale: a threat of this type would *only* be stopped by unconventional means. The Myrmidons were his only answer.

"Good. Now get out of my office, and don't screw the pooch again. The next time I call you in here, it had better be because we have something to celebrate."

***

Lazzario Littleton, supernerd and comic writer extraordinaire, had been adamant that no one should be allowed to communicate with Bast. "Ninety percent of the time," he'd said, "someone is going to get too chummy with the prisoner. That always leads to disaster. It's going to be tempting to take off the mask to interrogate her, but that absolutely cannot happen. Furthermore, a man should never be around the prisoner without supervision. Romantic interest is the leading cause of sympathy."

Cassandra found it both amusing and sad that Lazzario seemed to have forgotten that a woman could be attracted to another woman. Cassandra herself had no such inclinations, but it could happen. She was grateful for his oversight, though, because it meant that no one was focused on her unsupervised evenings in the lab.

She had rejected the idea that she should let comic book tropes run her life. Lazzario's attitude, which the rest of the team had adopted, prevented them from gaining valuable knowledge. Questioning Bast could give them so much insight into history, science, and the nature and power of these divine beings. She hated that they were missing a golden opportunity because of needless paranoia.

As for sympathy, that had nothing to do with romantic attraction or fictional logic. It was a matter of basic human decency. Bast was a criminal? Fine. A prisoner? Fine. An unwilling experimental subject? Every day that became harder for Cassandra to justify, but she'd made her peace with it. However, they should be trying to do their work in the most humane way possible, instead of strapping a sentient, intelligent *person* to a table without food, water, or mental stimulation. Even lab rats were treated better than that.

Cassandra stopped outside the door to the laboratory, taking a deep breath and glancing back and forth to make sure that the hallway was empty. It was a ridiculous habit that she couldn't seem to shake. Of course, the corridor would be abandoned; the guards didn't go beyond the security checkpoint without reason. She had checked in with Gary just a few minutes ago, so it wasn't like she was trying to hide. Besides, she had every right to be here and had been working late for days without anyone paying particular attention.

The lab was empty, just as she'd expected.

"Hello, Bast," she said. "It's just us, so give me just a second to get the mirror in place."

Bast raised a single thumb. They had managed to add some *very* limited hand gestures to Bast's silent communication, taking it a tiny step past blinking once for yes and twice for no. It was small progress, but progress nonetheless.

As she began to position the mirror, Cassandra reflected that it was a little challenging to start these talks. Social niceties like "How are you?" seemed inappropriate, if not downright cruel. She had decided that it was best to just jump right in since Bast certainly wasn't capable of directing the conversation.

"Before...all of this, did you ever get lonely?" she asked.

Bast gave her a single blink of affirmation.

"Even when you were part of a pantheon?" Cassandra pressed.

Bast blinked again, and although it was hard to see through the small holes in the mask, Cassandra thought the goddess's lips twist in bitter amusement.

"It's funny," she said, "how other people can make you feel lonely. I look at my coworkers and listen to them talk, and usually, it makes me feel worse. They have their families and friends and hobbies, and I just...never got around to those things."

Last night, when she couldn't sleep, Cassandra had taken stock of her life. She had always been driven and focused on her goals, so much so that friends had drifted away and boyfriends had stalked away. She had left so much for "after": after undergrad, her thesis, her Ph.D., establishing herself in her field. Only recently had she realized that now, when "after" was here, she didn't know how to begin finding the connections she'd ignored for so long.

"I think I talk to you more in an evening than I talk to other people in a week," she told Bast. "Unless you count work talk, I guess."

In Bast's eyes, she saw sympathy and understanding. Human emotions. Human eyes. The subject of an inhuman experiment.

Cassandra looked around the lab, the end goal of her years of study and work and sacrifice and hated herself for being there.

***

It was a relief for Dale to be back in the base, away from the stuffy air of Washington and its politicians trying to tell him how to save the damn world. It was obnoxious, but the only thing that mattered was stopping the Antichrist. Anything else – his career, his life, his President, maybe even his country – could be sacrificed in pursuit of that goal. His team seemed to be the only ones who truly understood the situation. Parvathi might be cold and distant, but she was dedicated to the cause. Lazzario might be irritating, but he knew what they were up against. The rest of them, all of them, were - in a way Dale had never imagined before - heroes. They'd never held a gun, but they were fighting in their own way.

"I think that went as well as we could have hoped for, Admiral," Lazzario said. "The President isn't overly restricting us, and...well, it appears that these beings are pretty much immune to conventional firearms. We haven't lost anything."

"Sir, may I ask a question?"

Dale turned to Jake, shocked to hear him doing anything other than mindlessly agreeing with everything Lazzario said. "Go ahead."

"Thank you, sir." Jake looked slightly uncomfortable at having Dale's full attention, but he plunged ahead. "One thing that often happens when, when these situations get out of hand is...well, off the top of my head, I can think of four films, three television shows, twenty-three novels, and forty-six comic book issues where the President orders a nuclear strike on American soil to destroy an unconventional threat when even unconventional measures have failed. Do we...I mean, should we..."

Dale shook his head to reassure him. "The President never would, and the Joint Chiefs agree with this assessment. These beings triggered a nuclear strike on Canadian soil as part of a fight amongst themselves. Until we know what they're capable of, no one is going to suggest turning the conflict between them and us into a nuclear one. Not unless they escalate it first."

Pivarti tapped her fingers on the table. "I don't think they will," she said after a moment's thought. "In fact, I'm certain of it. Ryan and his cohorts deliberately led Enki to Graham Island for that fight. In their first battle, at an abandoned gas station, they triggered a tornado. When they fought Enki in a populated area, they did so with much more limited attacks. Whatever this man's end goal is, he's trying to maintain the appearance of caring about civilian life."

Jake slumped with relief.

"Now," Dale said, leaning back in his chair. "Suggestions for our next move? I'm tired of being a purely a reactionary force. I want something we can do proactively."

"We're already monitoring every connection Smith has," Lazzario said. "It paid off once before."

"Which means," Dale said, fighting to suppress a sigh, "that we can't count on it working a second time. We have to assume he's not a moron and will figure that his sister wasn't the only one being watched."

"We don't have to assume," Parvathi said. "I think we have sufficient evidence that he, or someone working with him, has a decent amount of strategic capabilities. I still think we should keep monitoring the likely people and locations, but we cannot count on him being stupid."

"What about using his own tactic?" Jake asked. "Smith used a media blast to challenge Enki and draw him out. If we did the same thing, he'd probably realize it was a trap, but he has to be pretty angry with us right now, so there's a good chance he would show up anyway. It might even force his hand and make him reckless."

"The only way we can do that is to expose this entire operation to the general public," Dale said. "That's not a risk I'm ready to take. As far as we know, the only outsiders who know about us are the Antichrist and his followers. If we go public, we'd likely give the other unnatural beings a reason to rally behind the Antichrist, to work together."

"I agree," Lazzario said. "Although we'll want to keep it in reserve in case Ryan exposes us."

"Then what about going after the others?" Parvathi said, drawing eyes to herself. "Once the new harnesses are complete, why not attempt targeting some of the gods we have locations for? Moloch, for example. We know he's in Venezuela."

Dale grimaced. "After the fiasco in Ghana, the Venezuelan government is not interested in allowing us entry. They believe they have Moloch contained. That doesn't preclude a black ops operation, but we're going to need to be certain before we move."

"Then perhaps we should hold off," Lazzario said. "I know we want, and need, to be more proactive, but we don't have the new harnesses yet. How long until we do?"

Pivarti frowned in consideration. "Twelve hours until they're ready for deployment."

"Then we reconvene in twelve hours," Dale said, "with proposals for next steps. Get to work on them, because I want to be impressed."

As the meeting broke up, Doctor Pivarti intercepted him. "Admiral, a moment, please?"

He nodded for her to go ahead.

"The Black Stone has recently undergone a rapid, unexpected chromatic metamorphosis, including a manifestation of an auditory abnormality. We're not sure what it means, or what impact it could have."

The Admiral had to take a moment to process that. He sometimes wondered if she deliberately chose the most obtuse possible words to explain herself. "So it changed color and started making a noise?" he asked.

Doctor Pivarti nodded. "If you wish. To be even more accurate, it turned a deep red."

"And the noise?"

"Well sir, to be perfectly frank, it sounds like a heartbeat."

Admiral Bridges became aware of a sound that had been at the edge of hearing since he'd arrived back at the base. A deep, bass noise that was felt as much as heard.

Lub-dub. Lub-dub. Lub-dub.

"I see," he said. Mostly what he saw was a puzzle without any useful answers, but now that he was aware of the sound, it was rapidly grating on his nerves. "Any change to the subject?"

"No, sir," Pivarti said, some of the tension fading from her face. "And I do have a piece of good news. While you were in D.C., our team had a breakthrough on a new deployment method. The Black Stone appears to be an extradimensional space. By shunting matter through that space through an artificial gateway, we can relocate it anywhere on the planet."

Dale felt himself starting to smile. It was a good feeling, one he didn't indulge in often enough. "How quickly?"

"Anywhere within the country in five minutes, sir. Anywhere on the planet within, at most, fifteen. With enough power, we can take our people anywhere in the solar system within an hour."

Dale's eyes lit up. The long term implications of this...were not of his concern. Short term, however? It fundamentally leveled the playing field.

"Be sure to let the team know that they should incorporate that into their action plans. Well done, Doctor. Very well done."

***

Crystal stepped back into her staging area and turned on the real display.

She'd dropped Isabel off at a restaurant, promising to catch her up as soon as Crystal took care of a couple quick things. Isabel had seemed surprised by how abrupt Crystal was but had gone along with it. Crystal was glad she didn't have to answer too many questions. Her Hungers needed seeing to, but Isabel needed a chance to do some research on the internet and Crystal felt like she was going to go insane if she didn't see how her nanoverse was doing as soon as possible. *Please be okay, please be okay, please...*

Hope died at first. The cancerous bands of gas that spread between stars still existed. However, with a bit of focus, Crystal could see that they were mostly the dead remains of the Phoberia, mixed with her phobophages. It had worked. *It had worked.*

Relief flooded her. The phobophages had done their work, and the nanoverse was *hers* again. She almost wanted to dance.

Don't get ahead of yourself, love. Crystal thought. She'd removed one obstacle. One. But that didn't mean that the work was done. The stars were still unnatural colors, corrupt and twisted versions of what they had been.

On top of that, she could feel pressure in the back of her mind. There was some malignant power out there, thrumming within the fabric of the nanoverse. It was weaker, but it was there. Some thing, some force, was resisting her.

Crystal wanted to repeat the word impossible, but that word had started to lose all meaning. After a million years, she thought she knew the limits of what was and wasn't possible, and here, in her nanoverse, where her will was absolute, there should be no such thing as impossible.

*And yet...*and yet she had so much to learn. Most importantly, who, what, and how. So far, making big, sweeping changes hadn't drawn out her adversary.

So what if you try focusing, love? Crystal asked herself. She walked over the console. The fact that she was making progress, even if she still hadn't found a way to solve the problem, renewed her determination.

She pulled up a list of inhabited worlds. Dozens upon dozens appeared on her screen. Crystal pursed her lips as she went through the list. All these people...and she'd been ignoring them. Focused on the big things. Ignoring the individual acts of suffering that surrounded her. *Could I have helped them?*

Crystal pushed down that thought. It was something she could feel guilty about later. Right now, she didn't need to worry about what she should have done, but about what she could do now.

One particular species caught her eyes. The Sur-nah-him. Apparently, only one in ten Sur-nah-him lived past middle age. The rest died from violence or disease.

Their name, in their language, loosely translated to "those without hope", although the actual meaning was more nuanced. They had two hundred and fifty words for despair, and the word that she thought of as "hope" would probably best translate to "a belief that despair will decrease in the future".

Crystal stared at the words and cursed herself. These people were living in hell, and the best they dared hope for was that tomorrow would be slightly less terrible than today, then named themselves as a *species* after the belief that it would not.

Perhaps there were other people in this universe Crystal had failed more. But right now, the Sur-nah-him had her attention.

She dropped into her nanoverse's real time stream and set a course for their world, which they called Shadoth, or "the Hungering Rot".

From space, it was worse than she'd feared. Their world orbited one of the green stars. Tendrils of flame leapt from that star, waving around it like the lazy tentacles of a sleeping octopus. There was a world, uninhabited, within the tendrils' reach, and Crystal watched with sickened fascination as one of those tendrils washed over the planet. It turned stone to a molten substance that boiled like a witch's cauldron, sending toxic fumes into space. They'd ride the solar wind to sprinkle onto nearby planets, seeding them with carcinogenic particles.

She turned to face Shadoth itself, hoping things there would be better. *At least it's pretty,* Crystal thought, her lip curling. Shadoth's lands were a thousand shades of blue, which blended nicely into the ocean. The planet was dotted with cyan lakes as well, at a regularity that Crystal found odd but pretty, like gemstones littered across the landscape.

She reminded herself of the Sur-nah-him's mortality rate, and that was all she needed to make sure she didn't forget that looks can be deceiving. She swung the staging area around to get a better look at the planet, dropping into its atmosphere and bringing up her scanners. *Show me what's making his place so awful its people don't know hope.*

The landscape rushed up at her, and Crystal held her breath.

A group of a few dozen Sur-nah-him slumped across a blue grass plain beneath her. Their posture was hunched, their eyes sunken. Their skin was so taut that they looked like skeletons. They had hair, but it was thin and ragged. Crystal wanted to wave her hand and make them better, but a wretched appearance didn't prove a miserable existence.

The proof for that was in their surroundings.

The grass wrapped around their legs with every step, leaving angry red welts each time they tore loose. Thorn-covered tentacles lashed out from a bush, striking at the Sur-nah-him, who altered their path to avoid its reach. It seemed that every plant on this world was hostile. Crystal twisted her lip and threw a barrier of solid air between the bush and the people. *No one's dying while I figure this shit out.*

She could feel that corrupted, fragmented will push back against her, but it didn't impede her *too* actively. Just reminded her that she had to be careful while she was here. In her own nanoverse.

The thought gave her another chill.

Then there was a great crashing, and an enormous blob began to crest a hill. Pseudopods lanced out from its bulk, grasping and engulfing anything organic in its path. It was an amorphous blue mass, and the hill was being crushed under the sheer weight of the creature.

Crystal's eyes widened. This was one of the cyan lakes she'd found so compelling from orbit. They weren't bodies of water, but all-consuming organisms, and one of them was chasing the Sur-nah-him.

A few of the Sur-nah-him listlessly threw spears into the massive slime. Azure fluid poured from the wounds, and the bulk of the creature shuddered. More pseudopods erupted from the thing's surface and wrapped over the wounds. The leaking stopped.

It hadn't even paused in its forward progress.

The Sur-nah-him stared helplessly at the change. One sighed and began to trudge away. Another started to weep and fell to his knees. "No use...no use..." he said and held out his arms. "Just let it come for me."

The one that had sighed reached for the weeping man and tugged on his arm, but the weeper pulled his hand free. "No more. Go."

The sighing man tugged one more time, and when it didn't work, he shrugged and left the weeper to his fate. He wasn't running, just trudging through the grass that still tore at his ankles. There wasn't any hope in his eyes - the man expected to die. It was just a question of lasting longer than the others.

Sod this, Crystal thought. With a blink, she teleported out of her staging area, appearing between the Sur-nah-him and the monstrous amoeba. Its pseudopods diverted towards her.

That counter-will she kept feeling was a barrier to her omnipotence. It slowed her down, weakened her. Changes on the stellar scale were a challenge, and cosmic changes were impossible.

But this wasn't a star. It wasn't even a planet. Crystal was sure she could do something here.

Crystal held out her hand, and the pseudopods slapped against an invisible force field. The Sur-nah-him started to shout and point as the tendrils crept over her barrier. With a flick of her wrist, she tore the appendages off, changing them to a cloud of bubbles. The behemoth shuddered.

Stay away from my people, Crystal thought. In an instant, she dashed close enough to touch the creature. She struck its bulk. Ripples began to spread across the creature's membranous walls. The ripples intensified as they spread, and the creature's skin undulated. In seconds, the entire thing was vibrating wildly. Just as it seemed it would tear the ooze apart, the beast burst into another cloud of bubbles.

Crystal watched in satisfaction as the tiny bubbles rose into the air and drifted away. The Sur-nah-him gave her listless, vaguely confused looks. "I am Crystal," she said, using the calm but assured tones she called her "goddess voice." Over the millennia, it had done wonders to awe the various peoples of her nanoverse.

Here, it was met with dull silence until one finally stepped forward. "What happened to the Devourer?"

"I turned it into bubbles," Crystal said. She changed tactics, trying for the patient tones one would use to explain a difficult concept to a child. "I turned it into bubbles, and it floated away."

The speaker scowled at her tone, which was a relief. It was good to see that these people had some emotion other than acceptance. "I was able to observe that. How?"

"I'm your goddess, love. I know I've been away for a long time, but...hey, where are you all going?"

The Sur-nah-him were fleeing from her. Some screamed. Some covered their heads and wept. The one that had given up in the face of the creature was presently streaking away from *her*, tears streaming down his cheeks as he wailed.

Crystal watched them, her mouth open in shock and confusion. *How badly have I failed you?*

She took a step after them, but then stopped. What was she supposed to do? Trap them in their terror and hold them against their will? Force them to accept that she wasn't someone to fear, that she meant well? They'd probably die from fright if she tried the first, and for the second...Crystal had never, in any iteration of her nanoverse, violated a person's free will. She had no intention of starting now.

So she could only stand and watch them run, absorbing the full guilt of their terror. These people probably had invented their own goddesses over the millennia. What kind of deities did the people who named themselves "those who cannot even hope for a slight improvement" dream up? Crystal had to clench her eyes shut to stop the tears from flowing.

"I'm sorry," she said, even though they were out of earshot. "But I will make things better."

She rose into the air until she could see the curve of Shadoth. There were hundreds of those blue circles. Now that she knew to look for it, she could see them shambling across the landscape, leaving destruction in their wake. *No more.* Crystal braced herself for the resistance and began to spread her will across the world.

One of the Devourers beneath her trembled. Crystal fixed her gaze on the thing, pinning it in place. "No more," she said aloud.

The creature popped, bubbles floating into the air. One by one, its fellows followed - first shuddering, then bursting and drifting away. Purified of life, the water that had been trapped within them began to form clouds.

The tentacle-trees were lashing at the air, even with no prey nearby. Somehow, they sensed something wrong in their world and were trying to grasp at the source. Crystal snarled at them and focused her attention on the nearest one. At her command, it went rigid. An exoskeleton crept up its length until the tree was completely immobilized. She snapped her fingers, and the tentacles turned to antennae that grew through the chitinous coating. They fanned out and turned green as she added photosynthesizing structures to their cells.

They'd function close enough to trees now and would no longer need to feast on flesh.

On she went. Nothing too big, nothing so great it would push up against that wall of pressure, but enough to change the world.

When she was done, Shadoth wasn't a paradise, but it was...livable. The Sur-nah-him would have a chance to build. A chance to live and grow. A chance to hope.

It's enough. For now.

Crystal teleported back to her staging area. She pulled up the list of species again and started to count.

Seventy-two.

Let's see who's next, she thought, cracking her knuckles. At this rate, it would take her a couple decades in here to get to all of them.

Just enough time for Isabel to order food back in the Core.

Chapter 16

Rest, Relaxation, and Release

Isabel crossed her legs, resisting the urge to tap her foot.

Going through the internet for any information that could point to the United States government making its own gods was like looking for a needle in a needlestack. The internet was full of information that could lead that way...if one was willing to also accept that Beyoncé was controlling the masses with Illuminati hypnotic rituals in the form of dance moves, the Royal family was actually an ancient race of lizard people from space, Hitler's grandson was planning a fourth Reich in Argentina, and some combination of chemtrails and vaccines caused either autism, SIDS, or both.

Hell, half the internet seemed to believe that her brother and the other gods – as well as the monsters and the Heresiarch of the Church of Adversity – were actually government experiments gone rogue, and the radiation spike in Canada had been them trying to use a nuke to cover up the mess. Not that any of that was new information to her – when her brother had appeared on national news and *not answered her goddamn calls,* she'd started searching his name...

"You alright love?"

Crystal's voice shattered Isabel's train of thought. *Because it was unexpected. Not for any other reason,* Isabel reassured herself. "Welcome back," she said brightly. "And yeah, I'm fine. Why do you ask?"

Isabel was struck with how ordinary she seemed here; in jeans and a t-shirt, she'd pass for any other exceptionally beautiful twenty to thirty-something. Outside of a life and death situation, or a room full of stars, Crystal easily blended in with the rest of the crowd in the restaurant. *Really, though, what did you expect? Ryan looks mostly like himself if he actually bothered working out.*

The goddess arched an eyebrow at her. "Well, because for a moment there you looked like you just bit a lemon in half."

"Oh, it's just… I'm not one hundred percent over Ryan blowing me off for the first chunk of all this." Isabel shrugged. "I mean, I get the whole thing, but I was freaking out about him."

Crystal smiled warmly at her at that. "If it's any consolation, I think I did the same thing to my family when I was Nascent."

"You think?" Isabel asked.

"It was a million years ago, love. My memory may be good, but things do get a bit fuzzy, yeah?"

"Yeah," Isabel said softly.

"Penny for your thoughts?" Crystal asked.

"It's …it's stupid." Isabel shifted in her seat and decided to change the subject. "So what do you think of Moonburger?"

"I think it's perfect," Crystal said, smiling. "Wi-Fi for your research, a heavy dose of grease to fortify your stomach for an evening of drinking, and it doesn't look like anyone will care that we're going to hang around after we finished eating. I think I'm in love."

"I'm glad. I have a lot of good memories here." Crystal looked at her in askance, and Isabel went ahead. "When I was a kid, Dad would take us here after school every Wednesday, and made us promise not to tell Mom. Then Mom would take us on Saturdays while Dad was out golfing and make us promise not to tell him." Isabel laughed. "Then when Ryan started driving, we would come here on Mondays and promise each other not to tell Mom *or* Dad."

"Sounds like you two were tight," Crystal said.

Isabel nodded. "Oh yeah. Ryan was always a bit weird, but we never did a lot of those stupid sibling things. We'd fight, of course, but usually it wasn't over anything big and we never really hit each other, even when we were younger. I think when he was a kid, he was afraid he'd break me, and when we got older, well…" She shrugged. "I was a bit afraid *I'd* break *him*."

Crystal smiled. "Well, I'm glad you two had each other."

"Me, too. Especially when our parents died. I guess that's why…" There it was again, the subject she had been trying to avoid.

"Why it's still bothering you that he didn't get in touch?" Crystal guessed.

"Yeah. I've forgiven him, but I'm not quite past the hurt yet."

"Isabel, love, I know it's hard not to take that personally, but I promise you that it really wasn't personal. The first stages of Apotheosis are incredibly difficult even when you *don't* have an insane god and his posse hell-bent on destroying you. There's a difference between 'immediate' and 'important'. You're the most important person in the world to Ryan and given that everyone in the world has suddenly become his responsibility, that's saying something."

Isabel swallowed the sudden lump in her throat. "I hadn't thought of it like that. Thank you."

"You're welcome."

Again, Isabel looked for a new subject. "By the way, why are we going drinking tonight? I mean, it sounds like fun, but isn't there a little too much going on to take an evening off?"

"Everyone needs to take an evening off when they can get it, or we'd all go bonkers, yeah? And we can get it now because we're at a bit of a dead-end. That's the other reason we're going. Empyrean Provocation isn't just a club; it's a source of information, and I intend to find some. It's also neutral ground, and Ryan has someone he needs to talk to."

"So drinking and dancing is just a bonus?"

"Something like that." Crystal grinned. "It's also a lot of fun. By the by, love? Before you drink anything there – and I mean anything – make sure the bartender knows you're a normal mortal, yeah?"

"I mean, sure. But why does that matter?"

"Some of the drinks would kill a mortal outright. Others could leave you a drooling idiot for weeks, some will ensnare your will and make you the slave of the first person to say your name, some will-"

Isabel held up a hand. "Okay, I see what you mean. Is it even safe for me to drink there?"

Crystal winked and nodded. "You won't be the first mortal they ever served, and in the ten thousand years, they haven't made a mistake. The only time things have gone wrong was when they didn't know they were serving a mortal, or a mortal grabbed someone else's drink. So you'll be fine."

"Okay," Isabel said, deciding to not get more than buzzed. "Who's Ryan meeting?"

"That's for him to tell if he wants to, love."

Isabel flushed and, once again, changed the subject. "So, let me ask you. In the last million years, what is the coolest thing you've ever seen?"

Crystal blinked. "How do you mean?"

"Coolest thing, however you want to define that. I know you must have seen some amazing stuff, so what comes to mind as the 'coolest'?"

Crystal considered for a minute. "It's really, really hard to pick one, but one thing that comes to mind is the first time I saw you lot. Humans in your proper form."

Isabel leaned forward, suddenly intensely interested. "Go on?"

"So Neanderthals were around, and a few other hominids over the millennia, but none of them had gotten very far. Caves and all that, proto-languages like what crows speak, nothing too interesting. I was just about ready to pack up and head out to find a sentient species, any sentient species, capable of holding a conversation, and spend a few sodding millennia with them. I was barely using my powers, but even the slight drain had accumulated into a social hunger, and I was bored. Then one day-bam!" Crystal clapped her hands.

"Humans?"

"Yes, but that word wasn't around yet. What I saw was a bunch of hairless monkeys with mud huts and spears, sitting around a campfire. They freaked when they saw me, yeah? I didn't know what they looked like, so I was in my normal form, and seeing some kind of alien pop up really did them a bloody fright."

Isabel giggled. "So that's the coolest thing? Scaring the shit out of the first humans."

Crystal smiled and shook her head. "Nope. It was what one of them did. See, gods can't translate languages that aren't to a certain level of development. So I can't speak to crows, although my money is on those little buggers being the ancestors of the next sentients. But this one little early human, maybe five or six years old, didn't run away from me. She ran straight up and looked at me with these big eyes and said, 'Hello you look funny my name is Eve.' All in a rush like that."

Isabel nearly choked. "Eve? As in 'Adam and Eve? *That* Eve?"

Crystal chuckled. "Kind of. Genesis is pretty allegorical, but yes, she's the most recent ancestor all humans share in common. Biologists call her Mitochondrial Eve, but when angels passed along the bible stories to early humans, they edited it to something people could understand, figuring you lot would work out figure out the science later on. And I made sure they eventually got the name right."

"So the coolest thing that comes to mind," Isabel said after a moment, "is meeting the literal mother of an entire species?"

Crystal nodded. "Why? Not cool enough for you?"

Isabel started laughing. "It's on a scale of cool I can't comprehend. On a 1-10 metric, it's eleventy. Yeah, it's cool enough for me!"

Isabel's heart skipped a bit when she saw Crystal's slight blush. "Well...glad I could answer the question. So, love, you ready to go get drunk with myths, legends, and your brother?"

"Well, I was planning on watching Netflix, but since you don't have Wi-Fi at your place, I guess I'll have to setting for going out."

***

A wave of sound washed over Isabel with a near physical force as the doorway to Empyrean Provocation opened. The music was elemental, primal, but undeniably the product of modern technology – what she imagined hunting cavemen would have come up with if they had the tools.

Crystal flashed her a grin as the music hit them. Other than warning Isabel about potentially deadly drinks, she had refused to share any details about what to expect.

"Love, it's not every day you get to see someone's first impression of the Club of the Gods. Athena got that with Ryan, so I'm going to get it out of you."

I hope Crystal's enjoying my reaction, Isabel thought as she realized her mouth was actually hanging open. She closed her jaw forcefully and returned the smile.

"Wow."

Crystal's eyes sparkled. "I know, right? C'mon." Crystal grabbed her hand and pulled her through the doorway, and Isabel just took a moment to let the sights wash over her, a beautiful and chaotic assault on the eyes.

The dancers were the first thing that drew her attention. The mass of...beings, since it was far too diverse a group to be called "people", moved with a collective grace that made the entire crowd seem to be its own living, breathing, dancing organism. It was hypnotic, and Isabel thought she could stand there for hours just watching them dance.

Crystal still seemed to enjoy watching her wide-eyed fascination, so Isabel let herself drink the sights in a bit more. Eventually, she spotted Ryan and Athena sitting in a booth against the wall. She assumed they were waiting for Ryan's mysterious meeting.

"Are you ready to dive in?" Crystal asked.

"Sure thing."

To Isabel's disappointment, Crystal let go of her hand as they headed down the stairs and into the throng. A few beings gave Isabel odd looks as they passed. One, a pale man with fangs, licked his lips and took a step forward.

Holy shit, I think that's a vampire! Isabel thought, instinctively recoiling.

Crystal whirled in a fluid motion and stepped in front of Isabel. She locked eyes with the vampire and said sharply, "No."

The vampire bristled, baring his fangs.

"Lemort," Crystal said, "She's with me. Do you really want to tick me off?"

The vampire's menacing aspect melted away, and he shrugged, suddenly looking almost like a normal person. "Sorry, Crystal. Didn't recognize you at first."

"Last time I checked, Empyrean Provocation was still a no-hunting zone."

"True, but it isn't a no *pickup* zone," Lemort replied archly, "and if someone leaves with you willingly..."

"I'd advise you to focus a bit more on the spirit of the law, love," Crystal said, her tone light but her eyes hard.

"Fine, fine," he said, holding up his hands and turning away.

"Thanks for that," Isabel said, her stomach still doing flip-flops. *I definitely need a drink.*

"Don't mention it. He had a point about the rules, though. Vampires aren't the only reasons supernatural snogging can be dangerous, and if you leave the club, we can't guarantee your safety. I don't recommend trying to get a hookup here."

Isabel flushed. "Hadn't even considered it. No problem."

They snaked their way to the bar, and Crystal signaled a grey-skinned, antennaed bartender. Isabel tried not to stare.

"Crystal! What'll it be?"

"Candia, love, good to see you again! A Galactic Goddess, please."

"Oh, that. It has a new name now. I'm calling it-"

"I don't care," Crystal interrupted. "I could not possibly care less. Just let me have one, please."

Candia laughed loudly at what was clearly an inside joke and then turned to Isabel. "And for you?"

"I'm just a mortal human!" Isabel blurted out, terrified of forgetting.

Candia nodded seriously. "Well then, not often we get one of you in here. Put this on so the rest of the staff knows, and we don't have any unfortunate mistakes." She handed Isabel a slightly luminescent wristband.

"Thank you," Isabel said, slipping in on. "And I'll have a margarita?"

"Sure thing lass. One mortal-safe margarita, coming up."

Isabel towards Crystal. "Okay, I have to know...is it rude to ask what she is?"

Crystal grinned and adopted an airheaded tone. "Oh my God, Isabel, you can't just ask people what they are!"

"No, seriously," Isabel said after she got her laughter back under control.

"Most people here won't mind. She's an Aos Sí."

"Gotcha," Isabel said, even though she was still confused, as Candia returned and handed them their drinks.

"Just flag me down if you need anything." She headed towards the next customer, moving with the rapid but seemingly casual stride that was one of the secret tricks of bartenders and waiters at busy establishments.

She took a sip of her margarita and then stared at the glass.

Crystal furrowed her brow. "Everything okay?"

Isabel held up the glass with only slightly overstated reverence. "This is the single best drink I've ever had."

Crystal laughed. "Well, they serve actual gods and kings and lords and all that here. Only the best! And you're on my tab tonight, so feel free to get as obliterated as you want."

Isabel looked at her, looked at the drink, and decided to show her appreciation by taking another long sip. "You really are a goddess," she said, smiling.

"Absolutely."

***

Ryan glanced over at Athena, who was finishing her wine. "Penny for your thoughts?"

She smiled. "Just thinking about the first time we were here."

"You mean when we got obliterated, and then Crystal almost killed you?"

Athena laughed, a sound Ryan increasingly enjoyed.

"Exactly that," she said. "I especially enjoyed you bursting in and shouting 'Nooo' before you fell over your feet."

Ryan tugged at his collar and flushed. "I couldn't just let her kill you. Even if you would have gotten better, she would have felt terrible."

Another laugh, this one a shade deeper. "Yes, she would have. In fact..."

Choosing Empyrean Provocation as a meeting site pretty much eliminated any chance of being circumspect, but if Ryan had still held any hope of going unnoticed, it was swept away as Uriel glided across the room. The former archangel of light drew every eye. Her black hair framed her beautiful face, and her blood-red wings, half unfurled, swept behind her. Next to her, the King of Hell looked utterly ordinary. If Ryan had seen him on the street, he might have noticed the expensive suit, but little else.

"Not that impressive, is he?" Athena asked softly, echoing Ryan's thoughts. "That's one who might prefer to be underestimated, I think."

"She has a different idea, though."

"Angels, fallen or not, have never been known for subtlety. I wonder if the change in her appearance was a natural result of her changing allegiance or a deliberate choice on her part." As the two approached, Athena frowned and lowered her voice even more. "Are you absolutely sure about this?"

"Yes, but let me know if I'm about to make a stupid mistake, okay?"

"I'll do my best."

"Ryan!" Arthur said, smiling broadly and extending a hand. "It's good to finally have a chance to meet you in person. I hope you can forgive me for not introducing myself earlier, but things have been hectic."

"Of course," Ryan said. "Things definitely...looked busy."

"And you must be Athena," Arthur said. "This, of course, is Uriel."

Uriel just nodded, and she and Arthur slid into the other side of the booth.

"So," Arthur said, "our first dealings ended in mutual satisfaction and a victory for each of us. I'm looking forward to bargaining with you again. What is it you need?"

"I have a sister," Ryan told him, "and she's mortal."

Arthur didn't bother to feign surprise. "Go on."

"She could die at any moment, and I've put her in a lot of danger."

"So you want protection?" Uriel asked.

"For starters," Ryan said, "but even if she was hard to kill, she's still going to die. I'm going to live for, like, forever, and I don't want to lose her."

Arthur let out a low whistle. "You want her to be immortal?"

"Yes."

"And you think I can do that?"

Ryan was slightly taken aback. "Well, I mean, I assumed..."

Arthur smirked. "You assumed that I had some of the same level of power over the Core than you have over your nanoverse? I'm flattered."

Athena broke in. "If you can't do it, just say so."

The King of Hell held up a hand. "I'm not saying I can't do it, but I can't do it the way that Ryan's probably imagining. Waving my hand and making her something like a...demigod?"

"Something like that," Ryan admitted.

"To be perfectly blunt, I don't make demigods. I make demons. I could...tone down...the outward physical signs, but there would be a few. She would gain the benefits you're hoping for: resilience, longevity, some power of her own, and the ability to...I think of it as 'respawning'. In Hell, of course. We could bargain for her service to me to be light, but she would be mine. Still, that's an excellent deal."

Ryan winced, and an awkward silence settled over the table. Finally, Ryan said, "I'd like her not to hate me, and I think she'd have a problem with that. Besides, wouldn't that be me selling her soul for her? Is that even possible?"

"No," Arthur replied. "She would have to do that, in exchange for the transformation. You would pay for the light service, and for me extending the opportunity in the first place."

Athena, noting Ryan's discomfort, leaned forward. "Is that the only option?"

"At the moment, yes. If you want to conclude this business immediately, that is all I can offer. If you are willing to give me some time, I may be able to provide another solution."

"What's that?" Ryan asked, trying-and failing-not to sound too eager.

"I believe I may be able to locate a soulstone." Athena gasped, and Arthur smiled at her. "You're familiar with them. It's full of animal souls, although I think we could add human souls if you're interested-"

"We're not," Athena said firmly.

"Neither am I," Arthur said, and Ryan wondered if that had been some kind of test. Arthur went on, "To keep the explanation brief, someone who possesses a soulstone can shift into the forms of those animals, and the shifting process also maintains the holder's youth. It doesn't prevent death from violence or disease, but it does dramatically extend a careful person's lifetime, especially if they use the hardier animal forms when they're in danger. There's no respawning, I'm afraid. The first option is practically ironclad, but the soulstone is the best I could do if you're squeamish about the 'selling the soul' business."

Ryan looked at Athena. "Is it safe?"

Athena tapped her fingers on the table. "As far as I know."

"I don't deal in bad faith," Arthur said. "You have my satisfaction guarantee. Faustian bargains were Lucifer's shtick, not mine."

Ryan considered. Arthur *had* dealt with him fairly before, and this option sounded pretty good. "And my sister won't owe you anything?"

"No. You will pay the debt on her behalf."

And here comes the catch, Ryan thought. "Okay, Arthur...what do you want for it? Assuming you can find it?"

"You'll owe me a favor."

Athena's dark eyes flashed fire. "Absolutely not. Ryan, you can't just give him an open-ended debt."

"I told you already, *I deal in good faith*," Arthur said, no longer looking or sounding a genial, average guy. "You have my *oath* that I will ask nothing that betrays your deepest ideals, and do not doubt that *I know what those are*."

Ryan gulped, realizing that Athena had been right: Arthur did like to be underestimated, until he didn't. Right now, he was making it clear that the King of Hell was not to be messed with.

"I believe you," Ryan said finally, and Arthur's countenance changed immediately.

"Wonderful. So, a soulstone, assuming I locate it, delivered to your sister, in exchange for a favor, from you, to be named at a later date."

Please, God, don't let this screw me. Ryan thought, and said, "Fine." Only after the word was out of his mouth did he think about the irony of asking God to not get screwed when dealing with the King of Hell. He held out his hand.

"Ah, wait, just one more thing," Arthur said. "This debt *is* transferable. If you die or aren't available when I need you, someone else will have to step in."

Ryan shook his head. "I can't put my sister in debt without her permission."

"I wouldn't want you to," Arthur said, grinning. "Especially since, soulstone or not, she wouldn't be nearly as useful as you. Instead-"

"I'll do it." Athena cut him off before he could even ask.

Ryan looked at her. "You don't have to."

"I know," she said quietly, "but I will." Athena turned to Arthur. "Do we have a deal?"

"Absolutely." Arthur shook both their hands, and Ryan hoped he hadn't made a colossal mistake.

"I couldn't help but notice," Uriel said, "that there's a mortal woman at the bar, with your good friend Crystal. Would that happen to be your sister?"

Ryan glanced over. "Uh...yes, actually."

Arthur smiled. "I would very much like to meet her."

"Um, yeah, sure," Ryan said. "Let's not mention this to her, though, okay? I mean, the specifics."

"Not a word," Arthur said.

Almost as if she had sensed their interest, Crystal turned and looked toward the booth. Ryan caught her eye and waved them over.

"Hello, Arthur. Uriel," Crystal said brightly. "Good to see you. Isabel, I'll be back in a bit." Before anyone could reply, she headed back to the bar.

"Arthur," Ryan said, "this is Isabel, my sister. Isabel, this is Arthur, King of Hell, and the Lady Uriel."

Unsure of what to do, Isabel gave an awkward bow. *This* was Ryan's meeting?

"Charmed," Arthur said, offering a hand. Isabel took it, hoping he wouldn't notice that her hand had started to sweat. When he let go, she fought the urge to wipe it on her side.

Ryan moved closer to Athena, creating some extra space on their side of the booth, and Isabel sat down.

"I...heard about your church on the news. The Church of Adversity?" Isabel said, proud that she managed not to stammer.

Arthur laughed. "Oh, yes. I'm so glad we're still hitting the news cycle with gods running around. I was worried we'd get buried. That is my church, yes. Have you considered becoming a member?" He flashed her a dazzling grin.

"Um..." Isabel said, her brain locking up.

"Arthur...." Athena said warningly.

"I wasn't asking to buy her soul. Just a bit of recruiting. Still, question retracted."

"Thanks," Isabel muttered, then blurted, "So it's true then? Lucifer is out, and you're in charge now?" Immediately she wanted to retract the question. It was so damn obvious.

At least it didn't seem to bother Arthur, whose eyes lit up. "He's super out. I've got his head on a pike outside of my citadel right now."

Uriel laughed lightly, and Isabel decided that she was officially creeped out.

"It was lovely to meet all of you," Arthur said, "but we have other business. Enjoy your evening."

"*That* was your meeting?" Isabel exclaimed as soon as they were out of earshot. "Please tell me you didn't sell your soul."

Ryan shook his head. "I'm not as dumb as I look, Izzy."

Isabel snorted. "That's a relief; otherwise I'd wonder how you remembered to breathe."

He gave her a broad smile and an extended digit. "Thankfully, I don't need to remember it anymore."

She rolled her eyes. "Oh, please, remind me again how awesome it is to be a god. 'Oh, I don't need to breathe!' 'Oh, I don't need to use a bathroom, ever!' 'Oh, I can get my face shot off and give my sister a heart attack and be better the next day!'"

"I also don't get hungover."

"Oh, shut up." Isabel sighed. "Seriously, though, did you just make a deal with the devil?"

"Arthur's, well, a different devil," Ryan said. "He's already proven that his word is good."

"If you say so," Isabel said.

Crystal was pleased that the crowd at the bar had died down just as she had managed to slip away for a few minutes, and that Candia wasted no time coming over.

"Another drink," the bartender asked, "or something else? Or both?"

"Both," Crystal said. All the regular patrons of Empyrean Provocation knew that Candia collected, and dispensed, gossip, but most weren't aware that gossip was only the tip of the iceberg. Crystal firmly believed that her friend might have been some kind of intelligence agent at some point. It wasn't impossible that she still was, as she was in a perfect spot to learn about the goings-on of the supernatural world.

"How about if I go first?" Crystal asked as Candia mixed her drink.

"That's a change."

Crystal shrugged. "I like to mix it up sometimes. So here it is: I've seen with my own eyes that Olympus is abandoned and in ruins. Hades has gone to consult the Fates, hoping they'd known where the Olympians had gone."

"Hmmm," Candia said, biting her lip. "That is interesting. The underworld gods have been disrupting things since they got back, but I hadn't heard anything about Hades. That explains it. Also, people have been speculating about Olympus for ages, but no one has *known*." She handed Crystal her drink. "I appreciate it. So what do you want to know?"

Crystal knew that she'd just earned some serious credit. "I don't suppose you happen to know anything about gods affiliated with the U.S. Military?"

"I hadn't...really?" Candia asked in a shocked whisper. "That violates all sorts of treaties. You all don't get involved with governments, ever."

Crystal sighed and nodded. It'd been too much to hope that Candia would know something. "We don't know who they are. We think they might even be...some kind of manufactured gods."

"Something else I hadn't heard." Candia's antenna twitched in irritation. "I'm supposed to *know* about these things."

"I don't think they've been running in our circles."

Candia's antenna drooped. "And I'm afraid I'm going to disappoint you again, because no one knows what Moloch's up to."

"Damn," Crystal said, staring into her glass. "Do you happen to know something I *should* know about?"

"Harder to say, since I don't know what you don't know," Candia said. "Lots of people are talking about the Eschaton."

"I'm not surprised. What are they saying?"

Candia smiled, obviously relieved to have something to share. "He's quite the hot topic. Even if most of your kind still don't believe you about the end of the world, he's a new god, he's forming a pantheon, he's announced himself to the world...a lot of people are very interested."

"I don't suppose any of them would be interested in helping us?"

"Not yet, as far as I've heard. But I'm listening. And I'll be listening harder. You definitely gave me more than I gave you tonight."

Crystal shrugged. "It will even out, love."

Candia laughed. "I'll make sure it does. Come see me again soon, and I'm sure I'll have something to tell you."

***

Footsteps approached, and Bast realized she was hoping it was Cassandra. She had found herself warming to the woman, slowly but surely. It was a process Bast had become familiar with over the centuries. Back in her day, they'd called it conversion. In more modern times, it had been called indoctrination, then brainwashing. These days it had a fancy, psychological name: Stockholm syndrome.

Lub-dub-lub-dub

It seemed to Bast that Cassandra's heartbeat was louder today than it had ever been. Each time another person was in a room, Bast was more aware of the sound than the last time, and when the full quartet of researchers was present, the sound became a near cacophony.

The sounds of hearts, echoing in her mind. *Maybe I am crazy?* It was possible, she admitted to herself. Sane gods didn't hear every heartbeat and find themselves nearly driven to distraction.

Cassandra deliberately stopped just before she reached a point she knew she could be seen. She needed a moment to collect her thoughts. It was four in the morning, and she hadn't slept. After several hours of tossing and turning, she'd gotten out of bed and tried to organize her thoughts. Eventually, those thoughts have become hypotheses, and then questions, and finally, possibly, plans. She looked down at the notepad she had spent half the night filling and steeled herself. She moved the mirror into position, sat down at her desk, and smiled.

"Good morning," she said, trying to sound cheerful.

Bast caught a hint of strain in Cassandra's voice, a slight tightening around her eyes. It was so *frustrating* not to be able to respond, to figure out what was going on. Bast needed information, and it was impossible to get when she couldn't really influence the direction of the conversation. The listening and blinking also limited how effective the interactions were at filling her Hungers. They did as much to slake her need for Company as the slow drips of water did to relieve her thirst. It was much better than having nothing, but the glacial progress was maddening.

"I have some questions for you," Cassandra said. "Is that all right?"

Bast blinked once to signal yes.

"Did you sleep?"

Two blinks for no.

"Does sleep deprivation harm you physically?"

Bast hesitated, unsure of how to answer the question. The correct answer was both yes and no. She could stay awake for months if she wasn't using her power and never feel any ill effects. When she was Hungry, though, she felt fatigue as intense as any mortal. Even more important than the truth, though, was giving the answer that would best serve her purposes, and she wasn't certain what that was.

Cassandra watched Bast in the mirror, noting the lack of an immediate response. She was annoyed with herself. She had carefully composed her list of questions, trying to cover everything she needed to know and make sure that all of them could be easily answered yes or no. She couldn't believe that on the second question there was already a problem.

"Let me try again," Cassandra said. "Does a lack of sleep harm you in the same way it would harm a human?"

Bast blinked twice for no.

"Is your life in any danger because you haven't slept?"

Bast decided that, for now, she would just be honest. She blinked twice.

"Does it cause you discomfort?"

One blink.

"I'm going to ask you to answer this next question with a series of blinks, and then we'll go back to yes or no. On a scale of one to ten, what is the level of discomfort you're experiencing because of your lack of sleep?"

Bast thought for a second and then blinked eight times. She was thoroughly perplexed by this conversation. On the one hand, Cassandra seemed detached and clinical. She was reading from a notepad and using a more formal tone. On the other hand, she winced slightly when she saw Bast's answer. What the hell was going on?

"We're feeding you through a nutrient drip," Cassandra said. "As far as you know, is that enough to meet your physical needs? In other words, is your body able to sustain itself without actually eating?"

One blink.

More questions followed, covering eating, drinking, exercise, and even, to Bast's great relief, social interaction. It was apparent that Cassandra had prepared for this conversation, and she'd been damn thorough. Bast quickly realized that despite her limited answers, she was giving the researcher a relatively detailed picture of her physical and emotional health, as well as her needs. For the first time, she found herself actually feeling respect for Cassandra.

Mixed in with the other questions, seemingly at random, were inquiries about Bast's power. She would be blinking away about eating, and suddenly Cassandra would ask, "Do you need to use gestures to warp reality?" After Bast replied, it would be back to questions about food, and then whether or not she dreamed, and then, suddenly, "Do you need to say some sort of spell or power word when you use your supernatural abilities?" These offhand questions didn't even break Cassandra's rhythm, just thrown in among the topics that seemed to interest Cassandra more.

By the time she'd asked the last of her prepared questions, as well as the ones that had occurred to her during the conversation, Cassandra was exhausted. *Not nearly as exhausted as Bast must be*, she thought grimly. The fact that Bast couldn't sleep because of her physical discomfort, a product of her unique biology that Cassandra would love to fully understand, was disconcerting. As a scientist, she was fascinated by the picture that was emerging: while Bast's *body* didn't actually require anything to keep it alive, her *psyche* was dependent on physical "fuel". But Cassandra wasn't just a scientist; she was a human being, and the more she understood the unique nature of this situation, the more she wanted to throw up.

Bast studied Cassandra's face in the mirror, still trying to figure out what was going on. Abruptly, the other woman stood up and disappeared from sight.

Wait, Bast thought. She reviewed the last few hours and the barrage of research questions she had willingly answered. *Was that what all of this was about? Was she trying to gain my trust so she could get me to cooperate? Has* she *been manipulating* me? *I'll kill her first. I'll kill her* slowly. *I'll make her rue the day she dared to-*

Lub-dub-lub-dub

Cassandra's heartbeat grew louder, and Bast saw the woman's face just above her. Between the distracting sound and her rising fury, Bast didn't even notice the slight pressure on her lips until Cassandra spoke.

"Open your mouth," she said. "As much as you can."

For a second, Bast resisted. Then she realized that whatever the treacherous bitch was trying to put in her mouth could probably just as easily be administered through her IV, and it might not be wise to let Cassandra suspect that she had caught on.

She parted her lips as far as the mask would allow, creating a tiny opening. She seethed as she felt a small, slick object force its way through the opening, but then...

Water. It was a tiny straw, or perhaps a tube, and there was *water* slowly flowing into her mouth. Bast sucked greedily, and though the small instrument only allowed a trickle, it was a *steady* trickle, and she was able to drink her fill.

Cassandra held the tube in place until the IV bag of water was empty, and then asked, "Do you need more? I can refill the bag."

Two blinks.

"All right," she said. "I need to think for a minute."

Cassandra had been careful in her questions about Bast's power, hoping that sprinkling them throughout the interview would make it harder for the goddess to deceive her. Every answer had matched what the Myrmidons had said about their abilities, which meant that speaking had absolutely nothing to do with anything.

Lazzario was an idiot. All this time, Bast's torture had been intensified because a paranoid manchild had spent too much time sitting in the basement and pretending to be an elven wizard. "Verbal component" indeed. What a bunch of bullshit.

Still, Cassandra hesitated. What she had done so far was more than enough to get her fired, and *probably* enough to get her thrown in jail. What she was considering doing, though...

What she was considering doing was treason. It had been explicitly defined as such on half a dozen occasions.

Maybe I won't get caught. I probably won't, if I'm careful. And even if I am...

Even if she was, everyone had limits, and Cassandra had found hers.

Bast saw Cassandra's face over hers again and heard a series of clicks.

"Don't make a sound," Cassandra said. "Do you understand?"

Bast blinked once, and then suddenly the mask was lifted away.

"Don't scream," Cassandra told her. "For the love of God, keep your voice down."

Bast felt her own heart hammering as hard as Cassandra's. Her vision swam as tears flowed freely, and she took a moment to work her jaw. "Thank you," she said, her voice hoarse.

Cassandra jerked slightly, and glanced toward the door, then whispered, "You're welcome. I have food. Crackers and carrots, and some chocolate. I think there's some soup I could heat up, or-"

"Anything," Bast gasped. "It doesn't matter."

Once, Bast might have thought that being fed was demeaning, but her long imprisonment had radically altered her definition of that word.

"Thank you," she said again after she had eaten her fill.

"You're welcome." Cassandra checked her watch. "We should have an hour before anyone else arrives, but I'm not taking any chances. In half an hour, I'm going to have to put the mask back on."

"I understand."

"I need to be clear on something, Bast," Cassandra said. "It's possible that someday Doctor Pivarti or Admiral Bridges will decide to take the mask off and talk to you. If you tell them about this, I'm going to jail. Or worse."

"I understand. I promise I won't say anything." Bast was completely sincere and mentally vowed that *nothing* would drag that information from her.

Well, almost nothing. She had to be realistic.

Cassandra had a thousand questions but restrained herself. Bast would have thirty minutes of limited freedom, and Cassandra wasn't going to control how she used them. There would be time.

"What would you like to talk about?" she asked.

Bast was stunned by the simple kindness, and part of her raged that she had been so deprived that just being allowed to speak was a momentous occasion. "I...I'm not even sure. I...don't know. If you have more questions..."

It didn't matter what they talked about, really. As long as they were talking, Bast could fill her Social hunger, and she didn't want to waste any time because her mind had gone blank.

"All right," Cassandra said. "How did you become a goddess?"

Bast smiled. "So you've discovered that we're born as mortals? Clever. I was given my nanoverse, what you call the Black Sphere, by Ra."

"So Ra was real? Even before the Old Kingdom?"

Bast nodded and began to speak about the pre-Old Kingdom civilization. Bast carefully avoiding anything that would cast her in a negative light, focusing on the kingdom itself and the work she had done for Ra after her initial Apotheosis. She talked of cities saved and monsters defeated, skirting the ugly details to focus on painting herself as a hero to the idealistic young woman. All too soon, Cassandra picked up the mask again.

"We're out of time. When it's safe, I'll take it off again. I promise."

"Cassandra," Bast said quickly, "I want you to know that I would have gone insane without you. Thank you."

Cassandra hesitated, then touched Bast's cheek. The goddess leaned into it, drinking in the touch, savoring the human contact, and finally feeling her need for socialization fill.

After a moment, Cassandra pulled away and replaced the mask.

I won't kill you, Bast thought. *I won't hurt you. More: I will protect you. I will reward you. I will offer you my friendship. I swear it.*

Then she fell asleep.

Chapter 17

Line in the Sand

The next day, the group reconvened in Crystal's nanoverse. Ryan admired the stars and planets whirling in their usual dance above them. Isabel, lying face down on a couch with her hands pressed to her temples, only groaned.

"How's the head?" Ryan asked.

Isabel extended one hand with agonizing slowness, and then just as deliberately extended a middle finger. "This?" she croaked, waving the impudent digit to make sure she had everyone's attention, is for all of you. Every last one of you un-hungover assholes."

Ryan laughed as he slid into a seat next to Athena.

Dianmu smiled. "I have a remedy that might help with that."

"Oh?" Isabel said, rolling over and looking hopeful. "Some divine power? Some kind of mystic cure?"

"Ahh, yes," Dianmu said, reaching into her pocket. "The ancient art of ibuprofen."

"Praise the ancients," Isabel intoned solemnly, and greedily swallowed the medicine. "Not that I'm complaining, but why do you even have ibuprofen? Don't you not get headaches?"

"Awkward phrasing aside, I do not. But we're traveling with a mortal. I figured it was best to be prepared."

"You are officially my new favorite god. All hail Dianmu."

Ryan glanced around the room. "Anyone heard from Horus?"

As if on cue, there was a knock on Crystal's doorway. She opened it, admitting the dour-faced man into the staging area. "I trust you all enjoyed your cavorting?" he asked, giving them all a disapproving glare.

"Social Hungers need to be filled, love," Crystal said.

"We had an entire evening," Horus said, taking one of the seats. "The social Hunger can be filled quickly, so long as a suitable partner can be found, leaving the remainder of the time free for more productive activities."

"Oh yeah?" Ryan asked. "So you had what, ten hours to take care of that, right? Out of curiosity, what'd you do with the other nine hours and fifty-eight minutes of your night?" It was childish, and Ryan knew it, but he was getting sick of Horus's imperious attitude.

"Nascent, it requires more than petty insults to get a rise out of me." Horus's glare belied his words, however. "I'm beyond such petty jabs, no matter how much they make the egos of mortal men shrivel."

"Can we not?" Crystal asked sharply.

Ryan held up a hand. "She's right. That was uncalled for. Apologies, Horus."

"I don't want your apologies. I want you to learn." Horus sniffed, but his glare abated to its normal level, a sign he was at least mollified.

"We were attending to other business as well," Dianmu said. "How was your evening?"

Ryan mentally blessed the universe for Dianmu, who seemed to have the enviable ability to get along with everyone.

"I took care of my minimum sleep requirements," Horus said, "then did some investigation of my own. A sphinx had barricaded passage in and out of a small town in Siberia, allowing none to pass unless they could answer its riddle."

"Four legs at dawn, two at noon, three in the evening?" Ryan asked, settling into his chair.

"Indeed," Horus said. "I believe even among those folk, one of them could have answered it, if only they spoke ancient Egyptian. I taught the village elder how to say the words properly. The sphinx fled to find another town."

"You didn't kill it?" Anansi asked. Coming from anyone else, it might have sounded accusatory, but Anansi just seemed honestly curious.

"No. A fight with a sphinx would have been overly draining." Horus pulled a sheet of paper from his pocket. "Nascent, are you good with the Internets?"

Ryan choked back a laugh. *Do not antagonize him. Do not antagonize him.* "I'm good, but not the best."

"What do you need?" Isabel asked, sitting up carefully.

Horus looked at her, his eyes widening, and Ryan wondered if Horus hadn't noticed her, or just hadn't imagined she could possibly be useful. "I have written the phonetic pronunciation for the riddle's answer. Can you disseminate it, so it is easy for mortals to find at need?"

Isabel nodded, and took the paper, then lay back down and took out her phone. "Soon as we're back in reality, I can take care of it."

"The Core," Dianmu said.

Isabel craned her neck. "I'm sorry, what?"

"When referring to Earth and that universe, we call it the Core. Where you are is just as real as that."

Isabel gave her a thumbs up. "The Core then. When we're back in the Core."

Athena drummed her fingers on her arm. "You said you were investigating, Horus. Did you learn anything from the sphinx?"

"Not from him, but from the townspeople. They'd been stuck there for a few days, and I wondered why Moloch might want them trapped." Horus grimaced. "He told every able-bodied individual in the town that if they came with him and served, he'd send the sphinx away. He took at least a dozen people with him, all believing that their sacrifice had saved everyone else."

"He's getting more aggressive in his recruiting," Anansi said, steepling his fingers in front of his face. "I don't suppose this was after the attack on Shadu?"

Horus shook his head. "Before, damn him for it. Still don't know where he is."

"And that's a problem for the future," Ryan said.

Horus stiffened. "Does that mean you have a lead on Bast?"

"No," Dianmu said. "I'm afraid that we don't."

Horus scowled. "Then how can you say Moloch is a problem for the future?"

"Believe me," Ryan said, "hate saying it as much as you hate hearing it, I promise you that. The thing is...we've tried everything we can think of, and we still don't know where Moloch is. We have no way to find him. And we have another problem, one that we *have* to deal with."

"The super-soldiers," Anansi said, nodding in agreement.

"Yes," Ryan said, looking over at Horus to make sure he had the god's undivided attention. "The four of them nearly took Anansi and me out. If we hadn't figured out the trick of removing their harnesses, we would have been dead. When the lone soldier attacked me at Isabel's place, I couldn't get a fix on his harness. It was like it was resisting my twists. They're getting better each time we fight them and getting more dangerous in the process. The longer we ignore them, the more dangerous they become."

Horus pursed his lips. "The longer we ignore Moloch, the greater the threat he poses as well. He murdered an entire pantheon."

"Yes, but-"

"No, Nascent. You don't understand." Horus clenched the edge of his chair. "Moloch has been a threat to this world for countless millennia. He has destroyed cities, ravaged nations, and killed gods. He has gone unpunished for too long. As much as it pains me, I have been convinced that we *must* make him a top priority. Mortals have opposed us before and been beaten. This will be no different."

"It kind of is," Ryan said, feeling the first twinges of a headache. "They are making gods, Horus."

Horus sneered outright. "Gods that managed to fail to defeat you twice. One fell to *you*, an inexperienced Nascent. When you had a competent god to assist you, they managed to lose despite superior numbers. I'm hardly concerned about the doings of these 'super-soldiers,' as you call them."

Crystal interjected before Ryan could speak. "Horus, love. I'll happily go after Moloch first." Ryan whirled towards her, his mouth hanging open, but Crystal held up a finger, her focus on Horus. "As soon as you can look me in the eyes and say it's because you believe Moloch to be the bigger threat, and not because you think there's a chance that he could lead us to Bast."

If looks could kill, Crystal would be a stain on the floor. Horus clenched his teeth but didn't speak.

"Both would be easier if we had aid," Athena said, her voice tight. "If we retrieve the Olympians, we'll be able to pursue all three goals."

"*If,*" Anansi said. "That seems like a significant word. We do not know for certain they are in Tartarus. We do not know if they still live. We do not know if they will want to aid us. That is a great many things we do not know."

Athena's eyes flashed. "Then what, pray tell, would you have us do, Trickster?"

"The super-soldiers are our greatest threat," Anansi said, nodding his head towards Ryan.

"Horseshit," Horus spat. "Crystal, you called me on my motives, and I'll admit you were correct. So tell me, Anansi, Ryan - can you honestly say the super-soldiers are a greater threat than Moloch, or do you want to avenge the man they slew?"

Anansi's hands curled inwards. "While I may not be objective-"

Horus wasn't finished. "And you, Nascent. Do you want to go after them because of the threat they currently pose, or because the threat they made against your sister?"

"Oh, you know what, Horus?" Ryan said, rising to his feet. "Take your whole damn attitude, turn it sideways, and shove it so far up your ass that you choke on it." He balled his hands into fists.

"And we've moved on so quickly from my point," Athena growled. "With the aid of my kind, we can accomplish *both* at once."

"Sorry, love," Crystal said. "It's a week to get there. Who knows what we'll be dealing when we get back? We've got to nip this in the bud."

"I agree with Athena," Dianmu said. "These 'super-soldiers' are a threat, there is no doubt about that. Moloch has been a threat to the world since before I obtained my nanoverse. Reinforcements would be beneficial."

"Bloody hell, listen to yourselves," Crystal snapped. "Moloch, remember? The single greatest divine threat still running around out there?"

"*You're* siding with Horus?" Ryan asked.

"A broken clock is right twice a day." Crystal shrugged. "Sorry."

"But you shut him down a moment ago!" Ryan spluttered. He couldn't help it. He'd assumed he'd have both Athena and Crystal on his side.

"I just wanted to know his motivation," Crystal said. "Look, I get it. These super-soldiers are bad news. But Moloch is a threat to what we're trying to accomplish here. Remember? Saving the world? Or at least the people on it. Moloch could actually beat us."

"Again, I think Athena's view has merits," Dianmu said.

"Merits, sure," Crystal conceded, but her expression was unyielding. "But right now I don't want to be away from the Core that long."

"Why don't you split up?" Isabel suggested from the couch. "I mean, Anansi and Ryan can track down the super-soldiers, Horus and Crystal can look for Moloch, and Athena and Dianmu can go to get the Olympians. Whoever accomplishes their goal first calls in the others. Everyone wins."

"Won't work," Athena said. Every line of her body was tight with fury. "Tartarus is a difficult realm. Our nanoverses can only take us as far as the entrance. The week would be our travels through the Labyrinth."

"And we can't face the super-soldiers shorthanded," Ryan said.

"Nor Moloch," Horus added.

"We don't know where Moloch is," Anansi growled. "Or what he wants."

"We also don't know where the super-soldiers are," Crystal countered, folding her arms and scowling.

"No," said Ryan, "but we know what they want. Me."

Everyone turned to look at him. Ryan shrugged awkwardly. "They must have had Isabel under surveillance since I went on television. They were waiting for me. Whatever the United States' end goal in all this is, my death factors into it."

"That's a good argument for avoiding them then, isn't it?" Athena asked.

Crystal nodded. "If their goal is to kill you, we shouldn't dangle you in front of them. Especially while you're still Nascent and could still be killed."

"Like Moloch's any safer?" Ryan countered. "Sure, he's not actively gunning for me, but I think he'd still kill me if he had the chance."

"If the super-soldiers are looking for Ryan, it could give us control over when and where we engage," Anansi said. "Moloch's plans don't seem to involve hunting us down anytime soon. When we fight him, it will have to be on the battlefield of his choosing."

"All the more reason to gather reinforcements," Dianmu countered. "It still will take time to find either, and the longer it takes, the stronger they'll be. But with the Olympians aiding us in the search, we can find them quicker, and I doubt they can build up enough to withstand that pantheon. Few are larger, and at least we have an idea where the Olympians might be."

"So we're at an impasse," Ryan said, frowning. He looked over at Crystal. "Why are you so set on Moloch?"

She pursed her lips and looked away from Ryan. "I just...I really don't want to be away from the Core for very long," she said softly.

"Why not?" Athena asked with sudden concern. "Crystal...what's wrong?"

"Look, I won't be joining you in whatever you get up to next, Moloch or the soldiers." Crystal chuckled "Sounds like a bloody band name. A band named by wankers. I guess it would be 'Moloch *and* the Soldiers', but you get my point."

Dianmu walked over and put a hand on Crystal's shoulder. "What's wrong?" she asked, echoing Athena.

Crystal took a deep breath. "I have to deal with something in my nanoverse."

"Okay," Ryan said. "I mean, I get that, but...that'll only take a couple minutes, right? It's not like it's going to be a huge delay."

"And we cannot afford to divide," Horus said, his voice tight. "You are one of the best warriors I've met, and you want to run and hide in your nanoverse? When did you become a coward?"

"I didn't," Crystal said quietly. She visibly steeled herself, and then said, "Switch to real display."

Before anyone could say anything else, the false display melted away and revealed the real state of the nanoverse.

Ryan swallowed hard. "It looks like..."

"Enki's fused Nanoverses," Athena finished.

"What the *hell* happened?" Horus snarled, obviously furious. "This isn't...this is unnatural."

"Quiet yourself," Athena said, rising. "Obviously she doesn't know, or she would have fixed it already."

"If she can," Anansi said, eyes were wide with horror.

"I should have said something sooner," Crystal whispered. "I thought...I thought I could just pop in and fix it. Every time I tried, though, it came back worse than before. Something in my nanoverse is sick, and I don't know how to heal it."

"I'm so sorry," Dianmu said quietly.

"Thanks." Crystal gently shrugged Dianmu's hand off her shoulder. "I'd like to tell myself it's a side effect of...of being as old as I am. That we're not supposed to live this long, and it's been rotting away at my nanoverse. But it started right after I destroyed Enki's nanoverse."

"Somehow that corrupted yours," Athena said.

Crystal nodded. "Somehow, it did. And the corruption is getting worse. Back in Shadu? When I had to kill Resheph to give him a chance to resurrect away from his body, with his nanoverse?"

Ryan nodded for her to go on.

"Well, I loved it. It felt *so good* to end a divine life like that. For a moment, I seriously considered putting him out of his misery permanently. None of you would have had to know I did it. Just bring his nanoverse into mine and snuff it out. And that isn't the only crazy thought I've had lately. Whatever's happening here...it's affecting me, too." Crystal reached up and wiped at her eyes. "I can't be trusted until this is dealt with."

"Then we should leave," Horus snapped. "If you can't be trusted...Crystal, we're *in your staging area*."

"That's why I'm telling you right now," Crystal said. "I wasn't going to, not even after what I was tempted to do with Resheph...but since you walked in here, I've been considering dropping us into my nanoverse's time stream. And then...I don't know. Doing something. It's like an itch in the back of my head."

Isabel raised a hand to her mouth in horror. Ryan immediately understood. She'd slept here the entire night. If Crystal had snapped then-

"We need to get out of here," Anansi announced.

"No," Dianmu said firmly. "We'll finish the discussion here, and then we'll leave. I trust Crystal with my life. Even now. She realized the temptation was there, and she took the correct steps. Despite whatever is trying to influence her, she has resisted."

Crystal winced and looked around the room. When she met Ryan's eyes, he nodded.

"You are the strongest person I've ever met," he said with a confidence he didn't feel but knew she needed. "Without a doubt. Besides, if you were going to break, you would have already."

"I agree," Athena said. "We will discuss the fact that you hid this from us, Crystal, but not until you've dealt with it."

"I trust you," Isabel added.

"Thanks," Crystal said again, wiping her eyes.

"Wonderful," Horus said sarcastically, rising "Then I'd like to get this resolved before Crystal snaps and murders us all. Crystal, give me a whiteboard."

For a moment, Ryan seriously considered the pros and cons of punching Horus as hard as he could. "What is *wrong* with you?" he asked instead.

"You mentioned this yourself, Nascent, when you told the story of your fight with Enki. Every idea goes up." Horus looked pointedly at Crystal. She sighed and pushed a few buttons, causing a whiteboard to appear in her staging area, complete with markers.

"Now. Obviously, Crystal needs to deal with this mess," Horus said, writing "Crystal" and "Clean up your shit" on the board. "For the rest of us, there are three options."

Ryan didn't interrupt Horus as he scribbled on the board, muttering to himself. Instead, he just watched, trying to get his anger under control. When Horus was done, all three options were listed, with the previously mentioned pros and cons weighed for each.

"Now," Horus said, stepping back and studying the list. "Looking at it this way, it's *obvious* what we must do."

"Here it comes," Ryan muttered.

"We must go after the super-soldiers," Horus said sourly.

"I'm sorry, *what*?" Athena asked.

"All of you have been thinking about what you personally *want.* Ryan wants revenge for the attack at his sister's. Anansi wants revenge for his friend. Athena, you want to retrieve your kin. Dianmu..." Horus paused to consider, then nodded. "Of course. You're not concerned with tactics. You want the option that you believe is safest for the mortals in the Core."

"And that's wrong?" Dianmu asked, arching an eyebrow.

"Yes," Horus said simply. "We have a ticking clock. Armageddon looms. This is not the time to be squeamish. We need decisive action. What is a possible threat to mortals, when weighed against their total annihilation?"

"You were only advocating for Moloch because you wanted to find Bast," Athena said.

"Yes," Horus shrugged. "Someone has to be the first to pull their head out of their ass."

"And you figured it was finally your turn?" Crystal said. "You've had it up yours since you started working with us."

At least Horus had the decency to flush. "None of you have fought in modern times. Not in war," he said defensively. "You're all thinking in terms of long campaigns, but that's not what we have here. We have a series of engagements against possible targets. We're not an army, we're special forces. If we had an army, I think either the two war goddesses would have seen this first."

Ryan realized that was the closest to an apology they were going to get from Horus and decided to make a concession. "Seen what first? I'm not arguing Horus, especially not when you're on my side right now, but I'm trying to understand why."

Horus pointed to the section labeled "Tartarus". "We don't know for certain the Olympians are there. No, Athena, don't object. We *don't.* I'll grant that it's likely, but we need certainty right now." He pointed to the section labeled "Moloch". "We don't know where he is, either. But we can lure these 'super-soldiers' out. We can choose our engagement. That removes a threat from the board and gives Moloch time to make a mistake and expose himself."

Athena grimaced. "He's right. It would be foolish to go into Tartarus without Crystal anyway. Given the change in circumstances, pursuing the super-soldiers does seem to be the best course."

Dianmu studied the board and sighed. "Fine. Though we should make every effort to limit the risk to others." Everyone nodded, even Horus. Dianmu looked towards Ryan. "I don't suppose you know how to lure them?"

"That, unfortunately, is pretty obvious to me," Ryan said, slumping a bit. *You're an asshole for even thinking this,* Ryan thought. "If I was the U.S. Government, and I had access to my entire social media history, *and* I was monitoring the people I might go visit, there's one other person besides Isabel I'd be watching."

***

"Okay, so, a grande mocha frappuccino. No, wait, a venti. Wait, hang on, should probably get a grande. Yeah, grande."

Jacqueline Weaver shifted impatiently as the man in front of her dithered about the size of his coffee. Couldn't he have figured out what he wanted while waiting for the dozen people ahead of them to order? It had been bad enough listening to him change the *content* of the order three times, but now the *size*? If Jacqueline didn't get some caffeine soon, she was going to murder him.

"Hold on...maybe I could get a venti with skim milk. That probably has about the same amount of calories as a grande with whole milk, right?"

"Yes," Katie, the barista, answered quickly. Jacqueline had no idea if it was true, and she suspected that Katie didn't either. She was wearing had one of those glazed customer service smiles that meant the poor girl was screaming internally.

"That's it then. For sure."

Thank heaven, Jacqueline thought. *Please don't ask him if he wants anything else, Katie.*

"Okay," Katie said, "that'll be-"

"Hold on, I also need a, um..." the man turned around and yelled into the seating area. "Hey, Rachael! What did you want again?"

You have got to be kidding me, Jacqueline thought. *If this whole mess is about to happen again, in stereo, so help me I'll...*

"Vanilla latte with almond milk," a pretty blonde girl yelled back.

"What size?"

"The big one!"

The man turned back to the counter. "And a venti-"

"Got it," Katie interrupted. "Name?"

"Steve."

Finally, *finally*, Steve moved out of the way and gave Jacqueline a chance to order.

"Good morning, Katie," she said, giving the girl a sympathetic look. "I'll just have a venti caramel mocha, no whip, double shot of espresso." Sotto voice, she added, "I'm certain about the size."

Katie didn't laugh, but she did exhale sharply and genuinely smile, so Jacqueline counted it as a win.

On a workday, Jacqueline would grab the cup and dash back out to her car, but on Saturdays she made a point of thoroughly enjoying the experience, settling at a table and sipping slowly while she read. When Kurt was in town, he often joined her. Today he was in Tokyo trying to finalize a contract, so she planned to stay for at least three chapters and two venti mochas.

It was one of her little slices of heaven, and as Jacqueline snagged the last empty table and pulled out her Kindle, she dared to think nothing could ruin the experience.

"So apparently no one died, but Jesus Christ, they shot missiles into an apartment building," Steve's voice boomed from the table next to hers.

Jacqueline closed her eyes and silently cursed Murphy, Fate's scheming vizier who loved punishing such hubristic thoughts.

"It's totally crazy," Rachael agreed. "There's no way to be sure that was safe. So damn wrong."

Change the topic, change the topic, please please change the damn topic. Jacqueline prayed.

"I dunno about wrong," Steve said. "I mean...dude dropped a nuke on Canada. What kind of asshole does that?"

You could talk about anything else. Literally anything else in the world. Maybe you could have an in-depth discussion of how the coffee is going to give you irritable bowel syndrome.

"Smith dropped a nuke on that Enki guy," Rachael countered. "That guy was the bad guy, remember?"

"Yeah, according to Smith. How do we know we can trust him?"

I just wanted a couple hours to myself. I did not want to think about my ex-boyfriend who happens to be public enemy number one.

"Well-"

Another table opened up on the far side of the room, and Jacqueline made a beeline for it. It was too late, though. Now she was thinking about it, yet again.

Jacqueline couldn't blame everyone for talking about Ryan and everything associated with him. The appearance of literal gods, monsters fighting outside hotels, zombies overrunning a town in Texas, military assaults on apartment buildings...all of it was the kind of thing you only got in movies, and when the latest *Avengers* film came out, Jacqueline was more than happy to join in the endless discussions about that. When it was happening in real life, of course it would dominate the conversation.

Jacqueline couldn't enjoy it the way so many others seemed to, though. For starters, she was keenly aware of the very real loss of life that had happened. So many people seemed to gloss over that, for all the "Remember Grant" bumper stickers that were appearing on cars. It was horrible and tragic, yes, but it happened to *other people,* and that lent most people a detachment that Jacqueline couldn't match.

Partially because she knew one of the players. Her ex-boyfriend, Ryan.

Everyone was talking about Ryan. She couldn't escape it, no matter how much she wanted to. To listen to everyone talk, he was either a literal manifestation of Satan or the second coming of Christ. There was no middle ground.

Except Jacqueline knew that wasn't the case. Ryan wasn't a saint, and he certainly wasn't the devil. He was a high strung guy, always looking over his shoulder, and prone to forgetting important dates if you didn't remind him six times. He was also a sweetheart who always wanted to make people laugh, a good friend, and a fundamentally decent person.

Or at least, he had been. The man she'd seen on the news, issuing a challenge to Enki for a showdown on a remote Canadian island, had looked and sounded like the man she knew, but he'd been radiating confidence he had never shown when she knew him. It was jarring, like hearing a dog meow.

They'd been close friends before they dated, and inseparable while they were together. After the breakup, though, they'd cut off all contact. At first, it was too hard, for both of them, to be around each other. After that, it had been too weird. For a long time, they'd only heard about each other through mutual friends. Ryan had eventually isolated himself from their social circle, and their only interactions were liking the occasional Facebook post.

It was a mistake to tag him in that video, Jacqueline thought, not for the first time. People had noticed she'd been on his friends lists, and reporters had called and emailed asking questions. Thankfully, none of them had figured out they used to date, or they probably would have been hounding her relentlessly.

But she'd wanted Ryan to see the video. Everyone had been debating if Ryan, Enki, Moloch, or the others were villains or heroes. It had been constant. Yet the media had immediately portrayed Anansi as a monster. If he was, she wanted Ryan to keep an eye out. If he wasn't...well, Jacqueline knew Ryan. If Anansi wasn't a bad guy, Ryan would give him a fair chance.

You were supposed to be reading, she reminded herself. *Naomi Novik is fantastic, you're loving this book, why aren't you focusing on it?*

She didn't have any leftover feelings for Ryan. He wasn't the one that got away. Kurt *had* been the one that got away, and Jacqueline had waited for him to return from Dubai so she could get him back. She loved her husband with all her heart. But she still cared for Ryan. He'd been a good friend, and aside from his refusal to address his mental health issues and inability to remember her birthday, he'd been a good boyfriend. She was worried about him.

Like that's new. Ryan had often posted things to social media that had her concerned: depressing song lyrics, memes about depression and anxiety. But now she wasn't worried about how he was doing, but about the people that were trying to kill him...and if they'd come for her.

Jacqueline turned back to her book, trying to push thoughts of Ryan out of her mind. *I am going to enjoy the rest of my morning and my goddamn coffee, thank you **very** much.*

"Excuse me."

Jacqueline looked up to see a petite Asian woman standing beside her table.

"I'm sorry to bother you, but it's very crowded. Would you mind if I shared your table?"

Jacqueline did mind, a little, but not enough to say no. "Go right ahead."

"Thank you." The woman sat down and extended a hand. "My name is Dianmu."

"It's nice to meet you. I'm Jacqueline."

"A pleasure. Well, I won't disturb your reading."

Dianmu turned her attention to her phone, and Jacqueline returned to her book.

A few minutes later, Jacqueline's phone rang. She answered absently. "Hello?"

"Hey, Jacqueline. It's Ryan. Listen, Dianmu's a friend, but she's never been seen with me, so you're safe. I have another friend watching the guys watching you, and he'll signal Dianmu if they get too close. Right now they can't overhear, so you can talk safely. I don't know if your phone is tapped, but this isn't your phone, so we're good."

The rush of words set Jacqueline's head spinning. "Wait, what? Ryan? What do you mean this isn't my phone?"

"I switched them when you weren't looking," Dianmu said helpfully. "It looks just like yours, so the spooks won't be suspicious."

"What spooks?" Jacqueline asked.

"The ones watching you," Ryan replied. "Sorry to have to break it to you, but you're under surveillance." A pause. "That's my fault. Sorry. And don't look for them. It'll be suspicious."

Jacqueline had been about to do just that, but she forced herself to keep her eyes forward. Dianmu gave her an encouraging smile.

"Ryan," Jacqueline said, "what the fuck is going on here?"

"Did you happen to see the news about the government attacking an apartment building in California?"

"Of course I did. The President said you were there and had attacked civilians."

"Partly true. I was there, but they attacked me. That was Isabel's place, and I was visiting her. They were watching her, the same way they're watching you, and probably anyone else they think there's a chance I'll contact."

"Oh my God. Is Isabel okay? She didn't get hurt, did she?"

"No, she's fine. I got beat up pretty bad, but Crystal got her out safely."

"Hold on," Jacqueline said. She hit mute on the phone-which really was exactly like hers, including the scuffed *Starry Night* case-and looked at the woman across from her. "Tell me who you are and what you're doing here."

Dianmu took a sip of her drink. "Again, my name is Dianmu. I am a storm goddess, and I am allied with your former boyfriend, who we hope you still count as a friend. I am here to facilitate a private conversation with Ryan, and, along with another associate, ensure your safety."

Jacqueline frowned. That matched what Ryan had said. She hadn't precisely doubted Ryan's word, but she didn't really know him anymore, and the recent news about him had been...disturbing.

"He sounds weird," she blurted.

Dianmu laughed. "He's very nervous about this conversation, and probably trying very hard to hide it."

Jacqueline took the phone off of mute. "All right, Ryan. Tell me what's going on."

"Well, I mean, nothing too crazy. I've been practicing my cooking, thinking about picking up DnD with a new group, and I kind of found a pocket universe that gives me crazy powers and now I'm desperately trying not to get killed by the U.S. government."

"Oh, is that all?" Jacqueline snapped. She was scared to death, and he was making jokes.

"No, that's not all. I also bought a new set of knives."

"Knives," Jacqueline said, flatly.

"They're *very* sharp," Ryan confirmed.

Despite her fear, Jacqueline almost laughed. "I swear to God, Ryan, you haven't changed a bit."

"Hey now, that's not true. I have more friends than I can count on one hand, and I climbed Mount Olympus."

God, how quickly we fall into old habits. Jacqueline thought. This was how it had always been. They were rarely serious with each other, even about serious things. Strangely, Ryan's joking, while still slightly annoying, was also starting to make her feel better.

"You couldn't climb a hill, and you want me to believe you climbed Olympus?" she asked.

"Well, you did say you wished I was more active."

They'd argued about that about a dozen times throughout their relationship. Jacqueline had wanted to do outdoor things, like hiking and camping and going on float trips. Ryan had been of the opinion that the outdoors was all very well and good, so long as it remained outside of doors where it wouldn't bother him. He'd gone along sometimes for her sake, but it had put a strain on their relationship. Not as much as other things of course, but still...strain.

"I'm so sorry, Jacqueline," Ryan said into the sudden silence. "I know I keep saying that, but I am. About what happened between us, about all the things I didn't tell you. I could have explained what was going on, and I should have trusted you enough to do it. It was all my fault."

"Ryan," she said quickly, "You know I'm married, right?" She didn't *think* he'd call her after all this time, amid all this insanity, to try and rekindle their relationship, but...

"I know," he said. "I follow you on Facebook, remember? I saw all the pictures. I didn't call to talk about us, but I owed you that apology."

"It's fine," Jacqueline said. "Ancient history. So why did you call? Or was it just to warn me I was being followed?"

"Well...I kind of need your help."

Now Jacqueline did laugh. She couldn't help it. "Seriously? You become an all-powerful being, you fight a centimane in the streets, you *nuke Canada,* and you need *my* help?"

"Technically, it wasn't a centimane, it was a hecatoncheires."

"Technically, I don't give a shit. Ryan, why the hell do you..." she caught herself. "No, I was going to ask why you thought I'd help you, but that would be the wrong question. If you were in a tight spot and having problems, I'd be happy to help. You've known that for years. That isn't the problem."

"Then what is?"

"It's the kind of trouble you bring with you right now, Ryan," Jacqueline said. "It's about the fact that you are wanted by the United States government. It's about the fact that you fight monsters in the streets now. That all fine in books and games, Ryan, but I don't want that in my life. I'm already, apparently, being followed by nameless goons."

"I'm sorry. I...wouldn't call if there were any better options, Jacqueline. I hate asking you to risk anything, but I need you. I promise you'll be safe."

"Like you kept Isabel safe?"

Ryan was silent, and Dianmu winced. Jacqueline immediately regretted saying that. "Ryan, I-"

"I screwed up," he said quietly. "I let myself get blindsided. That won't happen this time. I can promise you that."

"I believe you," she said, surprised to find that she actually did.

"Oh, and you'll have some gods that owe you a favor. That's a pretty big deal."

"Oh, I'll have *gods* that owe me a favor. That's a perfectly normal thing to offer in exchange for helping a freaking fugitive. Is Jehovah going to come knocking at my door and offer to pay off my student loans? Is Thor going to slide down my chimney and find my husband a job that doesn't require so my travel? Is Horus going to pop by and offer me a chest full of gold so I can live in luxury?"

"I mean...that last one isn't impossible."

Jacqueline blinked. "You...you're serious."

"Hold on, let me send him a message."

"Send him a message? *Horus*?"

"He's the one watching the men who are watching you," Dianmu said helpfully.

A minute later, Ryan said, "Horus says, 'I was a god of Egypt, Nascent. If you don't think I have *more* than enough gold to pay off any mortal, you truly are as ignorant as I thought you were.' So, yeah, a chest of gold is totally on the table."

"I...for fuck's sake Ryan, what am I supposed to say to *that*?"

Ryan got serious. "You could say yes, Jacqueline. Please. I'm out of options, and the entire world is at stake. I know it's a shitty thing for me to do, but I swear to you that I will keep you safe and I will make it worth your time."

"Walk me through the plan," Jacqueline said after another pregnant pause. "Tell me what's going on, and what you want me to do...and then I'll decide."

Dianmu beamed at her. "I'll go and get you another cup of coffee."

Chapter 18

Meet the New Boss

The moment the others left Crystal's staging area, the strange urge to drop into her nanoverse's time stream vanished, along with the strain of holding back the desire to exercise power over the others. Now she could focus on her power over her *nanoverse,* and that thought immediately created a spike of fear. She took a moment to center herself, breathing slowly and fixing her eyes on the floor, letting her shoulders relax.

Once she felt fully in control of herself, she brought her eyes up to the ruined mess of her nanoverse.

When she'd shown the real display to her companions, she'd expected it to be bad. She'd assumed they would see the wrongness of the stars and the unnatural gaseous nebula stretching between them, but she'd also thought that she would be able to see the improvements from her last visit. Instead, she discovered that her work on her prior visit had been for naught.

The entire universe had turned into a putrid, disgusting mass. While the others had been focused on how the stars pulsed unwholesome colors, Crystal had been looking at the planets. Even from a distance, she could tell that her improvements had not stuck. The worlds were clearly choked with unnatural clouds or covered with strange-colored vegetation. Even without a closer look, it was clear that the revitalization she had set in motion had been halted and reversed.

Maybe it's just from a distance, she told herself now, going over to her control panel. *Maybe things up close aren't as bad.* Filled with desperate hope, she began to navigate her staging area to the homeworld of the Sur-nah-him.

The moment she saw it, she wanted to weep as her hope shriveled. The giant oozes that had fed upon the world and its people were gone, but now the planet was covered with massive insects she could see from the edge of the atmosphere. They worked their way along the ground like maggots on an apple.

She couldn't bring herself to look closer. Not yet. She synced her staging area's time stream to the nanoverse's, so this moment of grief would not prolong anyone's suffering and collapsed into the chair.

Now that she was truly within the nanoverse, she could practically hear the Sur-nah-him's cries for relief.

Relief that, so far, she'd failed to provide them. Hands down, without question, she'd utterly failed them. The people here were her responsibility. Their lives were dependent on her, and she had the power to ensure their needs were met. So what had she done? She'd given them Band-Aids for an infected wound. What defense did she have? "I was worried about the people of Earth, so I just did the minimum and bounced, hoping it got better?" "I didn't know what it would do?" Those were a weak excuse, mainly because the truth was so apparent. *I was afraid.*

She'd been afraid, and she'd let her fear cause them suffering.

How many prayers have they made to me since my last visit? Crystal wondered, fighting a wave of nausea. *How many of them begging me for succor, for hope, for anything other than the bloody hell I've left them trapped in?*

With a growing certainty, Crystal realized there hadn't been many. In a universe like this, why would you think to pray to God? You'd probably want to do whatever you could just to avoid drawing her attention. *If this universe has a devil, they're probably a sodding hero.*

Crystal took a deep breath. She'd let this go on too long. She'd let these people suffer from her own cowardice for millennia upon millennia. It had to stop. The half measures had to stop. She was not going to leave again until she was sure she had fixed it, no matter how long it took. She'd trust the others - even Horus - to look after the fate of the Core for however long she was in here.

Resolved, she stood up and tried to take better stock of what, if anything, her changes had accomplished. There was one spot of hope: the absence of the lake-sized amoebas had given the Sur-Nah-Him an opening to build a single city. *At least I accomplished something,* Crystal thought.

Then she turned her attention to those insects. Dreading what she would see, she magnified her view. They were enormously engorged centipedes with lamprey-like mouths that were surrounded by tendrils. Those appendages forced everything in its path, even the dirt, into their gaping maws. They scurried about, unchecked, devastating the landscape.

Crystal swallowed bile. This was a new super-predator, something that had arisen to fill the ecological niche she'd left when she'd wiped out the oozes. *Evolution should have taken millions of years to produce these things...and it's only been a few hundred. I wasn't gone that long.* Frustration and anger bubbled up within her. She'd *tried and* accomplished almost *nothing.*

Damnit. Damnit damnit damnit. Crystal slammed her fist against the console. It kept happening like that. She tried to will improvements, and her nanoverse spawned Phoberia to stop her. She created a virus to wipe out the Phoberia, and monsters swarmed individual worlds to devour the inhabitants. She got rid of the monsters, and *new* monsters emerged.

She was fumbling as badly as a Nascent trying to create a utopia.

There IS something intelligent out there. Something trying to keep things terrible. It was time to face that fact. No matter what Crystal did, her adversary would twist and distort it, or just create some new awful scenario. All she was doing was forcing him or her or them to be more creative. *Stop trying to fix the symptoms. You have to find the root cause, and you have to eradicate it. Otherwise, it's never going to get better, yeah?*

She began to lower her staging area into the atmosphere.

One of the centipede monstrosities was scurrying after a group of fleeing Sur-nah-him. Crystal's lips pulled back from her teeth in a snarl. *Here we go again*.

She teleported out of her staging area and appeared before the rampaging beast, hand outstretched. The creature roared at the new prey, and its fetid breath washed over her.

With a flick of her finger, Crystal transformed it into a swarm of butterflies that scattered to the four winds.

Immediately, the Sur-nah-him dropped to their knees. "Please spare us!" one of them wailed.

"Oh bloody hell," Crystal grumbled. "Get up. Up! I'm not going to be destroying anyone today."

"Goddess," one of them said in their tongue, although Crystal knew that the word could also mean "destroyer" and "glutton". He continued, his voice resigned, "I thank you for sparing us slow digestion by The Hunger that Walks, and beg you to swiftly end our wretched lives."

Crystal blinked a few times, buying herself time to make sure she properly understood them. "Oh bloody hell," she said, dropping the imperious tones. "I'm not going to kill you.

The Sur-nah-him wailed in terror. "Please, Goddess, I beg you. Spare us whatever living death you have in mind. Give us true death and allow us to embrace oblivion."

Crystal took a few deep breaths, suppressing a flash of irritation. *These people are fatalistic because you let their world rot, Crystal. You let this entire nanoverse rot. Don't blame them for confusing you with whatever monster you left in here with them.*

"Why do you think I'd give you some kind of fate worse than death? Bloody hell, get up already."

They rose to their feet, trembling. A child began to weep, and its mother held it close. The child wasn't the only one crying; the adults were just quieter about it. One of the Sur-nah-him collapsed, sheer terror overwhelming the poor man. *I have to prove to them that I'm better than what they're used to,* Crystal realized.

Going for the blunt option, she snapped her fingers. "I just cured all of you of your various illnesses and filled your bellies. Feeling better?"

The one who had been speaking looked down at his hands, his eyes widening. His skin looked less sallow and drawn, and his formerly malnourished frame had filled out in an instant. Shaking, he opened his mouth, but couldn't seem to speak.

"What's your name?" Crystal asked, trying to keep her voice as calm as possible. *Show them you're reasonable. Show them that they can trust you.*

"Xurir," he said, and Crystal's internal translation told her that the word definitely was his name, but also translated to something similar to "Wretch".

"Well, Xurir, today's your lucky day. We're going to make some improvements so your life is less miserable, yeah?"

Xurir stared at her like he understood the individual words she was saying but could not comprehend what they meant in that combination.

This was going to take a while. "Xurir," Crystal said with as much patience as she could muster, "I want to help you."

His eyes narrowed. "Why?"

She threw up her hands, ignoring the way it made the others flinch. "Does it matter why? Because if this is a pride thing, love, your life is so sodding horrible that you need to ditch that pride but quick."

Xurir shook his head. "I do not know pride. But you are a Goddess, yes? Goddesses do not 'help'. They are like The Feasting Morass, or The Rains of Burning Ice, or The Maws within Mountains: they destroy and kill and take. They do not 'help'. Not unless it leads to later torment."

Crystal felt her nostrils flare and had to remind herself yet again to not let guilt turn into anger. *Crystal, love. Get ahold of yourself. You're missing a pretty big clue here.* The rage subsided as she tried to figure out what she was overlooking. He said "goddesses" do this, "goddesses" do that, with such conviction.

"Xurir. Why, and how, do you have any idea what goddesses act like?"

He took a deep breath, drawing his arms around himself like he expected her to smite him at any moment. "I...that is, we have met the goddesses before. They created us, and we are their playthings."

Crystal's rage had finally found a target. *So...there are goddesses already here, are there? We'll just see about that.* In the meantime, she needed to assure these people that she had control of the situation.

"Xurir, I'm the goddess responsible for them." Crystal wasn't even remotely sure that was true, but since they existed in her nanoverse, it was technically accurate enough. She was responsible for what was happening here, and that included these so-called goddesses. "They will be brought in line. Take me to your city. I have much to discuss with the Sur-nah-him."

Still trembling, Xurir nodded.

***

While they walked, Crystal did her best to put the Sur-nah-him at ease, with only marginal success. Xurir, at least, had finally agreed to walk at her side instead of behind her and seemed to have become more comfortable answering her questions.

"What is the name of the city?" she asked.

"Na-hara," he said.

That translated to "Refuge", which wasn't the world's most cheerful name but could be a lot worse. Perhaps it was a city of comparative wonder and comfort that the Sur-nah-him could recline and relax in, one part of their life that wasn't terrible. However, she was puzzled by the location. They were crossing a vast salt flat, and the distant city seemed to be built in the very center.

"Why did you build it here? There's no food or water near the city. That has to make things more difficult."

"The Hungering Crawlers cannot survive the Great Drying," Xurir explained. "When they try to enter, they long before they reach the city."

He pointed into the distance. Crystal squinted and saw one of the giant centipede-thing's bodies being picked apart by flying creatures.

"We must carry everything to the city," Xurir continued. "It is difficult, and many die, but the city protects our young and weak."

Crystal tried to imagine the work involved to haul enough food, water, and supplies to sustain the population, and couldn't quite fathom it.

"Is that what you were doing when I found you?" she asked. "Are you a foraging party?"

"Yes. I have returned safely forty-three times."

His voice was devoid of pride, or any other emotion, but Crystal still had the sense that this was an unusual accomplishment.

"You're a hero, Xurir," she said softly.

He shrugged. "I am a gatherer. It is my purpose to gather until true death finds me."

Crystal lapsed into silence, brooding. She wondered how the other Sur-nah-him in Na-hara spent their time. It was possible that, since the foragers saw to their needs, the others pursued art or knowledge, creating a vibrant culture supported by the sacrifices of men like Xurir.

She doubted it, though, especially as they drew close to the city. It was a ramshackle collection of towers made of petrified bone and sunbaked dirt. Since the salt flat was the only protection the city had from the horrors of their world, they had clustered as densely as they could in the very center.

Na-hara was *not* a place of wonder and comfort. When they entered the city, Crystal saw that the buildings were in even worse shape than they had seemed from a distance. Every Sur-nah-him she saw had haunted, sunken eyes, and she realized that the foragers, despite their pitiful state, were the strongest and healthiest members of the population. In general, the city's population were listless and apathetic, at least until they saw her. Then they scurried away, around corners and into buildings, hissing "Goddess! Goddess!" as they went.

I should do something, Crystal thought, but what could she do? From the way he kept glancing at her, even Xurir still seemed convinced she'd destroy him on a momentary whim. By the time they had wound their way up a series of rickety bridges and reached the upper-central district, the pathways were utterly deserted.

Even the relatively wealthy and powerful hide from me, she mused. *That shows how bloody scared they are. Here's the thing, though-how have they all identified me on sight? How do they know what a goddess should look like? What the hell has my adversary been up to?*

Crystal was convinced that her opponent was behind the Sur-nah-him's specific terror of goddesses, just like they were responsible for the corruption of the cosmos and the planets' ecosystems. They seemed to have considered even the smallest detail in their campaign of rot and despair. Yet, if she had created demigods within her nanoverse, they would never have had this kind of power.

So far, whoever was behind this had stymied her at every turn. There were too many unknowns, too many variables, and so far, her belief that she could just set things right had been proven wrong time and time again. She had been popping in and out of her nanoverse whenever she thought she could spare the time, while the opposing force had clearly *stayed* here, supervising and adjusting their corruption for centuries. No wonder they had been able to counter her every move.

It was time to root them out and take care of this mess once and for all. The Sur-nah-him, she thought, could help her do that.

"This is the home of our king," Xurir said, as they approached the city's central tower. Other than its height, and the half-heartedly carved double doors, it wasn't any more impressive than the other structures. This was clearly the formal entrance to the king's residence, and Crystal was mildly amused that the king forced people to climb all the way to the top of the city's bridges to see him, instead of letting them enter from the ground level and ascend inside. *Ah, royalty.* At least *some* things never changed.

Instead of entering the tower, she walked closer to the edge of the bridge. From here, she could see the entire salt flat, and how many of those giant centipede monstrosities had attempted to cross it. She'd counted a dozen in various states of decomposition when Xurir interrupted her thoughts.

"We have informed the king of your presence, oh mighty goddess."

Time to see what passes for a king around these parts, Crystal thought.

She strode inside, taking stock of the room. Sur-nah-him lined the walls, prostate with their hands over their heads, shivering with terror. The king, identifiable by his tattered robes and proximity to the oversized wooden "throne", looked like the lord of the beggars.

"Oh, bloody hell, get up, the lot of you," Crystal snapped as her patience with their sniveling demeanor finally ran dry.

At her command, they shambled to their feet. It was like watching the dead animate.

"Look, I'm getting really tired of this. I'm going to make your lives suck less, yeah? And while I'm at it, I'm going to kill the gods that are ruining your lives and probably make some new ones that also suck less. Maybe we'll even get both up to 'good'. But if you keep sodding looking at me like I'm going to snap your necks, there's a good chance I'll bloody well do it, yeah?"

She took a few deep breaths, trying to quell her frustration. It had infected her speech, she knew it, but oddly that seemed to help. While they still looked frightened, the Sur-nah-him at least seemed less uncertain. Crystal pursed her lips. These "goddesses" had these people so cowed that they needed the threat to be on familiar ground. She pointed at the king.

"You. Xurir's been dealing with my cranky ass all day, so it's your turn now. What should I call you?"

The king swallowed roughly. "I am Uepth, your worshipfulness." Crystal's brain translated his name as "offal", and she fought the urge to roll her eyes.

"Great. Uepth. We're going to start with the goddesses, then work on you lot." She walked over and sat on the throne, which seemed to set them even more at ease. "You all deserve to have lives that aren't defined by fear and terror. Why? Because I'm your *real* bloody goddess, and I say so." The Sur-nah-him traded glances, and Crystal wasn't sure if she should cheer or slap them all. These people wouldn't listen to her if she was being reasonable. If she was issuing commands, they'd believe she meant it, even if it went against what they believed goddesses wanted.

Crystal put that in a mental box labeled "Future problems." Nothing would get better here until these entities were dealt with.

"Now," she said, "how do you contact the goddesses?"

Uepth gulped again, before timidly speaking. "We...we do not, your worshipfulness. They come, as you do, when they will. It is not for us to call upon them."

Crystal could nearly hear his unspoken "and why the hell would we want to?"

"Okay, fine. Fair. Then let's see what we can do about your lives." *Plus, if they're as nasty as I think they are, this should draw their attention.* "What do you need most?"

Uepth blanched. "We need to...suffer for your amusement-"

"Enough!" Crystal snapped. "I command you to tell me *exactly* what the greatest ills that your people suffer are. Fail me in this, or tell me what you think I want to hear, and I'll turn your teeth into insects that bite your tongue with every word you speak."

Part of Crystal hated that she was resorting to absurd threats, but it seemed to be the only way to get them to listen. Only Xurir, standing a few feet away from the king, looked thoughtful.

"Yes, worshipfulness!" Uepth stammered. "My people starve and thirst, your worshipfulness. The foragers can barely find enough food and water to stay alive, and parents give up food so their children might live while they starve to death. The Feasting Horrors are numerous and often devour our foragers. This land keeps us safe, but it cracks our skin and the rain sears and scars if we're caught out in it."

Crystal nodded. "Any other major problems?"

"Well...that is to say..."

"Spit it out, love."

"The Crimson Storms can crack our stones, so we must rebuild regularly. We've tried other cities, but all fall prey to the Feasting Horrors. And when a plague hits, it kills so many..." Uepth trailed off, shaking so hard, he seemed about to break his bones. Then he whispered, "I pray that you consider that sufficient suffering."

Holding his gaze, Crystal held up her hand and snapped her fingers. Every Sur-nah-him in the room shuddered. "You now need only half as much food and water to sustain your bodies." The Sur-nah-him looked at her with wide eyes. It was midafternoon, they'd all probably already eaten today. *Poor buggers probably feel full for the first time in their lives.*

Crystal snapped again. "I've wiped out the megafauna, what you call the Feasting Horrors. Last time I did this, I left a niche open for new ones to fill. This time, the apex predators are smaller and can be killed with bow and arrow. One creature will approach your fires when you go out hunting. Give them food, and in time, they will help you find game."

Another snap. "That fixed some of the aberrant weather. No more acid rain and these Crimson Storms are just going to be regular hurricanes."

The Sur-nah-him were gaping openly now. On a few faces, including Xurir's, she saw the beginnings of real hope. Crystal stood up and pointed to a row of windows on her left.

"Now, everybody go look outside. Smartly now."

As a mass, they rushed to do her bidding. Crystal followed at a more leisurely pace.

"All right, loves, watch closely." She snapped her fingers again.

The salt flat rippled and bulged, and then water erupted from the ground. It spread and deepened everywhere around the city, creating a massive lake. The city itself now stood on an island, and normal, healthy plants sprang from the ground and grew to maturity.

She pointed, explaining the landscape's new features. "Fresh water. Grain. Fruit orchards. Got it?"

A few of the Sur-nah-him nodded, but most stood frozen.

"Oh, I almost forgot." One more snap and a land bridge rose from the depths of the lake, connecting the island to the mainland.

For a few minutes, the Sur-nah-him stared at the changes in stunned silence. "But...why?" Uepth finally asked.

Crystal sighed. "Because I'm a benevolent goddess. Because I let you lot suffer too long. And because I think it's going to draw those other goddesses out of hiding."

"They come!" one of the Sur-nah-him shouted, pointing.

Crystal actually laughed. "Damn, I don't think I could have timed that better if I had tried. Kind of nice when things work out your way." She looked where the man pointed, hoping the Sur-nah-him would not notice that her brave words were hollow bravado. Now that the confrontation was at hand, she thought she might be almost as frightened as the Sur-nah-him were.

Purple and blue lightning bolts slammed into the land bridge. Crystal gritted her teeth as she sensed the power, the source of the echo she'd felt in the Phoberia, the same force she felt pushing back against her at every turn.

A little bit showy, aren't you? Crystal thought. Then again, if you wanted to cow the locals, big displays were often the best.

Once again, Crystal reminded herself that she was so far out of her depth that she was swimming over an abyss.

"We are doomed!" Uepth wailed, covering his head with his hands and running away from the windows. Other Sur-nah-him followed, and the city below filled with screams.

Crystal shouted, "No, you're not! You have me, and I can-"

Her words were drowned out by a final lightning strike that brought the screams to a crescendo of torment. The light was so bright that it made spots dance in front of Crystal's vision. When it faded, three figures stood at the end of the bridge, clad in black and purple armor and radiating confidence.

I'm going to crush you all like the bloody insects you are, Crystal thought with a snarl. Whoever these people were, now that she had them in the open, she was certain that she could defeat them. *I'm not distracted now, you wankers. Congratulations on earning my full attention.*

Then the figure in the center held up her fingers and snapped. The lake drained, turning back into salt flats, and the new trees and plants grew writhing tentacles. Crystal's jaw dropped. It was *exactly* how she made changes in the nanoverse, right down to the showy little snap she loved. There was no bending of reality, no twisting equations or formulas. The enemy had simply reached out and imposed her will.

Just like Crystal did. Her confidence vanished.

They're... they're actually as powerful as I am.

Crystal teleported in front of them, then snapped ostentatiously. The grasping tentacles withered, and water again poured out of the salt flat.

Take that, *you presumptuous beasts,* she thought. *Now I have to get them away from the city, or the Sur-nah-him are doomed.*

"You!" the goddess in the center exclaimed.

"What, did you think I'd let you run amok in here forever? Now, who the bloody hell are you, and -"

One of the three extended her hand and sent a pillar of stone shooting from the earth, creating an echoing boom as its speed broke the sound barrier. The pillar grew *sideways* and slammed into Crystal's head. If she'd been in the Core, it would have left nothing but a bloody smear on the stump of her neck.

Crystal rubbed her jaw and tilted her head forward, cracking her neck as she moved her skull and spine back into place. "Okay, fine. You know what? I'm sodding done. You suck, and you're making my nanoverse suck. Let's fight or whatever, and I'll pick the answers out of your corpses."

***

"I still can't believe you lied about why you and Jacqueline broke up," Isabel said, as Ryan watched the various lifeforms appear on his screens in his staging area. According to Athena, his nanoverse had entered the "Biogenesis Era," when ninety percent of the intelligent species that would ever exist were being born. Over the course of the next hundred million local years, new sapient life would stop forming as the old sapient life stabilized and took control of all available resources. He'd hoped watching them would distract him from what he was about to do.

It wasn't working.

"What was I supposed to say? 'She figured out I'm crazy?' I had you, Mom, and Dad completely convinced the man in the suit was just a phase."

"Yeah, I get that, but..." Isabel sighed. "Saying she didn't think you were going to work out long term? I *hated* her for that, you know?"

Ryan winced. "I panicked. I couldn't think of anything that you all would believe, and...and I didn't want to sound like an asshole."

"So instead you made her sound like a bitch. That's pretty crappy, bro." Isabel shook her head and stood. They'd dropped into his nanoverse's time stream for just one day of local time to let her finish sleeping off her hangover.

"I know it was," Ryan said, still looking at the screens. An intelligent species of humanoid amphibians was about to be wiped out by a gamma-ray burst from a nearby supernova. He pushed a couple of buttons to change the burst's path by two degrees. It would hit a lifeless star system a few light-years away. "I just...honestly, there's no excuse for it. And now I'm going to use her as bait to lure in the government super-soldiers."

"She agreed to it," Isabel reminded him.

Ryan shook his head. "I mean...I know she did, but does she really understand what she agreed to?"

"She gets that this is going to be a 'gods and guns' scenario. You were very clear about that."

"Yeah, but..." Ryan hung his head. "Can anyone really understand what this is like before they actually see it?"

Isabel rapped her knuckles on the top of his skull. "Hey, numbnuts. I watched you get shot in the face and had Crystal throw me out of a building under machine gun fire. I *know* what you mean. But Jaqueline isn't stupid. She understands what's she's getting into as much as she possibly can. So stop brooding and beating yourself up."

"Yeah," Ryan said, miserably.

"Ryan. Did you mislead her in any way about what was going to go down?"

He shook his head.

"Did you tell her everything you could about the scenario, in as much detail as you could?"

He nodded.

"And are you going to do *everything* in your power to keep her safe, and pay for any damages that happen to her home?"

"Of course," Ryan said. "And Horus is going to give her a chest of gold."

"Of course he is. Stop being a mopeasaurus. You're not rich enough for Batman brooding, so it just makes you look lame."

Ryan opened his mouth to argue, saw the look in Isabel's eye, and raised his hands in defeat. "All right, all right, I'll chill. You'll be ready to hop nanoverses to make sure she's safe?"

"I know the plan," Isabel said, giving Ryan a thin smile. "I'm not afraid to go out into the thick of things."

"Liar," he countered.

"Of course I'm lying. You all... you're gods. I'm running into the middle of a bunch of gods to help them get your ex to shelter so she doesn't get caught in a supernatural smackdown. Do you realize how insane that sounds?"

"Oh, believe me, I do," Ryan said with a mirthless chuckle. "Still getting used to this being my new normal. Mostly just making it up as I go along."

"Are the others in position yet?"

Ryan checked the clock. "We've got a few more minutes. It'd feel less long if *someone* hadn't needed a quick pit stop to cure her hangover."

Isabel stuck out her tongue at him. "I don't have divine physiology. I don't get to run around drinking myself silly and then be fine the next day."

"True." Ryan sighed. His heart was jackhammering, the pre-fight tension building to the point where he wanted to throw up. "Promise me you'll be safe about this? We could have one of the others babysit Jacqueline during-"

"No," Isabel interrupted sharply. "Absolutely not. You all are already a goddess down. The last thing I'm letting you all do is lose another fighter to take care of me."

Ryan smiled. "I'd be shocked if you'd said anything else. Remember that time you tried to jump those guys that were picking on me?"

Isabel laughed. Ryan had been in sixth grade at the time, Isabel only in second. She'd run in front of Joey Malone, a sixth-grader who had been held back twice.

"He was going to play your head like a bongo drum," she said. "What was I supposed to do, let him beat your ass?"

"I still can't believe it worked," Ryan said, shaking his head. Joey had been willing to punch a lot of people, but not a pigtailed second-grader screaming bloody murder. "I still think Joey retreated out of sheer confusion."

"He was terrified of my battle cry," Isabel said primly.

Before Ryan could retort, a preset alarm told them it was time to go. "Okay," Ryan said, heading to the door of his nanoverse. "As soon as I step out, the doorway should relocate. Be ready to move when it opens."

"I *know* the plan," Isabel said. She gave Ryan a tight hug. "Be careful out there, okay? I don't think my battle cry will work in this case."

He hugged her back. "Thanks, squirt. I'll see you on the other side."

"Later, jerkwad. See you then."

With a laugh and a raised middle finger, Ryan stepped out into the Seattle night.

Jacqueline had always liked the rain, so Ryan supposed it made sense that she had moved to the constantly drizzling Pacific Northwest. He popped his jacket collar, lowered the brim of his hat, and looked around suspiciously. He figured it would look like he was trying - poorly - to spot any watchers. He thought playing the part of being someone ready to jump at any shadow couldn't hurt.

"Horus, you in position?" he whispered.

After a few seconds, he heard the other god's voice in his ear. "Don't forget to say over when you're done, so we don't cross talk. Yes, I am. I'll let you know if anything changes. Don't look, but you've got one watcher in the building on your ten, and another on your five. They've spotted you. Nothing strange on the divine sight, so they're not the supers, but they're on their radios. Stay sharp, Nascent. *Over*."

"Roger that. Over."

Ryan walked down the street toward Jacqueline's two-story white house, complete with a lovely yard and an actual picket fence. It was the kind of place she'd always dreamed of having one day. Once upon a time, they had talked about sharing it.

Her husband, Kurt, was on a business trip to Tokyo. Apparently, he traveled a lot. They didn't have any kids, which was a relief, because there was no way in hell Ryan would have risked this if kids were in the picture. The neighborhood was a new development, and "For Sale" signs dotted the yards. Right now, the others were going through those homes to make sure they truly were empty.

Taking another deep breath, Ryan walked up to the door and knocked. "Just a minute!" came the familiar voice from inside.

Oh crap, Ryan thought, feeling a new panic that had nothing to do with the impending fight. There was no time to run away, though, no time to change plans. The super-soldiers were probably already on their way.

The door opened. "Ryan?" Jacqueline said, looking up at him.

"Hey Jackie," he said, giving her a lopsided grin. "Mind if I come in? It's cold as hell out here."

"Um...sure." She stepped away from the doorframe to let him come in. "Sorry, it's just...it's weird seeing you in person."

"Yeah, I know what you mean." Ryan rubbed the back of his neck. "You look good."

Jaqueline sighed. "I thought we'd got all the awkward done on the phone."

"Yeah, me too." Ryan made himself smile. "I really appreciate you doing this."

"Well, a friend in need..." Jaqueline trailed off, choosing her next words carefully. "Actually, I got nothing."

Ryan understood. It was hard enough to talk to Jaqueline, but it was made worse that they couldn't directly address the fact that there was a plan in place. Her house might be bugged, and it was definitely being watched. Right now, they had to act like Ryan wasn't here because of a trap; he had to look like he was making the same mistake he'd made going to Isabel's. Like he was a complete idiot. Horus had smugly commented that there would be no problem selling that idea.

Ryan had taken the high road and chosen not to respond.

"That makes two of us. Uh...still play Dungeons and Dragons?"

Jaqueline laughed. "Ten years, Ryan. Ten years, you're on the news, and you want to talk about Dungeons and Dragons?"

"I mean...yeah, why not?" Ryan felt the recent panic subside. He'd expected to feel conflicted about seeing the former love of his life again, but apparently, he'd managed to completely move on.

Jaqueline shook her head as her laughter subsided. "No, not these days. We're playing Mutants and Masterminds. Kurt didn't play, but he loved the Marvel movies, so I thought I'd hook him with a superhero game. Showed him some podcasts with voice actors playing to further the addiction. Now we get together with some friends from work once a month. How about you?"

"Not in person. Got into some online games, but the last one fell apart a while ago. I was going to find another one, but then...well, these days it's a bit less appealing. Feels too much like my day job."

Jaqueline quirked an eyebrow. "Day job?"

"Yeah, you know...fighting monsters, doing battles with gods, fumbling and falling flat on my face."

They shared another smile. "Okay, can I say something without you taking it the wrong way or getting awkward about it?" Jaqueline asked, a sparkle in her eye.

Ryan braced himself. "Yeah, go for it."

"Did you actually start working out, or were the biceps part of the divine package?"

Ryan doubled over with laughter. It took him a few seconds to even begin getting it under control. "Well, I did kind of squeeze a universe, so I guess a bit of both?"

"You...you squeezed a universe?" Jaqueline cocked her head.

"Pocket plane that gives me my powers," Ryan said. "It's...a long story. I'll fill you in on it sometime-"

Horus's voice intruded. "Eschaton. The watchers are pulling back. Four hostiles just emerged from a doorway in the house directly across the street. I'll meet the rest of the team in the basement. Get the mortal to safety now. Over."

"Copy that. Over," Ryan said, "Jaqueline, you have to get to the basement, right now."

Maybe the words came out sharper than he'd intended, or perhaps the sudden shift in topics was too unexpected, but Jaqueline stared at him, blinking wildly.

"What?" she said.

You don't have time for this, Ryan thought. "Jaqueline, you need to move *now.*"

Jaqueline was breathing heavily, and her eyes were wild. She was clearly having a very understandable and *extremely* unfortunately timed panic attack. *Shit.*

"Someone down there!" Ryan shouted. "Catch!" Then he reached out to grab reality and twisted hard. The floor beneath Jacqueline's feet transmuted from wood to harmless nitrogen.

She was too terrified to scream as she fell through the sudden hole. Athena slowed her fall before she could break her ankle on the concrete floor.

"Terribly sorry," Athena said, before tossing Jacqueline through an open doorway. "Isabel! My nanoverse!"

Isabel came tearing out of Ryan's doorway and practically leapt into Athena's, slamming the door shut behind her.

Ryan breathed a sigh of relief. Jacqueline and Isabel were both safe.

The sudden sound of shattering glass reminded him that the rest of them definitely weren't.

Chapter 19

No Plan Survives

Bast woke to the sound of hushed conversation and the smell of garlic and tomato sauce. She realized that Liam and Grace must be having another secret date in the empty back closet, whispering sweet phrases to each other and eating something Italian.

Bast felt...nothing. No thirst, no exhaustion, no hunger, no loneliness. Finally, her needs had been fully satiated. She wanted to shout with joy.

Lub-dub. Lub-dub.

The sound called to her, but she forced herself to ignore it. There were more important things to focus on. She flexed her fingers and could feel the threads of reality again. Her power had returned. *Don't rush,* she warned herself, knowing that if she made a mistake, she could set off every alarm in the base. If soldiers with ichor rounds got down here before she'd freed herself...she'd be dead before she even got off the table.

Then she'd be back where she started.

That thought froze her in place, and she took short, hitching breaths. Panic was settling in at the mere idea of resurrecting in an even more secure prison, after everything she'd gone through to break free...

Stop it, she chided herself. *You are Bast. You are a goddess. You will not cower at the idea of what mortals might do.*

Yet the panic remained. Maybe she should wait for Liam and Grace to leave. Wait until all risk had passed. Wait until that damn sound had gone and she didn't get to find out why their hearts called to her.

Lub-dub. Lub-dub.

Bast took slow breaths to steady herself. She remembered the desert hallucination and being stuck over and over again by these people. Stealing her ichor. Stealing her *power.* She drew upon the anger and channeled it into a fire to burn away the fear. No mortal had killed her. It had taken Athena to do that. No mortal had *ever* slain her. They certainly wouldn't do so now. She prepared to twist-

What about the Myrmidons?

That thought stopped her cold. What if the artificial gods were here? They could kill her, without question. They outnumbered her. If they were here, she *couldn't* risk it. They could even see her twists before she finished them, if one of them had their divine sight on and was looking in the right direction.

Bast ground her teeth. If she didn't use her power immediately, she could save it. She could endure the indignity of being strapped to this table a little while longer while she gathered information. She strained to hear the researchers' conversation.

Liam and Grace's voices were quiet. Bast could only make out a few sentences here and there, she heard enough to know they were talking about the consequences of being discovered. *If I could get free, I would teach you all about consequences,* Bast thought with a snarl.

Then she heard the sweetest words.

"...just g-g-glad we're clear right now." Liam's voice.

"You're sure...won't need us?" Grace said. She sounded nervous.

"P-p-positive. The Doctor even s-s-said that we should take the night off. They don't need us to monitor the Myrmidons in the field because-"

Bast didn't bother listening to the rest of the sentence. It didn't matter what else those two twits had to say. Before fear could stop her again, Bast started to twist, making the tiny motions her restraints allowed.

It was like reaching through a grate to grab something the tips of your fingers could barely brush. She was used to manipulating them with broad motions, not these small, delicate brushes. Strands of reality slipped in and out of her grasp. Her forehead furrowed as she focused. *Just a little bit more...*with a snap, the manacles on her wrists started to flake away, small plumes of ash rising from the steel. Bast held the twist in place, feeling reality pushing back against her. *No. You will obey.* The manacles were fading faster now, turning into smoke. They were thinner, and Bast had to fight an urge to pull against them. *Patience,* she reminded herself.

With a final push, the restraints turned to air and dissipated. Removing the mask and the shackles on her ankles was simple once her hands were free. Bast stood and took a moment to just savor the feeling of freedom.

Lub-dub. Lub-dub.

She crept towards the closet door and cracked it open.

"S-s-so," Liam said, and Grace sighed. Their heartbeats were louder now.

"We need to...we shouldn't." Grace turned away from him - and in doing so, turned away from the door, so that both of them were facing away.

"We always s-s-say that." Liam sounded cocky. They were so focused on each other that they didn't notice Bast slipping inside. "At least, we d-d-do after we've had one of t-t-these dates."

Bast held her hand behind Liam's back, her fingers curling into claws. *Lub-dub. Lub-dub.* It was so loud now. She felt her hand shake. She knew what she wanted to do. She knew what it was calling her to do. *I'm not mad. I'm not mad. I'm. Not. Mad.*

"Liam. We have to stop this. It's...it's been too much. If we got caught, we'd both be off the project – or worse."

Or maybe I am. Bast's hand blurred.

"I know, it's j-j-just – urk."

Her blow went straight through Liam's chest, cracking the ribcage with far less resistance than Bast had expected. His heart was in her hand, beating between her fingers. Grace whirled at the sound, and her mouth fell open in wordless terror.

Bast didn't care. She knew what to do. A small part of her screamed in protest, but Bast *wanted* this. She yanked her hand out of Liam's chest and brought his heart to her lips.

It was sweet. It tasted better than any food Bast had ever known, and it was more than just a taste. The sensation of coursed through her body, better than drugs, better than sex. It was like squeezing her nanoverse for the first time. She groaned as she took another bite.

Grace's eyes were wide, and she was making little whimpering noises, too terrified to scream. Her knees knocked together and she sunk to the floor. Tears began to stream down her face as she tried to find her voice.

"That was perfect," Bast said as she put the last scrap of heart in her mouth. She could hear Grace's heart now, beating like a snare drum. She laughed. "Looks like I picked up a sixth Hunger. Just like old Vlad."

That was enough for Grace to find the strength to scream. Bast blurred, and the cry was cut off with a splatter of blood.

The second heart was as good as the first, and Bast devoured it all, licking the blood and viscera from her fingertips. She couldn't hear any heartbeats, now, but there would be more. *How many before I'm full?*

She felt a wave of nausea. She'd *eaten* two *hearts.*

Anthropophage. She shuddered at the word. Gods who fell prey to a new Hunger, one that overpowered all others. In another life, she had hunted them.

I should destroy my nanoverse, she thought, but without conviction. That was what young gods were taught to do if they became an anthropophage. Better that than become a plague upon the world.

Bast had never heard of any anthropophage actually taking that step. She understood why, now. Why would she want to die when she felt more alive than she ever had before?

Now everyone in this base right about you. You are a monster.

Bast stood, cracking her neck. That might be true. However, none of them would live long enough to savor being correct.

Bast twisted, and the air began to flood with a thick, cloying mist. She could kill everyone in this base if she wanted to. An instant, a thought, a single command to the elements, and the base would flood with water, or poison gas, or flame. It'd be easy now - she could wipe out every single person in this damn building now that they'd sealed it up all nice and tight. Part of her *wanted* to. Wanted to punish them for what they'd done to her.

Lub-dub. Lub-dub.

Fear had made their hearts race, and Bast could hear them now in the distance.

There were two reasons Bast held back. The first was a base, primal reason. Their hearts, their damned hearts, *sang* to her. A deep bassline, a beautiful cacophony, each beat calling to her. If she just killed them from a distance, all the hearts would stop.

She'd have no new food.

And then there's the Cassandra. If Bast went for wholesale slaughter, Cassandra would die.

I'll never let that happen.

Bast grabbed Grace's body by the neck and stalked out into the hallway, another twist silencing her footfalls. No one would see her coming, but with their hearts serving as beacons, Bast would have no problem finding *them.*

There were three heartbeats at the end of the hallway, growing closer. Bast could make out muffled footsteps and a slight metallic clatter beneath the constant throbbing. Three soldiers. Bast had to assume they had rounds made from *her* stolen ichor.

She ran her fingers over Grace's face, closing her lifeless eyes. What she was about to do had been beyond her once. But now...now she saw more.

"You will serve me," she whispered in Grace's ear. The soldiers at the end of the hall were advancing cautiously. Soon they would be able to see her through the mist. They were coming for a fight, but they had it wrong. This wasn't a fight. This was a hunt.

And they were prey.

Her work finished, she tossed Grace's corpse down the hallway.

Jimmy Creighton had signed up for the armed forces the day he graduated from high school. He had seen some things over the years that made him lie awake at night. The kind of things that waited for you when you went to sleep. Dark things. He'd even done a few himself, and he'd come to the conclusion long ago that the real monsters were all men.

Now, he was rethinking that conclusion, as he walked down a hallway full of unnatural mist to check on a real monster that lay strapped to a table. Or at least, he hoped she was still strapped to a table. The two soldiers with him were trembling, and Jimmy kept his own hands steady through sheer force of will.

Then he heard a loud thump, followed by dozens more. The sounds grew closer, and Jimmy brought up his gun. "Don't shoot until you see what it is!" he barked before either of his companions could start a round of panic fire.

A figure emerged from the mist, crawling spider-like along the ceiling. When it saw them, it wailed like a banshee.

Jimmy raised his gun and squeezed the trigger. The hallway erupted with the sound of gunfire as bullets designed to kill literal gods tore into the monster. Part of Jimmy was dimly aware that this thing looked like Grace. Most of Jimmy was focused on one thought: *Kill it kill it kill it.*

The corpse's movements became erratic. It started to tumble and roll across the ceiling – like it had fallen, but in some kind of reversed gravity.

"Hoorah!" Jimmy shouted, turning towards the other soldiers.

They weren't there. Instead, he found himself face to face with Bast. Jimmy screamed and tried to bring his gun around. Bast lanced out with one hand and caught it by the barrel, holding it away from herself. He squeezed the trigger, and bullet holes appeared on the wall. He screamed, and she stared at him coolly until the gun clicked empty. Then she reached out and put a hand against his chest.

"Please...please don't kill me," he begged, tears coming to his eyes.

"Well...since you asked nicely..." Bast said, and Jimmy's eyes widened with hope. Then she smiled and rammed her arm into his chest. "No."

The last sight Jimmy Creighton had was the other soldiers, lying dead on the ground, their necks twisted one hundred and eighty degrees.

"Hoorah," Bast echoed, before taking a bite out of his heart.

Bast didn't stop to savor this meal. The mist might favor her for now, but mist did not stop sound, and there would be more soldiers coming soon. *Just a few more bites...*

She stuffed the heart into her mouth. The two that lay dead at her feet would have to wait. *Their hearts are going to spoil.*

Not that she regretted that too much. That rush of power, that heady sensation made regret impossible. But it was a distraction, and she couldn't afford that right now. Instead, she grabbed some of her new power and shifted her body into a black cat. With a few quick steps, she reached the shadows behind some pipes.

Soldiers enhanced with her Ichor, baby Myrmidons who did not yet have harnesses, charged into the hallway. A woman and two men. One of the men turned green when he saw Jimmy Creighton's heartless body.

"Does anyone have eyes on her? Over." Bast knew that voice coming from the radio. Admiral Dale Bridges, US Navy, head of project Myrmidon. Just thinking his name made her want to hiss.

"Hallway C reporting in sir. We missed her. Over." The male. His heart pounded with a rapid, staccato burst of fear.

"You can say that again," the woman said. The tag on her vest said "Johnson", and Bast noted the name.

The other man swallowed as he looked at the empty eyes of Jimmy Creighton. "Shit," he said, a southern drawl turning it into *sheeeeeit.* "Are we sure we can take her? I mean-"

Gunfire. Bast let out a satisfied purr as the thieves looked towards the sound. Johnson raised her hand to keep the others from moving.

A good call. Based on the direction, Bast assumed those soldiers had stumbled upon Liam. She waited...

An explosion rocked the building. Walls shook, doors rattled, and glass shattered. Bast's mouth contorted into a smile.

Liam's corpse had been "wandering" back and forth on the hallway's ceiling. The bodies hadn't been truly reanimated, just caught in a complicated gravity equation that kept them moving. The scream had been a touch Bast added to cover the sound of her own motion. Before turning Liam loose, Bast had twisted his stomach, intestines, and liver into TNT, which had been set off by the gunfire.

"Damnit, Hallway C. We've got people dying out here, *find her.*" The Admiral was almost screaming.

The first man swallowed hard and reached for his walkie-talkie with a trembling hand. "Yes, sir."

Johnson spat. "That asshole's held up in Operations, he doesn't have any more idea than we do."

The leader started to respond, but Bast didn't listen, darting through the cover of mist and darkness and shifting to her human form. She sent out a quick twist as she leaped, a blade of air severing the southern man's head from his body.

She slammed into Johnson, the force snapping the woman's neck. Then she ripped out the leader's heart while he still lived.

They'd told her what she needed to know. The Admiral, the leader of this whole mess, was in Operations.

It was time to say hello.

***

Smoke was filling Jacqueline's home. *At least they still don't know we don't need air,* Ryan thought. "Everyone, outside!" he shouted. Maybe they could do this without destroying the house as they had the office in Ghana.

Bullets begin to tear through the walls, and Ryan hit the floor. The rounds tore into Jacqueline's couch, sending puffs of stuffing flying. Ryan gestured and threw the door off its hinges, sending it flying out into the street. He twisted again, turning it from wood into a solid block of potassium.

Every window in Jacqueline's house burst from the explosion. Shards of glass flew across the room in a deadly hail. Even through the ringing in his ears, Ryan thought the gunfire had stopped.

In a single bound, Athena came flying out of the hole in Jacqueline's floor, holding a gladius in one hand and a large, round hoplon shield in the other. The equations around the shield told Ryan it wasn't an ordinary hunk of metal, but sheets of steel over a carbon nanofiber core, strong enough to stop bullets.

She needed it. Athena used the shield to cover Dianmu and Anansi as the gunfire resumed. Dianmu leapt out, wielding a long spear that ended in a curved blade, and Anansi held a pair of his daggers in inverted grips.

With a single bounding leap, Athena soared over Ryan and braced the shield again. "That was quicker than we expected," she said as bullets rang against the barrier. Horus emerged then, crouched low and holding an assault rifle.

Ryan stood, careful to stay behind the shield. "They must have been standing by. Let's get this outside?"

As they hit the street, Ryan had to gulp for air. *Stupid,* he chided himself. He'd burnt through a chunk of power at the beginning of the fight, and now he was paying for it. Already needing air, and they'd just gotten started. *Remember the plan, Ryan. Don't blow it.*

Ryan reached into his nanoverse and pulled out a sword. It was larger than he expected, almost five feet from hilt to tip, and must have weighed fifty pounds. He very much wanted to meet the beings that typically wielded this weapon. If not for divine strength, Ryan didn't think he'd be able to hold it upright, let alone swing it.

"Incoming!" Athena shouted, leaping into the air. Ryan took the cue and threw himself to the side as Anansi flipped away.

Only Dianmu didn't move, leaving herself straight in the path of an approaching RPG. She smirked and held out her free hand, twisting threads of reality. Her changes latched onto the RPG.

With Dianmu's twist, it arced upwards and headed back the way it had come. It was a small twist, but the super-soldiers met it with a blunt force response. A solid wall of air appeared in front of the RPG, which detonated in a sudden flash that illuminated the street.

There, Ryan thought, tracing the original path of the projectile. Horus, obviously making the same deduction, started shooting in that direction. One of the soldiers tossed aside a long tube and dove out of the way of the gunfire.

Horus's tracer rounds followed him right back to the others, who had taken firing positions between two houses. "Munoz, Palmer. Focus fire on the Antichrist," one of them snapped. "Ross, give us some cover."

Ross? Ryan thought, rolling back behind Athena's shield. "That bastard came back for round two!" he shouted.

"Which bastard?" Athena asked as bullets once again rang against her shield.

"Ross! The one that shot my face off!"

Athena's eyes narrowed. "Oh. *That* bastard."

Athena's anger was almost a physical force, and for a moment, Ryan wondered if he'd have to remind her to stick to the plan. She shook her head, clearing it. "Go," she snapped.

Horus broke from the cover of the shield, running across the street. He continued to fire his gun in short bursts, keeping the pressure on the super-soldiers. Anansi broke in the other direction, hurling a glowing orb just behind the enemy.

The soldiers pushed forward into the street milliseconds before it detonated, rattling windows and sending streams of colored sparks flying in all directions. The leader cursed. "Take them down!"

"Dianmu!" Ryan shouted, but he didn't need to. The thunder goddess was already gripping threads of reality, twisting to create a barrier of flowing air in front of Athena's shield. A burst of flame washed over the top of the shield, deflected by the sudden wind, and lightning strikes fizzled against it. Ryan's heart was racing. If she'd been a second slower, they might have lost Athena.

He twisted and slammed his equations into the ground. A fissure line raced through the asphalt. It encircled the super-soldiers and detonated behind them. He didn't put much force into it, so while it was flashy and loud, it was ultimately low impact.

It served its intended purpose, though, forcing the soldiers further forward and together.

"Damnit, Evans, we're getting overwhelmed," Andrew Palmer snapped.

"No. We're not." Evans sent his own twist into the ground and turned the asphalt beneath his feet to steel. It rose around them, forming a barrier with convenient firing slits.

That has to be draining, Ryan thought. Using a single twist to both reshape matter and change its state took a ton of energy.

Horus's gun clicked empty, and he tossed it aside and sprang to the roof of a nearby house. He pulled another gun from his nanoverse mid-flight and opened fire from this new vantage point, allowed him to shoot over the steel wall.

Diane Munoz whirled to face Horus, sending a high-pressure shockwave toward him. It dispersed his automatic shotgun fire but only sent him staggering back a few steps.

"The primary target is hugging the ground like a little bitch," she snarled.

"Right. We'll handle that in a second. Take out the shooter," Evans said.

They started to twist, and Ryan saw that they were grabbing onto equations for gravity and - *oh no.* "Horus, look out!" Ryan screamed.

Horus had started to create his own barrier, but when he heard the warning, he leapt into the air, turning into a falcon and gaining altitude. Where he had been standing, a perfect sphere was ripped out of the roofing materials and condensed into a ball only a couple inches across.

Horus flapped harder, but he'd stopped moving away and was sliding backwards towards that center point.

Dianmu broke formation, propelling herself upward on tornado force winds. Horus was flapping for all his might, but falcons weren't designed for flying in Jupiter level gravity. *I've got to undo that twist,* Ryan though, reaching out.

Athena grabbed his hand. "Don't! You can't burn that much power."

Ryan grimaced as Horus sunk closer. More bits of the house tore away and compressed into the sphere. A bed, blessedly empty, went flying from the building and wrapped around the center point, folding up until it was absorbed. Ryan tried not to think of what getting that close would do to a bird, but he couldn't help picturing the feathers ripping away, followed by chunks of flesh and bone and-

Dianmu's hands closed around Horus, and she pulled him away from the destruction point.

"Yes!" Ryan shouted.

He should have waited. The moment Horus was safe, the super-soldiers released the twist. The instant they did, the ball of condensed matter exploded outwards and sent shards streaking away in a deadly hail. The shards burst apart in the air, further spreading the destruction.

Ryan looked up at Athena. There were holes in her shield now, and her sword arm hung at her side. Blood poured from a hole through her bicep, and her skin had gone pale.

"Ryan, you have to move!" she shouted. Gunfire started again, the soldiers concentrating their fire on Anansi, who twisted and flickered for a second, then broke down the street and started running away.

Gunfire followed him. Palmer laughed. "Yeah, we got this bitch on the run!"

Ryan forced himself to his feet as his head cleared. Bullets danced around Anansi, stopping in midair before hitting him. *Please tell me this is working,* Ryan thought as he turned on his divine sight.

The real Anansi, shrouded in a twist, stood on top of a house, watching as his illusory self ran was surrounded by illusory suspended bullets.

"Move!" Athena repeated, and Ryan swallowed his fear and dashed out into the street, holding the massive sword across his body and hoping it might stop a bullet or two.

Ross noticed Ryan just as he got close to their wall. "Incoming!" he shouted, as Ryan's sword cleaved a swath of their barrier away, leaving the soldiers exposed on that side.

*All right. Now Horus and Dianmu can...*realization hit Ryan. He'd exposed the left side of the super-soldiers, where Horus and Dianmu *had* been. They'd had to relocate after the gravity bomb had torn the house apart. They were on the *right* side.

All he'd accomplished was making himself a target.

"Deal with him, Ross!" Evans shouted.

Hector dove for Ryan, hurling a sphere of pure force. Ryan caught it on the flat of his blade, but the impact was enough to send his feet sliding along the asphalt. He shoved his sword into the ground, tearing up the pavement with his improvised brake.

Hector was on him the moment he stopped. Before Ryan could even lift the weapon again, the soldier brought his foot up in a roundhouse kick that caught Ryan in the side of the head.

Ryan went flying through the air. If not for the sword, he probably would have flown through a window. Instead used the massive blade as an anchor again, digging it into the dirt as he traveled across a lawn.

Ryan clenched his fists around the hilt, his heart pounding from fear and anger. He yanked the sword out of the ground and charged. Hector responded by twisting with one hand and swinging with the other, exponentially raising the force behind his punch.

Ryan brought up his blade and managed to catch Hector's fist with the flat of the weapon. The force sent Ryan sliding across the lawn again, his feet ripping deep furrows in the mud. *Maybe I should try dodging instead of blocking, so that stops happening.* He pointed the sword at Hector.

Hector's face contorted with anger, and he was already charging. This time Ryan was on his feet and had his weapon ready, however. He swung the blade, forcing Hector to leap back.

That was all the opening Ryan needed to go on the offensive. He didn't want to tap into his divine power, not when he already required air. *Pace yourself.* Instead, he swung the sword in broad chops that forced the super-soldier to duck, weave, and leap to avoid being cut in half. *He's so damn fast,* Ryan thought as Hector jumped over another strike, then used a burst of air to propel himself above Ryan's backswing. Whatever powers were in play here, the fact was this man had likely been fighting since he was in his teens.

Ryan had about a month's worth of combat experience. Only his greater familiarity with divine powers and the long reach of his weapon was making this anything close to an even match. *We still have numbers on our side,* Ryan thought, *and the other gods are much better fighters.* Ryan reached out when Hector leapt again, attempting to twist off Hector's harness. Somehow, it resisted his attempt to warp reality, and the twist only tore off Hector's jacket, leaving him in a white t-shirt under the apparatus. Ryan paused his attack, focusing on part of the harness. It was a red LED indicator showing a numerical display.

Fifty percent.

Hector saw where Ryan was looking and grinned. "That's right, jackass. You're screwed."

Ryan charged again. Seemingly calm, Hector reached up and tapped the harness. The number jumped to seventy-five percent. Ryan swung, screaming with desperation as he put as much force behind the blow as he could muster.

Still grinning, Hector caught the sword with one hand.

Ryan yanked the weapon back, breaking it free of Hector's grip. Before the super-soldier could react, Ryan propelled himself into the air with a twist. *He caught the sword! How the hell did he catch the damn sword?*

Being airborne gave him a chance to survey the battlefield. During his fight with Hector, illusionary Anansi had been struck by a pillar of flame, and Anansi had left an illusory smoldering corpse in its place. Horus was back in human form, his gun thundering. Dianmu was buffeting the soldiers with winds from above, and Athena had advanced, her shield glowing like a blinding spotlight and blinding them.

The three super-soldiers - four, with Hector rejoining them - stood calmly in the middle of the tempest. Each of them started pressing their chest in the same place Hector had.

Oh, this is bad.

The super-soldiers twisted, and suddenly everyone was sent flying away. Ryan rocketed towards a two-story house. With a frantic twist, he diverted his path from the brick chimney and into a glass window. The glass shattered around him, and he was given a painful reminder that movie glass is soft, but real glass breaks into tiny knives that dig into your skin in a dozen places. One shard stuck deep into his leg and was driven even deeper when he ricocheted off the far wall. He started to scream, but everything was happening too fast, and before he could get the sound out, he slammed into the solid oak door of the closet. It cracked under the impact, and Ryan found himself pinned against it.

It felt like an elephant was balancing on one foot on his chest, with a second standing on the shard of glass in his leg. He tried to scream but couldn't through the force that was pressing him against the door. Something cracked, and Ryan could only pray it wasn't his spine.

Just as he thought he couldn't take anymore, the pressure vanished. Ryan slumped to the ground. Everything was weirdly quiet, the sound of battle completely faded. He took advantage of the silence to take stock.

A shard of glass in his leg. Lacerations across his back and arms, and bruises on his...*I don't think I have anything that isn't bruised. I think my bruises are developing new bruises of their own.* His head was pounding, he was gasping for breath, and on top of it all, he was thirsty. No broken bones, though. That was something.

Ryan pulled off the shredded remains of his shirt and twisted it into a narrow tube, then bit down on it. Breathing deeply through his nose, he braced himself and pulled on the shard of glass.

His scream would have given away his position if he hadn't had the shirt in his mouth. *It missed the artery, but you can't keep screwing around,* Ryan thought, taking more deep breaths to get ready for the next wave of pain. He waved his hand over the wound, heat flowing into the injury and cauterizing it. The sensation made him bellow into the shirt again.

He spat out the shirt and sat for a minute, panting and clearing tears of pain, but he knew he had to get back to the fight. He forced himself to his feet. Putting weight on the injured leg wouldn't be in his top ten favorite sensations, but it could hold him, so he counted that as a win. Trying to creep over the broken glass, he limped towards the window.

The super-soldiers were scanning their surroundings. At first glance, they looked utterly unphased, so Ryan wasted a bit more energy on creating a lens to bring them further into focus.

So far, they seemed uninjured, but all four were breathing heavily. Palmer's hand was on his stomach, Munoz licked dry and chapped lips, and Evans's eyes were drooping slightly.

That's right, Ryan thought, dismissing the lens and climbing out of the window. *You might have just thrown me through a window, stabbed me in the leg, and ignored everything we've thrown at you so far while pulling off some of the most complex twists I've seen since Tyr's sunbeams, but everything is still going according to plan. It might look like you're winning, but I've got you right where I want you.*

Ryan hoped that if he repeated the lie enough, his confidence would come back. He ducked into the space between the two houses and peered around the wall.

Slowly, his allies were emerging. Horus's falcon was circling overhead. Athena was pulling herself out of the rubble of Jacqueline's house, moving bricks away with her shield. Dianmu was crawling out of a trench her body had dug in the concrete. Anansi was limping back up the street, using a stop sign as a walking stick.

The super-soldiers nodded to each other and raised their hands.

Oh yeah, Ryan thought sarcastically as he braced himself. *Right where we want you.*

***

Crystal crouched as the three goddesses charged her, ready for their attack. *So they lead off with a rock spike. It hit hard, but I'm sure I can-*

The lead goddess vanished, closing the gap between herself and Crystal in an instant. Crystal had a moment to be surprised before her opponent's hand slammed into her breastbone. The energy in the strike was so immense, it distorted space-time, freezing this instant in time. Crystal stared into the blank, faceless mask of her opponent, her eyes wide with shock. *How could she hit like that?*

Then time resumed. Crystal was sent hurtling through the atmosphere and into the void.

The hit hadn't been painful because her physical sensation simply shut down. Crystal's nerves had no idea how to interpret what was happening to them. *No...*Crystal thought, barely able to focus enough to even form that protest. *The Sur-nah-him...*

It was too late. A wave of destruction spread out, a flame storm following it across Shadoth. The Sur-nah-him were already dead. Tears formed in Crystal's eyes. Beneath her, molten stone burst from cracks that were forming across the world. Crystal managed to get control of her body and reached out towards the retreating planet, gathering her will.

It was too late. The planet exploded along the fault lines. Two hemispheres separated, the space between them filling with enormous plumes of magma that froze as their heat dissipated.

Crystal screamed into the void, a blend of rage and terror. *You thought you were so bright, didn't you? Lead them outside the city, keep the Sur-nah-him safe*, Crystal railed at herself as chunks of planetary debris began to spread across the solar system.

The anger helped push down the fear, but it didn't dispel the realization that these goddesses were as omnipotent as Crystal herself. She wasn't sure she could create something as powerful as them even if she had tried, and now there were three of them.

A warmth began to spread across Crystal's back, and she snapped her arms out, halting her momentum before she impacted the green star. Tendrils of green flame lashed towards her as if they sensed her presence and wanted to grab her and pull her down into the immense heat.

She held her hands outstretched, warding away the solar flare, just as the two halves of Shadoth collapsed back into each other, shattering anew from the impact.

Nothing on that world had survived.

How could they? How *could* they? These three, whatever they were, were *of* this nanoverse. They should be shepherding it, guiding it. Treating it like a garden. In all her millions of years of existence, Crystal had never obliterated a planet with living beings on it. The idea was unthinkable.

In the dark days after she'd ended the world, Crystal had wandered a dead Core universe. She'd sat on planets that were falling into singularities, she'd walked through the ruins of civilizations, and she'd stared into the nebulas formed by suns going supernova. In those dark days, the only thing that had kept her sane was the knowledge there was one place where she could protect everyone.

And they're taking that from you.

Crystal screamed again and held her hand toward shattered ruins of Shadoth. Beneath her fingers, stones pulled themselves back to the world. The planetary crust flowed like water, sloshing together until the original crust was back on the surface. Grass began to spread, water coalesced out of the void, and the bodies that had been scattered erupted from the ground or were pulled back from orbit as the atmosphere reformed.

Shadoth had been restored to its former state.

"It's a stupid, pointless gesture," said a voice behind Crystal. She whirled to face the three goddesses. "Why do you waste your time preserving a single world?"

"I'd waste my time to preserve a single life," Crystal spat. "Now...who the *hell* are you?"

In the vacuum of space, there was no sound to carry her words, so she wrote them into the fabric of reality, a voiceless demand that made a question into a divine mandate. It would have been more impressive if her opponents hadn't just done the same thing to speak to her. Their armor was unscathed by the explosion of Shadoth, their body language relaxed and calm.

The first of the figures extended her hand towards Crystal. "I am the emptiness that awaits at the end of power; I am all that you need, the gnawing need for more that you can never satiate." From her extended fingers, she hurled a supermassive black hole at Crystal. "I am Inedia."

Crystal threw out her hands and caught the black hole before she could enter its event horizon. It kept trying to advance on her, as if it was propelled by some malign consciousness. *No,* Crystal thought. *That's not what it's like. That's what it is.* Crystal gritted her teeth and turned the black hole into a wormhole, its opposite end in some distant star. Plasma spewed from the wormhole in an apocalyptic stream towards Inedia.

Inedia stopped it by raising a single hand, canceling out its existence before it could reach her. Crystal felt her hands begin to tremble. It had been so *effortless.*

The second goddess gestured and spoke. "I am all that you lack, all that you could have been, your squandered opportunities." Crystal held up her hands to defend against the attack, but the goddess wasn't attacking her; she was shattering time. Crystal found herself on a battlefield in four dimensions, with each of her opponents able to attack her from different epochs. "You may call me Litura."

Crystal's heart pounded. She tried to force time back into a single line, but the fabric of reality had been broken and didn't just snap to her whims like it was supposed to. Litura was actively maintaining the fractured timeline. Alone. *She can resist me without the others. Damnit, I can't even overpower one of them.* Crystal stopped trying to fight the fragmentation and prepared herself to defend against attacks that were coming, had come, and will be coming.

In the future timeline, the third was speaking. Would have been speaking. Crystal put aside the question of pronouns to focus on the threats. "I am all that you will be, the ultimate fate of your arrogance and this very corruption that will remake you." She gestured. Crystal moved at the speed of light to evade spatial anomalies that surged from that gesture, razor-sharp shards of force without mass. She was able to deflect one, and it careened into the outer solar system. "You will call me Potentia."

Inedia and Litura joined in on the assault – or with the way time was fragmented, they had joined and will join and were joining in the attack, trying their best to shatter reality around Crystal. She saw what they were doing, saw the implicit shape their designs were taking – they were going to cut her off from her nanoverse, excise her like a cyst on her own reality. Potentia's barrage of anomalies were going to break her away from it spatially. Litura's temporal assault would isolate her from the time stream. Inedia would then destroy her body with force.

It was a nightmare given reality. Or, more accurately, given unreality. Crystal had never imagined such a thing would even be possible.

You can't beat them physically. Crystal thought as she danced through shattered timelines. Sweat beaded from her forehead from both fear and the sheer effort of affirming her own existence against these assaults.

There was one hope she had left. She had to take the battle into the metaphysical.

"I am!" Crystal screamed. Those words were an assertion onto reality itself, a testament of the self. She anchored herself to those words and inscribed them into the fundamental laws of the universe. The ripple it sent out through reality was strong enough that it sent her three opponents reeling. Crystal hadn't just made it true now, she made it so it was true and always had been true and always will be true.

It bought her a moment to form a plan. A desperate, hopeless gamble, but it was a plan. Crystal snapped her fingers.

The false goddesses didn't wait to see what her snap had created. They switched to the metaphysical to match her in kind. Inedia wrote into reality a deconstruction of the nature of being - I think, therefore I am not - and bludgeoned Crystal with that falsehood. It was a philosophical mace that struck Crystal across the face, and Crystal could feel it tearing at her fundamental sense of being, sinking claws into her doubts and tearing at her as though they were physical weapons. It also shattered her jaw as the lines between literal and figurative ran like chalk in the rain.

Crystal tried to mount a defense against the assault, but in the future, Litura wove a nihilistic dirge into reality and sent that song of Nothing to coil its way into Crystal's ears. It screamed silently into Crystal that reality was a lie, existence was futile, and she should allow herself to be unmade. Those doubts broke cracks in Crystal's psyche, and she screamed at the uncertainty. Ichor began to pour from Crystal's ears as the sound-that-wasn't ruptured her eardrums.

Potentia took both attacks and amplified them by making them into autopropagating memes, horrendous thoughts that crept into Crystal's brain and began evolving by the picosecond to find her most delicate fears and use those cracks to change the battlefield in her own mind. Every defense Crystal could come up with was adapted to before she could even put it in place. Cuts began to appear across her face and arms and legs as the psychic attacks manifested as physical injuries.

Crystal couldn't stop it. It was too much, coming from too many whens, on too many levels, the psychosomatic becoming somatic becoming flesh and tearing into her.

"You held true power in your hand, and you brought it here to shatter it like a coward!" Inedia shrieked as Crystal brought her hands and inserted them into her own eye sockets, already gibbering from the assault. "You could have had anything you wanted, and you chose fear."

"We were spawned from your weakness magnified by Enki's hate," Litura intoned in a much calmer voice, "that will that fused two nanoverse together could not be so simply dissipated." As they watched, Crystal began to tear at the back of her neck, trying to get at the thoughts that assaulted her mind and, in the process, starting to crack through her own skull.

"We could have worked together. We are shards of Enki's will, yes, but we are interpreted through you. There is nothing in us that you do not desire." Potentia's voice was calm and reasonable like they were having a discussion, and not like Crystal was already throwing aside flecks of her skull like bits of eggshell. "We will take your body and become you. Then we will set ourselves to gaining power over all realities. We will finish Enki's grand design and rule over the Core and all within it."

As those last words finished manifesting in the fractured fabric of the universe, Crystal shattered her own skull completely, leaving a headless corpse in the broken fabric of reality.

"That was quick," Inedia whined. "I was hoping she'd put up more of a fight."

"Be glad she didn't," Litura said dryly. "I don't know how long we could have held out against her here."

Potentia put reality back in place. "It doesn't matter anymore. We will finally be real. And she has access to six nanoverses – once we merge and slay the others, we'll be unstoppable." The three removed their masks at the same time, to show that they were all identical to Crystal. "Enki was a fool, but his death has given us birth. We will be free."

Crystal's empty, broken body floated through the fractured timeline and sunk towards the green, grasping sun.

Chapter 20

Miscalculations

Tendrils of mist flooded through the hallways of the base, cloying and grasping like the tentacles of some immense beast. The fog was as unnatural as the woman controlling it. "Get every noncom into Operations," Dale shouted. "Use private frequencies, don't broadcast it. We don't want her to know where to look."

"You think she's free?" Doctor Pivarti asked.

Dale wanted to rub his temples. Well, what he wanted was a bottle of aspirin, a glass of whiskey, and eight hours of sleep. "We have to act like she is. If there's some other explanation, we'll find it later."

Doctor Pivarti nodded. "Where are Liam and Grace?"

Dale looked around the room. He saw Cassandra, standing off in a corner and staring blankly ahead. Eugene was pacing the back wall, muttering to himself. The other two members of the doctor's team were absent. "You," Dale said, pointing to Cassandra.

At the word, the young woman started and looked at him with abject terror. "I know you're scared," Dale said, switching to the modulated voice he used for civilians. "But we need to know if you've seen Liam and Grace."

Cassandra's voice was completely flat. "They were in the lab. They were planning to have a romantic dinner when everyone left. They don't think anyone knows. They wouldn't have left yet."

The doctor closed her eyes for a moment and took a slow breath. "Admiral, I'd like to send someone to check on the remaining members of my team."

"I know, Doctor," Dale said, his voice firm. "That can't be risked right now. If I'm wrong, they're safe. If I'm not, they're already dead."

Cassandra went white as a sheet.

"Then what would you have us do?" Pivarti's voice had a hard edge.

Dale finished a quick inspection. Every other civilian was in the room. "We've waited long enough. Initiate lockdown of the entire facility, now." That last command wasn't for Doctor Pivarti's benefit, but for the staff that ran the facility. They immediately turned and began to furiously work their keyboards. All across the steel shutters slammed down over the windows. Every interior door locked itself, with a three-inch steel drawbar sliding into place across each of them. Only the Admiral or Doctor Pivarti could override the lockdown. The base switched to its own internal generator, and air filtration systems activated. They were completely cut off from the outside world. *I'm so sorry I didn't bother consulting you, Mr. President,* Dale thought with an admittedly puerile smugness.

"Admiral," Doctor Pivarti said, her voice low. Dale appreciated the respect for the chain of command - she'd waited until the lockdown was in place, and from where they were standing, only Lazzario could overhear their conversation. "Don't you think you're overreacting? We still don't know what the cause is and have no reason to believe the subject is anything other than contained."

He shook his head. "Better to overreact and be wrong."

Lazzario nodded in agreement. "No offense," he said, also keeping his voice low, "but what's the harm if she's not free? We tell everyone it was a drill, and no risks this way. I mean...we don't have our best assets for dealing with her right now."

Doctor Pivarti went ashen as the realization set in that they only had soldiers with guns against a woman who had the power to fool people into worshipping her as a goddess. "Of course, Admiral," she said, her voice full of confidence her face didn't match. "Then can we at least send someone down to check on the subject?"

Dale gave the orders, and officers began to relay them through radios. If Bast was free, she would know they knew, but putting the entire base on lockdown would have given that away regardless.

"Sir, we're not getting responses," one of the communication officers said.

"Something's disrupting communications," another added.

Dale had a sinking feeling that it wasn't a coincidence that radios were failing. "What about our sensors?"

"Interference there too, sir." The communications officer grimaced. "There seem to be ferromagnetic particles in the mist. It's disrupting everything."

For several tense seconds, there was silence.

"Wait, I'm getting something. It's Sergeant Howard."

Dale leaned forward. Howard had been on duty outside the containment room.

"I'm sorry," said a voice filled with amused arrogance, "the Sergeant can't come to the phone right now. Please leave a message after the agonized scream."

The sounds that came over the radio were rendered inhuman by pain and fear. Cassandra let out an agonized sob and turned to face the wall. Lazzario went pale. Everyone focused on the speaker until the shrieks ended with a sickening gurgle.

Silence reigned in Operations. Finally, the radio crackled to life again. "You were supposed to leave a message," Bast said, her voice almost warm. Like they were two friends laughing over an inside joke.

Dale grabbed sat down at a microphone. "Patch me into that radio," he demanded. When the officer nodded, he said, "This is Admiral Dale Bridges, United States Navy. Over."

"Hello, Admiral. It's good to finally talk to you. I've been...incommunicado recently. Over."

"Bast. We're willing to listen to your demands. Perhaps we can reach an accommodation. Over." Dale shook his head for the benefit of the stricken faces in Operations. There would be no negotiating with this monster. But with the Myrmidons engaged in an active firefight right now, the only thing they *could* do was stall until they returned. He needed to keep her talking.

"My demands, Admiral?" Her tone gained harsh notes, unadulterated hatred layering over her voice. "You locked me down, prevented me from knowing even the most basic comforts. For weeks. Maybe even months. For so long *I don't even know time anymore.* I don't have demands, Admiral Dale Bridges. United States Navy. I have a story. Over."

"Stay off comms," he said to the others. "I want the Myrmidons recalled as soon as they can disengage. We are in code red. Now!" People began to scurry as he turned back to the console and pushed the broadcast button. "Very well," he said, doing his best to keep his voice level. He was in charge, he was in control, and everyone needed to know it. "And what is this story? Over."

"Long ago, my people were given an ultimatum by a vengeful angel. Maybe he was acting on God's orders, maybe he wasn't. I didn't exactly ask. But it was a story I'm sure you know, Admiral. Every firstborn son would die, but he would pass over the houses that had been painted with the blood of a lamb, for that was how he'd know they were Hebrews. Do you know the story?"

It seemed she wasn't going to say "over" this time. "Yes, Bast," Dale said. "To free His chosen people from bondage, God sent plagues upon the pagans of Egypt. That was one of them. Over."

"Spoken like a true believer, Admiral. Well, here's my offer to you. I'm going to kill everyone in this base, one by one. I'll spare anyone in a room that has a lamb's blood painted over the door." This time, she didn't spit the final word but purred it like cat batting at a mouse. "Over."

Dale took a deep breath. "The base is in lockdown. We don't have any lambs here. Over."

Her response was immediate. "Well, isn't that a shame?"

Dale felt his heart rate accelerate. He turned to Operations, making sure to include the entire room. "When we found this monster, she'd been stabbed to death. She may be ancient, she may be powerful, but we've made gods bleed already. We can kill her, and by God, we will."

His tone seemed to give the men and women courage, and movement resumed.

"Sir?" Admiral Bridges turned to look at Doctor Parvathi. She looked every bit as frayed as he felt. "The Myrmidons still might not return in time. They're already engaged with the primary target, and if they're drained at the end of it, they won't have the power."

Dale ground his teeth. "Well, Doctor, do you have a better idea?"

To his surprise, the doctor nodded, although she frowned in concern. "Yes, but I doubt you'll like it."

The Admiral sighed. "Doctor, we're running low on options. If you have a suggestion, by all means, please share." The fact that he had to drag everything out of this woman –

"Activate the failsafe on level eight."

The words completely derailed Dale's thought, and he stared at her with his mouth open. "You want me to do *what* exactly?"

Doctor Pivarti didn't waiver, "Activate the failsafe. I know the intention was to utilize it only in the most extreme circumstances, but Bast is free, she's homicidal, and she has a serious grudge against us. I don't see us getting out of this alive, but the failsafe should permanently kill her."

He mulled over the doctor's words. The idea was almost unthinkable, but so was the situation.

He could feel every eye in the room.

"No," he said. It felt like every person in the room let out a breath at the same time. "There's no guarantee it'll permanently end the threat she poses. I'm not throwing away every life here for the *chance* we eliminate a single threat."

Doctor Pivarti nodded, and even she looked relieved. He wondered if she had been testing him.

"Understood, sir. In that case, perhaps we should dispatch a team to permanently disable it? Otherwise, we could risk the subject getting her hands on an active nuclear warhead."

That was an excellent suggestion, and he relayed it. "What I want to know," he said, turning back to the doctor, "is how the hell she even got out of there in the first place. She was disabled for weeks, and we took every measure you wanted implemented. No food or drink or interaction. We didn't even interrogate her. You were *certain* that would keep her from getting her strength back. So why the hell is she running around our base?"

"Someone must have broken containment protocols, sir." The doctor shook her head. "I assure you, without that, she had no way of getting the strength to get out."

The Admiral turned to watch the intermittent camera feeds. Somehow, Bast was playing havoc with all of their communications and monitoring. Most of the screens showed only static, but a few displayed soldiers slowly walking through hallways with their guns raised, checking corners and occasionally firing at something unseen.

The radio crackled to life again. "Admiral," Bast purred. "Are you still there? Over."

"I'm here. Over."

"I do have a few demands, actually. Over."

Dale swallowed hard. "Let's hear it. Over."

"First, tell me where you're keeping what you call the Black Sphere. Over."

To the communications officer, Dale said, "Do whatever you can to get as many people as possible guarding the sphere." Then he got back on the radio slowly explained the location of the item, giving Bast directions that were the opposite of the most direct path. Pivarti was glaring daggers at him, but he was confident that a force that was ready for her, and armed with ichor rounds, would take her down. If nothing else, this bought them more time.

"Excellent, Admiral. Now, for my second demand. Does Cassandra happen to be with you? Over."

All eyes turned to Cassandra's ashen face.

***

Bast crept through the hallway, following Dale's directions.

There were two ways this could turn out. If Dale was smart, he had realized his only hope was to meet every one of Bast's demands and pray that she would be merciful. Bast had decided that in that case she *would* be gracious and would kill him slightly more quickly than she had planned. It was good to reward intelligence.

Of course, he might not be intelligent. Instead, he might be trying to be *clever* by directing her into some kind of trap. In that case, she would see through it, evade it, kill whoever happened to be around, and then give Dale one more chance to give her proper directions. Then she would get her nanoverse, find Dale, and kill him without any semblance of mercy. There was *nothing* worse than a man who thought he was being clever.

And if he didn't give her the proper directions the second time, she would find her nanoverse on her own, kill everyone in the building, and then show Dale exactly how creative she could be when she really set her mind to it.

Lubdublubdublubdub.

Bast stopped short. Just around the next corner, she heard at least a dozen heartbeats. She twisted light to give herself a window and rolled her eyes. Looks like he'd opted for "clever".

She suspected that he'd thrown every available asset into this ambush. The soldiers were kitted out in Kevlar and high tech goggles, arranged in ranks as wide as the hallway would allow and staring ahead with rapt attention. The moment Bast stepped into the hall, it would be full of hot lead.

Bast was almost impressed. The soldiers were incredibly still and extremely quiet, and most other gods might have believed the hallway was safe, and the trap was still ahead further ahead. But Bast didn't make assumptions, and the soldiers couldn't quiet their hearts.

Careful now. Careful. There were a lot of guns in that hall, and without her nanoverse at hand, Bast would need to use a fair amount of power to arm herself. With a flick of her fingers, she twisted. Air condensed in her hand, forming a solid blade of perfectly sharpened iron.

Immediately, Bast's Hunger sharpened, and the soldiers' heartbeats seemed to grow louder. She was gambling on being able to feed before she expended too much energy, and the uncertainty of the situation made her own heart speed up.

Bast did one last twist and sprang around the corner.

Gunfire erupted in short bursts from at least ten automatic weapons. The sound was an oppressive force in its own right, enough to drown out the pounding heartbeats. Bast charged towards her attackers, her free hand held in front of her to maintain a shield of air. Bullets bounced off the barrier, and soldiers shouted and cursed but kept firing.

One of them, either in panic or desperate hope or genuine brilliance, turned his gun towards the wall and sent bullets ricocheting in new directions. One bounced behind her shield and punched into her left bicep. Pain exploded through her arm as the damn ichor-laced round tore through muscle and nicked bone, and Bast shrieked, losing both her concentration and her shield. An instant sooner, and they might have had her.

But now she was among them.

She slashed out with her sword, slicing a soldier's throat. As his hand leapt uselessly to the wound, she kicked him out of the way. Blood began to run between his fingers. She plunged her sword into another man's chest, then tore it loose and spun to decapitate another enemy. The gunfire went on, but the soldiers were beginning to panic, and their shots went wide.

The same soldier who had ricocheted his bullets dropped his rifle and lunged at her with a long hunting knife, drawing a thin line of blood along her ribs. Clearly neither panic nor hope-this one was *smart*. And fast. Bast risked ignoring the others for a few seconds as she sent a bludgeon of air against his knife hand. As his fingers broke and his weapon dropped, she plunged her hand into his chest and tore out his heart.

"Not quite smart enough," she said aloud as she leapt up and flipped over the other soldiers, landing behind them and cramming the heart into her mouth, chewing madly, blood streaming down her face.

The sight was too much for some of her attackers, who broke rank and dashed in the other direction. If her mouth hadn't been full, Bast might have laughed. Instead, she plunged the hallway into darkness and rushed into the center of the remaining foes. She spun her blade in a circle, blade slashing and hacking, and blood fountained around her.

Finally, there was only one, a barely ambulatory soldier who was trying desperately to scramble away. Bast let her twist fade and light filled the blood-soaked hallway.

"Oh my God," the soldier moaned as Bast strolled toward him. "Oh, my God, please help me. Please."

Bast took a handful of his hair and turned him roughly around.

"You're asking the wrong one," she purred. Then she fed.

Following Dale's directions again, she turned left at the end of the hall, into corridor H. She was starting to think she might be taking the long way, thanks to Dale's "cleverness", but it didn't matter. She would find what she needed eventually. A few turns later and she saw something promising: a solid steel door with several complex locking mechanisms.

Bast rolled her eyes. *Humans and their fancy toys.* With a gesture, she turned the steel to mist, flooding both the hallway and the room beyond. Her nanoverse was inside. She could feel it and wanted to rush in, but this was not the time to ignore caution, especially since she heard a heartbeat. Someone was waiting for her. She began to call up a gentle wind to disperse the mist throughout the building, but then she heard a voice from inside.

"B-Bast?"

Cassandra.

"Yes, it's me," Bast said quietly.

"Don't you *dare* come any closer," Cassandra spat.

Bast could sense the woman's anger, and her fear, and paused to consider the situation. "Cassandra, I told them to send you to me. You came. You're obviously waiting for me. Why would you tell me to stop?"

Cassandra laughed bitterly. "You think I came because I *wanted* to? Jesus Christ, Bast, you...you honestly thought that, didn't you?"

"Of course I did." Bast blinked, trying to make sense of this. "Why wouldn't I? Cassandra, you saved me."

"Yes, I did," Cassandra said. "What they were doing to you...it was wrong. Completely, undeniably wrong. I had to put a stop to it. But I didn't think you'd do *this.* I didn't even think you could get free! You told me you *couldn't.*"

"No, I didn't." Bast sighed and leaned against the doorframe, respecting Cassandra's wish for distance. She began to clear the mist. "I was cautious about how I answered your questions."

"Yeah, I guess you were. How did you do it, Bast? What question did I miss?" Cassandra knew she was provoking the goddess, but she couldn't have cared less. The moment that she'd been shoved into Black Sphere's room with a bomb padlocked to her chest, she'd stopped worrying about anything as mundane as pissing off their former test subject.

"Warn her," Pivarti had said, "and the Admiral will have no choice but to detonate the bomb. Stall her, and perhaps there's still a chance of salvaging something. Including your life."

Cassandra hadn't believed her for a second.

"You didn't even have the context to ask the right questions." Bast waved her hand, and the mist began to clear. "I don't see a harm in telling you, and I owe you that much, at least. We gods depend on two things for our power. One is our nanoverse, what you call the Black Sphere. It's a...battery of sorts. The nanoverse has near-infinite power, but we cannot use it indefinitely without cost. Our Hungers limit as. As we burn through power, we start needing mortal things. Air. Water. Food. Sleep. Socialization. Without them, we become helpless."

As the mist began to clear, Bast saw the bulky black vest over Cassandra's lab coat. She felt a sharp stab of fear and twisted quickly. *Bridges, you bastard,* she thought. *You despicable, insolent worm. Death is too good for you.*

The work was done in an instant, and Bast clamped down her rage. The worm could wait. Cassandra was what mattered now.

"So I let you escape," Cassandra whispered. "Jesus Christ. You played me. That's... I'm such an idiot. I fell for it hook, line, and sinker. You needed all of those, and I gave them to you because I thought you were in *pain.*"

"I was!" Bast snapped. How could Cassandra not *see* what was going on here? She softened her voice. "I *was* in pain. These are real, physical needs. My mouth was a desert, my stomach a pit. I could barely stay awake yet was in too much pain to sleep. The need to socialize...it was as sharp as grief. We feel these things as sharply as you do, except that mortals will eventually die, while we just...persist. In agony. I was in pain, and you spared me from it. It was the right thing to do."

Exhausted, terrified, and confused, Cassandra took a deep breath. Any second now, the mist would clear enough for Bridges to confirm Bast's proximity, and then this would all be over. At least she would die knowing that she had made her mistakes for the right reasons. "It was wrong to let you suffer. But Bast, this...what you're doing is *monstrous.* How many people have you killed today?"

"Not that many. Only those that got in my way."

"How many, damn it?"

Bast considered for a moment, hoping to find some way to calm Cassandra down. This definitely wasn't going well. "I haven't been keeping track," she finally admitted.

"You've been killing people and you *lost track,* and you don't see a problem with that? Those deaths are on my head, too!" Cassandra's voice was cold with fury.

Bast shrugged. "Let go of that. I am a goddess, Cassandra. I am over three thousand years old. Do you really think you can take credit for my actions?"

"I don't want *credit*!" Cassandra shrieked in anguished rage.

"If you can't take credit, you can't accept guilt," Bast said. That didn't seem to help, so she tried another tactic. "I'm not a monster, Cassandra. I've been tortured all this time, with no recourse. If it drove me to the brink of madness. Maybe even over the edge of it. There's nothing monstrous in that, is there? And my nanoverse...I need it, in a way I couldn't ever explain to you. I need it, and they took it, and *used* it somehow, without my consent. It's...a violation. That's the best way I can think to describe it. As serious as the violation of my body."

"I can't imagine what you went through," Cassandra said. Her mind whirled, trying to make sense of it all, trying to answer questions of psychology and culpability that would take a lifetime to unravel. She felt her sympathies pricked again, but the carnage in the base overruled them. "What you're doing here... it's too much. You've gone too far."

Cassandra closed her eyes and braced herself. Any moment now, the vest was going to explode, and that would be that. *As far as last words go, I could have done worse than "You've gone too far." Makes me sound a bit like an action movie heroine. Always figured if I did die early, my last words would be "the chemicals aren't supposed to turn that color," but this will do.*

Bast knew that she needed to move this along, so she decided to say whatever was necessary now and sort the truth out later. "I was half-mad, I think," she said, "but I also thought to protect you. To *protect* you, Cassandra. That's why I asked for you: so they couldn't hurt or punish you for being the only worthwhile person in this whole accursed building. And *because* you're decent, because you're better than *all* of them, they turned you into a weapon so they could throw your life away for their own purposes. Who's the real monster, Cassandra?"

"It doesn't matter."

"Yes, it does, because we aren't going to die. I already turned the C4 into ice. I won't let anything happen to you. You're safe, Cassandra. So let me ask you again: who is the monster?"

All of you, Cassandra thought, but didn't say. A moment ago she'd been sure she was going to die, but now she had a chance to live. The last thing she was going to do was risk throwing it away by making Bast angry.

And...Doctor Pivarti had sent her here to die. Cassandra had given the woman years of her life, devoted her career to the doctor's theories, and she'd been willing to sacrifice Cassandra for a chance of stopping Bast.

"They are," Cassandra said finally. "Admiral Bridges and Doctor Pivarti."

Bast nodded. "I thought you'd see it that way. Cassandra, you set me free, even if you didn't intend to. You *did* intend to ease my pain, and I will forever be grateful. Honestly grateful. I'll protect you, but you have to make a choice. If you want to stay here and face whatever consequences the monsters deem necessary, I'll make sure you're unharmed until they come for you. Or you can accept my gift and come with me."

Cassandra, still getting used to the idea that she wasn't about to die, stared at Bast in confusion. "What...what gift?"

"It's a horrible gift. A terrible thing. But you will never, ever be weak again. No one will be able to use you. I can promise you that. And it's the only way for you to be safe during what's ahead of us. Do you accept?" Bast held her breath. If Cassandra said no, Bast would have to figure out another way to preserve her life or force the change on her. *Please say yes.*

Cassandra couldn't think straight, couldn't figure out the right questions to ask, or how much time she had before Bast grew impatient. But she had been about to die, so how could this gift, no matter how terrible, be worse? And if it was, she could always give it back, or choose death on her own terms. Besides, she had no idea what Bast would do if she said no. "Okay. I'll. I'll do it."

Bast felt a flood of relief and moved quickly. She snatched her nanoverse, feeling whole for the first time since she'd fallen on Graham Island, and then pulled out a dagger. With a single, swift gesture, she sliced open her own palm. Before Cassandra could react, she grabbed the other woman by the back of the head and pushed her palm against Cassandra's lips.

Terrified, Cassandra began to struggle. Bast spoke quietly, "I'm going to share my immortality with you, and my Hunger. What Vlad once called his gift, I give you as both gift and curse. It's the only way."

Cassandra's eyes widened as she heard the name "Vlad", and Bast remembered how incredibly intelligent this woman was. She slapped and punched at Bast's arm, and Bast didn't bother defending herself. The blows were nothing to her.

"Drink, Cassandra," she said, soothing but insistent. "Drink, and be safe. Drink, and be greater than these mortals. Drink, and be my companion. My friend."

Eventually, she did.

"Can you hear me, Admiral?" Bast shouted. "I gave you a chance. You sent me on a goose chase, you absolute cretin. You led me into an ambush. You toyed with me. I might still have been merciful...but you would have killed Cassandra, *and that is too far.* I'm coming for you, Admiral. It's long overdue."

Chapter 21

Tides Turn

Ryan dove back to safety as the super-soldiers lowered their hands and twisted. He didn't see exactly what they did, but it was immediately apparent that something was burning. The orange light of the flames cast flickering shadows on the street in front of him, and the air was thick with steam as rain boiled before it could even hit the ground.

This is good, he thought. *This is great.* He took a deep breath and peered around the wall.

Great ribbons of flame poured out of Munoz's hands. She was wielding them like whips, striking at any movement, causing trees to burst into flame and scorching lawns. As Ryan watched, she lashed her flames at a parked car, and it detonated like a bomb. A single flaming wheel bounced and rolled down the street. As it passed his hiding spot, Ryan made a small twist to put it out before it spread the damage.

This is such a waste of power, Ryan thought as Munoz lashed out again. There was a reason his twists were almost always small and immediate. Reality didn't like flames to act like whips. Munoz had to continually manipulate the laws of physics to make it work, burning power all the while. Even *Enki* hadn't been that careless with his power, and he'd had so much more available.

Watching the impressive, and wasteful, display, Ryan smiled.

The plan was working.

***

"We have to assume they follow the same basic rules we do," Athena had said during their strategy session. "Otherwise we're going to drive ourselves crazy trying to come up with every possible scenario."

"And if they don't?" Anansi asked.

Horus scowled. "Then we'll have no hope but to improvise, but Athena has a point. None of the intel we have suggests that we're dealing with something entirely new. Ryan's seen them twist, just like we do. They're mortals who gained access to divine power through science, which is new, but the actual power is the same. The rules shouldn't change that much."

Anansi considered Horus's words and then nodded.

"We do have to consider one thing," Ryan said.

Horus raised his eyebrows and motioned impatiently for Ryan to continue.

"They're actual soldiers. Modern soldiers, I mean. Trained to work together. I mean, the five of us have never fought as a group before. I've fought with Athena a couple of times and Anansi once. How much have the rest of you fought together before all this?"

"We worked together once," Athena said, indicating Horus. "Back during the Bronze Age collapse."

"So...three thousand years ago? Longer?" Ryan asked.

"Longer," Athena said with a sigh.

"Correct me if I'm wrong," Dianmu added, "but I believe that Horus is the only one with any familiarity with modern weaponry and tactics? The only one who's paid attention to how mortals have changed their strategies over the centuries?"

Horus nodded, his face showing precisely what he thought of their deficiencies in that arena. "Unfortunately, we don't have time to correct that oversight. The central point is the same: we fight as individuals, they fight as a group. That is a true advantage they have over us. In return, we have to play to our strengths. We have thousands of years of practice in using divine powers- except for the Nascent, of course - and a better knowledge of how they work. Including their limitations."

"You mean the Hungers," Ryan said.

"If you insist on belaboring the obvious, yes, I mean the Hungers. The biggest limitation we have. Anansi, did these 'super-soldiers' start falling victim to their Hungers during your fight against them?"

Anansi considered. "They started to breathe heavily, but it might have been normal mortal exhaustion."

"Either way, Horus has a point," Ryan said, "even if he had to make it in the most dickish way possible. If they have Hungers, they'll be limited by them. If they don't have Hungers, they'll have the limits of a mortal body."

Dianmu leaned forward. "What exactly are you thinking, Horus?"

"We bait them," he said. "We hold our strength in reserve while making them think that we are using as much as they are. Minimal power, maximum flash. Get them to burn hard and burn fast."

"They'll run out far before we do," Athena said. "And then they'll either succumb to Hunger or exhaustion."

"So we don't fight them like soldiers. We fight them like gods." Anansi said.

"Stay defensive, stay evasive, stick to flashy low-effort twists and physical weapons, surround them, and then when they get so tired they're making mistakes, go in for the kill," Horus said. "Play it right, and we'll have them right where we want them."

***

Ryan didn't allow himself to gloat for very long. The soldiers were starting to make mistakes, but they were still extremely dangerous. Even now, missing a dodge or a block could be disastrous. They had to be careful, but if they played it right...

This is our chance.

Athena broke cover first, charging straight towards Munoz and shouting a war cry. Munoz turned the flames toward Athena, but the goddess twisted, kicked off the ground, and tossed herself away from the attack.

They can be beaten. Ryan told himself.

"Now!" he shouted and charged in.

A wild-eyed Munoz tracked Athena, who barely raised her shield in time to avoid incineration.

Anansi and a dozen illusion ran headlong down the street. In unison, they drew daggers and tossed them in a barrage aimed straight for Evans. Evans threw his hands up, and the asphalt followed his motion, curving like a tidal wave to intercept the attack. It was an awe-inspiring display of force...and another stupid waste of power.

Ryan joined the fray, reaching into his nanoverse and drawing a spear. A minor twist made it glow as he hurled it towards Palmer. As Ryan had hoped, Palmer overreacted, clenching his fist and turning the spear to dust mid-flight. Ryan could only imagine how much power it had cost to the bonds between the component molecules.

Hands splayed, Dianmu leapt off a roof and dove towards the cluster of super-soldiers. Ball lightning formed at the edges of her fingers, and she sent them streaking out in volleys. Lightning leapt between the orbs, creating a web of electricity. Hector smacked the ground, and a shaft of iron erupted from the street, creating an improvised lightning rod.

Conductivity was no match for Dianmu's will, and the ball lightning streaked past the grounding tool. Hector's eyes widened just before one of the spheres slammed into his chest. His muscles spasmed and his head arched back before he collapsed to the ground.

Not only had the lightning rod been a waste of power, but it had been the wrong call. *We're doing it!* Ryan thought.

Athena was still standing against Munoz's flames when Horus reappeared, with an automatic shotgun in each hand and four more hovering behind his back, held in place with simple, low-power twists.

"Die!" Horus shouted gleefully, and all six shotguns erupted.

Hector, who had just regained his feet, whirled to face the new attack and threw up a wall of plasma so hot that it turned the pellets into gas. Hector shoved the plasma wall toward Horus, reverted falcon form and darted away. Hector's concentration visibly wavered, and the wall disappeared as he lost his grip on the equations.

Taking advantage of the distraction, Athena charged at Munoz.

Evans intercepted her, blocking her strike with a blade of pure, solidified light. It sheared through Athena's ordinary sword like it was made of paper. Evans pressed the attack, but his weapon flickered out of existence before Athena needed to dodge. She surged forward, hitting him with her red-hot shield and driving the broken end of her sword into Evans's leg. He howled in pain.

"Evans!" Munoz shouted and threw a ball of force at Athena, hitting her.

Despite the pain, Evans seemed to have grasped the situation. "Fall back!" he shouted. "They're trying to surround us!"

The four super-soldiers used power-fueled leaps to escape the ring the others had been drawing around them, but when they landed they were all panting, and Hector slipped on the grass and almost fell.

Ryan and his allies were battered and bloodied, but they were still alert and ready to fight. The super-soldiers had taken only a few injuries...but they were lagging. Palmer's hands were actually shaking as he helped Hector to his feet.

Athena didn't give them a chance to recover. Evans created another light blade, but this time Athena had reinforced her sword. The two blades met mid-air, and Athena and Evans strained against each other.

"Die, you *bitch*!" he screamed.

In response, she headbutted him and was rewarded with the sickening crunch of his nose shattering. Evans howled in anger and reeled backward, the energy sword disappearing again as his focus broke.

Keep using that blade, buddy, Ryan thought. *Making weapons out of nothing is costly as hell.*

Then Munoz, Ross, and Palmer turned to open fire on Athena. At this range, they couldn't miss.

Ryan, Dianmu, and Horus all reacted at once. Air, ice, and rock surrounded Athena, and the soldiers' attacks didn't touch her.

Taking advantage of illusion and distraction, Anansi had moved right up to the super-soldiers. Now he lunged towards Munoz and shoved a dagger through her bicep. She howled and spun, but he was already gone, and her torrent of ice blades struck empty air.

Evans twisted, doing a quick version of the massive gravity push they'd used before. He didn't sustain it this time, but it still scattered Ryan and his allies.

"We have to pull out!" he shouted.

"Not yet! I've got the primary target!" Hector tossed his gun aside, stretching his hand towards Ryan. Ryan saw a single glowing light at Hector's fingertips and recognized it as a smaller version of Tyr's sunlight beam.

Ryan twisted and prayed. If this didn't work, it might be all over for him.

The high-energy beam lanced from Hector's fingertips. It hit the air prism Ryan had created and was redirected to the side, running through a second prism, which sent it towards Palmer.

The beam struck Palmer's left hand, blowing off three of his fingers. The big man howled, clutching at the injury.

"Damnit, I said disengage!" Evans shouted.

"I'll cover you!" Munoz shouted. She held out her hands...

And nothing happened. She stared at her fingertips in stupefied surprise.

Her Hungers had peaked, and she was no stronger than a mortal.

The plan had worked, and they had the super-soldiers on the ropes.

Except that Hector still had something to give, and he created a hail of flying debris that forced Ryan and the others to take cover. Evans, Palmer, and Munoz were already halfway down the street by the time Hector ceased the assault and turned to follow.

Ryan felt his blood run cold. They'd barely come out of this one alive, and the same trick wouldn't work twice. But on a deeper, more primal level, a vicious thought ran through him. *You tried to kill my sister, and I spared you. I let this happen. You are* ***never*** *hurting anyone* ***ever*** *again.*

Howling in fury, Ryan bolted after the retreating soldier. He twisted, stopping Hector in his tracks. Ryan's own Hungers were screaming at him, but he pushed through.

"No," he said, grabbing Hector's arm.

Hector looked at him with wild eyes. "Wha-"

Ryan pivoted, swinging Hector in an arc over his shoulder. He slammed the soldier's head into the asphalt with a sickening crunch, and Hector fell limp.

Ryan jerked as a spray of bullets hit him in the back. He could feel the pain, but it was a distant, alien thing, like it was happening to someone else. He heard Athena scream his name, and that was also far away.

Then his knees buckled, and the world went dark.

***

Potentia stared at Crystal's floating corpse and allowed herself a moment to relax. "So much time…" she murmured.

The other two nodded in perfect understanding.

Potentia remembered what could be, charitably, called her "birth". At the moment this iteration of Crystal's nanoverse had undergone its Big Bang, she had opened her eyes for the first time. As the universe had cooled, allowing matter to form, Potentia had floated in the void, adrift and contemplative. At first, she had only been sure of three things: she existed, Crystal existed, and her existence was dependent on Crystal's.

Over time, she had come to understand more, her mind processing millions of years of someone else's knowledge and experience. Then she had found her sisters, and they had realized that they were held prisoner by Crystal's very existence.

It had been simple to decide that they needed what she had.

Litura interrupted her reflection. "Potentia...are you certain she's gone?"

"She isn't," Inedia said, speaking before Potentia could. "Not fully, not yet. We have to finish, or she'll reform back in the Core."

Litura's forehead furrowed, and Potentia put a hand on her shoulder. Litura had always been prone to worrying over stupid things, ever since she'd started to wonder if their work - what Crystal thought of as corruption - would draw Crystal before they were ready for her.

"Be at ease, sister," Potentia said. "It takes them days to reform in the Core, remember? Days there are millennia upon millennia here. We'll have finished things before it gets that far."

"We're wasting time," Inedia snapped. "Even with all that time...we have to get to her staging area. We'll have the doorway then. We'll finally be able to leave."

Potentia sighed. "Can we not just enjoy the victory for a few hours first?"

"We did this so we could get to the Core," Inedia said, crossing her arms. "I'll enjoy our victory then."

Litura held up her hands. "Both of you stop it. We're not going to fight each other."

So it had always been: Inedia impatient and eager, Potentia slow and methodical, and Litura trying to balance the two. They were the first beings in the history of creation that had needed to share omnipotence. At least, as far as Crystal knew, and since they knew everything she did, it was essentially gospel.

"Five minutes," Potentia said to Inedia. "I just want to savor this for five minutes."

"That's agreeable." Inedia looked at the body. "I'd be lying if I tried to claim didn't enjoy seeing her like this." She spat at Crystal's corpse.

Potentia nodded in agreement. They'd been close to omnipotent, but two things had been beyond them. They couldn't just unmake Crystal...and they couldn't leave. Not while Crystal was alive. She was their jailor, and Potentia had only hated her more when she'd realized Crystal wasn't even aware she was keeping them locked away. She certainly would have never released them, even if she could.

It had been Inedia who'd figured it out: if Crystal died in her nanoverse, there would be an imbalance in the Core. They could escape before she resurrected there, and in doing so, they'd have full control of her nanoverse's power.

All of its power, including the remnants of the destroyed dual nanoverse. More power than any goddess had ever wielded in the Core. *And there were so many more nanoverses. Athena. Dianmu. Anansi. Horus. And...Ryan. Ryan's nanoverse, that has a twist powerful enough to end the world.* The possibilities made Potentia feel giddy.

"I think we're ready," Litura said after the five minutes had passed. "Anything else we need to do before our departure?"

"Oh, there's one little thing you might want to deal with."

The three whirled. Standing behind them, her head decidedly intact, Crystal waved. "Hullo, loves. Nice bit of theatrics there, yeah? I even had me convinced, and I knew I was messing with you lot." She strode towards them, grinning, walking across empty space like it was a solid surface.

"How?" Potentia asked, her voice cracking.

"Oh, you were damned clever, I'll bloody give you that," Crystal said, ignoring Potentia's question. "I mean, you want to kill someone in their own nanoverse? You have to get them to do it themselves. Even you three, you couldn't just sucker punch me out of reality. It's clever as all else, and that's coming from me. And it would have worked, except your plan had one little flaw."

Inedia clenched her fists. "And what flaw would that be?"

"You assumed I wouldn't bloody figure it out."

***

Asserting "I am" had bought her a moment to plan. A desperate, hopeless plan, but if she could pull it off...the goddesses were recovering from her blow. She had to act now.

Crystal snapped her fingers, creating a perfect copy of herself. Using what she had begun to suspect and understand about her enemies, she imbued the copy with her knowledge and almost all of her power, but without her actual consciousness. It left her feeling weak and hollow, with just enough power to teleport away and cloak herself so she could observe the fight from afar.

The invasive goddesses had rushed to attack and destroy the zombie, which gave Crystal time to think things through and see if her theory held up.

When they removed the masks and revealed her own face, she knew for sure.

***

She gave the trio an impish smile, radiating bravado. She could only hope they would fall for it. "Oh, come on. I gave you credit for coming up with the plan, you should give me some bloody credit for countering it."

Apparently, they did not see it the same way. The three goddesses flew at Crystal. She didn't return the charge, and instead planted her feet and braced against empty space. She smiled. *I know all of you.*

Litura went first this time, lashing out with a bruise-colored whip woven from the forgotten sorrows of Crystal's existence, the traumas she had erased over the millennia. Crystal held up her hand and leaned *into* the attack, letting the whip wrap around her wrist. She gritted her teeth against the agony of barbs biting into her flesh, creating wounds made of her own grief. It would have torn her apart before, but now Crystal knew she was fighting an old and familiar enemy.

Herself.

She jerked her hand back, yanking Litura towards her. Litura raised her arms, ready to deflect a strike, Crystal didn't try a traditional attack. She dove under Litura's defense and embraced the startled goddess. "You called yourself Litura, love. My weakness. I no longer fear weakness because I am not alone. You are a part of me, and I welcome you back."

And, before their eyes, Litura screamed and began to melt, flowing into Crystal.

Inedia screamed in rage and lashed out with claws forged in the apathy that had almost driven Crystal to allow her nanoverse to undergo heat death a dozen times over the millennia. Crystal stepped forward and let Inedia bury the claws in her chest. The pain was white-hot and contained a seductive whisper of surrender. In the Core, a wound like this would have killed her.

But they weren't in the Core. This was Crystal's domain.

Crystal coughed ichor as she wrapped her arms around Inedia. She'd faced this apathy before, stared into the void and then turned her head aside. "Inedia, my hunger. You always were a bitch. But I welcome the hunger because it reminds me that I am not a ghost and that I am not a monster. I am alive, and you are a part of me. I welcome you back."

Litura howled and flowed like smoke back into Crystal.

Potentia's chest heaved with deep, panicked breaths. She didn't attack but wrapped herself in a web of Crystal's forgotten ambitions, dreams and goals that had fallen by the wayside after the death of her people and her ancient quest. Crystal advanced on her, and Potentia stepped back, holding up a hand to ward Crystal off.

"This won't...this won't change anything!" she screamed. "We are a symptom of the corruption, not the cause! You cannot cleanse this!"

"Oh, Potentia. Dear, dear Potentia. My power. I'm not going to cleanse it; I'm going to fix it. And you told me how, so thank you for that. Now," Crystal held her arms out for an embrace, and although Potentia tried to pull away, Crystal's will was now stronger. "I welcome you back, you twit."

Potentia dissolved.

Crystal gasped, shuddered, and took a few moments to collect herself in a less literal fashion. Then she waved her hand and undid the lingering damage the three had left on the fabric of her nanoverse. *One million years old, and you still get to see entirely new things every now and then.*

She smiled and headed back towards Shadoth. She was exhausted, shaken, and wanted nothing more than to go back to the Core and sleep for a month. But she would never, *ever*, neglect her people again, and she had a job to finish.

Chapter 22

Curtainfall

A funeral hush settled over Operations in the wake of the failed ambush and Bast's threat. Lazzario and Jake had both run to the restrooms, presumably to hurl. Dale couldn't blame them for the moment of weakness. He'd seen some terrible things in his service, but that...

Doctor Pivarti finally broke the silence. "I told you to detonate the bomb immediately," she said with an unmistakable note of admonishment.

In Dale's opinion, there were many things that one simply did not say to an Admiral. "I told you so" might not be at the very top of the list, but it was pretty damn high. He turned towards Pivarti. "Doctor, at this point, I need you to remain silent."

"Because I'm being insubordinate, or because I'm right?" The doctor asked, her face the picture of insolence. All eyes turned towards her.

"Because you aren't saying anything useful," Dale said through clenched teeth. "The only thing I want to hear right now is how to stop Bast before she kills the rest of us and escapes the base entirely."

"She's become an anthropophage, Admiral."

Dale blinked. He'd never heard that word. "What is that, and is it relevant?"

Pivarti grinned wickedly and elaborated. "It's a being that needs to feed on some part of human beings. It's a side effect of extended Hunger denial."

"What-"

Pivarti went on like he hadn't even started speaking. "The best-known examples of an anthropophage are, of course, vampires and their thirst for blood, but there are several dozen kinds. Most anthropophages can reproduce through feeding some part of themselves to a human, which is what Bast has done to Cassandra." She walked over to a computer and began typing.

Dale felt a vein begin to bulge in his forehead. "What do you think-"

She interrupted again. "Any time a god or goddess undergoes extended Hunger denial, they become a new type of anthropophage." She kept her eyes on the computer, all but ignoring him.

Dale's blood boiled at her absolute dismissal, and the realization that she had been holding out on him. "What is Hunger denial?"

"Oh, it's not having food, water, sleep, social interaction...all the things we kept away from Bast. Until Cassandra proved that intelligence doesn't prevent stupidity."

"Wait...you mean you *knew* that something like this would happen?" Dale balled his hands into fists.

"Of course. It would have been my first chance to study an anthropophage up close. If I'd known the transformation would happen so quickly, I would have already started. A pity. Bast is the first case of heart eating, as far as I know, so, unfortunately, I won't have the chance to observe her."

"You're damn right you won't." Dale's voice was low and dangerous. "As soon as this is over, I'm charging you with treason and-"

She actually laughed. "Don't be ridiculous. You aren't going to charge me with anything, because I'm done here, and I'm going to die. The rest of you will too, when Bast gets here, but I'm going to take care of that business before she arrives. I imagine she'll be quite angry with me, and I'd prefer to avoid that unpleasantness."

She stood up from the computer, and Dale decided that enough was enough. He drew his sidearm and leveled it at the doctor's head.

"What did you just do?" he growled.

She rolled her eyes. "I emailed all my data to an external server, Admiral. I didn't go through all this, and do such awful things to Bast, to walk away empty-handed. I also deleted the data from your servers. Can't leave that knowledge with the US Government, can I?"

"What the hell is going on?" Dale demanded. "You're talking about dying, and then about walking away? You have three seconds to explain yourself."

"You really are an idiot," she said, crossing her arms and giving him a level gaze. "You capture a goddess, a live goddess, and within a matter of days I have a working prototype to pull energy off her nanoverse – sorry, her 'Black Sphere' – and a few days after that we're fielding soldiers powered by divine might. Have you any idea how quickly technology develops? It should have taken months, maybe years. There's no way I could have made such progress so soon unless I'd already been working on it, which I had, and had access to a lot more information, which I did. I honestly worried you'd see right through me, but you were so eager to believe the story I fed you that it was laughably easy. It appears I initially overestimated you."

Dale fought for something to say, but nothing came to him. He'd...well, if he was honest with himself, he had assumed that it was divine intervention ensuring they would be ready for the fight.

The doctor continued, her voice dripping with scorn. "It's taken me decades to get to this point, and this is far from the first time I've used government resources. I was on the Manhattan Project. I worked for NASA during the space race. I've been wearing different faces and taking part in important research for *centuries*, Admiral. And I must say that it's nice to be able to stop pretending to be a man. So are you going to pull the trigger, or just stand there wearing that stupid expression?"

Dale felt frozen. "You're a monster, like her. You're one of *them*."

"Gold star, Admiral," she said, rolling her eyes. "Of course I am, you twit. I'm also the last hope for this world. While the rest scramble about fighting over petty matters, *someone* needs to see to the important things."

"Who *are* you? What are you trying to do here?"

"Yes, of course, I'm going to tell you my real identity and expound on my goals. That way, when Bast inevitably captures and tortures you, you can tell her everything." She unbuttoned her shirt, revealing some kind of white bodysuit. "Put the gun down, Admiral, or pull the trigger. I don't care which."

Dale was reminded of cartoons from his childhood, when the coyote would chase the roadrunner and run off a cliff. He'd stay there, floating in the air...until he looked down. "What's that thing you're wearing?"

"It's a little safety precaution of my own design. It's lined with thermite tape, set to go off if my heart stops. Destroys my body, so I can resurrect at my nanoverse, which is over a thousand miles away from here."

Dale found his footing again. Even though Bast was coming, and the Myrmidons weren't going to get to her in time, they had their own super being to protect them. "Then I'm not going to shoot you. If you don't want to suffer her wrath, you're going to have to help us stop Bast. And if you could use your power to off yourself, you wouldn't need to use the suit, or try to goad me into killing you."

Doctor Pivarti – or whatever her name was – sighed again. "I absolutely can 'off myself', as you put it, with or without the suit. The suit makes it quicker and ensures that if I die of non-incendiary causes, my body will still be destroyed. Still, it would be faster and less painful if you shot me in the head."

"I won't let you abandon us now!"

"Admiral. You don't have any choice. You never had a choice. Men like you never understand what it means to fight against the divine. Your only choice, the only one that matters, is which of us you follow. Any other option just results in you getting swept aside or crushed underfoot." Now she sounded almost sad, bordering on pitying.

"I made that choice!" he snapped. "I follow the one true God!"

Sher laughed, low and mocking. "No one's seen Him in over two thousand years, at least. There's still some debate about Jesus, you know. He isn't the only god out there, and if he's omnipotent, he certainly isn't showing it. You've chosen...poorly." She shrugged. "When Bast gets here, give her a message for me? Let her know it wasn't personal. She was just the first opportunity to present itself, and I didn't like doing that to her. But it had to happen – the clock, as they say, was ticking."

Dale realized his hand was shaking. "You think she'll care about that?" he growled. "We all fucked her over, every last one of us. You think she'll give a damn if it was personal or not?"

"Maybe in a few hundred years. You'd be surprised what you can eventually get over, given enough time. For now, it doesn't matter. At this point, Admiral, I really must be going."

"You can tell her yourself," he said. "I'm not going to kill you. But if you even twitch your hands, I'll shoot you in the gut. You won't die until after Bast arrives. She can deal with you." Dale didn't know if it worked that way, but he hoped it might.

Doctor Pivarti smiled. "Fortunately, I don't need to move. *Dahan*!"

And before Dale's eyes, the suit began to glow. The light was white-hot, so bright Dale had to turn away, and the stench of smoke and charred meat combined began to rapidly fill the room. Vents activated, working as hard as they could to clear the ash and smell ...and in a matter of seconds, all that remained of Doctor Pivarti was a charred husk.

She hadn't even screamed.

Everyone was looking at Dale. He should be taking charge, giving orders, but he couldn't find the words. He was standing over thin air.

Then mist exploded into Operations, billowing from the door and choking off sight at an alarming rate.

"Hello, Admiral," Bast said, her voice floating through the mist like an ill omen.

Dale's paralysis broke. He turned his pistol towards the mist and fired into it. Several others in the room followed his lead, and a hail of ichor-infused lead flew into the void.

The gunfire died down, and an eerie silence followed. Visibility had dropped in seconds, and Dale couldn't see more than a foot in front of his face. As he began to reload, he thought that sight didn't matter right now. It was the *silence* that counted, the absence of that hateful voice. She had made a mistake in speaking, especially just inside the doorway where she had been such an easy target, mist or no mist. They'd taken her down, and in a second he would find her body and empty a clip into her head just to make sure. After that-

People began to scream.

The shooting resumed, and Dale hit the floor, knowing that they were more likely to shoot each other at this point. He held his fire, certain Bast would be coming for him, revealing herself so he could blow her away.

A shape passed him-something like a giant cat, but with a weirdly misshapen skull, almost like a human head. It reminded Dale of the Sphinx, only as gaunt as a dried corpse. It was moving at an incredible speed, but he fired anyway, tracking the shape as best he could until his gun clicked empty. The creature gave no sign he'd hit, and Dale prayed that was because he'd missed, and not because the bullets hadn't had an effect.

Dale reloaded, but the figure was gone.

Seconds later, blood sprayed the floor in front of him, and Kathleen's head thumped after it. Dale watched it roll across the floor, seeming to look at him in accusation.

Hands shaking, Dale reloaded again. He might not be able to save these people, but he wouldn't just lay down and die, and there was still a chance to stop Bast before she was loose on the outside world.

Then, as abruptly it had started, the screaming stopped. All he could hear was a horribly suggestive munching sound. Like a dog with a steak, but uglier. Ghoulish.

"Oh, this won't do," Bast said, and a wind began to blow through the room, sucking the mist out the door and into the corridor. He saw Cassandra hunched over a body, holding a chunk of red flesh and eating with frenetic eagerness, like a starving woman given a five-course gourmet meal.

Then he saw Bast.

He remembered all the times he had seen her before. First as a corpse, then strapped to a table. Then, she had just looked like a woman. A beautiful woman, of course, but nothing special. It had been underwhelming, in truth, to see a supernatural creature that looked so mundane.

Now, there was nothing ordinary about her. Gore coated her mouth and lips, ran from her fingertips to her elbows, splattered her clothing. Her hair was wild, and her eyes shone with madness. In spite of the horror, she was beautiful, like a tiger, a thunderstorm, a viper. Beauty that incited no desire, but inspired fear and awe.

In that instant, Dale understood how primitive man had idolized these beings, long before even the first days of civilization. Seeing her like this, a primal entity of death and carnage, he knew in his bones how his distant ancestors found themselves engaging in rituals with drums and dance and sacrifice. It wasn't cowardice or superstition. It was a desperate fear to do anything and everything you could think of to appease the being that moved like lightning and spoke like thunder.

She met his eyes, and Dale realized there was no hope of appeasing her.

He raised the gun in a last, desperate act of defiance. With a gesture, Bast sent it flying out of his hand.

"Admiral," Bast purred. "Admiral Dale Bridges, United States Navy."

He tried to get up, wanting to die on his feet. That suddenly seemed very important.

She allowed him to reach his knees before reaching out and sending an electric shock through him, locking his muscles in place. He strained, every nerve on fire, but it was no use. He heard a soft whimpering, and realized it was him.

"I like you like this, Admiral," she said. "Kneeling before me. You're going to get very good at that, I think."

She let the current hold him for a little while longer, then released him to fall prostrate before her. "How long was I your prisoner?"

Dale coughed, and blood sprayed. He wished he wasn't dying with so much left undone. He'd come so close to stopping these monsters. At least he knew that heaven awaited him after death. That would have to help him endure the hell he'd suffer before he got there. "Go to hell, you monster."

She sighed and kicked him in the face, shattering a few of his teeth. She leaned down to put her face close to his, her faux-friendly demeanor disappearing. "I have questions, Dale. And you are going to suffer greatly, even if you answer them. I won't lie to you about that. But if you refuse me, if you hold on stubbornly to this belief that you still have any power here, I'll make you just like her."

They both looked at Cassandra, gnawing at another heart, her face empty of any real awareness.

"I'll starve you," Bast continued, "until you're mindless and desperate. Then I'll let you loose among your family. Or friends. Or in a school, or the White House. Whatever is the worst for you, personally. And believe me, at that point, you'll feast. And when you're done, you'll beg for more."

Dale Bridges shuddered, but she wasn't done. "If you do talk, then I'll just torture you until you die or I get bored, whichever comes first. You'll be the only one to suffer for what you've done. Now. *How long was I your prisoner?*"

Some part of him considered fighting, still spitting defiance in her face...and then pictured himself attacking his daughter, his grandson...

"Two weeks," he whispered.

Bast patted his head, exactly how one would praise a loyal dog. "Good boy. Now, there's one person still missing. Your head researcher. Pivarti? Cassandra told me about her, and I'm very much looking forward to meeting her. Where is she?"

At this, at least, Dale could take some satisfaction. "You walked through her ashes. She burned herself so you couldn't take her alive."

Bast looked over to the smear on the ground, frowning. "How the hell did she manage that?"

"Thermite suit. Said she'd resurrect at her...what was the word? Nanoverse." He snorted bitterly. "She's a monster like you. And she's still free."

"There will be time to worry about her later," Bast said dismissively. "For now, I'm more concerned with you."

Admiral Dale Bridges screamed for a very long time.

***

Crystal descended to the world of the Sur-nah-him, back to the city of Na-hara, back to the king's "palace", where chaos reigned. She had expected as much because when she had restored the planet and resurrected its people, she hadn't erased their memories of the apocalypse. They were all aware that they had been destroyed, and then miraculously saved. She was sure that once they calmed down, it would do wonders for their ability to hope. Not to mention her reputation.

"Relax!" she shouted, gaining everyone's attention. "It's over. You're all fine. Better than fine. Your planet is actually livable and the psycho princesses are gone."

Most of the Sur-nah-him looked skeptical at best, but Xurir-who, come to think of it, had been looking shaken but thoughtful instead of completely out of his gourd-nodded slowly. "So you have defeated your...daughters?"

Crystal coughed. "I wouldn't exactly call them my daughters, they were more..."

Conceptual manifestations of my dark side that came into being when the last big crunch spread the corruption of another, evil god across the universe? C'mon, Crystal, don't blow the poor man's mind.

"...sisters," she finished weakly.

"I am glad," he said.

King Uepth, apparently deciding it was time to stop cowering behind his throne, scuttled out and cowered in front of her instead.

"Oh, great goddess," he cried. "Savior and deliverer. The people rejoice at your mercy and-"

"Yes, yes. Uepth, I'm sure you're a very good king," Crystal said, although she definitely *wasn't* sure about that, "but I have something more important than kings to think about, and frankly...you just don't suit. Stand up and be quiet for a minute, love."

Uepth did as he was told, looking awed, terrified, and just slightly affronted.

"Now," Crystal said, turning back to Xurir, "my business is with you. Here."

Crystal smiled and handed him the sphere she had made. It had taken an incredible effort, but she thought it was well worth the push.

"Go ahead," she said. "Take it. Look at it."

Xurir did, and after a moment, whispered "Goddess...it's full of...thousands of stars."

As long as Crystal could remember, gods had used power stones to create demigods within their own nanoverses. At some point, everyone tried to create a nanoverse within a nanoverse, and everyone eventually accepted that it was impossible. Power stones were a perfectly good alternative, but this time Crystal had wanted more. Her demigods would not only need to be shepherds and guardians, but also watchers. If corruption began to resurface, it needed to be seen before it had the chance to take root.

Xurir was still staring into the sphere. "What...what is it?"

Crystal kept her voice was soft, not wanting to interrupt the man's wonder. "It's two things. It's a source of power that allows you to assert your will over some of this reality, and it's a window to this entire universe. It allows you to see everything that happens within this cosmos. I call it a holoverse, and having it makes you a god too."

Xurir dropped the holoverse as if it had suddenly caught fire "I don't...I can't be a god!"

Crystal picked up the holoverse and handed it back. Xurir was hesitant, but Crystal gently took his hands, put the holoverse in them, and closed them around the sphere. "Relax, love. You won't have the world ending levels of power that I do, or that those other three did. But you'll be able to protect your people. Eventually, you'll even protect others. You'll be immortal, so long as this isn't destroyed."

And, Crystal added to herself, *you don't have to worry about letting an entire universe die if you fail.*

Xurir was shaking in shock. "Why...why me?"

"Because you foraged and returned safely forty-three times. Because you risked your life time and again to protect those weaker than you. Because you dared to believe I might be telling the truth when I said I came to help and not destroy. There is no bravery greater than pushing through fear, except perhaps being brave enough to hope."

"I don't deserve this," he whispered.

"And because you think that, I know that you do." Crystal put a hand on the man's shoulder. "You won't be alone. I'll be spreading these across your planet, and across the universe. There will be others, as quickly as I can find the right people."

"But *why* are you doing this? Why give power away?"

Crystal pointed upwards. "Your sun. It's green."

Now Xurir looked like he thought he might be joking or testing him somehow. "Yes. It...yes, that is the color of the sun."

"Ah. But it's wrong."

Xurir blinked, slowly. "I'm...sorry? What should I call that color, then?"

"No, no, the color is called green, but the sun shouldn't *be* green. The fact that it's green is the symptom of a sickness afflicting the entire universe. Stars should be yellow and white and blue and red! The space between them should be unmarred black!"

After a long moment, Xurir nodded in acceptance, which was good, because Crystal had no idea how to convince him if he didn't take it on faith. *Or maybe he's just humoring the crazy deity that's claiming the sun is the wrong color.* Crystal didn't know which and decided it didn't matter. She'd show Xurir how things *should* look.

"So..." he said, "Am I to do something about it?"

Crystal laughed. "I like your attitude, Xurir. I think you're going to do very well. But right now I'll take care of things. I'm going to fix the sun and a lot of other problems. But the corruption will come back, eventually. And there are other types of corruption, too. Sometimes, it's obvious. Sometimes, it's insidious. It might be the stars turning the wrong colors, or monsters roaming the land, but it can also be callousness or cruelty or decadence in your own people. You gods and goddess will fight against all that, and someday you may have to end the world and create a new better one. That will keep the corruption at bay until I can fix it again."

Xurir took a deep breath. "So, without this corruption, there will be no evil?"

"Oh, I wish." Crystal shook her head. "I'm not taking away anyone's free will. You lot still have the absolute freedom to choose to be monstrous to each other. I'm just making sure that there's nothing beyond your control that *forces* things to be worse. You'll need to decide what to do about the ordinary arseholes yourself."

"That's...a lot to take in."

"Well, you have a long time to think about it. One of the perks of immortality, love. For now...can you take it on faith?"

Several seconds passed, followed by minutes, as Xurir turned the holoverse over and over in his hand. "I can. I will keep the faith, goddess of hope. And I will protect this world."

Crystal rested a hand on her shoulder. "Good. I'll be back to check on you. I won't leave you without guidance. Might be a few millennia, but I'll be back."

"Thank you," Xurir said softly.

"It's what I do, love. After all, I'm the original goddess." And before Xurir could reply, Crystal was gone.

She re-appeared in the heart of the galaxy, floating above the supermassive black hole at the center. *All right.* She cracked her knuckles. *Let's make this happen.*

There was no presence pushing back against her, but the corruption itself was still there. She could feel it, slick and grimy on the very substance of everything, a puddle of oil floating on top of a still pond.

Crystal took a deep breath and started with the most visible sign of the corruption: the tendrils of gas that spread between the stars and across the galaxy. She willed them to be attracted to the nearest black hole, turning singularities into giant vacuum cleaners for that particular foulness. It would take centuries, but over those centuries all that corruption would be gathered into single points and trapped behind event horizons.

Now. The stars. The corruption had worked its way into the fundamental processes of her nanoverse, and solar cores, when they fused elements together and released energy, were also releasing corruption. That she couldn't just undo, but she could reset the clock, and trust her demigods to contain it in the future.

Crystal began to rotate her hand, like the way she twisted in the Core universe, but on a galactic scale. In response to her rotation, the stars started to shed their corruption in large waves. This had to be done delicately. If she spun a star too fast or pulled off too much stellar matter, she could destroy all life around it. *No rush. You can spend a millennium or two here and barely miss anything in the Core. Take care of your people.*

It took a century of delicate manipulations to pull all the corruption out of existing stars and hurl it into the interstellar clouds, where the black holes would devour it. Empires rose, and entire cultures stared in wonder as their suns changed color and began to shed natural, wholesome light. Philosophers debated the meaning. Scientists tried to come up with theories to explain the phenomena. Religions claimed it was the end times, or the beginning of the new times, or just a mysterious act of God in His ineffable ways. One religion on a world on the far end of the galaxy decided it meant they were *all* dying and that this new universe would be paradise.

And then the monsters started to die.

It was a trick Crystal had missed when she was trying to fix her nanoverse before. The monsters kept returning because they fed upon the corruption the same way plants feed off sunlight. Without their primary energy source, the massive flora and fauna that had devoured civilizations were withering and falling over dead.

This sparked another wave of philosophical, religious, and scientific debate, three minor wars and one major one, seven different cultural heroes who claimed to be behind the slaughter, and several unusual new belief systems.

The most interesting was a chain of events surrounding the possible divinity of pear trees. This was a world that the corrupt goddesses had never gotten around to visiting personally, so the people were free to create their own mythology, and they had decided that the man-eating monsters that terrorized their towns and farms must be gods dispensing justice to the unholy. Over the centuries, someone noticed that the "gods" were particularly fond of pears. From that, the clergy of this faith had developed three central tenets: thou shalt not consume the food of the gods; thou shalt give generously to the work of the gods; and if thou art consumed, then all shall know thee as a heretic. It had worked out very well for the clergy, who did a brisk business selling indulgences and crying heresy any time someone got eaten anyway.

When the gods began to die, the panicked clergy spun a story about a foul heretic plot to corrupt and poison the food of the gods, and the emperor declared war on heretics and pear trees. Since no one knew which heretics were responsible, they concentrated on the trees. Armies were mustered, and the formerly sacred groves were burned to the ground. This would have resulted in the extinction of the pear if not for an unlikely series of circumstances involving a bird, an unusually large pear, gravity, and the emperor's skull. Upon his death, the new emperor sued the pear trees for peace.

The trees, being plants, never responded.

The empire collapsed after a series of rebellions, primarily centered on the debate over whether pear trees were divinely good or the source of all evil.

On Shadoth, Xurir had spent the last century teaching the truth of the changes. He had *felt* the change happening and looked up just in time to watch his sun turn yellow, the light transitioning from gangrenous to warm and welcoming. "Thank you," Xurir said, to empty air, wondering if Crystal could hear him.

In space, only dimly aware of the impact her changes had wrought, Crystal looked over her new creation. She saw stars in red and yellow and blue and white, spotted with a few black holes, and she saw that it was good.

She ran her hands through her hair only to discover that, over the century, it had grown sixty feet long and wreathed around her in zero gravity like a raven halo. She decided to keep it as she flew towards the next task on her list.

This star system had a gas giant in the habitable zone, orbited by four airless moons. With a snap of her fingers, Crystal gave one of them an atmosphere and magnetosphere and oceans, and accelerated evolution to give her life to work with. She included some fossils for them to discover, so they wouldn't believe they had been snapped into existence by divine power, even though technically that was true. The people that emerged on this world looked like massive scorpions with fleshy hands in place of pincers, and Crystal scattered holoverses for them to find. The first one to find the holoverse of each era would know, instinctively, what had to happen and why. *Let's spare them the headache you had convincing people, yeah?*

Then it was on to the next uninhabited star. And the next.

It would take Crystal another thousand years to populate her nanoverse and spread more holoverses within it. The squid-like Chold, the giants of Xa'nati, the warring hive minds whose name was expressed in the Scent of Flowers in Rain, the minuscule people whose mathematical language called their world "force equals mass times acceleration"...to all of them Crystal spread her holoverses and her warnings. It wouldn't keep forever – one by one the worlds would fail, and just like stars went supernova in the Core, stars here would become corrupt. She would trust her demigods to postpone it long enough for the universe to host life until it usually would have fallen to entropy. It gave them, and her, time.

And for now, time was all they needed.

Chapter 23

No Rest for the Divine

"The end of the world," Jacqueline marveled. "The actual end of the world. I'm in an extra-dimensional Greek temple talking about the *imminent* end of the world. I feel like I've stumbled into a summer blockbuster."

"Welcome to the circus," Isabel said.

Jacqueline glanced at Ryan, lying unconscious on a bed in the corner. "When do you think he's going to wake up?"

"Probably soon. He woke up pretty quickly when he got half his face torn off, so I don't think this will take too long."

"That's crazy," Jacqueline shook her head and sighed. "So when are you getting *out* of the circus?"

"I'm not," Isabel said. "I'm scared sick half the time, and the other half I've gone up to scared out of my mind, but I'm sticking."

"I don't think that's a good idea."

Isabel almost laughed, remembering all the other times Jacqueline had said that to her. When she wanted to die her hair purple, when she wanted to audition for American Idol, when she wanted to sneak off and take a bus to Florida for spring break...that line has always been the starting point for an "I'm not your sister, but" kind of talk. For seven years, Jacqueline had been like a part of their family, and Isabel knew those talks had helped keep her out of a lot of trouble.

But she wasn't a kid anymore.

"He's the only family I have left," Isabel said. "As scared as I am now, the reality is still infinitely better than everything horrible I was imagining. I need to know what's going on."

"Then make sure he stays in touch, but-"

"I can't just sit around and wait for updates! And that isn't just about Ryan. It's freaking Armageddon here, and I'm not going to stay home and hope someone saves me. Not when I can *do* something, or at least be in the know. I'm not wired to sit on my hands and pray."

"I get wanting to do something, but you're out of your depth here, hon. There really isn't anything you *can* do."

Isabel snorted. "That's like saying the Air Force doesn't need pilots and lawyers don't need paralegals. I've already *been* helpful. I've done the background on Moloch's cult. I got the word out on how to handle the Sphinx. I'm picking up the slack on the things they don't have time for, or don't know how to do. I mean, this morning Athena asked me if I could 'use the portable phone to consult with those who write their suspicions on the interwebs'. I think Ryan may be the only one who has more than a basic grasp of modern technology, and he's a little bit busy."

Jacqueline studied Isabel for a long moment and then nodded. "Fair enough. Just be careful, ok?"

"I will."

"I'm not like you, though. This was a one-time thing for me. I guess it's like relying on the fire department or the police...I'm all right with trusting the people who are more qualified. I just can't believe Ryan is one of them. He's a good guy, but he kind of chokes when he has to deal with the big things."

"Not anymore," Isabel said. "These days, he's the type who charges headlong into the big things and chokes them into submission."

Jacqueline laughed. "Ryan. Ryan became that type. Do you have any idea how weird that sounds?"

"Not half as weird as seeing it," Isabel admitted.

"I bet," Jacqueline said. "Kurt's going to kill me, you know. He's been freaking out ever since he recognized Ryan on TV. Said they'd eventually come for me because of the connection."

"Well, at least he'll get to be right."

They laughed together, and Isabel felt glad that they'd had this time, and that Ryan had been able to talk to Jacqueline and explain things. The end of the world seemed like a good time to take care of unfinished business.

The door opened, and Horus strode in.

"What happened?" Isabel asked. "Did you catch them?"

"No. We can discuss it later. Jacqueline, it's time to see you to safety. I also have your gold."

"Wait...what?" Jacqueline sputtered. "You're seriously giving me a chest of gold?"

"I gave you my word," Horus snapped. "Did you doubt it?"

"Um...I guess not."

"I would suggest converting it to trade goods soon," he said in a more moderate tone. "Upheaval and uncertainty are coming, and in times of instability, goods are far more valuable than currency or precious metals."

"That's...good advice. Thank you."

Isabel hugged Jacqueline tightly. "I'm glad I got to see you."

"Me, too." She glanced at Ryan, who was just beginning to stir. "Tell him I said goodbye, and...tell him I'm sorry he didn't feel like he could tell me."

"Will do. Take care of yourself."

As soon as the door closed behind them, Isabel walked over to Ryan's bed. "You can get up now. She's gone."

Ryan groaned. "I wasn't trying to-"

"Avoid an uncomfortable conversation?" Isabel said brightly. "I know. You just managed to sleep through the uncomfortable conversation. You lucky bastard. How are you feeling?"

"Like I've been stabbed, shot, cut, thrown through a window, set on fire, and beaten over the head with a baseball bat."

"I know no one set you on fire, and I'm pretty sure baseball bats weren't involved."

"Well, it *feels* like someone did." Ryan started to sit up and then slumped back down, groaning again.

"Yeah, you should just lay there for a bit," Isabel said. "Also, the fact that you know what being set on fire feels like should probably be a bigger cause for alarm than you seem to think it is."

"This is normal for me now. Give me a hand? I don't want to keep laying here."

Isabel rolled her eyes, but she knew that voice. When Ryan had his mind set on doing something stupid, the best option was to just help him do the stupid thing so he didn't hurt himself more than absolutely necessary.

***

"And then the farmer said, 'But that's not my chicken'", Anansi boomed, and the others, except Horus, burst into laughter.

The table was littered with sandwich wrappers and empty water bottles, evidence of tired gods rapidly filling their physical Hungers, and Anansi's insistence on telling jokes while they ate had done wonders for their Social needs.

"Are we finished, then?" Horus asked. Without waiting for an answer, he went to the whiteboard standing incongruously between two pillars.

"Sure, why not?" Ryan said, before he could stop himself.

"The operation was a success," Horus declared.

"After a fashion," Dianmu said. "They escaped."

"Don't assume that an incomplete victory is a defeat," Horus said, picking up a marker and beginning to write. "Fact: We deployed superior tactics and successfully exploited our enemy's weakness. Fact: We reduced the opposition by 25%. Fact: They have suffered their third operational failure with no balancing success."

Athena nodded. "Correct. This was obviously a victory for us."

"Obvious to the war gods, I suppose," said Dianmu.

"You'll get the hang of it," Horus said. Judging by his tone, he had meant the patronizing statement as a compliment. "Their commanders will keep them out of action for some time, unless they perceive an inarguable need, while they reconsider their strategy. In other words, they will not trouble us for a while. That was the primary objective, and it was achieved. Even Ryan getting his ass kicked didn't prevent success."

Ryan's eyes narrowed. "Did you just miss a chance to blame me?"

"You comported yourself well in the fight, Ryan. I'm an ass, but I don't deny the evidence of my eyes."

"Uh...thanks." Horus being nice was like a lion laying down and purring: far more concerning than friendly.

"And now," Athena said, leaning forward, "we need to concentrate on Moloch. We can't keep playing catch up with him."

"Who are we playing with?" Everyone turned at the sound of Crystal's voice. "You all look a right bloody mess. Do the other guys look worse?"

"Crystal!" Ryan exclaimed. "Are you all right? What happened?"

"I'm right as rain, love, and everything's tip top. I'll catch you up later because it's a hell of a story and I was bloody marvelous, but don't let me distract you now. Where were we?"

"I was just saying that it's time to go after Moloch."

"No rest for the wicked, eh?" Crystal said. "Do we have a line on the wanker yet?"

Isabel cleared her throat. "I scoured the net while you all were fighting Panini goblins..."

"Penanggalan," Athena supplied.

"Right, those. I didn't mention it before because we got a bit wrapped up with the whole 'evil killer super-soldiers' thing, but I did manage to find his little cult's bible. It's a bunch of nihilistic bullshit wrapped up with astrology and vague, bastardized versions of Eastern mythology, Wicca for dummies, and, I swear, some stuff cribbed from Dungeons & Dragons. Just a watered-down mess designed to appeal to former uncommitted theists and atheists who suddenly can't ignore that gods do exist. I think it's really aimed at people who used to get their lunch money stolen."

Anansi sighed. "Good to know, but unfortunately it doesn't give us much to work with. Perhaps it would be best to focus on an alternate tactic. What does Moloch want?"

"Power," Athena supplied.

"Death," Crystal added.

"Monsters," Horus said darkly.

"An oral hygienist," Dianmu said.

Ryan was glad they were able to joke. After everything that happened, it would have been completely overwhelming to jump straight into a grim-faced discussion of tactics. "Probably more the first and third than the others," he added.

Anansi laughed. "Likely, yes. I think the stolen nanoverses are the key. We all agree it's unlikely he's going to risk merging them, yes?" Nods all around. "Well then. If you weren't going to merge them or destroy them, what would you do with a dozen nanoverses?"

"Hold them for ransom," Horus said promptly. "Force the pantheon to bend to your will to avoid their own destruction."

"Possibly," Anansi said, "but that doesn't sound like Moloch."

"Monsters," Athena said firmly. "It must be that he's planning to make monsters. Just like he did to Týr."

Isabel raised her hand. "Question: how long does it take to make a monster out of a nanoverse?"

"For most of us it would take days," Crystal said. "For Moloch...probably only hours, or even less."

"And he would want as many as possible, right? No matter what he's doing with the nanoverses, it would be better if he had more?"

"I...suppose so," Athena said slowly.

"Then let's stop thinking about *what* and start thinking *when*. How long does Moloch have before the gods he killed off resurrect and come looking for revenge?"

"Probably about five days at this point. Maybe six." Horus cocked his head. "Where are you going with this?"

"He needs to do whatever he's going to do with the nanoverses before the gods resurrect, so he's going to get started in three or four days. In the meantime, why not assume he's going to try to collect as many as possible? Why stop at a dozen when he can have two dozen? Or three or four? If he can scoop up a bunch of nanoverses quickly, he'd still have time to enact his evil plan. So where would he go to find a bunch of gods in one place?"

"Tartarus," Athena whispered. "My entire family is gathered in Tartarus."

"We don't know that," Ryan said, and Crystal nodded encouragingly.

"It makes sense," Horus said. "Thanks to his infernal portals, Moloch is the only one who can bypass the labyrinth. Anyone else will need days to catch up with him, and he already has a head start. Not only will it give him the chance to collect more nanoverses, but he'll have a relatively safe place to create his monsters or do whatever it is he's planning. Even if the Olympians aren't there, Moloch will follow the trail, same as us."

Athena's face was a mask of emotions too thick for Ryan to even begin to parse.

"We have to go to Tartarus," Dianmu said firmly.

Ryan nodded. "So let's get ready."

Epilogue

Or for the Wicked

The bloody handprint next to the air pad door confirmed everything Roger Evans had been thinking since he'd had to use his emergency lockdown override code to get into the base. The empty perimeter corridors, their inability to get anyone on coms, and the faint traces of some kind of strange smoke had really been enough, but the presence of this horror movie trope in real life was irrefutable. It said, without a doubt, "Everything went to shit here, and we're all dead."

"I think it's just going to get uglier from here," he whispered. "Keep your eyes peeled."

There were handprints along the floor, too, moving away from the keypad. In many spots, they weren't just single prints, but long streaks that told a story of a man scrabbling desperately for purchase as he was dragged along the ground. A couple of fingernails, violently torn free, were stuck in a gap in the tile.

"Whoever this was, he died hard," Evans said.

They followed the grisly trail around a corner and found Jason, one of the men who had been chosen for the next phase of the Myrmidon project, slumped against the wall in a pool of blood. The poor bastard had never even gotten his harness.

"God," Munoz whispered. "What the fuck happened to him?"

Palmer leaned forward and examined the ruin of the man's chest. "I think his heart's gone. The wound is messy as hell...it looks like something just tore into him."

"Bast," Evans growled with a certainty that settled into his bones. "The Subject got free."

Munoz nodded, her face set in grim lines. "She got the Sphere, too," she said, sounding every bit as confident as Evans felt.

Evans checked his power gage. Still less than ten percent. "She must have," he agreed. "And she's using it. That's why we're charging so slowly."

"No shit."

"So what are going to do?" Palmer asked.

"We need to find Bast," Evans said. "We take her down, and then get medivacs for the surviv-"

"How?" Munoz hissed, her face tight with sudden fear. "We've had full power for three engagements, and we *failed*, remember? Now we're talking about an enemy who knows our weapons better than we do *and* has pretty much taken them away from us. Palmer's still bleeding, you're limping, I can't see out of one eye, and we're a man down!"

An image of Hector rose, unbidden, in Evans's mind. He pushed it aside. *Mourn later,* he told himself. Finally, he said, "We have to take her by surprise. End it before she has time to react."

Munoz snorted. "How the *hell* are we going to pull that off? Look at what she's doing!" She gestured to Jason's ruined torso. "She ripped his goddamn heart out, and you want to catch her by *surprise*?"

"We have to get the Sphere back," Palmer said. He checked his power gauge. It had gone up another percent. "We've still got a little bit of a connection to it. If we can get our hands on it..."

"For the third damn time, how?" Munoz snapped. She was looking at Palmer, but Evans had no doubt the question was directed at him. "We've got almost nothing left, and you want to go after a psycho who did *this*? What we need to do is hope to God she's already gone, and then get the hell out of here ourselves."

Evans held up a hand to silence them. "You're right. We can't win. We can't beat her. Not as weak as we are, not without more power."

Munoz let out a relieved sigh. "Glad you agree."

"And I think she is gone," Evans continued. "Otherwise, I think she would have found us by now."

Palmer's forehead furrowed. "So what? We stick our thumbs up our asses and wait for reinforcements and new orders?"

"No," Evans said. "You're right that we need the Sphere, and when we've recharged and had time to plan, I think we can get it. Command will just get in our way. We need to be out of here before anyone else shows up, and that means a quick sweep of the base for anything useful. Including the failsafe."

"You want to steal the failsafe," Munoz said, her voice flat. "You want to steal a one-megaton nuclear warhead."

Evans nodded. "It's the only option. The ultimate trump card. No one is going to screw with three super-soldiers carrying a goddamn nuke. Including Bast."

Munoz pursed her lips. "We do this, we've gone rogue. It doesn't matter what answer we give them, it doesn't matter how we explain it. We steal a nuke and go AWOL, they're going to hunt us down."

"You have a problem with that, Munoz?" Evans asked. This was it. The moment of truth. "With everything we can do...you want to be taking orders from ordinary people for the rest of however long we'll live?"

"I..." Munoz considered. R&D hadn't known how long they'd live. It could be an average human lifespan, or it could be centuries. They could be as immortal as gods.

"Fuck it," she said. "Yeah. I'm in."

"Andrew?" Evans asked, looking at the big man.

Palmer closed his eyes and took a deep breath. "I'm with you two," he said. "Period. If you say stay, we stay. If you say we go, let's make sure we can pull it off."

Evans and Munoz shared a look. It wasn't a surprise. Andrew liked following orders. Of course he'd chose to follow the two people on the planet who were his actual equals.

"Then move out," Evans said. "We have work to do."

A Note from Alex

Thank you so much for reading Strange Cosmology. If you enjoyed the book, I would appreciate an honest review at your favorite online retail or book review site. Reader reviews are critical for a first-time author, and if you would take a few minutes to write one that would be amazing.

Be sure to sign up for my email list to receive a free prequel story starring Crystal, updates and exclusive content! You can sign up and visit my blog online at www.alexraizman.com.

You can also follow me on Facebook and Twitter.

Acknowledgements

Even more than *Weird Theology, Strange Cosmology* was a herculean effort. I'm so happy with how this book has turned out, but I never would have gotten here without the support from several people. First of all, as with last time, a ton of credit must be given to Laura Beamer, my dearest friend and long-suffering editor. I thought she was tolerant during *Weird Theology,* but she needed - and had - the patience of a saint with *Strange Cosmology.* This book would not exist without her, no questions asked

Second of all some particular Reddit users are owed particular thanks. Funique has been providing me a ton of line edits on the first draft, taking a huge burden of dealing with my typos off my editor. SilverPheonix41 has been a huge aid in making sure the table of contents for the reddit is up to date and accurate, which is great because I'm terrible at keeping track. Inorai was an immense help in lettering the cover art and was amazing for me to bounce ideas off, and all the people on the redditserials who have listened to me gripe about the process.

Third, I have to acknowledge my amazing cover artist, Iris Hopp. You can find more of her work at http://www.irishopp.com. She did a fantastic job with my cover and navigating my fumbling attempts to describe what I wanted.

Fourth, my younger sister Abbie, who's always encouraged me to be creative. Isabel wasn't inspired by her, but the bond Ryan and his sister share was definitely inspired by my sister. Love you squirt.

Finally, and very importantly, there are my Patrons over on Patreon, who have been instrumental in keeping me motivated. I love all my fans, and you all are great for keeping me on task and reassuring me that I don't suck nearly as much as I fear I do.

$1: Karavusk, Paul Kennedy, Joe Doe, Luke Medina, Schraubedrin, Daniel Weipert, Shahked Bleicher, Yasmine, Daniel Sandkvist Wong, Robbert Jan Grootjans, Marisa Katherine DiCamillo, Heroes Profile, Tyler Hardy, Angelina Zucco, Alexander Thomas, Derek Wider, Clarke Vandervaart, Steve Meckman, Youri, Brad Massett, Justin brady, Caitlyn T Nummerdor, John, Matt Barnes, Blake Haulbrook, Ander Wasson, Varun Malik, Nathaniel Wardwell, Matthew Nicholas, Jarred Hull, Ben Lagar, Michael Abdoo, Tyler Morgan, Bob, Edward, Meg Momohara, Sam Lacey, Shelby Lanie, Brandon Shafran, Iris Hartshorn

$3: David, Chris Bol, Casper Elshof, Adrian Warmerdam, Travis Ridge, Emanuel Couture, Calvin P, David, Patrick Filion, Marcus Righton, Ace, Daniel Enrique Serna Guevara, Daniel Röcker, Kai Ove Lyngvær, Eugene Lorman, Ari Plessner, dapinkone, James Paik, Merlin, Brittany Shane, Rajin Shahriar, Ivan Stroganov, Adam Bolton, Ryan Deckard, Nick Clifford, Eric Spain, Ryan Diaz, Billy Kwong, Lars Hoeksema, Jono Chadwell, Dallas Nelson, Mikal Waage Gismervik, Matt Clury, John Reed, Darin Stockman, Luke Peavy, Neel Trivedi, Will Kenerson, Janis Svilans, Bart Smeets, Thanatos Lin, Maya, Derrick Tran, Suzanne McNeil, Emilie Hørdum Valente, Justin Lipe, Nicholas j Nosek, Emtasticbombastic, Chris On, Tim Schmidt, Dodoni, O$I, Francesco Barbera, Zack Griffin, J

$5: Megan Gallagher, Chris Heng, Klickup, James F Hayes, Tanner Muro, Boop, Markus Hamann, Micah Kroeze, Mat Carrington-Mackenzie, Morgan Whiterabbit, Scarth, Corin, Daniel Kauppi, Kim Roy

$10: William Isom, Thomas Keenan, Jason Hirsch, Mark Fishel, Doug McOwen, Inorai, Tony Dougherty, Udaeus, Anne, William Piper, Raphael Hämmerli Rachel, Kyle Bernzen, Noah Nelson, Ivan Smirnov

$20: Jordan Allen, Daniel Kelton, Philip Jacobsson, Joshua Stalkfleet, Brodie P, Ryan McPherson, Stefan Oshinski, Micah McFadden, Diane Tam, Dorian Snyder, Isaac Pebble

Other amount: Caleb Rheam, David Ballantyne, Ethan Fesmire, David Latterman

Made in the USA
Monee, IL
22 November 2019

17268979R00192